EASTER ISLAND

A Novel

D0049808

"A beautiful story,
a journey of mystery and surprise
that readers will want to take
again and again."
—Chicago Tribune

"Recalling A. S. Byatt's Possession…
Vanderbes weaves together
history, science and romance,
while maintaining an
undercurrent of suspense."
—Time Out New York

JENNIFER VANDERBES

EASTER ISLAND

Jennifer Vanderbes

DIAL PRESS
TRADE PAPERBACKS

EASTER ISLAND
A Dial Press Trade Paperback Book

PUBLISHING HISTORY
Dial Press Hardcover edition published June 2003
Delta Trade Paperback edition published June 2004
Dial Press Trade Paperback edition / September 2005

Published by
The Dial Press
A Division of Random House, Inc.
New York, New York

Book design by Virginia Norey
Map by Michael Gellatly

The Dial Press and Dial Press Trade Paperbacks are registered trademarks of Random
House, Inc., and the colophon is a trademark of Random House, Inc.

Library of Congress Catalog Card Number: 2002031588

ISBN 0-385-33674-8

Printed in the United States of America
Published simultaneously in Canada

www.dialpress.com

BVG   15 14 13 12 11 10 9 8 7 6

For my parents and my brother

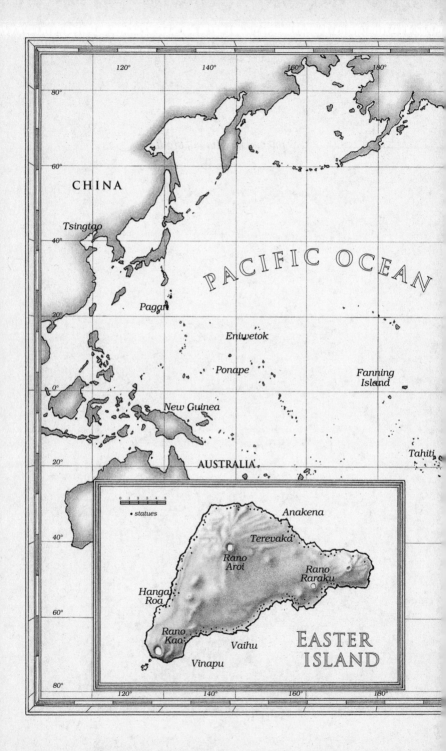

120°   140°   160°   180°

80°

60°

CHINA

Tsingtao

40°

PACIFIC OCEAN

20°

Pagan

Eniwetok

Ponape

Fanning
Island

0°

New Guinea

Tahiti

20°

AUSTRALIA

0 1 2 3 4 5

● statues

Anakena

40°

Terevaka

Rano
Aroi

Rano
Raraku

Hanga
Roa

60°

Rano
Kaa

Vaihu

EASTER
ISLAND

80°

Vinapu

120°   140°   160°   180°

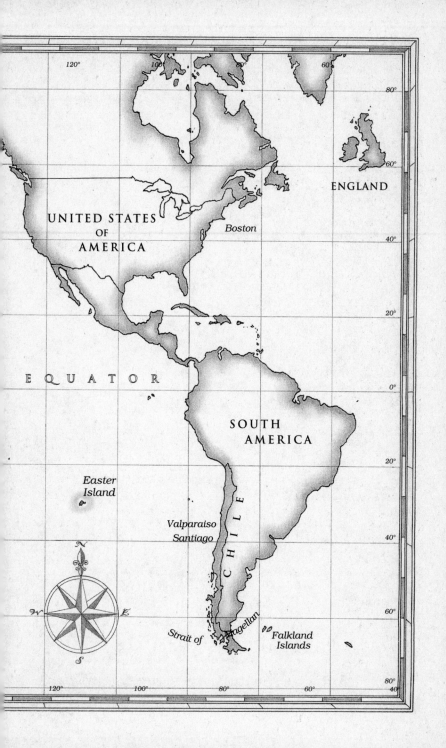

One evening, as Hau Maka lay beneath the full moon on the island Marae-toe-hau, he had a dream.

The dream soul of Hau Maka flew toward the rising sun and she passed above seven lands, each of which she inspected. But none of the seven was to her liking. So she continued on her journey, flying farther, over the vast and empty ocean, and for a long time she saw no lands below, only the rolling sea, until finally she reached a sandy shore. Here, the dream soul descended. She stood upon a glistening white beach and saw in the water the fish Mahore. Then the dream soul walked across the land and saw plump fruits of all colors, which she tasted, and were to her pleasure. Each fragrant flower she smelled, plucking a white one to tuck behind her ear. And then the dream soul climbed to the highest point on the land from where she could see the ocean and sky meeting all around her. As she looked at the island, she felt a gentle breeze coming toward her. . . .

Here was where she wanted to live.

When Hau Maka awakened, he found the King Hotu Matua and told him what his dream soul had seen.

"We shall find that land," said the king.

—The Legend of Hotu Matua, and the
discovery of the island Te Pito O Te Henua

1

The decisive moment for Germany's fleet in the Great War was, indisputably, its ill-timed arrival at the Falkland Islands. Having avoided detection by the Allies for three months since the outbreak of hostilities, it was their great misfortune to head straight for the Falklands just hours after the British fleet put in to coal there. Had they borne in and launched an offensive, they would have caught the British in the disarray of refueling. Instead, and for unknown reasons, all eight ships, under the command of Vice Admiral Graf von Spee, tried to escape. Compounding this fatal decision was atypical weather—a bright, cloudless sky hung overhead; there were neither the usual fog banks nor the low-lying squall clouds to afford even momentary concealment. The British, with their superior cruisers, were quick to pursue. From all sides gunfire bombarded the Germans. After three hours of battle, von Spee's flagship, the *Scharnhorst,* turned over on her beam, heeled gradually to port, and slid into the icy Atlantic, a cloud of black smoke shooting up from the boilers as she submerged. Only a coal collier, which was later interned in Argentina, and the small cruiser *Dresden,* which was to be run down and blown up in three months, escaped the fiery battle. Within hours, the rest of the squadron met its fate at the bottom of the sea.

The question, then, is what brought about this decisive event. What accounts for von Spee's inopportune arrival at the Falklands? Why did he order his ships to flee? How did so gallant and skilled an admiral, a man known for his precision, bring about the destruction of the German East Asiatic Squadron and turn, forever, the tides of the Great War?

—*Fleet of Misfortune: Graf von Spee
and the Impossible Journey Home*

2

14th January 1912
Hertfordshire

My dearest Max,
   I'm unsure as to where you are, but I'm sending this to Grete
at Gjellerup Haus in the hopes she's had word from your
household and will forward it.
   Alice and I have found ourselves in quite difficult
circumstances. One month ago Father passed on and I left my
position in Lancashire immediately. Please don't be angry with
me for not writing sooner. I needed time to determine in exactly
what station this placed me and, I'm afraid to say, it's worse than
I first suspected. How I should like to curse the textile industry
and this endless muddle of strikes. The cost of Father's faith in
English labour, it now appears, has been nearly his entire life
savings. By my most modest calculations, the sum left can
sustain Alice and me no more than six months. I cannot accept a
new position unless I can bring her with me & even your
extravagant letter of reference (indispensable demeanour? really,
Max) cannot outweigh the obvious difficulty of Alice let loose in a
respectable household. The solicitor, who looks to be younger than
myself, seems convinced an impoverished twenty-two-year-old
woman could not possibly tend to the needs of a nineteen-year-
old. He "most emphatically advises," for Alice's welfare, for my
own welfare, and for the good of the community, that I place her
in one of the Crown's colonies at Bethlam or St. Luke's. Well, I, in
turn, have told him in most unladylike terms that I should sooner

*lock myself away than Alice. Incarceration is the growing fashion
these days. Even as I write this, the Feeble-Minded Control Bill is
edging its way through both houses of Parliament. Progress—
that's what the doctors and the legislators like to call it. If it
passes, I'm not sure what we will do. Alice has only me, now, and
I cannot let her down.*

*I know we made no promises to one another. But all this past
year I was happy so long as I dreamed I might see you again.
What could be grander than to think of you giving up everything
and coming for me? Forgetting your responsibilities, your life,
arriving on my doorstep with a handful of lilies from your garden.
How silly that hope now seems. Did you ever realize how childish
I could be? But with Father gone, my sense of the world has
darkened. I've lost the conviction that life eventually works itself
out for the best.*

*I know your frustration at my position. I, too, wish things were
different. But to be angry at my situation is also to be angry with
Father. How can I blame him for trying to better our prospects? I
hope you believe, as I do, that my education was a far more
valuable gift than any investment. That I cannot do with it, as
you have always wished, something more than help children
conjugate verbs and crayon maps of the world, is simply the lot I
have inherited. It is best that I accept it. Please don't think me
weak for my resignation. I still share your spirit of fight, only I
haven't the means to indulge it right now.*

*I am here in England and I've not had word from you for
months. Your duties no doubt prevent you from writing, but no
longer can I afford to hope you will one day appear at my door.
We've always known you have obligations to your family & your
career. What point is there in my wishing you will awake one day
able to extract yourself from the life you've led for years? I
understand clearly now that it will never happen—I will never
again see you.*

*I cherish the time we had together. Not for a moment do I regret
our conversations on that shaded bench, the walks in the
garden—it still makes me laugh to think that you, of all people,
know the name of every plant and shrub. Who would have
suspected your love of nature? It's awful really; I cannot see a
flower without thinking of you. But when you left, I could no
longer stay in Strasbourg. I could not face your family alone, with*

only the faintest hope you might return for a day or two in several months.

I know you worry Alice will consume my life, and you think I must look after myself. And these past few weeks, in my mind I've listened again to all your arguments. But, dearest, I have to ask myself: what life? Alice is, in truth, the only companion I've ever known. For nineteen years she has been my life. To tend to her is to tend to myself. Please understand.

I suppose I must finally come to it: Professor Beazley (Father's colleague in the Department of Anthropology, and yes, the "jungle man" of whom I sometimes joked) has agreed to look after Alice and me. The University has granted him Father's position and he has made intelligent investments with his family's large estate (if only he could have advised Father) that should keep us quite comfortable. We are to be married within the month.

Will it really be so difficult to teach him a thing or two of charm? Perhaps a short lesson in the art of laughter? Never have I known a man so ill at ease; only reading and writing, and the occasional mapmaking, seem to relax him. Maybe if I constantly keep a book propped before him we might forge something of a normal house! No. Oh, Max, what is wrong with me? I shouldn't joke at his expense. After all, if he hadn't proposed—well, Alice and I would soon be wandering the East End. Can I really ask for more?

Max, please do not imagine I've chosen Professor Beazley over you. I have simply chosen to care for Alice rather than wait for the impossible. I wish I could tell you this in person, but I haven't that luxury. Perhaps this will make things easier for you. Perhaps you've always known this would happen. Long before I did, I think you sensed there was little hope for us. But for me this marks a change, a painful awakening. There is no one but you to whom I can write, no one but you who would understand.

Isn't it strange? I will be a married woman by the time this reaches you.

Forgive me.

Elsa

Elsa sets her pen down, folds the letter, and tucks it between the pages of her morocco journal. Edward will soon be home. She will post it in the morning, after he has left for the university.

Behind the tall glass windows of the sitting room, dusk is falling. Elsa stands, strikes a match, and lights each branch of the candelabrum. The shadows move across the curtains, the burgundy wallpaper, the thick lacquer of the walnut armoire. From every corner, elegance gleams. And carefully, like a child cautioned against sudden movements, she gathers her black skirt and inches toward the divan. Elsa still cannot imagine this place as her home. It reminds her too much of the houses she has worked in, of the vast, chandeliered dining rooms, the cold carpeted entrance halls. In Strasbourg, in Max's house, she moved with even greater caution, always kneeling to straighten the corner of a rug, fluffing each gold-fringed pillow as she rose from the sofa, as though the prudence of her movements might make up for, or disguise, the negligence of her emotions.

As she settles on the divan, Elsa feels content with what she has written. Just the right balance of affection and firmness has been struck. She knows that the tone—so much more adult than her other letters—will surprise him. Now *she* is the one offering apologies. Max won't have expected her to end things; he has always known the depth of her feelings. But surely he will understand the circumstances. Even if it means upending his ideals about liberty, his belief that all objectives can be reached through ardor, skill, and determination. That was, after all, what he said he admired in her—her ardor. And it was what she loved in him. But of what use is it now? For all his sympathy, Max has never known what it means to be trapped.

Elsa glances at her journal, the envelope's corner protruding from its pages. How odd that a few sheets of paper bear her decision, that at any moment she can hold them to the candle's flame, or never post them at all. But her decision is final, and has little to do with Max's knowledge of it. After all, it will be months before the letter reaches him. Perhaps it's for herself she has written, to understand once again her predicament, the unsatisfying idea of what now seems her future.

On the table beside her lies Edward's most recent book: *The Indigenous Peoples of British East Africa.* She extracts the ribbon marking her page and begins reading. The book so far engages her—and how nice, finally, to have the luxury to read such a comprehensive study. Religious practices, domestic life, transfer of property: To each of these Edward has devoted a detailed chapter. Her father always praised his field research skills. The language, though, she finds too formal—*A monthly ritual to grieve the dead allows adolescent members of*

the tribe to display emotion in the form of tears, yelps, or occasional song—
but she hasn't told Edward so. "It's engrossing!" she has announced
across the dinner table, the white tablecloth stretched between them
like a snow-covered boulevard. "Edward, you really have known such
excitement! You've seen such wonderful places." And she has
watched a brief smile nudge the reserve from his face: "I am delighted, my dear, that your attention is captured by those studies
which have occupied the bulk of my days. The world is filled with
other wonderful places ready for study. Perhaps someday you can
share in my endeavors. Really, I am touched, in the utmost, by your
interest in my work." It is, thinks Elsa, the least she can do. And how
could she not be intrigued by such far-off lands, and the faint promise he might take her to one?

In the center of the sitting room's carpet, Alice is sprawled on her
stomach, drawing pictures. Her stocking feet, flung up behind her,
crisscross in distracted excitement. Her long brown braids, Elsa's
morning handiwork, has already unfurled into a riot of curls. Every
few minutes Alice leaps up and rattles a picture in front of Elsa:
"Beazley," she announces with a smile. From years of hearing their
father use that name, Alice cannot be persuaded to call him Edward.
"Wonderful, dearest," Elsa replies. Then she straightens Alice's dress,
tucking away the lacy edges that have crept up the bodice, the straps
that have wandered out of place. A fortnight earlier, Alice lay slung
across the chesterfield, her skirt twisted like a bedsheet about her
waist, her stark white bloomers perforating the dark shadows of the
room. When, having returned from the university, Edward stepped in
to say hello, Alice's indecency startled him. She should at least prevent him further embarrassment. Now, beneath the fastidiousness of
Elsa's hands, Alice squirms and sighs and huffs—the opening notes
to her temper's looming aria.

"Allie dear, I've an idea." Elsa whisks her expression into exaggerated delight. "Would you draw me *another*?"

Then Alice drops down, her black skirt ballooning, and begins
again.

Of course, before Edward returns, Elsa will have to hide the drawings. They emphasize too strongly the hollows beneath his eyes, the
crease of concern across his forehead; they will no doubt surprise
him. "It's strange to say," Edward remarked several nights earlier, "but
you *do* make me feel so much younger." He is fifty-five and has never
been married. An elderly woman has kept house for him for years,

but the presence of two new women in his home clearly unnerves him. Each day, he consults Elsa about the curtains, the wallpaper, and the house itself—*We shall arrange everything to suit you, Miss Pendleton.* (Please, she reminds him, try to call me Elsa.) Edward seems as uneasy in this house as she is. It belonged to his parents and fell into his hands as the only child when his father died. For the past fifteen years he has lived amid the brocade curtains and the china and the glistening cutlery of his childhood. But rather than growing accustomed to what has for so long surrounded him, he seems a guest in his own home. Only now, with the arrival of Elsa and Alice and their crates of pinafores and hats and yellow-back novels, does Edward realize he is not a visitor. He is the host, and his new role absorbs him. Anything Elsa touches or appears to avoid, he notes—*The mahogany side table, I see, is not to your liking; of course it can be replaced easily enough. And perhaps you think the table linens should be a cheerier shade?*—as though women are yet another foreign culture of which he has embarked on a study.

Max is only five years younger than Edward, but having a family lent him a certain ease with women. With Max it was always, if not simple, at least relaxed. Sobbing, giggling—nothing could unnerve him. Despite his inherent sternness, he always understood the language of affection.

Elsa knows, however, that at some point in Edward's past there was a woman. A third cousin from Dover? The niece of the Royal Geographic Society's president? She was never told the particulars; only her father's allusions to the fractured romance revisit her. "Old Beazley has suffered his fair share of amorous afflictions. Enough to send him all the way to the African continent. I've often thought the world would still be entirely unmapped were it not for the impetus of a broken heart." Edward himself makes no mention of it, and if this woman left any impression, it is only one of unease. How else to explain his discomfort with women? He is, after all, reasonably handsome. He carries himself with a stolid intelligence, harbors an intensity of introspection she remembers admiring as a girl. She had always thought him quite playful, much more so than her father; from his travels he brought them wooden dolls with seaweed tresses, rosewood boxes with golden keys; at the end of their puppet shows he would applaud wildly, once snatching the flowers from the mantelpiece vase and tossing them to her and Alice as they curtsied. But with each year that passed, as Elsa moved closer to adulthood, he seemed to grow suspicious of her, even mystified, and reserve, like ill-fitting armor, settled over him. The presents vanished; the laughter quieted. An awkward formality tinged his once-blithe greetings. And now all his actions seem studied: the hand rising tentatively to touch her shoulder; the brass knob of her dressing room door inching like the dial of a vault near its final number. *Ill at ease*—her words to Max, emphasized for his consolation, were true. But is it fair, she wonders, to blame Edward for lacking the flirtations, the effortlessness, the experience, of a married man?

At least he wants to please her. She knows she can rely on his patience with Alice despite his clear distress at her behavior. Whenever Alice approaches, he steps back as though afraid. And the bloomer incident, for which he spent the whole evening spilling apologies— *I am not accustomed to knocking. An old bachelor with old habits. I beg of you both to forgive me*—has caused him to rush past the sitting room whenever he hears Alice within, or to make enough noise as he approaches that any indecent exposure can be adjusted. But was she not honest in her characterizations of Alice? Did he think she was exaggerating? He must have seen some of her hysterics with Father—he visited the house quite often while Elsa was abroad; Father said Beazley seemed fond of Alice. But Elsa also warned that she would not, under any circumstances, stand for Edward treating Alice as a dullard. Alice could read and write, could identify every country on the globe by its outline, could rattle off every species in Swaysland's guide to ornithology. Birds: They were Alice's true love. One of the first books Elsa read to her was *Birds Through an Opera Glass*, and ever since then Alice has asked for nothing but birdwatching books. When Edward proposed and invited her and Alice to move into the carriage house on his property until the wedding, one of Elsa's stipulations was that Pudding, the African Gray parrot their father had bought Alice for her birthday, accompany them.

"He's quite agreeable. In fact, he barely speaks," said Elsa, recalling the sad fact that Alice had been able to teach Pudding only a few words—*bird, kiss, superior* (their father's favorite adjective), and *Alice*—the words Alice thought essential.

"My dear Miss Pendleton. I would never think to separate Alice from her beloved pet. I myself am quite fond of animals. And I have even lived amongst peoples who worship them as gods."

"I would just like for you to be perfectly clear," said Elsa, "as to Allie's situation before any permanent—" She stopped, not wanting to sound too distrustful, too calculating.

"Before arrangements are made?"

"Well, yes."

"I understand. Before you accept my proposal you would like to ensure Alice's protection. Yes, Miss Pendleton, I can ensure that."

His words calmed her, and Elsa was thankful he understood her fears; but she knew her demands were a performance. She was pretending she had other options, that she might, if Edward didn't accommodate her, refuse his offer.

"But it's much more than protection, Edward. It is respect I want to ensure. Alice is different, yes. Sometimes difficult to comprehend. But she's much more intelligent than you suppose. She understands and feels a great deal she isn't able to articulate in the way that you and I would. But she is really quite like us. Only her emotions tend to sometimes get the best of her." Emotions, Elsa did not say, that come in the form of fits.

"Some would say, Miss Pendleton, that emotions *are* the best of us. If it is respect you are concerned with, I assure you, Alice has mine. In toto."

"Are you quite sure?" But as Elsa said this she sounded, even to herself, too insolent.

Quietly, Edward offered, "Yes. . . . Quite sure." But the words were tinged with discomfort.

"Good," said Elsa. "Excellent. Yes. We are perfectly understood, then."

Elsa glances down at Alice, still sprawled on the carpet, drawing slowly. Her large brown eyes, inches from the paper, swallow each detail of the emerging image. "A delicate beauty" is how their father described her, her features chiseled, the bones poised beneath the skin at graceful angles. Her face was a pale oval framed by thick brown braids. Since infancy, Alice's behavior drew awkward stares in public. But when she turned sixteen, people began to stare before any peculiarity had revealed itself. Pulling open the heavy wooden door of their house in St. Albans, stepping into the bright morning sun, she could seem, for a moment, the loveliest of young ladies, mulling over, as she twirled her parasol, the gentle phrases she would use to decline her latest suitor. But then a curtain of dullness would descend. It was not idiocy, Elsa knew, nor was it a feebleness or weakness of mind; it was a disengagement. As Alice's lower lip slackened, her eyes would seem lost, as though staring inward at some private thought, some personal theater, for minutes, sometimes an hour, until something—a spark in her mind, an abrupt noise beside her—flashed alertness back into her face, and she reawakened, stunned and eager. It was at these moments hysteria seized her. As her mind bounded back to the scents and sounds of a simple room, to the sight of familiar faces, Alice would mark her return with a squeal or a jump, sometimes stomping wildly on the carpet as her heavy braids flopped and swung, as if to celebrate a distance traveled, a place seen that no one, even Elsa, could comprehend.

"Beazley!" Alice shouts again. In the dim room, her slim white hands, like two crescent moons, curl around the edges of the paper. In this picture, Edward's brows converge in a violent V of concern.

"Lovely," says Elsa. "Shall we make another?"

Elsa closes Edward's book. Through the near-black windowpanes she can see the streetlamps have been lit, a necklace of gold along the dark line of Heslington Road. Several bicycles whisk by, and Elsa sees a white Rolls-Royce glide to a stop in front of a house on the corner. In their father's neighborhood there was only one motorcar, that of Dr. Benthrop, who used it for emergency house calls. But their father, even when Dr. Benthrop offered him a ride, preferred his bicycle. It was one of his many theories—an indolent body resulted in an indolent mind. When the Ladies Humbers were first sold, he immediately bought one for Elsa and one for Alice, and insisted they cycle thirty minutes each day. At first Alice refused to mount her bike. Not until Elsa, seventeen at the time, cycled around Alice in clumsy orbits would Alice touch the strange steel frame. It took six months of Elsa running alongside, one hand guiding the center of the handlebars, for Alice to keep her balance. What excitement, though, when finally Alice could ride. Elsa loved their outings, cycling along the narrow streets in the late afternoon, stopping at the chemist for Father, Alice placing the small pouch of sassafras root or bottle of wheat germ oil in her wicker basket. As they rode home, Alice would shout from behind "I'm after you!" and then Elsa would cycle faster, sweat prickling from the roots of her hair. The momentum delighted Alice, and when she finally dismounted—cheeks flushed, eyes tearing from the wind—she demanded to know when they could go again. Almost every afternoon they cycled like this. But when Elsa left to take up her first position in Heidelberg, their rides ended. Alice was despondent. And in a letter from her father Elsa learned that Alice, frustrated she was not permitted to cycle alone, had thrust a hatpin into the tires of Elsa's Humber.

In the distance, a church bell sounds six slow gongs. Alice, her crayon clasped like a scalpel, appears to make slow incisions in the paper. Alice needs her; of that much Elsa is sure. It would be unthinkable to leave her in another's care, to place her in a colony, away from the world. Too much like punishment for being different. And it would mean only that Elsa had not wanted the task of caring for her own sister. What she has chosen, a life with Edward where she can look after Alice, is best. And writing to Max, a necessity. Such is life, thinks Elsa. Such is fate. Choices are luxuries, and Max will have to understand that. How can I begrudge my own situation, thinks Elsa, with Alice here, a reminder, always, of how fortunate I am? I am fortunate, she tells herself. And a heavy-limbed resignation settles over her as she recalls the letter—*Can I really ask for more?*—as though persuading Max of her acceptance has finally solidified her own acceptance. Once he receives the letter, it will all be over, those distracting months left behind. How many evenings of one's life could be spent lying awake in troubled speculation? Such nights were a symptom of a life without responsibilities—a life that ended when her father died, when she returned home and stood in the cemetery, clasping Alice's hand. Only then did she understand how frivolous her former grief had been. As she stood before her father's coffin, her eyes refused to dampen. When it was time to say the final prayer, she fell silent. Weeks passed. She could not cry; she could not speak of her father. The loss had lodged within her for good.

And now, in the sitting room, Elsa thinks: There is not only this sadness, but there is Alice. And soon, a husband. She must banish all wondering about Max's feelings, her own feelings. She must think of herself as an adult.

The thud of the front door startles her. Edward calls from the hallway, "Good evening, ladies!" His voice is a strong baritone—a voice accustomed to lecture halls.

Elsa rises, collects the papers from the carpet. "Beautiful," she whispers as she rubs Alice's back. "I shall add them to my pile."

Alice abandons her pout of frustration at the sound of Edward's approaching footsteps. There is a great bustling outside the door, as though things are being tugged and tossed. This attempt at heralding his entry, thinks Elsa, is a bit extreme.

"Beazley!"

In the archway, Edward pauses. His hair is carefully combed, his beard clipped. He is tall and broad and a long black frock coat hangs tidily over his form. The weight of his satchel tilts him slightly to one side. "And how are my girls today?" Does he realize this also was their father's nightly greeting? Edward has adopted many of their father's mannerisms, prompting in Elsa the suspicion that their father asked Edward to do this, to replace him.

"We are quite well," replies Elsa.

It would certainly explain Edward's offer. After so many years of bachelorhood, could the idea of marriage—and to Elsa, no less, who had not shown him a hint of affection in years—have been so tempting? If Father did ask, Edward would never tell. His decorum would prevent such a bald confession. But the possibility that she has been bartered discomforts her. Is this new life something laid out for her, something expected, as though her father had said, *Elsa will fetch the tea for you,* and she was now simply carrying in the steaming pot? *Some thread of my own will,* thinks Elsa, *no matter how small, should be woven into my future. Even if I knew death was coming tomorrow, should I not be permitted to choose between poison and pistols?*

She crosses the room to meet him. "Welcome home, Edward." Resting one hand on his elbow, and straining her face upward, she kisses him on the cheek.

"Beazley!" Alice leaps up, her slender arms lassoing his neck. She pecks him with a series of kisses. "Beazley, Beazley, Beazley!"

As she squeezes him, he stands immobile as a statue, a marble saint surrendering to an odd ritual of affection.

"Allie, why don't we let Edward sit and rest?"

He slowly extricates himself from Alice's arms, lifts the leather satchel to his stomach, and spanks it affectionately. "There shall be no resting. Not tonight!" From the bag he produces a thick roll of papers, unfurls one, and palms it smooth on the lacquered side table. A map. Of South America. His index finger, hovering in the air, stalks the web of longitude and latitude. But as his hand descends, Alice snatches the map and drives it, with a yelp, toward the center of the carpet.

"Well!" he says. "It seems Alice likes the map!" Elsa takes the crayons from the carpet, shooting Alice a look of reprimand. Edward offers a mild but unconvincing laugh. His papers, particularly his maps, are dear to him. But scolding Alice seems, for Edward, unfeasible. Perhaps Elsa's requests for understanding have worked.

"Well," he pronounces, "maybe Alice would like to be our navigator."

"Navigator?"

"An opportunity has presented itself, Elsa. An opportunity to explore another, as you said, 'wonderful place.' A terra incognita."

"An expedition?"

"The Society has offered a commission."

"Really? For us? Now?"

"There is much preparation necessary, of course. Travel arrangements, equipment. It shall be months before we can depart. But, yes, my dear. If you shall consent to it." With a wide smile he opens his arms to her. His severity, his composure, his awkwardness, slips from him. "Consider it, if you will, my dear, a very long and adventurous honeymoon. But only, of course, if you approve."

Elsa rushes forward, but on the periphery of his embrace she halts. "And *Alice*?"

"She would come with us. I shouldn't have it any other way."

A rose of excitement blooms within Elsa. A trip! She wants to ask where, but she must restrain herself—what if Alice refuses? What point is there in imagining a place she may not ever see? Go slow, she tells herself. Be moderate.

"Allie dear, how would you like . . . to go on a journey?" Alice's eyes lift briefly from the map. Elsa turns to Edward, trying to curtail her eagerness: "I must consider this carefully. How it would be for her. If it would cause her distress. My decision depends on a great many factors."

Edward's hands plunge into the pockets of his coat. His head dips. "Most certainly."

Is he disappointed at her lack of enthusiasm?

"It is her decision," Elsa says firmly. "Or, the decision depends on her."

But what of Elsa's own desire? From the street below comes the jangling of carriage wheels, the sharp crack of a whip. She glances around at the towering armoire, the thick curtains, the dull and heavy gleam of this new home, this new life. The map, a yellow rectangle of possibility, seems to call to her from the dark carpet. *An expedition.*

"Allie, it would be a journey filled with bird-watching."

Alice glares at them both, eyes narrow with distrust. "What *kind* of birds?"

"Well, I'm not sure. Cape pigeons, I imagine. And petrels, and albatross." Elsa looks toward Edward, who nods. "Oh," adds Elsa. "And parrots."

Alice, as though bored, twirls her braid. "Pudding is a parrot," she says. She often speaks as though answering questions she has not been asked. "An African Gray parrot."

"Do you think that Pudding would like to meet an Amazonian parrot?" Elsa asks.

"The Amazon is in South America. Pudding can't fly to South America. That's silly. There is a large ocean in between."

"You're quite right," says Elsa. "That's very silly of me. But, you know, Allie, we could *take* Pudding there."

For a moment, Alice's face goes limp, as though envisioning Pudding in a strange land, watching him fly from perch to perch, turning his gray face to the sun. Alice shuts her eyes, opens them again, and resumes her study of the map.

"Allie, would you show me South America?" Elsa moves toward her. "On that map."

"Elsa, it *is* South America," says Alice.

"Chile," calls Edward.

"Very well. Show me Chile, Allie."

At this, Alice brightens and vigorously flattens the map as though trying to smear the paper into the carpet. "Sit down, Elsa. You have to sit down. So you can see."

Elsa crouches beside her.

"Ready!" announces Alice, poking at the western edge of South America. "Chil-ee. Chil-ee. Do you see? Look, Elsa."

Huddling together, Elsa and Alice stare at the pink and orange and purple countries nestling one another, like particles clustered to a magnetic continental core.

"Alice," Edward says from above, "move your finger a tad to the left . . ."

Alice's small finger sets off from the coast, sailing slowly across the blue and empty Pacific.

". . . ah, a little more now. Farther, a tad farther."

Shadowing the Tropic of Capricorn, her finger navigates a straight course through the sea.

Finally, Edward calls through the room, "There." The word is his arrival at this imagined destination. "There."

Elsa squints at the speck of land and puts her arm around Alice.

"That's where we can go," she says. "All the way there. All of us." She can feel Alice's breathing quicken. Alice has never traveled with Elsa; she has never left England.

"Through the *ocean*?" Alice mutters.

"Through the ocean, Allie. Just like Christopher Columbus. And Vasco da Gama."

"Like . . . Hernando Cortez?"

"Like Hernando Cortez, Allie. And like Ferdinand . . ." Elsa lets the name hang in the air.

Alice's eyes widen as she realizes the game. "Magellan!" she booms, her braids slapping her neck as she twists.

"And just like Captain . . ."

"Captain Cook! James Cook!" Alice's head now rolls in delight; giggles cascade on every side. And she then recalls her favorite joke: "No, don't cook James! Don't cook James!" Alice leans hard into Elsa's shoulder, nearly pushing her over. She squeals, and tickles, and sways, her exuberance scattering like raindrops. "Stop it, Elsa! You're being silly. Elsa, you're being silly."

"Yes," says Elsa, steadying herself against the force of Alice's excitement. "I'm being very silly."

At this, Alice giggles even more, then catches her breath. The familiar curtain falls. Rocking in silence, she scrutinizes the map, and then, with great concern, looks up. "Do they have a ladies' room?"

Edward laughs, a genuine and hearty sound, the first that Elsa has heard from him. "I see I will have to make adjustments for the concerns of the ladies on this expedition."

"Yes, Allie," says Elsa. "They will have some sort of ladies' room."

"I'm allowed to go?"

"Absolutely."

"Through the ocean?!"

"Yes, Allie."

"And you are going too? You will be there?"

"Yes," says Elsa, glancing up at Edward. "I will be there too."

Edward nods ever so slightly and his eyes flash with pride, acknowledging receipt of her consent.

For a moment Elsa wonders if this whole scene—his question, her deliberation, Alice's fervor, her answer—has been imagined by him beforehand, if Edward is not equally aware of her own strained pretense of freedom, and if he has not, in some way, been watching her with amusement. Could she, after all, have refused to go?

"Goodness me!" says Alice. "Goodness, goodness, goodness. I must pack my bag."

A clap. Elsa sees that Edward's hands have sprung together. Something like delight, or pleased confusion, sweeps his face. "Just a moment."

From the hall comes shuffling, the sound of tugging, and soon he emerges with a large trunk in tow. Brass hinges shine against the unblemished black leather. He drags it toward the center of the carpet, then disappears into the hall and returns with another.

Alice has already pounced on the first; he sets the second beside her.

"Inside of each, ladies, you will find a vanity case, a satchel, and a journal. You should compile any further necessities onto a list and I'll see that everything is—"

"This is mine?" Alice asks, unlatching the trunk before her.

"Yes," says Edward.

"And that one?" Alice points to the other.

"That will be Elsa's."

Alice looks with dismay at the trunk before her, abandons it, and scurries toward the other. "This one is mine."

"Alice, you can have whichever you like best," says Elsa, rising. She feels dizzied by the haste of the decision, the map of this unknown land, and the knowledge that her life is once again about to be transformed.

"Edward, this is quite thoughtful of you. It's a very kind gesture."

"It is nothing. Proper luggage is a necessity. Again, any other necessities should be compiled on a list. I'll make sure you have them, that we have everything. *In omnia paratus.*"

"Thank you, Edward."

"No expressions of gratitude are in order. You, Miss Pendleton, are performing the great courtesy of accompanying me. I have for a long time dreamed of this trip. I am delighted you desire to go."

It's clear he did not for a moment doubt her consent.

"Of course," says Elsa. "Of course I want to go. I was hoping that you would suggest something of the sort. I was, I suppose, even expecting it."

"Ah! Yes! Really? How well, then, you feign surprise!"

She feels a blush begin, but Alice's excitement saves her.

"Te Pito O Te Hen-oo-a?" Alice asks, her face inches from the map.

"Another language, Alice," says Edward. "A Polynesian language. It means 'the navel of the world.' The English, however, call it Easter Island."

"Is it far?"

"Oh, yes." Edward's voice is warm and satisfied. "It will take nearly a year to get there."

Alice is happy. Edward is happy. So why should Elsa let Edward's assumption bother her so? He only meant well. And she does, of course, want to go. After all, she's had enough of gloom. This is an extraordinary opportunity.

Elsa looks down at her trunk, then looks at Edward and at Alice sitting with legs splayed around the map, and she thinks perhaps this is a moment of significance, that she will one day recall these images and the excitement she is now feeling, the sense of mystery at what lies ahead. Miles from this house, from this city, she will think back to this as a beginning—but of what? As Elsa tries to imagine the future moment from which she will look back, she feels the present moment slip from her, as though as she stands there in the drawing room she has become the memory itself: She is the recollection of herself at twenty-two, in England, in her fiancé's house, her hands clasped, her eyes aglow, as her future self watches from a great distance.

"The mind," says Edward, startling her from thought, "is always eager to begin scouting, is it not?"

"What? Oh, yes," laughs Elsa, tugged back to the present. She is twenty-two again, simply crossing the room, moving toward her trunk. She throws it open like a giant book. Inside sits the vanity case, the soft leather satchel, the black and gold-leaf journal tied with a ribbon.

My imagination can do its reconnaissance, she thinks. But somebody must do the packing.

The next morning, at her dressing table, Elsa begins a postscript to her letter:

A trip I had been hoping for, well, it now seems it will happen.
I shall be leaving Hertfordshire for quite some time. . . .

3

It was February 1973.

With practiced self-control, Greer Farraday closed her eyes as the small Lan Chile plane began its descent. The pilot had announced that the eastern tip of the island would soon be visible from the plane's right side, Greer's side, but she wanted to wait until the entire island was visible, to absorb it in one comprehensive view.

With her eyes closed, the propellers thrummed even louder in her ears. All around her, *Oohs*! and *Magníficos*! and *Dios míos*! blossomed like a field of moonflowers. When finally the plane steadied and she opened her eyes, below her, like the jagged fin of a sea creature, the island rose from the water.

"*Vértigo?*" came a Spanish voice across the aisle. She turned to see the young man in the linen shirt studying her once again. His hair was dark brown, combed back, except for one thick strand that bisected his forehead. His cheekbones were high-ridged, his eyebrows two firm lines. He was handsome, and surprisingly unrumpled after the long flight. During the lunch service, when he had asked the stewardess for an extra piece of cake, Greer had offered hers: "I'm not eating it. *Lo quiere?*" He had accepted it with a smile, but his eyes betrayed surprise. She realized this was a breach of airplane etiquette—offering a portion of your meal to a stranger—and the dismayed stewardess returned moments later with a fresh piece, at which point Greer began reading her copy of Erdtman's *Pollen Morphology and Plant Taxonomy;* this would assure them she wasn't going to start offering around sips of her coffee.

With a shake of her head, she now said, "No. No vertigo. Excitement. *Emoción. Sí?*"

"*Ah, sí. Emoción.*"

Then Greer turned from him.

Excitement—that was what she was feeling. This was her first fieldwork in years. For months she'd been researching this island, writing letter after letter to arrange accommodations and lab space, packing equipment. She'd always wanted to study an island ecosystem but hadn't been sure she would, in the end, actually go. The preparations were such a useful diversion from life, from thoughts of Thomas, she began to fear it was their only purpose. But the day before, when her alarm rang, she had gotten out of bed, sealed her duffels, locked all the windows and doors, unplugged the appliances, turned the heat down—when that was done she double-checked everything to keep herself in motion—and finally stepped into the taxi, not looking back at the quiet house she was leaving behind. Now here she was, seven thousand miles from home, thirty-three, and alone. No one was depending on her. She was, for the first time in years, and in a way that felt almost frightening, free.

Greer pressed her forehead to the plane window, which framed, like a giant ocular, the long-awaited specimen of basalt. A mass of cumulus clouds hung just beyond its southern tip. Must be downwind, thought Greer. The warm air rising from the island is blown toward the sea, where it condenses. This was how the Polynesians had found their islands, settling every habitable landfall over eleven and a half million square miles of ocean a century before European explorers even thought to raise their sails. New Zealand was known as Aotearoa—"land of the long white cloud"—before the slender hulls of Polynesian canoes had reached its sands. Wouldn't it have looked to them, Greer thought, as though the cloud had given birth to land? Even in research it was easy to confuse cause and effect, to see the cloud first and think the land below was its shadow. The cloud, though, was the real shadow, a white silhouette, the island's ghost hovering above its igneous twin.

Greer could now see the whole of Easter Island—the southeastern vertex of the triangle of islands known as Polynesia. The island was itself an isosceles triangle, buckling inward at its three midpoints. In each corner there was an extinct volcano, bulbous and perfectly round, and dozens of smaller craters pocked the landscape. The island was oceanic, its raggedness the relic of an ancient deep-sea eruption. Leagues below, a fifty-four-hundred-mile scar stretched across the ocean floor; the East Pacific Rise, a volcanic mountain range, ran parallel to the western coast of South America, its occasional magmatic bleeding leaving well-known volcanic scabs: the Galápagos, the Society Islands, the Marquesas. Some two million years earlier, one of its volcanoes erupted and left another lifeless heap of cooled lava: Easter Island.

Easter was the ideal controlled experiment—this was what intrigued Greer. Never linked to a continent, the island had needed to wait patiently for flora and fauna to be carried to it by wind or ocean currents, and by a few determined birds whose feathers had swaddled seeds. Continental islands, like Bali and Tasmania, had been brimming with lemurs and mammoths and marsupials when the seas rose, and they were set adrift like overcrowded arks. But oceanic islands were tabulae rasae, naturalists' favorites. The Malay Archipelago had lured Wallace; the Galápagos, Darwin. But Easter made an even better subject. Fourteen hundred miles from another landmass, it would have taken thousands of years for plant life to reach its shores, far longer for Homo sapiens. This time spread meant the number of outside influences, the unknowns and extras that made any scientific answers so eternally dubious, could be reduced. Easter Island was, she thought, the perfect microcosm.

Greer thrummed her fingers one last time on the book in her lap and crammed it into her backpack. It pleased her to see her bundle of field gear—notebook, pollen guide, camera. She needed this trip— eight months of solid research. Draping her mind in data had always soothed her. Even as a child, looking into her father's microscope, she had discovered science was a room your mind could enter, a safe chamber of contemplation in which there was no space for sadness. Later, she came to realize it was a matter of scale. The minuscule— pollen grains—and the massive—geological time, the motion of epochs—made the day-to-day, made even the months and years of simple, human-size disappointments, seem trivial. Science had become, over the years, the blanket she reached for when she felt a chill from life.

And with her husband's death, a deep chill had settled within her. As she moved through the house in Marblehead, packing up Thomas's belongings, everything she touched—old photographs, his flannel shirts, his notebooks—dizzied her with memory and regret. When she couldn't bear to see his things, or their things, she sat on the porch for hours, watching the ocean. When winter came, she retreated to the basement lab, listlessly reading old data logs, examining new pollen collections. If she left the house, it was usually for a slow walk through Harvard's herbarium or the Peabody Museum.

The idea of this trip, though, had finally begun to pull her from her malaise. The arrangements kept her busy, kept her in contact with the outside world. For months, Easter Island had loomed before her as a goal, something, in the bewilderment of her grief, to look forward to. And here, finally, she was.

The plane nosed down now, and around her passengers clasped their armrests and checked their seat belts. But for Greer it was getting on the plane that had tried her nerves; arriving was easy. She simply tucked her hair behind her ears and pulled some chewing gum from her pocket.

The plane's wheels gripped the asphalt and the machine steadied itself as silence filled the cabin. Through the window, Greer watched the twin propellers slow, the silver blades revealing their true shapes: swirling steel samaras, iron descendants of the winged maple seeds she'd watched as a child spin to the ground. So few viable shapes, she thought. The winged seed of the Asian climbing gourd (*Alsomitra macrocarp*) had inspired early aircraft and glider design. Milkweeds (Asclepiadaceae) and western salsify (*Tragopogon dubius*) could drift across entire valleys with their feathery umbrellas. Greer had always liked to imagine the awe of the first humans to see these seeds. How long, she thought, before envy arose, before someone wondered: Could *I* do that?

The plane gently came to a halt. A brief applause swept the cabin, and immediately the passengers around her stood. They clutched their purses and straw bags, and something—an elbow? briefcase?—knocked the back of Greer's head. "*Perdón, perdón*" drifted forward. Despite her excitement, after nine hours of sitting patiently, it seemed absurd to hurry. Greer remained seated, letting the rest of the plane depart before her. When she reached the exit, the impeccably groomed stewardess beamed at her. "*Buen viaje!* Enjoy your visit!" she said, her tone arrestingly cheerful. Greer couldn't help but wonder what this woman did on bad days, how difficult it would be to smile like that in the midst of a divorce, after a lump had been discovered, or after your husband of eight years had died.

Greer was the last of the travelers to spill down the portable steps into the warm air of the tarmac. Before her spread a squat one-story building marked AEROPUERTO MATAVERI and below that *Iorana, Bienvenido, Welcome, Wilkommen*. A Chilean flag flapped from a tall pole.

This was the smallest airport she'd ever seen, but the island was only about twice Manhattan's size, and mostly uninhabited. She'd been told any correspondence, though she expected little, could simply be addressed: Dr. Greer Farraday, Correo Isla de Pascua. The Lan Chile flight arrived only once a week, and that, she knew, had started just a few years earlier. Nineteen sixty-seven—the same year MacArthur and Wilson published *The Theory of Island Biogeography*, the monograph that had been a turning point for her own work. Greer recalled sitting at the kitchen table and noticing an ad in the *Globe*'s travel section for Lan Chile's Santiago–Rapa Nui–Tahiti line. How perfect it seemed. Island biogeography, a fledgling theory about distribution and speciation on isolated landmasses, and Easter Island, the world's most remote island. But at that time, she was working in Thomas's lab. And Thomas's enthusiasm for an Easter Island study was tempered, as was all his enthusiasm, by anxieties about his magnolia research. There was no chance of Greer getting funds to go alone, so she stayed in Cambridge.

The door of the cargo bay hung open, and a man in coveralls was tugging out the long box with her Livingston corer, struggling with the uneven weight of the six-foot steel rod and piston. Greer walked over to help—she'd carried that corer often enough, and couldn't risk having it damaged—but as she approached, the man signaled her with an insulted shake of the head that he had things under control. Greer nodded, then shifted her attention to the crates beyond her corer: the ones marked EXTREMELY FRAGILE in which she had carefully packed her microscope, her slide mounts, beakers, and her centrifuge. Another marked TOXIC (YES, ONE WHIFF CAN KILL YOU) CHEMICALS pasted with skull-and-crossbones stickers held her jars of hydrochloric and sulfuric acids. She'd brought everything she would need to take core samples and analyze data—it was impossible to obtain scientific instruments on the island. Flanking her box of chemicals was a canvas sack bulging with letters—the island's mail delivery, she assumed. Past that, another crate, with PORTALES stamped on all sides. Portales—the name stirred a vague memory, but one she couldn't place. Greer thought it best not to hover and moved slowly toward the terminal.

The building was cool and dim after the bright sunlight. Most of her fellow passengers had left. A plump woman, hair pulled in a loose and slightly graying bun, held a sign that read FARRADAY and stared determinedly beyond Greer, out onto the tarmac. Her eyes were large and wide set, her nose broad, her cheeks full, slightly weathered by the sun—a face distinctly Polynesian. A white dress clung to the supple curves of her body, flaring at the knees, lending her a distinctly feminine grace, and she stood with one foot tucked behind the other as though at any moment she might curtsy. Around her neck hung a garland of white hibiscus. Family: Malvaceae, thought Greer. Species: *Hibiscus moscheutos.*

"Residencial Ao Popohanga?" Greer asked.

A look of apology softened the woman's face. She had the solidity of one who had seen sons, husbands, whole nations, fall, but the gentleness of one who feared admitting the milk was finished, or that the cookie jar was empty. "*Sí, sí.* Residencial Ao Popohanga. But no more rooms. Maybe Residencial Rapa Nui. Or Hotel Pascua. They have a table for the Ping-Pong. Very very nice."

"I believe I already have a room." She extended her hand. "Doctor Greer Farraday."

"Greer? Greer? Doctor? *Una mujer?* Ahh."

"Yes, I'm a woman," said Greer with a slight smile, trying to hide the frustration this moment still produced in her.

The woman's hand rose to her cheek. "I not know! *Doctora. Mujer.* It is good. It is very good. Very American, yes?" At this, the woman beamed, lifted the hibiscus garland from her neck, and laid it over Greer's head. She kissed Greer on both cheeks. The smell of gardenia and coconut oil lingered about her. "I am Mahina Huke Tima. *Iorana.*"

"*Iorana?*"

"It is hello and good-bye in the Rapa Nui language."

"Well, hello for now," said Greer.

"Yes, hello for now," repeated Mahina, her hand resting gently on Greer's shoulder. "Very very hello."

The Jeep wound slowly along a red dirt path, kicking up light chunks of volcanic rock, red dust rising like vapor from its wheels. Each time the Jeep approached a figure on horseback, Mahina, now wearing a wide straw hat, tapped the horn and called out a greeting. She seemed reluctant to clasp the steering wheel, her fingers dangling like tentacles. A few times, as she shifted gears, the Jeep bucked. A woman who has learned to drive late in life, thought Greer.

"How many cars on the island?" asked Greer. "*Cuántos autos en la isla?*"

"*Solamente un automóvil,*" said Mahina. "For the mayor. Others have Jeeps, like this, but not many. This Jeep, not mine. It belongs to my brother-in-law. I ride the horse. You ride the horse?"

"*Sí*," said Greer. But her Spanish was better for questions than answers. "Not for many years. But they say it comes back."

"Yes, yes. And you drive the car?"

"Yes," said Greer.

"The woman is *doctora*. And the woman drive the car! Very good. And how many hours you are on the plane?"

"Almost ten," said Greer. "*Diez*. From Santiago. Another thirteen or so from New York. One more from Boston."

"*Veinticuatro!* So much time on the airplane!"

A strong wind rose up and Greer fastened her hair into a lumpy ponytail. She had meant to cut her hair before the trip—the island would be hot in February—but had forgotten, and it now hung well below her shoulders, tousled and unwieldy. She glanced in the side-view mirror: Her narrow face was pale from winter, tired from travel, but she saw the same high forehead, the familiar dark eyebrows. It was odd—nothing in her expression revealed the sadness of the past year. No sign of what her husband had done, that she'd been recently widowed. She appeared young, healthy, a bit disheveled, but basically composed, not at all like someone trying to start a new life.

Greer looked toward the coast, where the water shimmered in the light, a sharp contrast to the dull landscape. Even though she'd read about the island's depleted biota, the terrain's visible starkness surprised her. Only bleached grass—family Gramineae, that dogged monocot—had made its way across the land.

The island began lifelessly, thought Greer, but it would have welcomed stray seeds or spores that reached its shores. Igneous soil was rich in lime, potash, and phosphates—nutrients key for plant life. When a volcanic blast in 1883 wiped out all life on the island of Krakatoa, it took only thirty-five years for the island to replenish itself. The eruption was a dream come true for naturalists, the closest thing to witnessing the birth of an island. Hordes of investigators documented the appearance of each new fern and flower on the pumice-covered landscape, until the island's former forest had returned. Of course, Krakatoa was only twenty-five miles from Java, a warehouse of flora and fauna. Easter Island was fourteen hundred miles from the nearest major supplier, Pitcairn Island. But when you did the math, Easter should have been forested. Two million years was ample time. So what accounted for this barren landscape? The prime suspect was some sort of extinction. A catastrophe that would have undone ages of ecological hospitality.

"Hanga Roa," announced Mahina as she turned the Jeep inland and jabbed at the brakes. For a moment Mahina tried shifting into all possible gears before she settled on first and gently depressed the accelerator.

"Hanga Roa," she repeated. They had arrived at the island's sole town. Small light-blue houses, their front paths obscured by lattices of dusty millers (*Senecio cineraria*) and blankets of orange nasturtiums (*Tropaeolum majus*), lined each side of the road. A broad cypress tree shaded three sleeping dogs, their ears twitching with afternoon dreams. Mahina turned left down a smaller road, this one dotted with flat cement buildings—stores, it seemed—roofed with corrugated tin. Out of nowhere, several children darted in front of the Jeep, racing to touch the lone coconut palm at the street's end.

Mahina scolded them in Rapa Nui, then turned to Greer. "We have the church, the *correo* for the letters, the school. We are small but we have here what we need. I think you will like it."

"I'm sure I will," said Greer.

"Now *mi residencial*," said Mahina as she turned left and parked the Jeep beneath a pungent *amygdalina* eucalyptus.

"Avenida Policarpo Toro," Mahina said. "To go to the lab-or-a-tory you walk to Te Pito O Te Henua Street, then left to Atamu Tekana Street. If you like, I draw you map."

Before them stood a one-story cement building. The pink blooms of two coral trees framed the dark wooden door. A small sign, lettered with black tape, was pitched in the ground: RESIDENCIAL AO POPOHANGA.

After climbing from the Jeep, Mahina went to the back and began to pull at Greer's two duffels. Greer protested, but Mahina insisted, lifting each bag with surprising strength. Just then, through a line of bushes on the side of the house, came an elderly man wearing a faded red baseball cap, rubbing his eyes; the volley of offers and refusals had clearly interrupted his siesta. The man spoke firmly in Rapa Nui to Mahina, gesturing toward the luggage, but something in his tone suggested great tenderness to Greer. And from the measured rhythm of shrugs and sighs, she had the feeling this scene had transpired many times. The man examined the Jeep and when, it seemed, he had discovered no damage, he grinned at Mahina. Mahina, unamused, signaled Greer to follow her into the building.

She hastily pointed back to the man, and said, "Ramon Liragos Ika. *Vamos*, Ramon!" she called, at which point he lifted Greer's bags and followed them inside.

A shower of delicate bells heralded their entrance into a spacious room. The air was cool, the walls dark. From the ceiling hung two rows of green glass spheres in rope nets. Mahina carefully set her hat on the desk beside the doorway and from its stuffed top drawer extracted a key dangling from a white poker chip. Greer followed her across the room and through a door opening onto a lush courtyard: African flame trees, bamboos, and tall cypresses. In the midst of this cluttered vegetation stood a near–life-size statue of the Virgin Mary, her blue dress flaking at the folds. At the opposite end of the court-yard was a narrow porch lined with four doors. Mahina led her past the first three, and at the fourth she lifted the key, unlocked the room, and with a shove of her hip, the door opened.

The room was small. A double bed and two wicker nightstands crowded the far wall. Above the bed hung a round plaque of the Vir-gin Mary. Beside the door there was a writing desk and chair made of what appeared to be mahogany. Burlap curtains covered the single window.

"Good?" asked Mahina.

"Very good." Greer needed at least six months on the island to take cores and do the analysis, but most of that time would be spent in her lab.

"Good for the *doctora*!" Mahina smiled. "Of course, no piano. No Ping-Pong. Also, other *residenciales* have blankets much nicer. But we are short walk to laboratory. Yes? And I make the best food."

Ramon rolled his eyes and placed Greer's bags at the foot of the bed.

"This is just fine," said Greer.

"The bathroom is there," Mahina said, gesturing to a narrow door beside the desk. "When you want the hot water for the shower, you must put it on outside. I will show you. Also, we can get another lamp. Or, we move the desk. And if you are not liking here, we find you other room."

The room was so small it was hard to imagine the addition of any furniture. But from the expression on Mahina's face, Greer had the distinct feeling other guests had shown greater enthusiasm.

"This will suit me perfectly. It's wonderful." The sparseness of the room, in fact, appealed to her. Her house in Marblehead had become a jumble of furniture and books and artifacts, piles of unsealed boxes of Thomas's clothing that she hadn't yet decided what to do with. On top of everything else, it was the mess she had needed to get away from.

"Dinner I serve tonight at eight o'clock," said Mahina, kissing Greer once more on both cheeks and retreating from the room.

Greer set her purse on the desk and toed off her leather sandals. The floor was pleasantly cool. From her bag she pulled and carefully unwrapped the apothecary jar with her magnolia seed, then held it to the light; there it floated, shiny and fat, in its bath of salt water. This had been Thomas's wedding present to her—they were going to see how long the seed could survive in ocean water. Eight years so far, more than she had ever expected. For a while she believed the seed was a good-luck charm, taking it on all her field trips, setting it on hotel nightstands in Belgium and Italy. But when Thomas's research grew frenzied, when Greer stopped fieldwork and spent most of her time in his lab, she'd let the jar sit on the mantel in Marblehead, collecting dust. In two years it had barely moved, but when she'd packed for this trip, she felt she couldn't leave it behind. She now regretted her decision. Looking at it reminded her too much of Thomas in their first years together, when he still cared for science, and for her.

Greer set the jar down and looked up at the plaque of the Virgin Mary. There was a drift seed named for the Virgin Mary. Mary's bean, *Merremia discoidesperma*, held the record for the longest distance traveled by any seed: over fifteen thousand miles.

Kneeling on the bed, Greer mashed her way across the sagging mattress, lifted the plaque from the wall, and placed it facedown on the wicker nightstand.

Better, she thought, and began to unpack.

✽

It was late afternoon when Greer headed over to the lab. Ramon had driven her there earlier with her equipment, but now, more awake than she'd anticipated, she thought she would explore the village. As she walked along the dirt road, several stray dogs followed her and then lost interest, and a confused rooster crowed in the distance. She passed a building with a sign that read HOTEL ESPÍRITU, a name she recognized as one of the other hotels that housed researchers. Through the front door emerged an older couple, mid-argument, their fingers dueling across the pages of the guidebook. They wore matching Hawaiian shirts.

"*Iorana!*" they called.

"*Iorana,*" said Greer.

"Let me guess," the woman said. "American. East Coast."

"Impressive," said Greer, wondering what had given her away.

"You see?" The woman turned to her husband. "Ten for ten. It's a skill, I'm telling you. I should work for the state department or an embassy or something. A countryman detector." She thrust the guidebook toward Greer. "So what do you think of these things?"

"What?"

"The *moai.*"

"I just arrived," said Greer." 'Just,' as in hours ago."

"Well," the woman said, nodding at her husband, "she is in for a real treat. You're in for a real treat. I'm telling you. Whatever photos you've seen don't do them justice. They're e-nor-mous."

"The photos were quite small," said Greer. "I imagine the statues must be larger."

The woman squinted, then smiled. "Funny."

"Well, enjoy your stay."

She turned the corner and continued past another row of houses. Each one, she could see, had an extensive backyard. Chickens bustled and clucked within small wire coops. Guava trees (genus: *Psidium*) and taro plants (genus: *Colocasia*) grew from the thick lawns. Only here, in the village, in carefully tended gardens protected from the wind, could plant life thrive.

Farther along were the cement buildings. No signs advertised their purposes, but Greer could discern a distinct character behind each facade; she recognized the post office and the bank; the market made itself known when a woman emerged hugging a mesh sack stuffed with canned goods. Greer stepped inside and let her eyes adjust to the darkness. A red-haired man smiled from behind the counter. "*Iorana.*"

"*Iorana,*" she replied.

He was pale, with a dusting of freckles across his cheeks. She'd read the island had a mixed population. Early voyagers had noted that some people appeared distinctly Polynesian, and others European, known as the *oho-tea:* "the light-haired." This was one of the reasons the origin of the islanders had been in question. A mixed race left many possibilities.

Greer wandered past bags of rice and grain, boxes of sweets and candies, an enormous pyramid of what looked to be canned peaches. Converting into dollars, Greer found the prices high, especially for the peaches. But all these items would have been shipped from the mainland, a costly endeavor. She pried one banana from a cluster and pulled down some boxes of cookies for the lab, carrying the awkward pile to the counter. She'd exchanged money at the Santiago airport and now handed the proprietor a wad of pesos.

"*Inglesa?*"

"American."

"Ahh. New York? Los Angeles?"

"Massachusetts. Marblehead."

From behind his desk he pulled a dog-eared atlas and opened it on the counter. "You show."

Greer glanced at North America and saw that small black X's had been placed over Los Angeles, New York, and Salt Lake City. "Here," she said, pointing to the East Coast. "Marblehead. Massachusetts is the state."

"*Riva riva,*" he said, pulling a pen from behind his ear and marking an X on the coastline. "Marblehead. Island? Yes?"

"Peninsula."

"Pen-in-su-la. *Riva riva.*" He closed the map and slowly counted out her change.

"*Gracias,*" she said.

"*Iorana.*"

Outside, in the fading light, she peeled the banana and continued walking in the direction of the lab. She'd brought with her a well-worn brochure with a map of the island, the lab's location having been circled by Mahina. The brochure offered in one brief paragraph the island's historical highlights: the legendary arrival of the first king, Hotu Matua; the construction of the massive *moai;* the undeciphered *rongorongo* hieroglyphics; Captain Cook's visit; the toppling of the *moai;* the emergence of the bird cult; the war between the long-ears and the short-ears; the cannibalism in the island's caves; the disappearance of the British scientific expedition; Admiral von Spee's eight-day anchorage during World War I. No mention, of course, of the island's geological history or its depleted biota. Amazing how little attention people paid to the narrative of the land itself. As though sixty-four square miles of stone were just a stage for late-arriving human actors, whose performance, in geological time, had happened in the blink of an eye.

Greer continued on, heard the slow plod of a horse's hooves in the distance. A slight breeze stirred the red dirt of the path. Out of sight, a dog was barking. The quiet reminded her of Mercer, the town in Wisconsin where she'd grown up. Summer evenings, before dinner, she would walk to the general store, watching women sweep dust from their porches, men with rolled shirtsleeves push their daughters on tire swings beneath broad maples. A quiet town, where little happened—that's how she remembered it. And the quiet here was the same, as though the island's past catastrophes had been sealed away, untouchable.

The windowless building sat before her like a giant gray brick. Little had been done to disguise its utilitarian purposes. No guava or cypress trees here, no nasturtiums or daisies. In white letters, SOCIEDAD DE ARQUEOLOGÍA DE AMÉRICA DEL SUR fringed the building's upper edge. Greer had arranged her lab in advance through SAAS, which had built this work space for researchers on the island a few years earlier. It was a bit of a scam, really—scientists paid for their own space and equipment yet had to acknowledge themselves as guests of the society in publications. Permission to do work on Easter Island was mainly the decision of the Chilean government, a lead society member.

Greer entered the building onto a long, bare corridor. Hand-lettered nameplates marked each workroom, and midway, on the right, hung her own: DR. FARRADAY. She opened the door and flipped the light switch up and down a few times before the three fluorescent bulbs flickered to life. Her crates were neatly stacked, the corer balanced atop them. Otherwise, the lab was nearly empty. The porous cement walls had been painted white, the rough floor, a shade of pink—coral, perhaps—in what seemed an amusing attempt at cheer. Two long metal tables, a wooden stool tucked beneath each, lined opposite walls. In the corner was a metal sink, a green garden hose snaking from its plastic pipe to a water source outside. Beside it stood a small white refrigerator for her core samples. A column of bare shelves rose above one of the metal tables. On the top shelf sat one dusty beaker—the only scientific instrument in the room—like a skull in a Renaissance painting, a reminder: *Science is here.*

There was certainly sufficient space for her equipment. She looked down at her crates; she needed something—a crowbar, a hammer—to pry them open. Nothing like that in her gear. And the building seemed deserted. She glanced at her watch: six-thirty. First thing in the morning she could ask Ramon for a lever and come back. She set her groceries on the table at the far end, took one last look around the cavernous room, and turned to leave. As she tried to close the door, it caught on an envelope on the floor. It contained a note:

> Doctor Farraday:
> *I have been a fan of your work for a very long time and I look forward to meeting you. I am in the last office on the right side of the hall. Also, we all have dinner at the Hotel Espíritu Thursdays 8 pm. You must join us and tell everyone about your work here. Iorana! Welcome!*
>
> Vicente Portales

Greer slid the note back inside the envelope, shut the door behind her, and tiptoed to the end of the hall. The last nameplate on the right read DR. PORTALES. Beneath it sat the crate she had seen on the airplane: PORTALES. Now she recalled the name. When she was taking samples with Thomas in Belize, she'd read about his work on Mayan hieroglyphics. But what stood out in the article was that he was young and already held a world record of some sort, something to do with hot air balloons, or mountain climbing. Something athletic.

Greer pulled a pen from her pocket, pressed the envelope against the corridor's cement wall, and wrote *Thanks, but I'm busy settling in.* She slid it beneath Dr. Portales's door.

She walked back to her own office, took the nameplate down, and between the words DR. and FARRADAY, she added, in small letters, the word GREER.

A dinner would have been nice, but it wasn't Greer he had invited. And soon Dr. Portales would realize she was not the Dr. Farraday whose work he admired, but his widow.

Greer turned and walked down the dark corridor. A sudden fatigue had descended upon her, as though she had been swimming for hours and her hand had just touched land; more than anything, she wanted to sleep.

4

The warship's interior was draped in velvet, the stateroom laid with Persian carpets, the steel walls hung with gilt-framed watercolors of the Bois de Boulogne. On the tables sat glasses of champagne, splayed decks of cards, jade ashtrays spilling cigarettes, cups of jasmine tea. On a bench beneath a map of the Kaiser's Pacific coaling stations lay an onyx chessboard, the king stranded in eternal checkmate. The rooms were thick with smoke, with people, with laughter. At that very moment, a *Kapitänleutnant* was telling a joke: *So there's a Brit, a German, and a Chinaman and the genie tells them each to make a wish. . . .*

We've heard this before! someone hollered. It was always the Brits, the Germans, and the Chinamen—the usual crowd on the warships at Tsingtao Harbor, in China's Yellow Sea.

Not this one . . .

All right, all right, go ahead. . . .

Then into the smoke-filled room floated the forgotten sound of the wireless, the radio's ancient crackle. There was a shuffle, and soon an officer broke into the festivity. The phonograph's needle was lifted.

The archduke's assassination, he said, it has begun a war.

There was a moment of silence as they all looked at one another. What these men had spent years practicing for, what they had spent the past month anticipating, had now arrived.

So the British stood and dusted their lapels. The Chinese set their cups down. A strange energy pervaded the room—a game, they all knew, had begun. And, like children agreeing to close their eyes and count to ten while someone hides, they extended politenesses. Hands were shaken, apologies offered. In German and English and Chinese, good-byes were said. Soon the Germans, hundreds of men barely twenty years old, were left amid the silence of their festooned warship, imagining, no doubt, that awful sound—one-two-three-four-five—unsure, though, who was counting and who was supposed to hide. They were in China, thousands of miles from Germany, from home. What did this mean?

For this answer, the men looked to Vice Admiral Graf von Spee, striding into the abandoned elegance, the halted party of peacetime, in his gold-trimmed uniform.

"Men," he said. "Prepare the ship. Strip it for war and await further orders."

So the tapestries were hauled down, the carpets pulled from the floors. Into the bay they tossed everything: armchairs, sofas, pianos, paintings. The men, leaning over the gunwale, watched as porcelain vases bobbed across the harbor, as guitars and mandolins cartwheeled in the whitecaps. These waters, in which their ships had been moored for years, now seemed foreboding. It was only a matter of time before the British tried to begin a blockade and sink them at anchor, then only a matter of time before the Russians, the French, and the Japanese, perhaps, began the hunt as well.

They knew they must escape—but to where?

Amid the chaos, someone in the wardroom, a young officer with foresight, surveyed the now-naked room of steel and said to his friends beside him, "And so history is written."

Von Spee, studying his logbook, heard this and looked up. With a hint of that arrogance for which he was famous, he said to his men: "And so we will write it."

—*Fleet of Misfortune: Graf von Spee*
and the Impossible Journey Home

5

Data Compiled for Professor Edward Beazley
by the Royal Geographical Society
Lowther Lodge, Kensington Gore

Te Pito O Te Henua, Known as Rapa Nui;
Commonly Called Easter Island,
South Pacific Ocean
Latitude 28°10′S, Longitude 109°30′W

1722 (Easter Day): Admiral Jacob Roggeveen (Netherlands):
First documented contact with a naked population of mixed race who worshipped huge statues, "squatting on their heels with heads bowed down. . . . The stone images at first caused us to be struck with astonishment because we could not comprehend how it was possible that people who are destitute of heavy or thick timber, and also of stout cordage, out of which to construct gear, had been able to erect them; nevertheless some of these statues were a good thirty feet in height and broad in proportion." Some natives were noted as having slit earlobes hanging to their shoulders, which they could tie up over the edges of their ears. Inhabitants were described as cheerful, peaceful, and well mannered, but expert at thievery. They swam and paddled to the ship in frail canoes. Through a misunderstanding, one native was shot aboard ship and a dozen were shot ashore. A tablecloth and several hats were recorded missing from the admiral's ship.
1770: Don Felipe González (Spain): *Reported that the natives had their own script. He estimated a population of three thousand, but no children were to be seen. He noted large statues speckling the coast.*

A declaration addressed to His Majesty Carlos III of Spain was presented to natives who signed their names (in the form of birds and curious figures) "with every sign of joy and happiness." The island was renamed San Carlos Island. After four days the Spaniards left and never returned to their "territory."

1774: Captain James Cook: *Reported a decimated, poverty-stricken population of approximately 600 men and 30 women. Noting several heaps of stones in front of narrow descents, Cook suspected a network of underground caves in which natives were hiding. The natives refused access to these areas. The colossi were no longer venerated, and most looked to have been toppled. A Tahitian on board partially able to understand native dialect determined that the colossi were not divine images but memorials to deceased persons.*

Cook noted in his journal: "We could hardly conceive how these islanders, wholly unacquainted with any mechanical power, could raise such stupendous figures. . . . They must have been a work of immense time, and sufficiently show the ingenuity and perseverance of the islanders in the age in which they were built; for the present inhabitants have most certainly had no hand in them, as they do not even repair the foundations of those going to decay."

The expedition left with a small supply of sweet potatoes.

1786: Jean-François de Galaup, Comte de La Pérouse (France): *Noted approximately two thousand people on the island; Frenchmen were admitted to caves and subterranean passages where women and children had been hiding; it is believed the peaceful conduct of Captain Cook allowed for this access. Attempts to introduce pigs, goats, and sheep unsuccessful.*

1864: *Brother Eugène Eyraud, a French Catholic missionary, settled on the island; it is believed that the majority of the population converted to Christianity. No statues were in upright position.*

1877: *Population: 111 (reports of a smallpox epidemic related to raids by Peruvian slavers).*

1886: *Visitation by George S. Cook, Surgeon, United States Navy, aboard the USS* Mohican.

1888: Annexation by Chile.

The Society wishes these questions pursued by investigators:
How were the colossal statues crafted? Transported? Were they
made by ancestors of current inhabitants or an earlier, vanished race?
What caused the uniform collapse of the colossi?
Is the script noted by González related to other known writing?
What has been recorded in this script?
Are natives related to other Polynesians or to South Americans?
What is the diet?
What is the family structure? The current ratio of men to women?
Is or has polygamy been practiced?

It is March 1912.

Through the gray Atlantic the White Star liner steams forward. Three thick chimneys crown the boat. Just beyond the compass bridge, past the captain's quarters, Alice and Elsa share a small wood-paneled cabin. Their new leather vanity cases rest on the dresser; on the butler table sits Pudding's cage. The room is elegant, tidy. It is in Edward's cabin, one door down, that they have jammed the crates of tents and saddlery and reference books. "Our equipment is rather important, and we can't have it walloped around in the cargo bay," he explains to any passengers who see him emerging, harried, from this maze of gear. Brushing off his jacket, he says, "We are going on an expedition."

In fact, at any opportunity, Edward speaks of the trip. At breakfast, at tea, as he passes the sugar across the finely laid table, he says, "Did we mention that after this we are making our way to the South Pacific?" Sometimes he asks, "Do you have family in Boston?" or "Is it business that takes you to Massachusetts?" merely to await the same question, so that he can respond, "Boston is a mere starting point for us!" He converses with architects, with American steel magnates, with lonely Cambridge dowagers, displaying with strangers, notes Elsa, an ease he is unable to muster with her.

On the fifth day, when they awake to thunderclouds bruising the horizon, they retreat to the red-carpeted lounge for a game of bezique. There they are approached by an elderly man who announces that he is Andreas Lordet of Belgium, that he is an experienced traveler, that for three years he administered the famous Lemaire copper mine in the Congo, and that he intends, for a brief interval, to join them.

The man sits; he looks wearily at the rain-smeared windows. He is waiting, he says, for his wife to join him. Then slowly, meticulously, he scans them: Edward first, then Elsa, then Alice. His eyes rest a moment on Alice, intrigued by the wad of playing cards held tightly in her hand, and by the way she holds the cards out in front of her, as though unsure of whether to offer them, magicianlike, or to embrace them. With a quick flash of his wrinkled hand, he summons the waiter and orders a gin.

"Congo," Edward says. "I myself spent extensive time in German East Africa. I am an anthropologist and we are now, all of us, in fact, beginning an expedition to Easter Island."

"Ah, yes. Anthropology," the man ponders. "Hmmmph." His eyes close, opening only when he hears the waiter approach with his drink. "*Merci*," he tells the man, followed by a long swallow of gin.

"Of course," says Edward, "the South Pacific is vastly different from the African continent."

"Africa! Yes!" he exclaims. Then, eagerly, he begins the story of his experience with what he calls "savage discontent"—a phenomenon about which he hopes soon to write a scholarly paper. An anthropologist such as Edward would no doubt take interest in his observations. And on he goes with tales of stolen revolvers and bands of natives, of poisoned arrows raining from the sky, finishing each story with a swig of gin, as though still astonished at his ability to survive such danger. "*Bien sûr.*" He thumps his emptied glass on the table beside him. "Yet, here I am. You see?" He knocks his fist against his chest. "One must have strength. Courage. *Resolve.* And then such uprisings will merely be"—his hand flaps in the air—"a cure for boredom."

"Wouldn't it be easier," asks Elsa, drawing a new card from the table, "to stay in Belgium and go to the theater?"

He turns to Edward. "Theater?"

Elsa reorders her cards with great concentration. She is tired of playing audience to this tedious man.

"Well. What you say of courage is indeed true," says Edward. "The foreigner has many new and unsettling experiences. The change in diet alone can be a cause for alarm."

"*Théâtre?*" the man repeats, giving the word its full French pronunciation.

You sound like a brute, Elsa wants to tell him. Uprisings as a form of amusement! She's heard enough. And why must Edward be so diplomatic? She knows he agrees with her—in his own book, Edward emphasized the need for imperial subjects to respect the peoples of their colonies. But a row? Edward won't have it. She'd like to remind him of his own book's final chapter, "Toward Greater Understanding," her favorite: the one part of his writing that made her think Edward, in addition to collecting and compiling data, harbored a deep sympathy for his subjects. But now she wonders at the sincerity of his feelings.

Suddenly, the man looks past Elsa. "Hélène!"

Elsa turns. A finely dressed woman of seventy or so strides toward them. A thick gold necklace clings to her chest. Three broad bangles anchor each of her wrists. Edward rises, and Andreas conducts introductions. Finally, the woman sits carefully on the edge of her seat and turns to her husband.

"Nous parlons de voyages," he says.

Edward says, "We are headed for the South Pacific. On an expedition for the Royal Geographic Society."

"Ah, *le Pacifique du sud.* Well, you must beware of mosquitoes. You have lots of quinine, I hope. You can never have too much quinine."

Do these people, Elsa wonders, love nothing more than to alert others of danger?

"Quinine?" asks Alice, who Elsa sees has accumulated almost an entire deck of cards in her fist.

"Qui-nine," answers Madame Lordet. "You use it for the treatment of the malarial fever. It is taken from the bark of a tree. A dose of three drops at bedtime is best."

"Fever?!" Alice's hands slacken, and several cards flutter to the floor.

The woman's head tilts contemplatively to one side.

"We have tents with nets," Elsa says. "Mosquito nets. Don't worry, Allie."

"Fever?"

"Ma chérie. Do not be worried," says Madame Lordet, her voice gentle. "You will just tell the mosquito to go away and leave you alone! You will say 'Shoo,' and he will fly off!"

Alice smiles, tosses her cards to the side.

"I think somebody has won the game!" Madame Lordet leans toward Elsa, necklace jangling, and whispers, "My niece in Antwerp"—she shakes her head with regret—"is just the same."

After the card game, Madame Lordet offers to take Alice to the parlor to cheer the Ping-Pong matches. "My Adèle just adores watching the balls go back and forth," she says, lifting a pale finger to illustrate the motion.

"Well," Elsa begins politely, "Alice has a variety of interests more stimulating than ball-watching." How tiresome, though, the endless assumptions. "You might ask her to draw your portrait. She's quite a good artist."

"An artist!" The woman smiles, shakes her head in wondrous delight, as though before her has pranced a monkey in a top hat. "*Merveilleux.*"

Elsa strains a smile and offers a polite good-bye, planting a kiss on Alice's honeyed scalp. From the table she picks up *On the Origin of Species* and tucks it in the crook of her arm. Edward smiles; the book, a handsome first edition, was his wedding gift to her. The night before leaving England, he presented her with a collection of Darwin: five books, each bound in burgundy leather, the spines lettered in gold, and her new, married initials—EPB—embossed on all the title pages. She has been carrying this volume from her cabin to the deck to the lounge without a moment, yet, for study. Now she can steal a few minutes.

Elsa climbs the steps to the boat's upper deck, but no sooner has she reached the windy promenade than she thinks of turning back. She is sickened by the idea of this woman dragging Alice through the parlor like a pet. Elsa tries to shake the image from her mind. Her father always admonished her for this—her desire to argue Alice's abilities. Alice was Alice, he said, no matter how she was perceived. Ignorance wounded only the ignorant. But for Elsa, it was a matter of defending Alice's honor. Even if each contemptuous stare could be disregarded, she couldn't help but feel that left unchecked, the weight of them all might soon press against Alice. And part of Elsa suspected her father was simply too tired, too old, for outrage. She had seen him outraged just once in her life: She had been nine years old, sitting in Dr. Chapple's London consultation room with her father and Alice, listening as the doctor explained the medical specifications of amentia—*state of restricted potentiality . . . arrest of cerebral development . . . insufficient cortical neurons*—at the time, an endless muddle of syllables to Elsa, but words she would hear again for years to come. What Elsa did understand was that Dr. Chapple said there were places they could send Alice—the Royal Albert Asylum in

Lancaster, the Sandlebridge School for the Feeble-Minded—places that would accommodate, and this phrase etched itself in Elsa's mind, *mental defectives*. Elsa finally slid forward in her chair and asked what to her seemed the most relevant question: "Can you fix her?"

"I'm afraid, my dear girl," said the doctor, removing his glasses for this final pronouncement, rubbing the bridge of his nose, "the condition of amentia, though its external manifestations can be reduced through a proper balance of stimulus and rest, is both permanent and untreatable."

Her father nodded silently.

The doctor then began scribbling. "However, take one part caraway seeds, one part ginger and salt, and spread it on bread with a touch of butter. This has been shown successful at temporarily quelling mild episodes of hysteria." Her father's gaze was fixed on the floor, so Elsa accepted the doctor's paper.

Once they were outside, on the steps of Dr. Chapple's office, after the door had closed behind them, her father raised his hand and slapped Elsa's face. He had never done this before.

"Understand this," he said. "Alice does not need to be fixed. She needs to be cared for. And you will not now or ever refer to any of Alice's behavior as a problem or defect. Do I need to repeat myself?"

Elsa's head dropped—she had meant only to see if they could help Alice. She refused to answer. Was she not the one who always fought on Alice's behalf? Suddenly a shriek erupted beside her— Alice, hand raised above her head, face flushed with anger, began to twist and spin, until the propeller of her arm landed with a firm thwack on their father's stomach. She swung back for another strike, but their father caught her wrist. His eyes were mapped with capillaries.

"Alice. My little Alice."

But Alice only glared at him, the vein on her forehead plump with rage, her narrow chest rising and falling with exertion. He released her wrist and Alice again launched her arm.

"Allie," said Elsa, grabbing her. "It's all right."

Their father stared down at them as though searching for the just response. This was too much for him; Elsa could see it. It was the first time he had shown such exhaustion, such confusion. He shook his head, then walked down the steps toward the busy London street.

"Elsa, I hit him!" Alice wrenched free from Elsa's grip. "I hit Papa. Did you see me?" She sprang to her toes and began to bounce.

Tugging Alice by the sleeve, Elsa hurried down the steps until they flanked him. "Father," said Elsa. "Please . . . Father."

He did not stop; he did not even look at them.

"I'm sorry, Father."

"Hmmnn? What is it?"

"I'm sorry."

"Elsa's sorry!" shouted Alice.

He seemed disoriented. "You must catch your breath, Elsa. Calm yourself. Why have you let yourself get flustered?"

"Elsa's sorry!"

"Elsa? Sorry? What on earth for?" He glanced up at the sky and sighed, a long, tired sound that seemed to have taken years to work its way out of him. "No. No one needs to be sorry. No one. Let's get home before dark."

And together they walked down the sidewalk in silence, as though nothing had happened.

On the boat's rain-washed promenade, Elsa hears the rumble of the engine, the sharp voice of a mother forbidding her child to run, the murmurs of a couple leaning on the railing to watch the sun break through the clouds. The rain has stopped, but a cold wind sweeps the deck. She trails her fingertips along the chilly rail and surveys the horizon. No England; no Europe. Is it really possible to leave the past behind? To begin anew? But Elsa knows all too well this yearning in herself. When leaving home for her first governess post, she had imagined she could start afresh, could unhinge her former frame of solemnity and let herself curl into a new, carefree girl, the kind she had always envied. But the frame was too old, and, despite her hopes, despite her efforts, it held firm.

Seating herself on a dry bench, Elsa opens *On the Origin of Species*. She's read some of this before—her father, of course, had a copy; and often it could be found in the libraries of her employers. But this is *her* volume. Burgundy leather, beautiful. She smiles at the thought that she can crease the pages. She can mark the margins. She can drip tea across the pristine ivory pages. "First edition" means little; what matters is that the book is her own, and as such should bear traces of her use. With this in mind, Elsa turns to the introduction and with her thumb and forefinger nicks the page's upper corner. There. She looks up, hoping, perhaps, that someone has seen her. A silly gesture, she knows, but it fills her with a sudden satisfaction, as if this small act of destruction, of rebellion, has for a moment offset the prudence of all her other choices.

Elsa begins reading, and with her pencil underlines passages of interest. This, too, gives her great pleasure, and she wonders if some primitive instinct is at work. Her pupils always scrawled their names on lesson books—front covers, back covers, random pages—as if they had an unwavering need to document the event of their learning, to mark the territory their minds traveled. Am I no different, she wonders, than a schoolgirl hoping that a few possessions will remind the world of my existence?

She reads on.

> There is a striking parallelism in the laws of life throughout time and space; the laws governing the succession of forms in past times being nearly the same with those governing at the present time. . . .

The words seem to flow through her. *Past times, present time*—yes, there is a largeness to it all, something beyond her, beyond this vast steamer and this endless ocean. Elsa pencils a note, turns the page, and suddenly senses herself smiling. I love this, she thinks. I feel like a true scholar. All those grammar and geography and mathematics lessons gone—here is Darwin; here is an amazing theory.

A burst of laughter distracts her—farther down the deck two young women in leghorn hats are strolling. Their eyes are locked on a young man reading, and as they pass him, there is another burst of laughter that draws his attention from the magazine. This brief game won, the women lean into each other, whispering, their hats forming a canopy above them. There is an ease in these women, a careless- ness Elsa envies. She has never been like that. Since childhood, she has lived in constant vigilance. Always she has had Alice to look after, her father to tend to. Alice needed her patience. Her father, her obe- dience. And when she became a governess, Elsa begrudgingly ac- quired the most difficult, for her, of dispositions—humility. Over time, these duties had produced in her a seriousness that made others uneasy. Made men uneasy. She was not, after all, ugly; her skin was smooth, her hair chestnut and silken, though a little thin. When she looked at herself in the mirror, her features seemed soft and balanced, and she thought she must be as pleasant to look at as the next girl. Still, the tension in her demeanor made men look past her to more lighthearted girls. Even Max, who shared her gravity, had drawn back from it at first.

Several days after his return from Kiel, he came to say hello in the schoolroom. Elsa was at the table with Otto and Huberta, reviewing English prepositions, when he walked over, extended one hand, and laid it for a moment on each child's head. Looking down at their lesson books, he asked Otto, the oldest, in English, "And how do you like the new governess?"

"*Sehr gut, Papa.*"

"Have we brought her all the way from England to help you speak German?" He turned to Elsa. "Have you settled in well?"

"Yes," she said.

"Prepositions?"

"Yes, sir."

"Excellent."

And with that, he left. An entire month passed before he spoke to her again. But she thought his disinterest a sign she was doing her job well. The staff was the foundation of a household—best unseen.

Their next conversation had to do with a pocket watch Huberta had taken from her father's office and, when Elsa tried to retrieve it, let tumble down the marble staircase. When Elsa picked it up, she saw the glass face had been cracked. And rather than have Huberta—who was hopelessly fitful and clumsy, who sometimes reminded her of Alice—disciplined, Elsa told the head maid she had broken it herself and that the repair costs should be taken from her wages.

The next day he interrupted her while she was giving lessons. He said there was a debt to be discussed.

"I'm sorry, sir?" Elsa closed the lesson books and rested her hands in her lap.

"My watch. What has inspired you to pay for the repair?"

Huberta, whose English was progressing rapidly, squirmed in her seat.

"I don't understand." But suddenly Elsa did: The watch was already damaged when Huberta snatched it. "Ah, yes, sir. I apologize."

He lingered for a moment, looking at his children and the books, his eyes resting on Elsa.

"It was given to me when I was thirteen."

"What was, sir?"

"The watch, it belonged to my father."

"Fine, sir."

"It has meaning for me."

"Yes, sir."

"For one who teaches conversation, your English is quite limited."

Elsa did not like to be goaded. This was a danger of her position she had resolved to guard herself against. Employers were moody. Some days—if it was rainy, if they had not slept well—they might decide to draw out the details of your life, or offer theirs. Afterward they feared you would take it too far, abandon your work and gossip all day, and so they grew colder, struck a pose of even greater superiority. If you had let yourself believe in the friendship, this was a blow. It was easier, and safer, never to test that path.

"I suppose so," she said.

"Very well, then. Continue with your lessons," he said. "And if the urge strikes, do teach them some compound sentences."

They did not speak again until the day she received a letter from her father about the drafting of the Feeble-Minded Control Bill. Elsa had gone to her favorite garden bench to read, and had become visibly upset. When Max, out walking, saw her, when he asked what was the matter and motioned if he might sit down, Elsa was too unhappy, too preoccupied, to respond. Her mind was with Alice, and so when he sat beside her, that was of whom she spoke—she described Alice's episodes, her abilities, the term *amentia*, the details of the legislation. Elsa's openness risked impropriety, but Max didn't seem to mind. He seemed intrigued by Alice's predicament, as though it were a great riddle offered up for him to solve. He stroked his beard and stared straight ahead as Elsa spoke. The wind rustled the tree above them, and as the sun set, long shadows, like awnings, fell from the hedges. There was a sense of sanctuary on that bench, and Elsa understood very clearly that his empathy for her could be expressed only there. It was her understanding of this, she suspected, that put him at ease.

Even after other encounters, after he began leading the children on long hikes that he insisted she join, for hours teaching them the names of the trees and shrubs they passed, even after he had sought her out several times, alone, when his wife, Margarete, was calling on friends, Elsa never behaved toward him as anything but her employer. It was a friendship, a simple companionship, which neither dreamed would escalate. They could talk easily, and they liked each other, though Elsa wasn't sure at first what it was she liked in him.

Max was attractive, but she never thought herself greatly impressed by that. He was intelligent, but Elsa had often met intelligent men at the university. Max, however, was the first person she'd ever met who needed no looking after. From time to time, she would overhear him lose his temper in some distant wing of the house, his voice rising for a moment about a telegram belatedly delivered, a door left unlocked, but it would subside quickly. He never looked upset, never tired, never nervous, and it was a bit of a joke among the servants that his self-sufficiency drove them mad. In him dwelled an awesome strength to which Elsa was drawn, though by attraction or envy, she couldn't say. And then, unexpectedly, she fell in love. She sometimes wondered if being so far from Alice had allowed her indiscretion. Had Alice been with her, it would never have happened. Of that she feels certain.

But Elsa is happy, now, to have Alice with her. And gradually her doubts concerning the trip are subsiding. Edward has promised they will turn back if the journey proves too much for Alice, but so far it thrills her. In Southampton, as the ship set out, she hooted and waved to the harbor crowd. She has explored and drawn each level of the steamer. And the amenities of travel—the books, the bags—enchant her. Several times a day, Alice opens her small leather satchel, examines the contents, then seals and stows it beneath the bed. In it she has arranged a comb and looking glass, a small pair of scissors for Pudding's nails, a photograph of their father, the perfumed silk sachet that Elsa bought her, a bundle of chalk and crayons fastened with blue ribbon, a pair of binoculars, the silver candy bowl from Edward's sitting room (which she scrambles to position on the dresser each time before Edward is permitted to enter their cabin—"Not yet!" she cries as he lingers in the doorway, sure to keep his palms held firmly over his eyes), and, despite Elsa's insistence that she would have no need for it, a German-English dictionary—the same item Alice watched Elsa pack the first time she left home.

Of course, the longest, most arduous part of the voyage is still ahead. Tropical climates, strange languages, peoples of unknown dispositions. The potential for danger is, Elsa knows, quite real. But wasn't there danger in England? The whole business of the Royal Commission on the Care and Control of the Feeble-Minded, their endless articles and proposals, the bill they tried to slip through Parliament to mandate institutionalization—it terrified her. Her father, in his last months, had posted three letters to the *Daily Telegraph* decrying *The Journal of the Eugenics Education Society* and their claims that sterilization could prevent the spread of idiocy. "Spread!" he coughed from his bed, hurling the journal to the floor. "Do they think this is smallpox?" Even more unsettling was one of the names on the masthead of the *Eugenics Review*—Dr. William Chapple—the man they had turned to years before to diagnose Alice's condition.

When Elsa and Edward were clearing her father's office, in her father's desk drawer she found the last few volumes of the *Review*. Why, she wondered, did he hold on to them? Did he think that in his drawer he might control their contents? How typical of Father to assume his constant obsession, his ten-page letters, would solve the problem. Never was he guilty of indolence, never of surrender. His hard work, however, could be so misdirected. Textiles—a serious investment, but dreadfully ill-advised. Looking around at the dusty books, the boxes of papers—the bulk of her inheritance—Elsa thought: I am penniless. It would take more than her vigilance to make sure Alice didn't find herself in the hands of maniacal doctors. Elsa pulled the volumes from the drawer and scanned the clutter for a wastebasket.

"Please, Miss Pendleton," said Edward from across the room. "Do have a rest. I'd be pleased to deal with this untidiness. This sort of thing is always trying on one's feelings."

"I'm fine, Professor Beazley," she said, the coolness in her voice obviously startling him out of his tender moment. He seemed disconcerted by her lack of bereavement, by the calm she had shown at the funeral. Why did Edward and everybody else expect she would be consumed by emotion? If she hadn't so many other concerns, she might have been. "I'm merely looking for a place to dispose of this idiotic rubbish." Elsa glanced around; everything, actually, looked like a trash bin—suitcases and crates stuffed with papers, books, and broadsides. Finally Elsa tore up one volume at a time and let the pieces tumble to the floor. "There. Now I won't mistake them for anything worth saving."

"I understand your irritation. The Eugenics Education Society. An awful business."

"Father no doubt told you all about it."

"Some. Yes." Edward shook his head. "It is an outrage, really. This is what Britain's medical experts concoct? Not a cure, not a remedy, not even an attempt to ease the discomforts of those who are troubled. But isolation? Imprisonment? Sterilization?" His hands flew up. "Good God."

This sudden passion surprised Elsa—Edward had been silent through the morning as they filled the crates. But the contagion of his anger swept her; and she was happy to be permitted a display of frustration.

"They're frightened fools, Professor Beazley. Not a single doctor in eighteen years has been able to explain what happened to Allie. Over twenty so-called professionals consulted, and none of them could say if she began this way; if she was injured in birth. The doctors can't move one foot toward identifying the source of such differences, and so what do they want? They want all those different people to disappear, because their existence reminds the doctors of their own incompetence."

"It is a case of Britain's sense of nationhood gone too far. This focus on the good of the political unit rather than the good of the individual. It's an appalling feature of our culture. Among the Hoonai and the Mugundi of East Africa, those born with impediments or unusual features are seen as children of the gods given to humans to look after."

"Perhaps I should take Allie to East Africa."

"Don't worry, Miss Pendleton. We won't let anything happen to Alice."

Yes, Elsa thinks, even then he said "we." *We won't let anything happen* . . . Before he had proposed, as though anticipating Alice would be his concern. And how coldly she had behaved. Could she have known he would help her out of the very situation that made her act with such detachment?

When he had spoken of this journey to the South Pacific, he spoke of Alice's protection, of the safety of foreign shores. "Elsa, both you and your father have always made certain that Alice was cared for by the people who love her. This voyage—well, it most certainly won't resemble England—but it will be with her family, with the people who care for her. It will be good for her. *Desideratum*. No risk of horrid legislation taking her from you, from us."

He was right.

Only Elsa hopes the people of Easter Island are as forgiving as the Hoonai and the Mugundi.

❀

Evenings, they work in the ship's lounge.

"Before we even arrive we shall be experts," says Edward, seated on the edge of a velvet sofa, sorting papers. He has boxes of correspondence from Royal Geographic Society members. Others, reading of the expedition in the papers, have written to offer services; thirty-two steward applications alone clutter his pile. Geologists have requested rock specimens from each port of call. Some correspondents have provided theories—*I must inform you, Professor Beazley, that your mystery island is part of the lost continent of Lemuria (see enclosed map), of which I am an original inhabitant;* others, warnings— *"And the waters prevailed exceedingly upon the earth; and all the high hills that were under the whole heaven were covered. And all the flesh died that moved upon the earth, both of fowl, and of cattle, and of beast and of every creeping thing, that creepeth upon the earth and every man." You venture thousands of miles when the answer to your "mystery" is right there in the Lord's Scripture? Do not incite His wrath!*

Separating the letters of immediate use has fallen to Elsa. But it is like searching for a clover in a field of grass; theories and warnings obscure each relevant fact. Yet she soon finds herself reading on even after she has extracted the data. *I have always wanted to travel myself. I once dreamed of an island in the Pacific. My son, taken last year by the consumption, wanted to be an archaeologist.* This glimpse into lives she will never encounter—it is just one more door of novelty the expedition opens. So leisurely, to faint tango staccatos drifting from the ballroom below, she compiles a list of Polynesian phrases. *Hello, peace, horse, food, freshwater*—in Tahitian, Hawaiian, Samoan, and Tongan. She also details the island's climate, its average rainfall and temperatures. Domestic plants and animals get their own list. And from this data her mind begins to form a picture of their mysterious destination: grassy slopes, hundreds of grazing sheep, strong winds hurling in from the sea.

"I don't have a book! Why don't I have a book?" Alice, seated on the floor, dutifully unfolding the letters for Elsa's pile, stops her work. She focuses on Elsa. "Alice must have a book."

"But you've your very own journal, Allie," Elsa says.

"I do. I have my own journal. What do I put in it?"

"Anything you like, Alice," Edward says warmly, looking up from the mess of papers before him. His work relaxes him.

"Pictures. Why, you should be the official expedition artist," says Elsa.

"My book is in the room. I want to get it."

Their cabin is only yards away, and Elsa tells Alice she may walk, slowly, to the room, retrieve her book, and return immediately. In a flash Alice is gone. Elsa closes her book and watches the narrow passageway. When Alice reappears, she has her journal in one hand, Pudding's cage in the other.

"Allie."

"He wanted to see the boat!"

"Set him down, there, beside the sofa. This is a lounge. If he begins to caw, we'll have to take him back."

"Keep quiet, Pudding. Or Elsa's going to take you away."

Alice dramatically perches herself in a chair, mimicking Elsa's studious posture, and spreads the blank book in her lap.

"What will you draw in it?" Elsa asks.

"Who is on the expedition?"

"We are. You, me, and Edward."

A mischievous smile curls Alice's mouth. "Three people."

"Three indeed, Allie."

Alice carefully counts three pages. She looks up at Elsa. "Portraits."

"Excellent. Three portraits." As Alice's pencil leaps into the book, a young couple, elegantly clad, strolls past.

"Good evening!" says Edward, and the couple return his greeting, but Elsa can see, in the way their eyes search Edward and his clutter of papers, then Alice, herself, and Pudding's sparkling cage, that they are unsure of what to make of this group before them. Pudding squawks, and the woman grabs the man's arm.

"A bird," the man says. "Just a bird, my dear."

"Allie," cautions Elsa.

"Pudding," scolds Alice.

"I told you we would have to take him back to the room."

"What's in your book, Elsa?"

"Allie."

"What are you writing in there?"

"Words for us to use when we meet people who don't speak our language."

"Put some in my book."

"Very well." Elsa takes the book from Alice's lap and writes:

Iorana: Hello
Ahi: Fire
Ana: Cave

"Now study those words so that you can use them when we arrive. Everybody is going to want to talk to you."

Alice smiles, then slides Elsa's notebook from her lap. "You need
drawings."

Below them, another song begins. A slow song, with violins. Elsa
imagines all the well-dressed couples clasping hands, swaying from
side to side. She imagines the two young women she saw on deck
wearing long white gowns, their eyes seeking out the man with the
magazine. She sees the Belgian couple gliding across the dance floor,
the woman's gold necklace lit by the porthole's moonlight. But when
she looks at Alice, Elsa brushes the image away.

"Drawings. Yes. I do need them, don't I? Do you think you could
make some for me?"

"Can he stay?" she begs, looking at Pudding.

"All right, Allie. He can stay."

❀

After two weeks at sea, they arrive in Boston Harbor and Elsa says a
silent good-bye to the vast liner, the elegant strangers, the ballroom and
game room and canopied promenades. Standing in the hubbub of the
dock, fortressed by their crates, they watch the waves of splendid greetings: valises dropped, arms flung open, names trilled, *Charles! Clarissa!
Father!* Trunks are tumbled into the boots of motorcars. Skirts are gathered in small fists as one black-buckled shoe, then another, sidesteps
into the backseat. Doors thud closed. The crowds thin, and cars rumble
away. How strange, thinks Elsa, to see people move from one container
to another. From ship to motorcar. And soon, no doubt, to flat, to house.
She has always liked being out of doors, riding her Humber or strolling
through Kew Gardens. Motion soothes her, makes her feel a sense of
progress and freedom. The evening after her father died, after she
learned the details of his finances, Elsa took Alice's bicycle (her own still
suffered the wounds of Alice's hatpin) and rode through the darkening
streets, cycling faster than ever before, her legs burning with exertion,
as though she could pedal through her mounting sense of doom, could
hurl herself forward, over it, into a new bright life.

And now motion *is* taking her into a new life. They have crossed the Atlantic and will soon sail the coast of two continents. How Elsa would love to tell these people: *We* won't be snatched away by a motorcar! *We* won't be tucked into narrow beds in tidy homes! We are adventurers! And she stands amid the clang and creak of the docks, smiling, her hand resting on a crate, until up walks a ruddy-faced young man who introduces himself as Ryan Fitzpatrick.

"Of Fitzpatrick and Sons?" asks Edward.

"Son number four. Best for last. Here to get you to your schooner."

He engages five porters and leads them down a long pier. Soon they are before the fifty-two-foot schooner Edward arranged for from England. It is a four-year charter agreement, subsidized by the Royal Geographic Society, and will allow them two years on the island and a year for travel on either end.

"Have a look," Edward says while he reviews a thick set of contracts with Ryan Fitzpatrick.

Elsa guides Alice down four steps, into the long main cabin. Paneled in a thickly lacquered blond wood, the space is bright and cheery. It is divided into a galley—with a stove and an icebox—and a dining quarter. The sitting area has two high-backed benches at the far end. This entire cabin is no larger than the attic rooms she was given by her employers. It is smaller than she imagined—but there is always the deck, where she will spend most of her time. Behind the stairs a thin wooden door opens into a spacious square cabin, the captain's quarters, with one large bed. She and Alice will sleep here.

"Do you like it?" Elsa asks. "Just like we had in Father's house when we were little."

Alice looks the room over. "Where will Pudding sit? At home he sits on my dresser. There's no dresser here."

"Perhaps we could put a hook in. Let his cage hang."

But Alice is already on the bed, crawling across the mattress, pushing at a hatch directly above. "An escape route!"

"Careful, Allie."

She shoves the glass until, hinges creaking with resistance, it bursts open. "Look, Elsa! Look!" Alice's head disappears above deck, and in a moment a squeal comes. She ducks back into the cabin.

"Allie, you mustn't go sticking your head out like that. You could hurt yourself. And who knows how sturdy those hinges are?"

But Alice's face is red. She leans toward Elsa, eyes wide, and whispers. "I saw Beazley."

Edward hires two Irishmen, Kierney and Eamonn, as crew to help him sail to the island and then to return on their own to Chile. The society will arrange crew for the return voyage to England. The men will sleep in the V-berth at the boat's front end. They are young, leather-skinned, and brawny, but come recommended for their reliability and their experience. They brag of the ports they have seen—the Chinese vendors in San Francisco, the thieves in Acapulco—as they heave from dock to deck the endless stores of coal and water, the provisions of paper, ink, tea, biscuits, fresh meat, the buckets of fruits and vegetables, the bags of bandages and cameras. Kierney, constantly flashing Elsa a gap-toothed grin, pauses to examine each piece of equipment as he carries it belowdecks.

"Look here, Eamonn. Have you ever seen this here thing?" He is holding a large vernier caliper, flipping it up, then down. "You think it might be for a doctor? For surgery? Holding the head in place while he cuts 'em open?"

"Just put it aft and tie it down so it don't jump up at you when we set off. You see that hold? You see all that empty space in there? We gotta fill it. You and me. And chattering ain't gonna get the work done."

"Aye," he says to Elsa with a huff, "he sounds just like me mum!"

After days of provisioning, packing, and checking the boat, on April sixth the men set the sails, and Elsa and Alice watch the boat come to life. Edward, proud and handsome in his new white suit, assumes a regal perch behind the wheel. Above them, the sails fill with the breeze, and the schooner departs the waters of Boston Harbor.

Carried by a steady wind, the first week is smooth sailing. Elsa sits on deck and studies the rigging and the equipment, learning the names: windlass, Aladdin cleat, Charley Noble. She adjusts to the peculiar rhythms of life at sea, the occasional swing of the boom, the swift hauling of heavy, wet lines. She accustoms herself to the tedious unfastening and refastening of the teakettle and biscuit tin each afternoon—everything has to be tied down so as not to fly across the cabin should the boat lurch, a lesson she learns quickly when, two days from Boston, a neglected melon thwacks her in the back.

Off Cape Hatteras, a sudden gale catches the boat. Slashing rains and winds ransack the deck, and as they heave to for hours, Alice races through the main cabin, clinging intermittently to Edward and Elsa, then vomiting over a navigation chart.

"Aye there, little lass! A boat is no place for this here kind of mis-chief!" shouts Kierney, wiping the soiled charts, fanning the stench from his face. "I'll gladly suffer the rain if it means a breath of good air."

Alice curls up beneath the steps. "Bad Alice," she mumbles. "Bad Alice. No mischief." And then her eyes retreat to their private do-main.

"Yes, do get yourself a breath of fresh air. And take your time," says Edward, gesturing toward the deck.

Kierney doesn't budge.

"No air, then? I suggest you collect yourself or you will have more than ample time to explore Recife. I think Brazil would suit you quite well."

Elsa can't help but smile at this—Edward is standing firm. And for the sake of Alice. In the dim cabin Edward catches her smile, and lets it spread, ever so slightly, to himself.

❖

June finds them off the northeast coast of Brazil. Weeks from the port at Recife, they are stilled in doldrums, fighting the northward flow of the Guiana current. But for a few grainy flaws on its surface, the sea stretches in stillness. The air is hot and thick and the sun itself seems to vibrate. For days on end, sitting on deck, Elsa watches the canvas squares hang motionless, her mind lulled by the stagnancy, her thoughts turning to her letter to Max. She sees him unfolding the pages, examining each phrase like a code, reading it aloud, measur-ing its sound. She has seen him study dinner invitations as if they were riddles. But will it be his first thought of her in months? Have his duties diverted him so completely? After all, she has been able to put him mostly out of her mind. Only in this sluggishness does she find herself closing her eyes and thinking of him, even though she doesn't want to. It only saddens her, a sadness that seems to agitate Alice. Sometimes, opening her eyes to the bright light of the deck, Elsa finds Alice sitting across the bow, staring accusingly, as if she knows Elsa's mind has been wandering to places she is not invited.

These looks of accusation always remind Elsa of what happened with Rodney Blackwell. Years before, when she was sixteen, Rodney, the son of the president of the Zoological Society, had briefly courted Elsa. He took her to cricket matches, to Kew Gardens, to the Royal Victoria Hall to see *Macbeth*, and once, after much pleading, he took her for a ride in one of the new motor taxis. They enjoyed, in a sedate way, each other's company. Rodney liked to discuss Descartes' *Meditations* or Irish Home Rule or the failings of parliamentary government; ideas and issues thrilled him. He felt no *emotional* attachment to her, Elsa knew. A pure intellectual curiosity led him through life. As a child, he had, for the sake of satisfying his interest, smeared honey on his hand and provoked a bee to sting him.

One evening, standing before the door of her father's house, he removed his hat and said, "Elsa, I should like to try a brief kiss before we part." Elsa had never been kissed, and she, like Rodney, had, if not the passion, at least the curiosity for such an experience. "Very well," she said. He stepped forward and pressed his tense mouth against hers. She could smell his hair, his cologne, could feel his cold nose against her own. When he stepped back, she said, "Fine. Something new. Good night, then." Elsa eased the heavy door closed behind her, tiptoed up the stairs to the bedroom, and saw Alice, in her white nightgown, seated on the window ledge. Alice was silent for a moment, then raced toward her. "I'm Rodney! I'm Rodney!"

"Allie! You'll wake Father." Elsa's voice was sharp.

Alice retreated.

"I'm sorry, Allie. Come here. Quietly."

"Why can't I kiss you?"

Elsa looked at Alice's hair, loose from its braids, a wreath of curls around her small face. Her brow was creased with worry. "Do you want to kiss me?" Elsa asked.

Alice nodded.

"All right," said Elsa.

Alice paused, as though she didn't trust this concession. Then slowly, she stepped toward Elsa. "I'm going to be Rodney," Alice said, eyes aglow, tucking a curl behind her ear. She straightened her nightgown, as though nervous, as though she really were Rodney, or another boy, asking to approach Elsa.

"Ready?" asked Elsa.

"Ready." They were still several feet apart.

"Do you want me to come toward you?" Elsa asked. "Or shall you come toward me?"

Alice hesitated.

"Rodney came toward me."

Alice sprung to the balls of her feet. "All right. All right. Elsa, close your eyes."

"I'm closing my eyes."

In the darkness, Elsa waited, listening to the hush of crumpled cotton, a slight sigh as Alice released the shadow of a mysterious thought into the night, and then the gentle creak of the floorboards beneath Alice's feet. Alice's warm breath bathed her face, and her lips, plump and moist, touched Elsa's and withdrew. Then the lips returned, more confident, nestling against her own. A soft humming began and Elsa could feel the sound waves thrum through her cheeks. It was no different, she thought, from what she had done with Rodney. And it was a truer kiss. Gentle, loving. Her life had been full of such private, intimate concessions to Alice. As a child, Alice sometimes begged Elsa for a small taste of her chewed food; when Elsa began menstruating, Alice panicked when she found a drop of blood in the washroom and insisted Elsa show her where it had come from. Of these moments, Elsa told no one.

When Alice finally pulled away, Elsa opened her eyes. A wide grin lit Alice's face.

"Did you like that?" she asked.

"I'll have hundreds of kisses," said Alice.

"Thousands, Allie."

Elsa unclasped her dress in the dark room, poured herself a glass of water for the bedside. When they were both finally beneath their covers, Elsa whispered good night.

"Thousands," mumbled Alice.

Then Elsa blew out the candle and pressed her cheek against the cold pillow.

After two weeks of floating aimlessly, a brief rain at last loosens from the sky. They all seize a bowl or cup and clamber on deck to catch the meager spray, their tongues lapping at the drops. Within minutes, however, the sky revokes its gift, offering instead another blast of heat, tinged now with oppressive humidity. Edward unbuttons his collar and steps below to check the stores. Moments later he returns with a look of concern. "We shall all halve our rations until we know we'll make Recife in time."

"What about Pudding?" Alice demands, gripping the gunwale to pull herself up. "He is supposed to have fresh water two times a day! Isn't that right, Elsa? I've always given him water two times a day." She squints at the sun with indignation.

Kierney, crouched on the foredeck, rolls his eyes and drinks the last of his rain-filled cup."There's a hierarchy at sea, Miss Pendleton. And birds, even birds who can say *superior*, ain't at the top of it."

"Pudding can have his water twice a day,"Elsa says."It will be fine, Allie. For goodness' sake,"she announces to the boat."We are not going to run out of water."

"I've seen it happen," says Kierney. "You name the disaster, and I've seen it."

"We shall be fine,"states Edward."This is merely a precaution."He turns to Alice."The bird may take from my ration."

For the first time, Elsa feels anxious. Could they really run out of water? She scolds herself for drinking too much, washing too liberally. She sets aside what's left of her day's ration for Alice. She can manage.

But the next morning when Elsa steps on deck, the small hairs on one side of her neck seem to tingle. The mysterious language she has been learning for months, the silent script of breezes, is now being written on her skin. As the cool air letters itself along her neck, Elsa calls below,"Allie, come quick! I think we've a trade wind coming."By noon, the boat bounds away, tightening at all sides with new life.

In Brazil, they call in Recife, Bahia de Todos Os Santos, Cabral Bay, and Rio de Janeiro. With each anchoring there are visits from harbormasters, customs officers, and doctors. Ashore, Edward visits the consul and searches for the latest copies of the *Daily Graphic* and *Spectator*. Elsa arranges for fresh mutton and vegetables from the port chandlers. The boat provisioned, she and Alice stroll through the harbor, nibbling on a fried fish wrapped in newspaper, Alice's feet dragging beneath her long skirts in their usual forgetfulness. Elsa loves these late afternoons, exploring the maze of shops and stalls and shanties bathed in the golden glow of tropical sunset. And at all times, she carries her notebook, now thick with information for the expedition.

She is pleased that Edward is allowing her to contribute. He seems to recognize to what lengths her father went teaching her science and history, and he often consults her: *Elsa, do you recall in what year Brazil became a republic?* She is hoping that, even though she lacks research experience, on the island he will permit her to help excavate, or interview, or detail the customs of the natives. But as they sail farther south, as she is constantly called on to cleat a line or find provisions or look up the Portuguese phrase for"clean bill of health," as Alice is given the chore of mending sails, it becomes clear he will have no choice but to enlist her full capacities. He *needs* help.

Elsa knows Edward did his research in Africa alone. For two years he trekked from the coast to the interior, established a camp, recorded data on Kikuyu marriages, births, deaths, initiation rites. He catalogued medicinal herbs, hunted lions and leopards, collected and analyzed primate fossils—all without a single colleague. That was fifteen years ago; he was forty. Once he was also an excellent sailor. He even crewed for Sir Thomas Johnstone Lipton—five-time contender for the America's Cup—a fact he now slips into their deck conversations with embarrassing frequency. But each morning as he pulls himself up the steps to the deck, wiping his brow, he looks somehow diminished, as if his body has betrayed his ability. In his younger days, he often sailed single-handed, and at a glance he knows what should be done—*clip the gaff, run the jib, turn downwind.* Sometimes, it even seems he can see his younger arms stretched before him, winching and cleating, phantom limbs. But always he passes along the task.

"Eamonn, let's set the outer jib. And, Elsa, would you mind tightening the main?"

"Not at all." Elsa cranks the winch with ease. Her arm muscles have hardened these past few months; her palms are now callused. "Are you feeling all right?" she asks.

"Excellent. Perfect. I'm in tip-top shape."

"Because if you wanted to work belowdecks, Edward, I'm sure we can manage things up here."

Her solicitude seems to hurt him, as if he imagined his few boasting words might, after all these months, have won her attention. He stares at the horizon. "As the captain, everything is my responsibility. I like to keep watch here, to look after things. In another few weeks, Elsa, you will be able to sail this schooner. You've become quite the mariner. It's wonderful. I hadn't expected it. That is not to say I did not think well of you, I admired all your abilities, but the life of the sea is not for everybody. I simply, well—" He halts; this half-compliment is tripping him. "What I mean to say is: You mustn't concern yourself with me."

In late August they reach the coast of Uruguay. They are again becalmed, slowed to thirty miles a day, drifting south on the Brazil current. They tack endlessly to no avail. On several occasions, when the current stills, they even drift north. From the hold wafts the odor of

spoiling meat and oranges and fish. The boat has taken on a swarm
of mosquitoes, and each evening, as they light the oil lamps in the
cabin, there follows a frantic smacking and swatting, the burlesque of
which might quell some tensions were it not for the threat of malaria.
At bedtime, Elsa begins administering quinine.

During these windless weeks, everyone grows edgy. Edward, in
particular, grows curt with the crew. While he is above deck late at
night, Elsa can hear Kierney complaining to Eamonn.

"Perhaps if Captain Beazley and his wife shared a cabin he
wouldn't be hollering at us so."

"Ah, clam it, Kierney. Drifting like this'll make a saint testy."

"Aye, but a saint would at least get a little squeeze from his wife."

"The captain's a gentleman," says Eamonn. "That's all, Kierney. You
just dunno what that word means."

"Gentleman. Lady. You can call it whatever, Eamonn. But if that's
what the moneybags call marriage, you won't be seeing me trying to
get meself into no aristocracy."

Eamonn laughs. "You'll be too busy trying to get yerself into a
wife!"

"Shut up."

As Elsa lies in the dark, listening to them, she thinks Kierney has,
in fact, hit on the source of Edward's agitation. Not the arrangement
itself—Edward seems as willing as she is, given the circumstances, to
postpone sharing a bed—but having a crew there to witness their
arrangement, to judge it. Privacy vanished the moment they stepped
on the boat. Surely Kierney and Eamonn, who Elsa suspects spend
their nights ashore rum-drunk with prostitutes, look down on
Edward. A wife who sleeps with her sister—to them, it must seem
ridiculous. And it doesn't help that in Rio, the consul's sister, partially
deaf from a severe case of tonsillitis—"You see, dears, it makes no
difference to me if someone is speaking Portuguese or English or
Bantu!"—assumed Elsa and Alice were Edward's daughters. Despite
protestations and clarifications, in the haze of her deafness and
several brandies she insisted that Elsa had Edward's same lovely
cheekbones.

To pass the slow days, Elsa and Alice sprawl across the bow for fish-
spotting contests. Alice exaggerates incessantly. *How many sharks, Alice
dear? Fifty? Well, I hope we don't fall in.* They watch the occasional sea

turtle glide by, and once in a while, when they pass through a shoal, a flying fish leaps aboard, sending Alice into hysterics. She giggles at the fish's side fins thumping the deck, until, the creature's distress beginning to alarm her, she finally tosses it back to the sea.

The cape pigeons also delight Alice. Edward hands her shreds of meat to throw to them and crouches behind his photo box to take several photographs of the birds. Then, with evident pleasure, he takes one of Alice, her arm extended over the gunwale, a smile stretched across her face as a gray speckled bird dives before her.

Alice and Elsa wear broad hats on deck, tie scarves about their heads when the wind is strong, but already their skin has darkened. At night Elsa rubs almond oil into their hands and arms and necks; they drift to sleep beside one another in a haze of salt air and marzipan.

At Buenos Aires, they meet supplies and letters from England. A week later, they put in briefly to water at Bahía Blanca—where native women make Elsa presents of penguin eggs and seashells—and then at Puerto Deseado. The tropical heat dissolves, replaced by clear and breezy days. But farther south, as they approach Patagonia, it grows colder; porpoises tumble about the bow, seals slither alongside. Two albatross, their wide white wings suspended in a gentle arc, wheel and circle about the stern, silently following the boat.

The patent log bobbing behind them registers speeds of six knots, but their sense of motion slows as daylight stretches interminably with summer's approach. Elsa and Alice prepare breakfast at three A.M.—dawn. When they retire at ten P.M., the sun still cuts through their cabin window. And late into the night Pudding stumbles dizzily on his perch.

"Are you sick, Pudding? Are you sick?"

"Good Alice. Bird superior. Bird. Bird."

"Allie," says Elsa, rising from the bed. "I think Pudding needs to sleep."

"Oh, no, Elsa. He's cross. I was watching the other birds and he thought I forgot all about him. But I didn't, Pudding, I didn't."

"Look, Allie," says Elsa as she drapes a shawl over the cage. "He just needs the dark so he knows to rest."

Only Alice sees this as concealment; she rises every few minutes to peek behind the shawl. "Pudding," she whispers, "where are you, Pudding?"

In bed at night, unable to sleep, Elsa thinks: Darkness is now like a blanket too small to cover one's entire form. You try to wrap yourself safely within, but daylight still finds a naked spot toward which it creeps.

The daylight is misty-gray, foglike, shrouding the landscape in constant haze. Its damp chill reminds Elsa of London. So far away now. They have been at sea eight months, and it will be years before she sees England again. St. Albans's clock tower, its Roman walls, the narrow streets where she cycled, her father's house. For the first time, she misses home.

Farther south, antarctic breezes tear through the cabin. Elsa dresses Alice in gaiters and a second pair of bloomers. At night, they cuddle close, their teeth chattering into each other's ears.

"*Cooollddd*," Alice says in the darkness.

Elsa presses her mouth to Alice's neck and releases a slow, hot breath. Alice giggles. Elsa finds a spot on Alice's scalp and blows again. Elsa can feel the steam collect on her own lips. Alice squirms with delight.

"I'm your very own stove," Elsa says.

Alice suddenly flips over. "Alice is a stove too." Her eyes flicker with excitement. "Hot, hot, hot!" she squeals. Her lips stretch into an exaggerated yawn and find their way to Elsa's neck. The blast is hot and moist. Then there is brief suction, a cold tickle on Elsa's neck as Alice nestles her lips on the gulf of skin and breathes in. This must be what mothers feel, Elsa thinks, when they listen to the breath of their infants. The sound soothes her.

Then, on the night of October tenth, Kierney shouts below, "I see the light of Cape Virgins!"

They have arrived at the Straits of Magellan. Elsa knows enough of sailing now to realize how difficult they will be to pass—a long, narrow, zigzagging path of roiling ocean. Max had called the straits a seaman's greatest adversary. "Scylla! Charybdis!" he said. "Odysseus was fortunate he did not have to sail through the Straits of Magellan!"

In Tierra del Fuego, they anchor for two nights, waiting for the wind to slacken. The British consul, interested in the expedition, invites them to dinner. "I have always meant to make the trip myself. Only my poor health prevents me. Asthma, you see." Over brandy he remarks on the perils of the straits, suggesting they enlist a tramp to tow them through.

But Edward, discouraged by their recent drifting, now takes great pains to prove his ability. He sits up straight. "We shan't be discouraged by minor danger."

"Edward." Elsa sets her glass down.

The consul grins. "Ah, you see? The ladies often have ideas of their own."

"Elsa," says Edward. "We're not amateurs. I've sailed with Lipton, considered one of the best. I hope you have some faith in my judgment in these matters."

"Neither my faith nor your judgment is in question," Elsa says flatly, aware she is spoiling the mood. The consul, to her right, shifts in his chair. "I only think we should take better stock of the situation before determining our course."

"Mrs. Beazley," says the consul, "it is the captain's ordained task to determine the course of the boat."

"The safe course."

"Very well, we'll take better stock," Edward cuts in.

An awkward silence fills the room. Edward avoids Elsa's gaze.

But on the third day, they do sail. The navigation of the First Narrows proves tricky. The water churns above the rusted wreckage—smashed hulls and broken masts thick with barnacles. Alert, hands ready to loosen or cleat a line, they station themselves on deck. "Remember, keep the sails loose," says Edward. "We don't want to catch any sudden gusts." Slowly, the boat noses through the narrow waterway and at the first hint of dusk they drop anchor; at least Edward acknowledges the risks of sailing without full light.

At six A.M. they awake to pass the Second Narrows at slack tide, and make it safely, though exhausted, to Punta Arenas. Here the land is flat and windswept; it is sheep country, grassy and low. "A tow!" Edward tosses the word overboard. He rubs his knee, looks up at Elsa. "You see, Elsa, I would not lead us astray."

"I see, Edward. I see that now."

"I am looking out for us. For all of us."

"I know." And she is sorry. Sorry she let her doubt reveal itself to him. He has acted with caution and kindness the entire way, and she hopes that when they are there and settled, she can prove her growing trust.

For a fortnight they sail the Patagonian Channels, a labyrinth of fjords and coves and bays. Hundreds of giant petrels and albatross circle the stern, their wings forming a loosely knit canopy of white. Alice settles herself on the foredeck, wrapped in a blanket, her arms folded across her bosom, her head tilted back. For hours she watches the birds intently, warned by Eamonn not to wave or shout at the petrels, known as "stinkers," for vomiting when frightened.

Elsa draws a map and plots the schooner's progress against Darwin's route. She is now reading *The Voyage of the Beagle*, devouring the descriptions of Rio de Janeiro, Bahía Blanca, Buenos Aires, the Falkland Islands, and Patagonia—all places they have passed. The pages have curled from the spray of seawater.

At Isla Desolación, they are detained by hail for five days, but as they zigzag north through the channels, the weather warms. Above them now, in misty splendor, rise the snowcapped Andes.

Christmas Day, they anchor in Golfo de Penas, off the coast of Chile. A light drizzle washes the boat as they dine on a special meal of salted beef and boiled potatoes. But the damp air holds warmth, and Elsa, for the first time in weeks, perspires beneath her dress. After their meal, despite the rain, Elsa, Alice, and Edward row the dinghy ashore. Alice insists on bringing Pudding. Once the dinghy is pulled onto the beach, they hike through a winding path of dripping vegetation.

"Elsa!" Edward calls from ahead. Pulling aside a cluster of wet vines, he peers into the dark mouth of a cave. "Shall we have a look?"

"Oh, let's!" says Elsa, breaking into a run. The exertion delights her. How wonderful to be moving! Alice, slowed by Pudding's cage, lags behind.

From his pack Edward pulls a revolver and a small lantern, which he lights beneath the shelter of his body. "Ready?"

But as he steps forward, Alice darts ahead. "Hullo in there! Hullo!" she shouts into the cave.

"Allie dear, careful." Elsa gently pulls her backward. "You can't just storm in there. There might be bats."

"Bats!"

"Bats can't harm you, Alice," Edward says. "And it's likely there aren't any. I'll go first, just to be sure. You hold Elsa's hand."

"I am not going where there are bats."

"Allie."

Alice shakes her head no.

"Then you can wait here and look after Pudding," says Elsa. "Edward and I won't be a minute."

"Why do you want to go in there if there are bats? Oh, no. Don't go in there, Elsa."

"We want to explore, Allie. We're going to be one minute. That's all. I promise you we'll be fine."

"Promise?"

"I promise."

Alice's eyes look from Elsa to Edward and back again, and finally she moves aside and squats by the cave's entrance, settling Pudding's cage in a patch of grass. The bird flutters and caws, agitated by the raindrops. Elsa unties her own cape and drapes it, like a hood, over Alice's head.

"Why don't you tell Pudding about the albatross you've seen."

"I already did."

"What about the flying fish?"

"Oh, no. He wouldn't like that. Fish aren't supposed to fly. If I tell him that he will think he can swim. I'm going to tell him about bats, Elsa. Big horrible bats in caves."

"Allie, we're going to be fine. I'll call to you from inside."

Edward passes Elsa the lantern and takes her hand. With his other hand he poises the revolver. Elsa calls, "We'll be right back."

Inside, the air is cool and moist. Their shoes thud against the hard ground; a slow drip pings against the rocks. The walls are slick with moss, the ceiling low, and they crouch forward through the narrow passage, Elsa's eyes intent on where she steps. Soon Edward releases her hand and squeezes ahead.

"No bats, Allie!" she hollers back, watching Edward crouch down, uncock his revolver, and tap it against the rock face. She holds the lantern out. "How deep do you think it goes?"

"I think we're at the end," he says. "Hear that?" He taps the handle of the revolver once more against the rock. "There's something hollow. Maybe another passage, but there's no opening I can see."

Elsa wiggles beside him. "Are you sure?" She'd been hoping for a brief adventure.

"Nothing is so final as a wall of rock."

Elsa swings the lantern in a half arc over the passage's end. "Not even a crack," she says.

Edward tucks his revolver through his belt and takes the lantern. "Follow my light," he says, brushing by her. He extends his hand back for hers.

"I can manage," she says.

She gropes the walls for balance, carefully places her feet behind his. Outside, the light is gray, and they turn from each other, embarrassed by their brief physicality.

"Good Lord," says Edward.

Alice's post beside the cave has been abandoned. On the ground, the cape lies in a soggy heap.

"Allie!" Elsa shouts. "We're out now."

"Alice!" Edward shouts, his voice panicked.

"She's not far," Elsa says. "She's no doubt waiting by the dinghy."

Hurrying through the wet overgrowth, they retrace their steps along the coast, calling Alice's name along the way. But when they finally spot her, she isn't waiting by the boat. She is in it, steadily rowing away from the shore, her head tilted back so that the rain falls upon her small, upturned face. Pudding's cage sits beside her, the bird's wings flapping madly.

"Alice!" "Allie! Allie!" Their frantic voices stumble over each other. But Alice keeps her head back. Her mouth seems to be moving, her thin lips forming strange shapes, but Elsa cannot tell if Alice is speaking to them or simply lapping at the raindrops.

6

Greer awoke to the late-afternoon sun filtering through the burlap curtains. She propped herself up against the headboard, knuckled sleep from her eyes. She looked around the dim room—wicker nightstands, cement walls. On the desk opposite her a stack of books rose in an unstable spiral—*Plants of Polynesia. The Settlement of the Pacific. The Theory of Island Biogeography. Textbook of Pollen Analysis.* Ah, she remembered, Rapa Nui.

She stepped out of the bed and pulled back the curtain. A warm glow bathed the courtyard, its eclectic vegetation reminding her of Rousseau's paintings. Greer once spent a month investigating each floral image in *The Dream* after reading a turn-of-the-century botanist's paper that accused Rousseau of inventing his tropical flora. "Jungle Jousts and Botanical Brawls" claimed Rousseau concocted aesthetically pleasing plants: broad emerald stalks with giant fronds, white blossoms on velvet-black branches. In *The Dream*, Greer had found a subtropical mimosa branch depicted at ten times its normal size, a Japanese clover blossom, and an agave native to the African desert. The plants were real but the proportions confused, and their biogeographic combination a greenhouse mishmash: a biota worthy of Dr. Frankenstein's imagination. In fact, that was what she titled her article—"Frankenstein's Jungle"—which she sent to several botany journals, all of which rejected the manuscript for its lack of scientific relevance. She then sent the article to a dozen art magazines, who likewise rejected it, this time for its inconsequence to art. It now sat in a drawer in Marblehead inside a folder bulging with other articles on hybrid, unpublishable subjects—subjects that, she now knew, once you were established in the scientific community would suggest to colleagues your robust intellectual appetite but, as a young post-doc, simply suggested a lack of focus, and imaginative, perhaps emotional, tendencies.

Greer pulled the curtain shut, lifted the books from her desk, and spilled them on the bed. She'd brought botany and pollen guides; her collections of Darwin, Wallace, Lyell, and Linnaeus; two contemporary volumes on the history of the island with excerpts from early European visitors. But she knew she would need their full accounts. Roggeveen's or Cook's journal might, after all, mention the island's flora. Somewhere in their building, SAAS maintained a good library, but the materials were locked away, and access required paperwork. It would have to wait.

As Greer settled on the bed, her stomach grumbled—she hadn't eaten anything since the previous day's banana. Now she threw on a cardigan and a long skirt, then stepped into her sandals. Grabbing some of her pollen texts and *On the Origin of Species*—always a good dinner companion—she made her way to the room with the emerald globes. Mahina was nowhere in sight. Greer called her name, then pulled back a beaded curtain behind the desk that revealed an empty office. It was six forty-five, almost time for dinner, so Greer settled into one of the high-backed wicker chairs flanking the card table and reread Darwin's famous passage:

> No one ought to feel surprise at much remaining as yet un-explained in regard to the origin of species and varieties, if he makes due allowance for our profound ignorance in regard to the mutual relations of all the beings which live around us. Who can explain why one species ranges widely and is very numerous, and why another allied species has a narrow range and is rare? Yet these relations are of the highest importance, for they determine the present welfare, and, as I believe, the future success and modification of every inhabitant of this world. Still less do we know of the mutual relations of the innumerable inhabitants of the world during the many past geological epochs in its history. Although much remains obscure, and will long remain obscure, I can entertain no doubt, after the most deliberate study and dispassionate judgment of which I am capable, that the view which most naturalists entertain, and which I formerly entertained—namely, that

each species has been independently created—is erro-
neous.

Deliberate study and dispassionate judgment, thought Greer.
Darwin, who after twenty years of meticulous study rushed like a
madman to publish his theory of natural selection before the young
Alfred Wallace beat him to the punch! It was a story Greer loved, one
her father used to tell. Darwin, fearfully holed up in his house in
Down, England, writing to Charles Lyell and Joseph Hooker for advice: Should he patiently compose his opus on evolution or slap together a makeshift theory before Wallace went public? His judgment,
in the end, was entirely passionate. He moved quickly, garnered his
fame, but not without the haunting question of the letters he received from Wallace that somehow disappeared, and of Wallace's
own natural selection manuscript, which Darwin received but
claimed to have set aside, unread, as though the subject bored him.
But was dispassion ever possible, Greer wondered, in a science that
required decades of observation to grasp one fundamental principle?
Natural selection—an idea so basic, so *natural*, it would appear self-
evident to every generation that followed. Above all else, science demanded passion. But what she admired in Darwin was his ability to
sound as though his ideas were of no personal consequence; he
could present himself as the clinical observer. That had always been
Greer's problem—she had difficulty masking her private interest,
had trouble making her judgments seem detached.

The bells above the door chimed, and Mahina strode across the
threshold with a look of concern. "*Doctora! Hola, Doctora!* You are well
now? I come at noon to make up room, and you are sleep."

Greer closed her book. "The travel must have worn me out," she
said. "*Cansada?* I feel fine now. But I haven't eaten anything. If it's not
any trouble, could I get dinner a little early?"

"Yes. Dinner. We find you dinner." Mahina closed the door behind
her. She was wearing a white skirt and a bright pink blouse with
seashell buttons. A hint of a lace brassiere showed through the fabric.
"You come." Without setting down her hat, she led Greer down a corridor and into a whitewashed room with four round tables draped
with floral tablecloths, neatly laid with shining tracks of forks and
knives. "Sit, *Doctora*," Mahina ordered, pulling a chair from the table
by the window.

"Please don't go to any trouble. Anything is fine. Maybe just some fruit. I can get it myself, even."

"*Pollo*," announced Mahina, glancing distractedly through the window. "*Pescado* tomorrow night. Tonight, *pollo*. Yes?"

"Perfect."

"Ramon!" shouted Mahina, and soon Ramon was in the doorway, instructions were issued in Rapa Nui, and he disappeared into a backyard, where the sound of clucking and fluttering erupted.

"*Uno momento*," Mahina said, then disappeared through a set of swinging wooden doors and reappeared outside. She waded through the garden, her hand expertly extracting two avocados and then a guava from the trees, setting them in the bib of her blouse. She knelt, grabbed hold of a stalk, and eased a carrot from the ground. She tapped the root against her thigh, loosening the soil. Soon there came the clanging of pots and pans from the kitchen, a sizzle, the sweet smell of browning butter. Greer inhaled deeply, basking in the scent. A home-cooked meal. The past few months, she'd been snacking on fruit, crackers and cheese, cold lasagna. She'd dined a few times with people from Thomas's lab who had her over for meat loaf and casseroles. And once or twice she'd gone out alone, for the company of strangers. That was, after all, what people told her to do. *Get back into the world.* But it wasn't as easy as it sounded.

Greer turned to Darwin's section on the inhabitants of oceanic islands, in which he explained patterns of island flora and fauna:

> I have carefully searched the oldest voyages, but have not finished my search; as yet I have not found a single instance, free from doubt, of a terrestrial mammal (excluding domesticated animals kept by the natives) inhabiting an island situated above 300 miles from a continent or great continental island; and many islands situated at a much less distance are equally barren. The Falkland Islands, which are inhabited by a wolf-like fox, come nearest to an exception; but this group cannot be considered as oceanic, as it lies on a bank connected with the mainland; moreover, icebergs formerly brought boulders to its western shores, and they may have formerly transported foxes, as so frequently now happens in the arctic regions . . . Though terrestrial mammals do not occur on oceanic islands, aërial

mammals do occur on almost every island . . . for no terrestrial mammal can be transported across a wide space of sea, but bats can fly across. Bats have been seen wandering by day far over the Atlantic Ocean; and two North American species either regularly or occasionally visit Bermuda, at the distance of 600 miles from the mainland.

Greer set the book down. Yes, oceanic islands hosted only plants and animals with that perfect combination of wanderlust and endurance. Most terrestrial mammals didn't have a chance at cross-water dispersal. A few years earlier, though, she'd read about an elephant on Sober Island that simply walked into the ocean and swam to Ceylon—a distance of only a third of a mile but still an impressive feat. Several tourists had photographed the tired creature as she climbed onto the new shore and made her way inland. Other sightings of lone swimming elephants were later reported. So some terrestrial mammals did have cross-water dispersal abilities. Rats and mice were often seen riding across the ocean on bits of flotsam. Rodents and bats were the only mammals, in fact, that inhabited most islands.

But strange evolutionary fates awaited creatures that made it to distant shores. What Darwin referred to as "becoming slightly modified" was a gross understatement. Modifications could get outrageously out of hand. Islands nurtured eccentricity, producing a faunal carnival of dwarf mammoths, giant reptiles, and flightless birds. The worst of these were the insects—beetles and cockroaches whose bodies had swelled over generations to the size of small continental rodents. Fortunately, as their bodies grew, their wings, as Darwin noted, "shriveled," and most of these arthropods were doomed to scurry across the floor of her room at night; no hope, thank goodness, of landing on her sleeping face. But for birds, flightlessness was tragic. The dodo, a bird whose ancient ancestor was strong enough to fly to Mauritius, a volcanic mass in the Indian Ocean four hundred miles east of Madagascar, found that after several generations its wings had withered. When humans imported pigs and monkeys, mammals that liked to eat dodo eggs, the birds had no escape. The last of these marooned birds had been observed in 1681.

"*Bueno,*" announced Mahina as she carried the plate across the room.

"Smells delicious." Greer pushed her books to the side. "Thank you."

Mahina set down an assortment of cooked vegetables. "*Pollo* soon, *Doctora*. For drink?"

"*Agua, por favor.*"

A moment later she brought a water glass, her eyes sweeping Greer's books. "The pal-ee-nol-a-gi?"

"The study of pollen," said Greer.

"*Ah, sí,*" said Mahina. "You study the pollen of Rapa Nui?"

"I'm going to take samples from the bottom of the lakes"—Greer mimed plunging a corer into the ground and twisting it out—"and then see what pollen is buried deep below. That way I can figure out what plants grew here years ago."

"*Bueno.* I read the doctors study the pollen for the cloth for *Jesucristo!* It is the pollen, yes, that tells it was for Christ."

"You read about that? Most people have never heard of palynology. Most people spend their lifetimes never thinking about pollen, unless they're allergic."

Mahina shook her head with pride. "Me, no allergic. I read in our magazine for the Virgin Mary. It comes two times a year, from Spain. This one came very late, almost one year, but I read it all."

"Were you convinced?"

"Con-*vinced*?"

"Do you believe what they said about the pollen?"

"I believe the cloth was for Christ, yes. But not because of the pollen. I not know enough about the pollen. I know enough of *Jesucristo.*"

"Then you won't be disappointed when I tell you the analysis done on the shroud was no good. The pollen on it matched plants from Palestine. But there are over seventy species of each of those flowers. A grain of your basic tumbleweed, supposedly from Jerusalem, looks identical to thousands of other daisy species. Also, people have always left flowers before holy relics; things get dusted with all sorts of pollen." Greer forked a steaming carrot, blew on it, and took a bite.

A look of sympathy softened Mahina's face. "The *doctora,* I think, believe very much in the science. Maybe not in *Jesucristo.*" She raised an eyebrow. "And maybe she not like the science used for *Jesucristo*?"

Oh, no, thought Greer. Why had she opened the door to this? She wasn't disputing the existence of God, she was disputing a study. She had no qualms with anyone believing anything: One God, ten gods, it made no difference. But piety had no place in science. And she couldn't help feeling that Christianity, which had spent centuries contesting the greatest developments of human thought, had a lot of nerve using a microscope to prove an object sacred. But her Spanish wasn't good enough to convey her points, and in English, her arguments would be lost on Mahina. She didn't want Mahina to think she was dismissing her faith when, in truth, she respected it. Faith wasn't easy to sustain.

"Let's compromise, Mahina. We'll say the pollen doesn't prove the Shroud of Turin ever touched the body of Jesus Christ. Nor does it prove it didn't." That would have to wait for analysis of the fabric, a test that would determine the cloth's age. Pollen grains on their own said nothing about time. Pollen never aged.

Mahina considered this. "*Bueno, Doctora. Bueno.*"

She disappeared into the kitchen again, leaving Greer to slowly eat the last of her carrots and onions, reemerging a while later with a plate of steaming chicken. "Now the *pollo. Moa* in Rapa Nui."

She watched as Greer took her first bite. "Delicious," said Greer.

Mahina smiled. "In Rapa Nui: *kai ne ne.* Delicious food."

"*Kai ne ne,*" said Greer.

"*Bueno.* Now you work, *Doctora.* I walk about here but you will please not see me." Mahina took the Darwin book, opened it in front of Greer where the page had been marked. "You are here for work. Important work. I not disturb you."

"You haven't disturbed me in the slightest."

"A *doctora* need the silence to work. To think. I can see."

Mahina left and reappeared with four wineglasses of varying sizes dangling from her hands, the stems wedged between her fingers. With deft movements, she set each one to the right of a place setting and then disappeared for another set. After she had placed them on all the tables, she surveyed her work and rubbed her hands together.

Although the book was still open, Greer had watched all of this. "Really, Mahina, you're welcome to sit with me."

Mahina clapped. "Ah. Mahina is here only for work." And with that she made her way back toward the common room. Greer finished her meal in silence, folding down pages of interest, then carried her plates into the spotless kitchen and left them in the sink.

When Greer returned to her room, she saw that her bed had been made, her shoes lined neatly against the wall, and her black duffel bags piled in the corner. The books she had left on the mattress were neatly arranged on one of the wicker nightstands with the help of a bookend that had not been there before. Above the bed, the plaque of the Virgin Mary had been restored to its watchful position. Beside it now hung a small crucifix.

Greer laughed. This was going to be an interesting few months.

She threw Darwin's book on the bed, leaving him to do battle with religion, and grabbed a jacket and her flashlight from her duffel.

❄

The SAAS building was again dark and deserted, and Greer was thankful the other researchers kept such normal hours. Years ago, in graduate school, as one of five women in her department, she'd been given access to the botany lab only late at night, when nobody else had wanted to work. She'd grown so accustomed to the quiet, to the darkness and the solitude, she found it a hard habit to break even when she had access to equipment during daylight hours.

Her crates sat beside the door exactly where she'd left them, but this time she had a lever with her. On her knees, she gently pried the splintery top off the first one, then carried her collection of chemicals to the metal table nearest the sink, arranging the bottles in their usual order—potassium hydroxide, acetic anhydride, sulfuric acid, hydrochloric acid, silicon oil—making sure the labels faced out.

She was meticulous about arranging her equipment, a trait she'd inherited from her father, a high-school biology teacher. In the basement of their house in Wisconsin he had set up a complete research station: carefully labeled jars of chemicals, color-coded drawers of slates and sandstones and seashells, shelves of alphabetized reference books, and a beautiful brass microscope he'd brought from Hungary that looked to Greer, the first time she saw it, like an ancient treasure.

Almost every night after dinner, her father retreated downstairs with a new sample to examine: a butterfly or a pressed flower he'd collected, sometimes a dead housefly or ladybug that arrived in an envelope from California or Maine; he often wrote to teachers around the country, asking them to send local organic materials. Dandelion seeds, pouches of soil, and dried redwood needles all made their way to their house in Mercer; and once, from a teacher in Tennessee, he received a package with a note that said: *This plant was grown not twenty miles from our school. Enjoy.* The box held a pack of cigarettes.

As a young child, Greer was mesmerized by his secret downstairs world, by the mysterious paraphernalia with which he was surrounded. And for years, because he didn't want his organization disturbed, Greer wasn't permitted to touch any of it. This only fueled her curiosity. She imagined he must be some sort of genius. A few times, when she persuaded her mother to let her follow her downstairs when she was dusting, Greer was able to examine the brass knobs and cylinders of his microscope, the beautiful glass bottles of his private alchemy.

Her mother treated his laboratory with less seriousness. Test tubes and slides held little fascination for her. They could have been pieces of a model ship, the fragments of a suitable hobby any husband might have. She preferred fiction to fact; she spent her evenings sitting on the porch with a novel in her lap. For her, the natural world was a canvas for narrative, a place of myth and legend. At bedtime, she told Greer stories of souls who lived in trees—lost lovers turned into wood, mischievous children turned into saplings—and these were secrets between them. "Papa only sees through his microscope," her mother said, the sweet scent of cold cream on her skin mingling with the smell of cigarettes. "You and I, we see *everything*."

Those were Greer's strongest memories of her mother: her smell, her bedtime whispers, and the way she had of making everything—*I'm going to the store for butter*—sound like a secret. Greer was nine when her mother died of a ruptured aneurysm.

This was when her father, in an effort to console Greer, finally let her use his lab.

Two months after her mother's death, Greer came back to the house one afternoon with a frog she'd caught in a creek. She cupped it in her palms and walked into the kitchen. "I caught a frog," she announced, "and I'm going to name it Harvey."

Her father took off his reading glasses and folded his newspaper. "Let's have a look."

Greer held it in front of his face, the wet, slick creature pulsing in her hands.

"That is not a Harvey," he said. He took the frog from her and told her to get a bowl. Greer then watched as he dangled her frog above a cereal bowl and squeezed its abdomen. Soon a cascade of small black pods dropped into the bowl. "Eggs," he said. "Do you want to look at them?"

She could hardly believe what he was suggesting. She followed him down the dark cellar steps, and with a tug of the rusted chain, the light clicked on. The disarray of the place startled her. Dirty beakers crowded the sink; the table was covered with dust. Her father pulled forward his microscope, grabbed a slide, then removed a tweezers and a dropper from a canister of utensils. "Take a few eggs, add three drops of water, then place the slide cover on top. Now gently slide the mount into the microscope. Right here. Slow, Lily Pad. You do not want to break it. Now wait one moment."

He put his eye to the ocular, adjusted the focus. "There we are. You try."

Greer strained onto her toes and pressed her eye to the brass eyepiece. Three swollen circles appeared before her.

"What do you see?"

"Circles," she said.

"What else?"

"Puffy circles, big puffy circles with thick edges, like they were drawn with a Magic Marker."

"But what do you *see*, Lily Pad?" His voice was edgy; there was a right answer. "What are you looking at?"

"Life?" she asked.

"Ah, Lily Pad." She felt his hand, firm and proud, settle on her back. "You and me."

Just as she began to feel the happiness of her achievement, the bulb above them sputtered, and Greer heard a drip from the corner. She looked over and saw a leak in the ceiling. She felt her throat tighten. The place she had waited so long to make use of had vanished, the threshold she had waited to cross now held nothing but disorder.

Now, years later, she understood the danger of letting grief enter your sanctuary.

Greer opened the crate that held her distiller—tap water contained pollen and had to be purified—and carefully assembled the pieces. She unpacked her centrifuge and set it on one of the tables, then lifted the lid, checked the eight empty buckets arranged in a circle, and made sure nothing had been broken in transit. She removed her plant press, wiped down all the pieces, and set it nearby.

The final crate, which held her microscope, proved harder to open. She gave the lever a gentle kick downward, but this sent the lever clanging to the floor. Greer then wedged the tool deeper and stomped hard. The wood splintered open, the lever dislodged, cartwheeling into her shin.

"Oh, bloody shit!" she shouted, hopping on her unharmed leg. A sharp pain shot through her, and for a moment she felt tears, but as she swung around she saw a young man in the doorway. It was the man from the airplane—the cake man.

He raised his index finger. "We have a medicine kit." He disappeared, his footsteps fading along the hallway, and Greer composed herself. When he returned with a wad of gauze in one fist and a glass bottle in the other, she had mustered a decent show of stoicism.

"I'm all right."

"It is important to disinfect. To avoid tetanus."

Greer was still hunched over, her hand pressed firmly to her shin, but the initial wave of pain was subsiding. She tried to straighten herself. "It's fine. Really."

"Do you mean *oh-bloody-shit* fine?"

"In theory."

He crouched beside her. "Well, yes. Of course it is fine," he said. "Only, it should be clean as well, no?"

He opened the bottle, doused the gauze, and handed it to her. The sharp smell of rubbing alcohol tickled her nose.

"It's fine," she said, dabbing at the cut. A thread of blood had risen in the crevasse of the wound. "Really."

"Fine," he said. "Fine. Fine. Hmmnn. My English is not so good. Forgive me, but I don't think I know this word." A smile pinched the corners of his mouth. "I must look for understanding in the language of the body. The blood, the body bent over, the face tightened with pain. I think perhaps that this word *fine* must mean the same as awful."

"No," sighed Greer. "It means really awful. Aching awful."

"English is a fascinating language. There is much you can teach me." He stood. "Once, and this was many many years ago, I fell in a broken hang glider, just after I had taken off from a peak to the north of Santiago. I landed on my leg. A clean break. The danger, of course, was not the bone but the mountain dust. The doctor said I was very fortunate I had cleaned my wounds quickly." He gestured once again to the bottle of rubbing alcohol.

"Vicente Portales?"

"Would that be fine for you?"

"The most fine kind of embarrassment." She lifted the gauze from her leg and saw that the bleeding had stopped.

"See? Almost like new," he said. "Well, at least I have seen here tonight that you are, in fact, very busy settling in. Of course, you do not have to come to dinner. I wanted only to say hello to our new guest, who I now know is Doctor Greer Farraday. I am indeed Vicente Portales. A cryptographer. And I welcome you to Rapa Nui and to our colleagues—Doctor Sven Urstedt and Doctor Randolph Burke-Jones, who would also like to meet you. And I will offer you this small piece of advice: If a person would like to avoid the whole world, it is an excellent choice to come to Rapa Nui. There is perhaps no better place. But if a person would like to avoid people on Rapa Nui, that person will have very little success, because, you see, it is a very, very small island." At this, he crouched down, removed from his pocket an elaborate Swiss army knife, flicked up a thick blade, and in four quick movements eased the lid off her final crate. "To help you settle in a little faster," he said, returning the knife to his pocket. "*Iorana*, Greer."

She listened as his footsteps faded leisurely down the hall.

"Thanks," she called, though she did not think he could hear her. Only the echo of her own voice returned.

The next morning, Greer awoke at dawn, put a fresh Band-Aid on her wound, and prepared a day pack: sample bags, cutters, field notebook, camera, a change of clothes. She lathered sunblock on her arms and neck, then walked through the just-waking streets of Hanga Roa to find Mahina's cousin Chico, whom she'd been told could rent her a horse. It seemed news of her plan had spread quickly—the short man with an unruly gray mustache stood in the middle of the street, holding the reins of a brown and somewhat emaciated horse, waving as she approached. After arranging a price, he gave her a boost on and handed her a worn map of the island with several *moai* drawn in.

"Best *moai* here." He pointed to a spot on the island's western side. "Ahu Tahai. Fifteen minute. No more. And here"—his finger tapped a stretch of sand on the northern coast—"is good for swim. Anakena. Maybe two, three hours."

She thanked him, and gave a slight kick to the beast's flank. It had been years since she'd been on a horse, not since she went riding as a child, and she liked the roll of her torso over the animal's back, the light trapezing of her feet. Often she had ridden alone across fields, watching her parents' house fade to a white speck in the distance, to collect minnows and newts from the creek. Her father had raised her from infancy on a diet of science. He filled her with stories of natural wonders: century plants that grew for decades, waiting to finally flower and fruit for one brief moment; an Asian orchid that could bloom for nine months. But her favorite was the story of the small heart-shaped seeds that fell from tropical vines, washed by rains into the sea. Millions of sea hearts were riding the world's oceans at any given time, drifting for months, years, eventually washing ashore on the beaches of distant lands to begin a new life. Sea hearts were such good travelers, her father said, that sailors stuffed them in their pockets for luck.

While her friends gathered after school to trade Ginny dolls and baseball cards, Greer went exploring in the woods, upturning rocks and rotten logs to see what miniature worlds lay beneath, hovering for hours above mildewy civilizations of spiders, slugs, and millipedes. Or she went riding across the fields, collecting wildflowers, sometimes dismounting and following a bee as it pranced from flower to flower, trying to see if she could discern a pattern in its preferences. She had long ago grown accustomed to solitude, to a quiet alliance with nature.

Greer continued slowly along the road out of the town, the ocean on her left a forget-me-not blue. Soon, cluttered rows of white crosses sprouted from the grass. Her map marked this as the local cemetery—started after the missionaries arrived and began preaching Christian burial. Before that, burials had been in the caves, or under the *ahu*, the long stone platforms on which the *moai* originally stood.

The path was lined with ferns, which Greer suspected had been on Rapa Nui a long time. Fern spores were among the lightest in the plant kingdom, no heavier than the average grain of pollen, and could be carried by wind for hundreds of miles. Ferns had been among the first flora to regenerate on Krakatoa; three years after the eruption on the Indonesian island, they made up over half of the island's plants, far above their usual fifteen percent. Greer liked to think of ferns as the floral Polynesians—itinerant, adventurous, adaptable—settling every landfall across entire oceans.

In the distance ahead, several giant stone figures lay fallen in the grass—*moai*—the statues that had etched Easter Island into the world's consciousness. According to Chico's map, this was Tahai, the group of *moai* closest to the village. Much more depressing, she thought, than impressive. Long noses pressed to the ground, backs bared to the sun. They looked like debris. Greer tried to imagine them standing, the way Roggeveen had seen them in 1722: a row of towering human forms. But that majesty was long gone. Greer didn't dismount; the *moai* weren't her purpose for being there.

She cut inland to look at the old leper colony, where the land was supposedly the most fertile on the island, and had been used by the lepers to grow fruits and vegetables; the produce had been difficult to sell at first, but people eventually overcame their fear. After a few minutes, Greer found herself before the scattering of abandoned huts in which almost twenty lepers had lived at one time. The last leper had died a few years earlier. Since then, the huts had been left to the violence of wind and rain. She circled the settlement until she found what looked to be a field for cultivation, dismounted, and took a soil sample. She then headed back toward the shore.

Dozens more toppled *moai* littered the coast below. From a distance, some simply looked like rocks. Through her binoculars, though, the slope of the shoulders and the indentation of the eyes fixed to the ground became clear. The twenty-foot statues of volcanic tuff had all been carved with identical features—they looked like slender giants with huge rectangular heads. They were neither lifelike nor ornate, but the size of them and the sheer number were impressive. She could see why they had captured the imaginations of Roggeveen, González, Cook, and La Pérouse. This was more than art, this was industry. Carving hundreds of stone giants, then positioning them along the island's coast—impossible to imagine.

The sun, now high in the sky, beat steadily on Greer's arms and legs, and she put on her sunglasses. For another hour she urged her horse along the rock-clogged path, stopping once at a cluster of low shrubs speckled with red berries. Genus *Lycium,* she guessed. This was the only wild plant among the grasses, and she clipped a branch and eased it into a sample bag. Dozens of horses and sheep grazed on the slopes. She passed two cattle ranches, where she had to lead her horse inland to bypass the fences, and saw several partridges jumping in the grass.

By noon she had reached Anakena, a crescent of white sand hosting several picnics. The American couple from the day before were sunbathing on a plaid blanket, a small radio propped between them. Farther down, several women in bikinis tossed a beach ball. A cluster of palm trees shaded the edges of the beach—these, she'd read, had been planted just a few years before—and three elderly women had propped themselves beneath one of the thick, scalloped trunks, fanning themselves with pamphlets. They were reveling in this minute patch of shade, the first Greer had seen all morning. It astounded her, really, how completely the island bared itself to the sun. Almost as if shadows, too, had become extinct. The island's sole oasis was this slim beach with its canopy of palm fronds. This was where Hotu Matua, the island's first settler, had landed his canoe, and where the famous lost British expedition had made its camp. Greer had planned to have lunch here, in a bit of shade, but now changed her mind. Too many tourists. She wasn't here to take photographs, to say to friends back home: *I went to Easter Island*. She was here, in some significant way, to understand.

She rode away from the beach, following the steep rise of the coast. For another hour she stuck to the shoreline, then veered off the trail into a tangle of grass and rocks. The horse stepped slowly. A strong, salty wind rose from the water, battering her face. This, and the sound of the waves below, briefly muted the thump of the horse's hooves. Seabirds swooped overhead in eerie silence. But soon the wind subsided and she heard a hollow *whoosh*. On the rocks below, a spout of water shot straight into the sky: a blowhole. According to her map, this was almost halfway back to Hanga Roa—a good place to stop for lunch. A worn track led down toward the water, so she dismounted and tethered her horse to the broken head of a *moai*.

Fastening the straps of her backpack, she eased herself down the cliff, carefully placing each foot on the loose rocks. Finally on flat ground, she had just shrugged her pack off, when she heard the faint sound of footsteps against the rough basalt. She looked around the cliff's face to see an old man in loose brown chinos and a beige sweater climbing the rocks toward the path, his footholds fast and light, noticeably more confident than her own. An islander. His hair was thick and gray, his eyebrows unruly. Nervously glancing at Greer, he passed out of sight. Just then a breeze carried the smell of food: roasted meat, the sweet smell of yams. On the rocks about twenty yards from her, she spotted a plate covered with a metal lid, a halo of steam curling from its edges. It was odd, this abandoned meal, but then again, the island seemed governed by its own rules and rituals.

Greer sat and pulled out the lunch Mahina had packed—two bananas, a cheese sandwich, and a warm bottle of cola. In the distance, a small jetty stretched into the water, frayed ropes hanging from its rocks. Beneath her, the sea splashed the cliff and she listened, with surprising contentment, to the rhythm of the waves. Greer had always liked the ocean, and in Marblehead those past few months, when the confusion of mourning Thomas seemed overwhelming, it was the ocean that had calmed her. But here, above this endless sea, in this place so far away, she felt more than calmness: She felt the first small hint of joy returning. She'd made it to Easter Island, and she was doing her first solo field research. Greer pulled out her notebook and began to write:

Day 1: *Initial survey of current vegetation of northwest coast of island: extensive Gramineae and ferns, without apparent shrubbery or ground cover. One sample (A1) of possible Lycium taken two miles beyond village of Hanga Roa. (Are berries edible to humans? What are the other possible faunal predators of fruit? Means of dispersal?)*
Soil eroded and dry. Approximately two dozen coconut palms grow at Anakena beach on the island's northern coast, but beyond that there is no—

The blowhole released another whistle, a spray of seawater fell over her, and when Greer looked up, above the steaming plate stood a ghostly figure. An old woman, pale and slender, barefoot, in a soiled smock. The wind stirred her long white hair. Her legs bent gingerly as she lifted the plate. Then she turned to Greer.

"*Iorana!*" Greer shouted. "Windy. *Viento! Fuerte!*" You never knew what difference a friendly word might make. "The view," Greer said, her arms sweeping out to the ocean, ". . . *el mar, hermoso.*"

The old woman scanned the horizon.

"*Hermoso!*" Greer repeated.

"*Vai kava nehe nehe,*" the woman said, her voice low and brittle, almost lost in the rumble of the water. She turned toward the cliff and disappeared.

Sliding forward, Greer saw a small crack in the face of the rock, a sliver of an opening. Of course, a cave. The whole island was perforated with relics of its volcanic past: lava tubes left by the magma that flowed thousands of years earlier. Beneath the yellow grass, beneath the basalt, these caves formed a subterranean world of elaborate passageways hidden from view, littered with the skeletons of ancient islanders. According to oral history, the caves had served as shelters and hideouts during turbulent times; in them, families had slept and cooked and waited, and, when needed, had buried their dead. The early Christians, too, thought Greer, understood the benefit of underground networks, digging burial chambers beneath ancient Rome, then, during times of religious persecution, taking refuge belowground, beside the dead. Strange how mausoleums often became sanctuaries.

Many of the island's caves were still thought undiscovered. The one before her, though, seemed to serve as the old woman's home. How many more, she wondered, were still inhabited?

Greer quickly finished her lunch—it was getting late—and resumed writing her morning's observations. She detailed the path she'd taken, the weather, the number of horses she'd seen. She had promised herself to take extensive notes, to document each step of her research as though she were, in fact, responsible for turning the notes over to the nonexistent society that funded her research. But now, at the bottom of the page, Greer added a small note inappropriate for an official log, the kind of note at which Thomas would have shaken his head.

> *An old woman who lives in one of the caves fetched a plate of hot food that had been left outside by an elderly man. She seems some sort of hermit. Interesting. She is pale, with white hair. One of the oho-tea race.*
> *Vai kava nehe nehe—translate.*

Smiling Greer closed her notebook, packed up the remains of her lunch, and made her way back toward the village as the sun fell in the sky.

After returning her horse, Greer walked through the streets of Hanga Roa toward the *residencial*. It was eight P.M., and the few shops along Avenida Policarpo Toro had closed. On the corner, a small restaurant seemed to be coming to life. A man in a brown button-down shirt carried chairs and tables to the dusty street, shook checkered cotton cloths across the tabletops, clinked down salt and pepper shakers. A few tourists had already been seated, extricating themselves from their visors and camera straps, piling guidebooks on the tables. Snatches of Spanish and German and English mingled in the street. This was the only life in sight. As she turned onto Te Pito O Te Henua Street, she spotted Vicente Portales walking with a newspaper tucked in the crook of his arm. Greer noticed the precision of his posture. He wasn't tall, but the way he held his shoulders made him seem so. He waved and approached her with an easy confidence.

"You see? A small island."

"Apparently."

His eyes took in her bulging backpack. "It seems you've had a busy day of exploring. Did you enjoy yourself?"

"Yes," said Greer, but she couldn't very well say she had preferred a long stare at the ocean to the world-famous *moai.* "It's an interesting place."

"Good word: interesting. Beautiful, no. But yes, very, very interesting. Perhaps the most interesting place I have ever been."

"How long have you been here?"

"A difficult question. For work five months. But I take trips to the mainland, on the Lan Chile flight, as you know. Well, I would very much like to hear about your work, what you are studying. The *sociedad* seems to know little about the people they host and yet if we share our knowledge we will all enhance the work of each other. Will you join me for a pisco sour?"

Greer had amassed enough questions about the island that talking to someone who knew the terrain appealed to her. And as he'd said, the town was small. She glanced at her watch. Mahina had said dinner was at nine tonight; she had an hour.

"So what exactly is a pisco sour?"

"It is one of the typical drinks of Chile, Doctor Farraday! You must try one. Unfortunately, we have no bars here. Vittorio over there"— he pointed to the man carrying tables and chairs—"is trying to start the first restaurant. But it is for tourists. We will have a drink Rapa Nui–style. Okay?"

"A Chilean drink, then," she said.

They walked down the street to the place where she'd bought her groceries. The door was now closed, but Vicente knocked. "*Iorana!*

Mario? Vicente *aqui!*" Soon Mario emerged with a groggy smile. "Ah! Marblehead! *Iorana! Hola,* Vicente!"

"*Una botella de pisco sour?*" asked Vicente.

"*Sí, sí.*" Mario disappeared into the dark store, returning a moment later with a bottle and two tin cups.

"*Maururu,*" said Vicente.

They wandered downhill to the *caleta,* where a dozen small fishing boats fanned out from the docks, and seated themselves on the low stone wall overlooking the harbor. Vicente spread his newspaper between them, flipping through the pages, until an article caught his eye. "This one I've read." He flattened the paper and set the bottle and two cups on it.

"You see?" He pointed to the paper's date. "Only three days old. Quite a valuable item on Rapa Nui. We shall try not to spill." He twisted open the bottle. "Now, I know only that you are here for core samples. You caused the *sociedad* quite some trouble asking for a refrigerator. One of their bureaucrats thought it was for your food." As he spoke, he pulled a bandana from his pocket and wiped off both cups. "Many accusations were made about the luxuries required by American researchers. Of course, they soon had one of their experts explain that cores must remain cold."

"Well, I'm here to study fossil pollen records. I'd like to find out what plants were here, how long ago, what happened to them. A decent lake core will contain pollen from several thousand years."

"Plants, yes," he said, pouring the cloudy liquid into each cup. "An important piece of the mystery. It will bring us one step closer to understanding this island."

"And you?"

"I am trying to decipher the *rongorongo.*"

"The mysterious tablets."

"No one has yet been able to decipher the writing. But to understand what's written on those pieces of wood would very much enhance our understanding of what happened on this island."

"What kind of wood are they made of?"

"Ah, a botanist's question! We believe some are the *toromiro* tree. Others are laurel, or myrtle. I believe there is one of ash. Of course, there are only twenty-one left. The nineteenth-century missionaries made the islanders burn them. Many, it is said, were hidden in caves, but they've never been found."

"I'd love to look at them. To look at the wood."

"Next time you are in Europe, perhaps. London, Paris, Berlin, Vienna, Leningrad. They are in museums there. Only three remain in this hemisphere. Two in Santiago and one in Concepción. I first saw them in Santiago, many many years ago, and that is what ignited my interest in decipherment. I was young, and their mystery lured me. But now . . ." He handed her a cup. "Your pisco sour, señora."

"*Gracias.*"

Vicente watched her lift the cup to her mouth. The liquid was tart and strong, like a margarita with lemon juice.

"It's good," she rasped.

"Pisco is made from muscat grapes from the Elqui Valley, what we call the Zona Pisquera, north of Santiago. A beautiful region for hiking or hang gliding, where the water from the Andes comes down. In Chile we all drink pisco. But most foreigners don't like the pisco without the sour mix—it is too sweet for them. And too strong. *Pisquo* is an aboriginal word which means 'flying bird.' We believe it was used to explain the feeling of one's head when one is drunk. In a few moments you'll see." He smiled and took a sip, his eyes lingering on the cup. "Do you like our little Rapa Nui tavern here?"

"Very nice."

There was something in the pleasure he took in this moment—sitting on a stone wall pouring drinks into tin cups—that made Greer think he came from wealth. As though all things simple or archaic were, for him, the true luxuries.

"But if there are no tablets left on the island, why do you stay?"

"You mean the place doesn't strike you as the kind of island on which to remain indefinitely? Yes, an excellent question." It seemed he had asked himself this many times. "Of course, at first I did hope to find more tablets here. But I have given up on that. You see, if the script is not alphabetic, if it is symbolic, then it is likely the symbols originated as representations of the objects relevant to the early Rapa Nui. The best way, of course, to determine any relationships between the characters and real-world things is to examine the real-world things. Language relates to life. It emerges from life. For example, the Rapa Nui now have a new phrase: *peti etahi*. It means 'peach one,' or, as you say in English, 'peachy.' *Peti* has entered the language just recently because the Chilean supply boat brought a new product to the island—canned peaches. Before, there were no peaches on the island. But now they are everywhere, and the people love them! Anything that is good, anything they like, is *peti etahi*."

"Have you found any correlations?"

"Many symbols appear to be birds, or part bird, part man. Some appear to be fish. And many, in fact, look like trees."

"Trees? That's surprising."

"It is my interpretation, though. The *rongorongo* is a great mystery, the most spectacular achievement of this island. The *moai* bring the tourists. But the *rongorongo*, well . . . we are speaking of something that has occurred only five times in the history of the world." Vicente held his fist in the air, and with each name lifted a finger. "Meso-potamia, Mexico, Egypt, and China. These are the only places where a written language was *invented*. Every other instance of writing has been borrowed, or revised, from those four. Four spontaneous inven-tions of writing. Plus here, on my favorite island"—his thumb went up—"number five. And the only script not yet deciphered."

"Your task," she said.

"Yes, my task."

"Sounds like convergent evolution," said Greer.

"Biology talk?"

"The same developments turn up in different species on separate continents, even in different epochs. The American cactus and the African spurge—oceans apart, but you'd swear they were related. Same swollen stems, same aureoles. Or the milkwort and the sweet pea. Entirely different families, but nine out of ten botanists couldn't tell their flowers apart. Even those helicopter seeds of maple and ash and tipu trees. Different species, different places, but they all come up with the propeller shape. Some developments just make sense."

"Like the creation of writing."

"Exactly."

"And it evolved in only five places. One of them right here," he said, patting the stone wall. "Quite something."

"It is," said Greer. "Only I hope the tablets don't turn out to be like some of the cuneiform. Ancient grocery lists, ledgers. It would be great if they really said something." She tapped her cup to his, took a long sip, and felt the alcohol rise to her temples. She ran her fingers through her hair. "'Romeo loves Juliet,' at the very least. 'Antony loves Cleopatra.' Something juicy."

"Not 'Romeo gave Juliet fourteen chickens.' "

"Combine the two—'Romeo gave Juliet fourteen chickens be-cause he loves her'—and then you've got something. The beginning of an epic."

Vicente laughed. Greer could feel him watching her, and leaned away. She didn't mean to be flirting. She was just a little tipsy.

"The decipherment sounds like an excellent project," she said, setting her cup down. "Challenging."

"It would be very good to know what they say." Vicente, too, seemed content to let the brief awkwardness pass. "But even when we decipher the script, there are very few left we can read. So much has disappeared from this island. Do you want to know why all these *moai* are still here? Because they are too heavy to move off the island."

Greer laughed.

"All of the early visitors here left with valuables. The islanders traded their artifacts for hats and bandanas. It's tragic. Who knows what is still out there? Right now I am at work obtaining records that may locate some more tablets. You've heard of the German fleet that anchored here during the First World War?"

"Admiral von Spee. Actually, he was a naturalist as well. Kept botanical records of the ports he visited."

"I've not read those accounts. I've focused primarily on his naval correspondence, his ship's log. The details of his cargo. A naturalist, yes. He was an interesting man. He sailed on the first German colonizing mission to West Africa. He was promoted to rear admiral in 1912, posted to Tsingtao, which is where he found himself when war broke out. A gallant man. Of course, he was sunk with his whole fleet at the Falkland Islands. He made a horrible mistake—tried to run for it. No one knows why."

"Fear isn't a good enough reason? If I recall correctly, there was a whole British fleet after him."

"And French and Russian and Japanese. But he was a great admiral, Doctor Farraday. Truly great. Men like that do not become afraid so easily."

"Sure they do."

"In all accounts by his officers, even by his adversaries, von Spee was a fearless man."

But fearlessness, thought Greer, was a feeling, not a temperament. No one, no matter how accomplished, could avoid fear. Who would have imagined Thomas Farraday would be scared of failing?

"Anyway, he was here," Greer said—she was having fun and didn't want to spoil it—"the gallant, fearless, botanically inclined admiral. At Easter Island. How does this relate to the *rongorongo*?"

"It is believed, and I am hoping these records will confirm, that the fleet made off with valuables from the island. Local legends tell of things disappearing from the island with the warships. It's my hope that the valuables—tablets, I am convinced—were sent ahead to Germany."

Greer looked up; the stars were beginning to shine in the night sky. A cool breeze rolled off the ocean. This was all she wanted—a nice conversation, in a new place with a new person. She pulled her legs up and arranged them Indian-style. "Will the Germans admit it if they have them?"

"No," said Vicente. "They will not, I think, want to admit to hiding the artifacts. But if I have documents to prove they do have them, that is a different situation."

"And you want to return them to the island?"

"Yes," said Vicente. "But it is a difficult situation with Chile. Chile, you see, will want them. Chile will consider them their own."

"The islanders might not like that."

"I am Chilean. Many people on Rapa Nui are Chilean, or have one Chilean parent. There is no antagonism now between Rapa Nui and Chile. Not yet. But there is a growing feeling from the islanders that we should not be here. We are called *mauku,* or, in Spanish, *pasto.* You know that word? It means 'weed.' It means we ruin good things."

"There are a lot of weeds here. The plant kind. And remember," she said, "one person's weed is another's flower."

"Well, even though there is little on the land, the islanders would still like the land for themselves. It is theirs, after all. During the fifties and sixties, the government forbade the islanders from traveling. So some of the Rapa Nui stole rowboats from the Chilean Navy, some even made sailboats and canoes, and they sailed for Tahiti, but they had no navigation equipment. It was an awful scene, you can imagine, when at dawn the village awoke to find so many of its men gone." Vicente shook his head. "Some men had not even told their families for fear of being stopped. Most of these boats were lost at sea. It was another horrible chapter for the islanders. Good men, men who might have been leaders, lost."

"You don't sound very pro-Chilean."

"I love Rapa Nui. I am at heart a Rapa Nui. This is the truth, what I feel inside of me." He touched his chest. "And I would like to see the people in possession of their island. But even if I am able to unravel the *rongorongo,* there will be resentment. I am not an islander. I will still be a *pasto*."

"Do you really think you can? Decipher it?"

"I suppose I must think so, or else I wouldn't try. But I'm waiting for something new to work with. I am hoping for my own Rosetta stone."

"The Rosetta stone was made of basalt, you know. This island is basalt. A good omen."

"Let us hope," said Vicente, sipping the last of his drink.

The sky above them was black now, the stars so bright they seemed to spill from the sky. A distant streetlamp cast a soft glow over them, but Vicente had faded to shadow. Greer pulled her flashlight from her backpack, clicked it on, and laid it on the rocks between them. "Better," she said.

He laughed. "Ah, Doctor Farraday, you'll soon get accustomed to the darkness here. I don't even own one." He held the flashlight up and examined it. "And you? You will be taking core samples? That seems like work which can produce good, definite results."

"Once you get past the messy and tiring part of the core taking."

"An intellectual pursuit with physical labor. I like that."

"I do too, until I'm up to my knees in a swamp."

"Well, no swamps here."

"The crater lakes will be plenty of trouble, I'm sure."

"Crater lakes?"

"The samples need to be taken from a damp area. Pollen can be preserved in water for thousands of years."

"Ah, yes. In the craters there is fresh water. But everywhere else is dry. And do you know what it is you want to find?"

"I try not to think about that, so as not to bias my analysis. But I'm interested in why there are no native trees here, no shrubs. Something happened—an eruption, an earthquake—something wiped out all the vegetation."

"It is as I have said: Everything here disappears. Plants as well."

"It seems so. I'll have to look at a core. Extract pollen at various depths, count the grains, analyze the assemblages. From that I can start to determine what the island used to look like."

"It is an excellent project," said Vicente. "I am a great fan of the botany sciences. When one's work is at an impasse, the work of others always seems much more exciting, much more important, does it not?"

Greer laughed. "The Gramineae always have more chlorophyll . . ."

Vicente raised his eyebrows.

"Botany talk: The grass is always greener."

"Ah, yes, I've heard this saying. On the other side of the fence . . . it is true. I cannot help but become fascinated by the German fleet. Why they came here. What they did. It happens to you as well? This distraction?"

Greer nodded. "I like to tell myself it's not a distraction. That the mind needs to look to the side sometimes to make sense of what's in front of it."

"Yes, well, perhaps you'll want to spend some time looking at the photos of the *rongorongo,* and I will want to spend some time taking a core sample. I have always been interested in that work. I was, as you know, a fan of Thomas Farraday." Vicente looked at her. "He was your husband?"

"Yes."

"I read much about his work."

Not enough, she wanted to say, to know he had died.

"I am sorry I mistook you for him. Of course, they wrote only 'Doctor Farraday.' I made an assumption. I hope you will forgive me."

"Of course," Greer said. He couldn't know it was the same assumption everyone made. But the mention of Thomas suddenly darkened her mood. She looked at her watch. "I hope you'll excuse me. Dinner's at nine. And I need to sort through my notes from today."

"You must not be late for one of Mahina's *umu* feasts."

"You know Mahina?"

"Ah, Doctor Farraday. Everybody knows Mahina. An extraordinary woman. Like I said, this is a very small island."

"Well, thanks for the drink." Greer tapped her cup to his. "And the conversation." As she stood and slipped her backpack over her shoulders, she felt a little dizzy. A strong drink on an empty stomach after a long day—a poor combination. "I'm sure I'll see you at the lab. And elsewhere."

"Now, Doctor Farraday, I would just like for you to know that I am still sitting here on the wall because I am guessing that you would prefer to walk alone."

"A fair translation," she said.

"Next to the *rongorongo*, everything else is easy."

He was charming, she had to admit. And at another time, she might have wanted him to walk with her.

"I'm just in a solitary mood," she said.

"That is allowed. But you must know this is hard for me. Chilean men are not accustomed to allowing women to walk home alone."

"Well, this American is very accustomed to walking home alone."

"Fair enough. For now. But when in Rome, Doctor Farraday . . ."

"Well, that's an entirely different story." She grinned. "Then we're dealing with *Italian* men."

"You have abandoned me, insulted my country and my manhood, Doctor Farraday, all in the course of less than a minute. What on earth is left for the next few months?"

"Work."

"I can see you will be an extremely good influence on me. Very well." Vicente poured himself another drink, and he turned the page of his newspaper, squinting. "Ah, there was an election yesterday and we will not know who won until the plane arrives next week. You see how everything here can become a mystery?"

"Good night, Vicente."

He raised his cup. "*Salud, mi amiga.* I am very curious what you will find under your microscope."

"Me too," said Greer. "Me too."

And she followed the narrow beam of her flashlight up the road.

7

From the outset, it was a question of provisions.

The two thousand officers and men who had turned to von Spee for instructions required food and fresh water. The ships' guns needed ammunition. And above all, the five armored cruisers could not move an inch without coal.

Coal: That simple fuel of ancient plant fossils would write von Spee's fate. The *Scharnhorst* alone, von Spee's flagship, burned almost twenty-five percent of its two-thousand-ton coal capacity in one day. After less than a week at sea the ship needed to anchor and refill its bunkers. But the German Empire had only one fortified coaling base in the entire Pacific: Tsingtao—the port the squadron was fleeing. Across the Pacific were a few *Etappen,* neutral countries with German supply contacts, and also the islands Apia, Yap, Rabaul—German colonies. But it was only a matter of time before the Allies seized these, silenced the cable and radio stations, and cut off von Spee from any potential supplies.

It was August 6, 1914, when the German East Asiatic Squadron, the *Kreuzergeschwader,* put to sea, beginning their long and arduous journey across the Pacific, toward the base at Wilhelmshaven, toward Germany, toward home. Allied against them now were Russia, Great Britain, and France, whose ships were quickly closing the oceans of the world to German merchantmen and men-of-war. Only the Baltic Sea, thousands of miles away, remained safe.

"From now on," von Spee wrote in his journal, "I am on my own."

In leaving Tsingtao, von Spee also left behind any hope for communication with home. The range of the ship's wireless was only several hundred miles, and cable stations were few and far between. Alone, unadvised, von Spee would have to follow the orders, now strangely prophetic, that the Kaiser had issued long ago to commanders in foreign waters in case of a war:

> *From that moment on he must make his own decisions. . . . The constant strain will exhaust the energy of his crew; the heavy responsibility of the officer in command will be increased by the isolated position of his ship; rumors of all kinds and the advice of apparently well-meaning persons will sometimes make the situation appear hopeless. But he must never show one moment of weakness. He must constantly bear in mind that the efficiency of the crew and their capacity to endure privations and dangers depend chiefly on his personality, his energy, and on the manner in which he does his duty. . . .*

So von Spee did his duty. He decided to cross the Pacific, to round the coast of South America, and then break for Europe.

The squadron's first stop on this long journey was Pagan, a small German-owned island in the Marianas. Here they found live cattle and pigs, fresh vegetables, flour, whiskey, wine, and tobacco. The men went ashore, listened into the night to the songs of the islanders, watched the moon rise above them. It was almost, for those few days, as if the war had not yet started.

But when the four supply ships they were awaiting failed to arrive, captured by the Allies, everyone, especially von Spee, understood that the search was now on.

—Fleet of Misfortune: Graf von Spee
and the Impossible Journey Home

8

Heaving the oars in uneven circles, Alice cuts a choppy course for the schooner. Kierney, standing on the stern, shakes his head in disbelief. "Eamonn, come up here and look at this. I think Miss Pendleton has had 'er fill of shore leave! I think this here might be some kind of mutiny!"

When Alice finally rams the schooner, squealing with delight, Kierney and Eamonn hoist her soaked figure on deck and swaddle her with blankets. Kierney then takes the dinghy back ashore to get Elsa and Edward.

"I happen to think Miss Pendleton would make a tremendous captain." He laughs as he rows them toward the schooner. But Elsa and Edward are silent. "In the beginning, I was quite surprised to find she liked birds so much. Knew all the names and such. And then that she liked to draw. She ain't half bad. She did a nice one of me with one of them cape pigeons at my shoulder. But I didn't ever think Miss Pendleton would be fond of rowing. A lady of endless hobbies, I tell you."

The rain falls harder now, dimpling the water around them. "Kierney, stop talking," says Elsa.

"Here, I'm just giving your sister a compliment! There ain't nothing to please you folks!"

"Kierney." Edward's tone is firm. He lifts his finger in the air, a pointed sword.

Elsa's gaze fixes on Alice, seated on the schooner's bow, her wet head wiggling above the cocoon of blankets. Alice has always been unpredictable, but this . . . Rowing off on her own—what could she have been thinking? A current could have swept her off. If the dinghy had capsized, she would have drowned. Why did she ignore Elsa's instruction to wait? Did Elsa have to also say don't take the dinghy? Don't try rowing to the schooner? Did she have to imagine every possible disaster in order to prevent it?

Elsa feels a slow rage rise within her. Here it is, she thinks. Everything she had hoped to rid herself of on this journey. The equation now seems simple: For every step Alice takes toward recklessness, she must take one toward caution. It is an equilibrium Elsa cannot fight.

Of course, her anger is not with Alice but with herself. Alice is never to blame; that, too, is part of the equation, a constant. It is Elsa's fault for thinking—for hoping—that Alice could change. Why did she believe that several months without a major incident meant that Alice had matured? Why did she still cling to the false belief that time could alter Alice as it altered others? Alice has always lived outside of time. Moments and events do not, for her, accumulate, do not add up to change.

I must be even more attentive, Elsa tells herself. This journey presents Alice with a new set of circumstances, and anticipating her reactions will require Elsa's alertness.

As they climb on deck, Alice sheds her blankets and throws her wet arms around them both. "Beazley! I took the boat!"

Elsa pries herself away, grabs Alice's shoulders. "That's the ocean, Allie. The water is freezing. It's deeper than you can imagine. Don't go rowing off alone like that. Ever!"

"She's fine," says Edward. "Here." He steps behind Alice and wraps a towel over her head. Alice is between them now, her eyes blinking sleepily. "Alice is fine," Edward whispers. "Let's not upset her further."

"She's not leaving my sight again."

"She'll stay beside us all day long, right, Alice?"

"You are not leaving my sight," says Elsa.

Alice nods disinterestedly. Why is it that Elsa can lie in the cabin at night, cuddling with Alice, feeling the greatest sense of connection, and now feels such disengagement? Alice's mental departures have always produced an eerie sense of abandonment in her. When Elsa was little, they made her feel like she'd been left alone in the dark, and she would pinch Alice to try to bring her out of these states—to no avail. Now she wants to shake Alice back to herself. Elsa needs Alice to understand that she cannot protect her alone.

It haunts her to know that two such disparate feelings—utter connection and complete disassociation—can exist between the same two people.

"She probably needed to stretch her limbs," says Edward. "We'll be more careful."

He's trying to soothe her, but she resents him now for his ability to believe that since nothing happened, everything is fine.

"This was an awful idea," she says. "This trip. This boat. What are we doing?"

"Elsa, please don't overreact. We're almost there."

"That won't make things safe."

"It will reduce the variables."

"You don't know that."

"Do you realize how close we are?"

Valparaíso is just two hundred sixty miles north. And retracing their journey at this point, Elsa knows, is no safer than proceeding forward.

Beneath Elsa's hands Alice's bones feel so small, so light.

"I need you, please, Edward, to help me. To watch her."

"I will," he says.

Elsa, almost mechanically, kisses Alice's head. "Stay with her now. I'm going belowdecks. I just need to lie down."

But in the narrow cabin, trying to rest, Elsa's mind retraces the wet, leafy path to the cave, Alice perched beside Pudding, Elsa's cape draped over her; it is as though her mind believes if it can examine the events closely enough, an answer will emerge. Elsa rolls over, pulls the rough wool blanket to her head, then tosses it aside. She doesn't deserve to sleep. Since childhood, she has felt that guarding Alice was a task given her by some higher power. And in those moments when Alice tripped on the stairs, when she knocked her head against a doorjamb, or when a passing group of children mocked her, Elsa believed she had failed. So she would assign herself penance— four nights without dessert; a week of sleep without a pillow; once she left her favorite doll on the steps of the Blessed Mary Church with a note attached: *For a worthier child.* How else did one accept sacrifice, except to believe it part of some heavenly plan?

Elsa steps out of bed and climbs to the deck, where Alice is seated, blanket-wrapped, against the gunwale.

"I thought you were tired?" asks Edward.

Elsa rubs the sleep from her face.

"Never," she says.

✿

Within four days they make the clamoring port of Valparaíso. From the dark blue water rises a forest of masts; a cacophony of Spanish, Italian, English, and French booms from the docks. Here is where they will prepare for the final leg of the journey, the last twenty-five hundred miles of open sea. New stores are needed. Everything in the hold must be examined and restowed. Kierney and Eamonn begin prowling the docks, chatting with skippers and captains and cooks, looking for new commissions. The men will sail the journey's final leg to the island but return to Valparaíso on the Chilean Company boat that collects the island's wool once a year. The boat is scheduled to make its annual trip in three weeks. But on their first night ashore Edward learns from the consul that the company boat departed the day before.

"It wasn't to sail for another few weeks," Edward says. "We'll have to hasten our departure if the men are to meet the boat and make their way back. We can't have them stranded on the island with us for an entire year." In two days they frantically arrange supplies, obtain their official papers of permission from the Chilean authorities for their archaeological work, and post their last letters—all professional letters, Elsa realizes, wishing in this final moment she had someone to whom she could write: *The last leg, we're almost there.* She wishes she could write to Max.

The night before they sail for the island, while the crew is ashore, Edward and Elsa sit on deck and examine the last of the gear.

"I want to thank you, Elsa. I couldn't have wished for a better assistant."

"Well, it's been thrilling. It is thrilling. Leagues more exciting than sitting in Hertfordshire."

"Do you realize that before us waits the adventure of a lifetime?" He looks healthy and vibrant, younger than he did in England. The triumph of passing the straits and of leading them this far has clearly invigorated him. "We'll be sharing in the greatest of experiences."

Leaning forward, he kisses Elsa on the mouth. After all this time, after all the nights of Edward squeezing her hand, or kissing her on the forehead, Elsa is startled by this sudden show of passion. A slight laugh escapes her. Edward pulls back.

"I'm sorry, I didn't mean . . ."

He busies his hands with a coil of rope. "I know this experience, this journey, will be good for us. You'll have every freedom you could possibly imagine. You don't need a degree, you don't need a certificate. You need only curiosity."

"You're not the least bit nervous about getting there?"

"You forget I've traveled before. But I remember my first trip. Bali." He looks up at the mast, the rigging, losing himself in the memory. "I was an assistant to a very experienced anthropologist who wouldn't tolerate the slightest show of nerves. But they were wreaking havoc in me. And then, once we arrived, it was entirely different. The imagined place disappeared and was replaced by real soil, real people. Nerves are at their strongest in the realm of the imagination." He turns to face her now. "But soon we'll be there, on the actual island, and it will all be different."

"I suppose the anticipation is greater in me too. I can't believe I'm actually doing this."

"Your father would be proud."

She takes a deep breath. There is a moment of silence between them as they watch the port chandlers pack up their goods for the evening, as these last signs of familiar civilization rumble their carts into the distance.

"It is an amazing thing to travel to a new land, Elsa. You'll see. Fear can never conquer curiosity."

The next morning, they set off. Since anchorage between Valparaíso and the island is impossible, they will have to make it in three weeks. Elsa, troubled by the crew's impending departure, sleeps little. For ten strenuous months she has lived with these men, and a strange fear of loss now consumes her. The individuals, the people, have little to do with it. When she left a governess post, she always dreaded saying good-bye to the children, even when they'd been monsters. She could never help herself from making, and believing in, ridiculous promises: *I shall try to visit in the spring. Do come visit me in Lancashire.* Or, now: *Eamonn, promise to find us if you ever anchor even remotely near England.*

"Mrs. Beazley, you just remember ol' Eamonn when you find all that buried treasure."

It is not that she *likes* the crew. But she has grown accustomed to their presence. And married life, as she has known it, has meant Edward berthed in another cabin. Her behavior with Edward almost depends upon the crew, their proximity justifying her reserve. Once they leave, what reason will there be for decorum?

For a fortnight they sail without sight of land, and the idea of finally reaching their destination begins to overwhelm Elsa. For thousands of miles they have sought this small patch of earth, believing in the story of an island they have never seen. Soon they will be spilled onto its sands, like a wish fulfilled.

On the eighteenth day, beneath a fierce noon sun, several seabirds swoop about the boat. Land must be close. But as Elsa sits on deck, looking at the full sails, the taut lines, the winches, she no longer has the feeling that they have brought themselves this distance. The boat seems to her a creature with its own resolve, and the ocean and wind, conspirators in some mysterious plan. This thought soothes her: If she can believe an unseen hand has guided them, she can believe in their well-being, in Alice's safety.

The next night, keeping watch beneath the low and lambent moon, Elsa sights the outline of an island.

"Allie! Edward!"

There are no lights on land. Only the vague traces of dying fires send wisps of smoke into the night.

This is it, thinks Elsa.

"We'll head to the south of that jetty and anchor for the night," says Edward. "It isn't safe to go ashore now."

They slow for the approach. Edward takes the wheel and Kierney and Eamonn let loose the gaff and lateen lines; the slack sails begin to quiver. As the boat glides toward the shore, they hear the thunder of waves smacking rocks.

"Drop!" Edward calls, and then the men crank the windlass in furious circles, the thick chain shuddering as the anchor hurls downward, plunging into the dark water beyond.

With the anchor dropped, the sails stowed, the lines tied, a haze of exhaustion settles over the deck. They all collapse against the gunwale, quiet, as though speaking will rouse them from this glorious dream of landfall. They listen to soft sounds of water lapping the ship's side, the rhythmic *creak—creak—creak* as the boat rocks gently in the night, the worry of so much weather-beaten wood.

After several minutes, Edward's voice cuts into the silence, "Time to go below and catch some sleep. Tomorrow will be a long day."

Elsa hauls herself up, takes Alice's hand, and leads her down to their cabin. Edward follows them below. Without speaking, they all prepare for bed. Like moths, good-nights flutter through the darkness.

And this night, for the first time since they've left Southampton, Elsa dreams of Max. He is in St. Albans, wandering through her father's emptied house, searching for her. He tears through the sitting room, the bedroom, the library, calling her name, over and over again, Elsa, Elsa, Elsa, until the word takes on the rhythms of a chant, *El-sa,* and as he searches room after room, his voice swells, layers, multiplies into the voices of hundreds, all chanting. *El-sa-el-sa-el-sa.*

She awakens, her forehead damp with sweat. The boat rises and falls, issues a prolonged *creak*. Then her stomach leaps. Above her, dangling through the open hatch, is a brown face. Its eyes, white in the moonlight, silently explore her, search her, and then Alice, and the narrow space between them. Elsa slides her arm around Alice's sleeping figure. She thinks of calling to Edward, but fears startling or angering the visitor. Then she remembers.

She whispers, tentatively, hopefully, "*Iorana?*"

A smile spreads across the visitor's face. "*Iorana,*" he replies in full volume, stirring Alice. Then comes the sound of dozens of voices, from the cabin, the galley, the deck, the water beyond. Rippling, in unison, they call, "*Iorana.*"

Hello.

9

In the darkness, the ropes lashing the corer to the horse's back looked like the threads of a giant cobweb floating in front of her. It was just before dawn and Greer was in the rear of a three-horse caravan traveling the northern coastal path. The middle horse carried her large equipment. Ramon rode in the lead. They were on their way to Rano Aroi, the island's smallest crater.

Greer would need several days to get her initial set of cores, and was eager to start. Extracting a clean core was a rigorous process, and this was her first time doing it alone; she and Thomas had always taken samples together, standing on skis or sleds, drilling holes into frozen lakes, balancing on makeshift rafts to plunge their corer into swamps. On their honeymoon in Tuscany they drove into the Apennines to collect sandstones. This was when things between them were good, when Thomas was himself, and as they hammered at the rock face, they were playful. *Husband, would you give this thing a solid whack? Good God, I am, Wife.* In bed at night, after they made love, waiting for sleep to claim them, they whispered about the colors of the sediment, the texture of the rocks. It was a pleasure they had shared: extracting a physical piece of history, listening to the earth grumble as it "confessed," they liked to say, to their hammers. Back in the lab, pointing to a sample, Thomas would wink at her: *Take that to the interrogation room.* But his liveliness, his delight in these processes, had vanished years ago.

Greer shifted in her saddle, trying to adjust to her gear. She had her field clothes on: long khaki pants, a sweatshirt, and knee-high rubber boots. Her backpack, weighing heavily against her, held her waterproof notebook, a camera, a large bottle of water, a first aid kit, a pair of thick gloves, three rolls of aluminum foil, and her plastic sample bags. Across her lap lay three zirconium extension rods, which flashed with light as the sun peeked over the horizon.

Greer was enjoying this long morning ride to her field site and tried to savor the anticipation, something she knew Thomas wouldn't have been able to do. He'd become so set on achieving answers that inquiry, for him, had grown burdensome. She still wondered, though, how exactly he'd lost sight of the scientific process, why the man who'd once held himself to such high standards had cut the biggest of corners.

She tried to focus on the landscape. As the sky slowly brightened, craggy shadows revealed themselves as rocks and signposts. The obsidian sea became blue. By the time they turned inland, two miles beyond town, the sun had laid a long sparkling track across the ocean.

"Rano Aroi," called Ramon, pointing ahead. These were the first words they'd exchanged in an hour. Something about the darkness had made silence feel natural.

"Wonderful," said Greer. "*Magnífico.*"

He stopped his horse and surveyed the crater. "*Sí, magnífico.*"

In the distance she could see the crater rising from the grassy slope—a knuckle of land. No trees or bushes obscured the view. Beneath the threads of morning cloud, only the crater loomed ahead: her first field site.

The path vanished into the grassy plain, strewn with volcanic rocks, and cautiously, the horses made their way.

It was just past seven-thirty when they tethered the animals to an outcrop, unfastened the corer and the platform, and hauled them to the crater's edge. Sweat coated Greer as she lugged her backpack and the extension rods along for the final hike. The corer, the rods—all this equipment had been designed by men, for men, and required sheer brute force to transport and operate. Even Ramon huffed at the weight. He was thankful, it seemed, when she told him, half in Spanish, half in pantomime, that she was all right now, that she needed to work alone, and that he could do what he pleased. The risk of having someone unskilled try to help with sample-taking was just too great. Mistakes were made too easily, data contaminated in the smallest, well-intended gesture. Ramon moved to a patch of grass, where he lay down, tucked one arm behind his head, and held a worn paperback in front of him.

Greer took out her camera and photographed the crater, the edges of its mouth barely contained within her lens. Below, the lake was matted with long, thick reeds—the *totora,* she presumed—that the islanders had used for decades to make baskets, mats, and roofs. The earliest European visitors had noted this plant. Strange, then, that it alone should still grow in abundance. What kind of a mass extinction played favorites like that? A profusion of ferns made sense. But reeds weren't known for wanderlust. They were seed plants, and their best shot at cross-water dispersal was stowing away in the plumage or stomachs of birds—much less reliable than drifting with wind. Greer would have to determine this reed's relationship to species on nearby landfalls; from that she could estimate its life span on the island. If she found close relatives nearby, the *totora* was a recent arrival. If she found only distant cousins, it had probably been there thousands of years, evolving in solitude.

Opening her notebook, Greer marked the date, time, location, and weather, then began her descent. She tucked half of the baseboard under one arm, and used a zirconium extension rod as a walking stick. The cool water rose to her knees. The reeds, easily seven feet, towered over her, reminding her of the cornfields she had walked through as a child, a world of thick green stalks and sky. But the reeds were brittle and snapped easily beneath her. Soon she had forged a path. As the shore faded from view, Greer recalled stories of scientists getting injured while taking samples. Of people breaking arms, getting their boots stuck in marshes. Of course, Ramon was just on the other side. If anything happened, she had only to call.

When she reached the midpoint of the crater, Greer set the platform on the broken reeds. The sun beat strongly. Sweat streamed into her eyes. She crouched and splashed some water on her face, then lifted off her visor, plunged it in the cool lake, and set it back on her head. The chill felt good.

She then went back for her corer and the other rods, and by the time she set down the last of her equipment, two trips later, Greer was panting. She hadn't carried this gear in quite a while. She bent for a moment, hands on her thighs, surveying the site—the platform, the corer, the rods—and as her breathing slowed she became aware of the silence all around her, broken only by the slight slap of water against her boots. Here I am, she thought. In the middle of a crater on the most remote island in the world. Reeds rising all around me; all I can see is sky. Not a voice, not a rustle to be heard.

This was solitude, she thought, utter and remorseless. And the image of herself standing there filled her with dread. This was what life could come to.

She had to break the silence. She had to move.

Greer stepped up on one side of the platform and eased the corer through the center hole. She slid on her padded gloves and positioned the piston.

"Come on," she said, calmed by the sound of her own voice. "Do this. Just do this."

And with that, Greer pressed all her weight against the long metal rod, throwing herself forward as the barrel cut deeply into the wet earth.

"Ah, look, it's Doctor Farraday! The very busy Doctor Farraday! She will settle the question once and for all! Please, Doctor, you must join us."

The sun had almost set, a cool breeze swept the island, and Greer was walking toward her *residencial*. She was thinking of the work that lay ahead of her—another few days taking samples, weeks of cleaning and analyzing. Her project now seemed more daunting than it had back in Marblehead. It had taken her five hours to extract the core segments—after tugging on the piston for an hour, she finally lay on her back, kicking at the handles. By the time she made it back to Mahina's, tired and somewhat disheartened, she'd devoured an early dinner before dropping off the samples in the lab. Now she was hoping for a shower, and some rest.

"Looks like it was a long day in the field!" From a picnic table outside the Hotel Espíritu, Vicente was waving. A torch was pitched beside each corner of the table. Two men—one brawny, one slender and somewhat hunched—sat across from him. Thursday, she realized. The researchers' dinner.

"Was it just a day? It felt like a week!" Greer answered cheerily, trying to make light of her weariness. She slipped her backpack off, setting it on the ground. "Those reeds are tougher than rubber. Whoo! The sun felt like a furnace. And when you get up on the rim the wind can really batter you when it gets going!" But she stopped herself; she could feel the exhilaration of finally, after a day alone, speaking with people. Ramon had been quiet even on the ride back to Hanga Roa, and her Spanish wasn't good enough to goad a stranger, and a shy one, into conversation. He'd mainly been interested in looking at the core. When she came over the rim, he set his book down in the grass as she unwrapped one for him. He had laughed, as though amused by the idea of pieces removed from the earth.

"Doctor Greer Farraday is our new resident palynologist," Vicente announced. The smaller man, in a gray dress shirt, offered only a nod. A pair of spectacles, thick as paperweights, sat heavily on the bridge of his nose. The other man, blond and tan, stood immediately. He was big. A yellow T-shirt hugged his chest. It read:

Swede e π

"Sven. Sven Urstedt," he said. His handshake was firm. "Meteorologist, amateur geologist. Pisces." His eyes, large and blue, traveled Greer. "We insist that you join us."

Happy to be diverted from misgivings about her work, Greer sat down. The elaborate apparatus of her room key with the poker chip cut into her thigh, and she laid it on the table. "I'll see you that," Sven said, setting his own key, attached to a red rabbit's foot, beside hers. "And raise you one." He poured her a glass of what looked like pisco sour from a small yellow bucket on the table. "To clear your thoughts. Now. Purple irises," he said. "No particular meaning, right?"

"Meaning?"

"You are leading the witness, Sven," said Vicente.

"All right. *Do* purple irises have any meaning?"

"What Sven means to ask is whether or not the purple iris, as a flower, signifies anything in particular. In the way a red rose has particular meaning. Or a black rose."

"As a gift, you mean?"

"Precisely," said Vicente.

"Not that I know of," said Greer. "But that's more a question for a florist. Ph.D. programs have been cutting back on corsage and bouquet courses."

"Doctor Farraday, flowers are meant to be cut!" said Sven.

Greer laughed.

"No distractions, Sven," said Vicente. "We are at an impasse."

"*Were* at an impasse."

"Sven, Doctor Farraday has made it clear she isn't sure."

"If we can't find anyone to tell us what the irises do mean, I think it's safe to assume they simply don't have a meaning. If they did, people would know. That is, I should think, the whole *purpose* of meaning."

Greer thought Sven had a good point.

"Well, it seems von Spee knew what they meant. 'They will do nicely for my grave'—that is a fairly strong statement," said Vicente.

"Von Spee was depressed. Moody. For God's sake, Germans can't take anything lightly." Sven swigged his pisco and thumped the glass down on the table. "One bouquet and . . . he sinks his fleet." He grinned, proud of this last statement.

Vicente turned to Greer. He was wearing a dark blue shirt that lent a richness to his olive skin. "We're speaking of Admiral von Spee. I have come across some documents that—"

"We're *done* speaking of Admiral von Spee. We are going to bore her to tears."

"All right," said Vicente.

The man in the gray shirt had still not looked at her.

"What about plain irises?" Vicente asked. "Do they have a meaning? Like the lily?"

"Vicente!" said Sven. "I like you much better when you are obsessing over the *rongorongo*. It is worth searching for meaning in that. In flowers—well, I simply cannot support you on that mission."

Lily, thought Greer. Lillian Bethany Greer—that was her given name. But growing up she disliked Lillian—it was too matronly—and Lily in particular, especially as she became interested in botany; some jokes couldn't be stomached for a lifetime. And in science, androgynous names helped. Applying to graduate school she became Greer Sandor: her father's name, reversed. And when she married, Greer Sandor Farraday. But Thomas, in private, had always called her Lily.

"Very well," sighed Vicente. "Another topic. SAAS is making noise about a conference."

"They've been making noise about a conference for two years," said Sven.

"But now they have threatened to send one of their people."

"People? They have *people*? No, SAAS is run by machines. Never have I seen an organization for archaeology so uninterested in, well, archaeology. They care about the light fixtures, the memos, the packets of guidelines. Last month we received a shipment, a whole crate, of ballpoint pens. For over a year now I've been trying to get access to Chilean weather satellite data. That is, after all, my work. South

Pacific weather patterns. Ocean currents and their relation to Polynesian migrations. But what do I get? Seventy-five—the exact number apportioned to my lab—blue ballpoint pens."

"Well, Sven, perhaps if they send one of their people the situation will improve,"Vicente said."You could voice your concerns."

"Oh, I've voiced my concerns. Anyway, no more work talk. Greer," Sven began, his hand swatting the former conversation from the air. "You look very musical. Surely you play an instrument. I'd guess the oboe."

"I've no musical talents whatsoever."

"Sven is an aspiring opera singer," Vicente said."And it has always been his dream—"

"Vision." Sven smiled broadly at Greer.

"—his *vision* that we might have some sort of talent show. Drama, music, games. Unfortunately, he is the only one among us with any talents."

"Yes, Vicente here holds the record for the longest hot air balloon voyage over the Andes, but of what entertainment value is that? *His* talents require elaborate equipment and funds."

"I'm afraid this is true," Vicente said with a shrug.

"Games?" This word came from the third man at the table.

"Yes, games, Burke-Jones. We need some games. Some entertainment. Don't you think?"

The man, his gaze still fastened on the tabletop, nodded. His hair was strawberry blond and looked as though it had once been thick with curls. It now lay matted across his scalp, a few lone ringlets clinging to his forehead, as though penciled in. Beneath the thick glasses, his eyes were puffy with fatigue.

"Croquet," said Vicente. "Or badminton. The British games, of course."

"I'll bet Burke-Jones can send a shuttlecock flying."

Burke-Jones smiled at this.

"Excellent," said Sven."Now, Doctor Farraday, although my abilities are enough to make up for everyone else's lack, it would be so lovely to have a partner in crime—"

"Crime," mumbled Vicente."Pray you never hear him sing."

"—a fellow aesthete, a performer, a lover of the arts."

Greer wondered if all their get-togethers were this energetic, this choreographed, or if she had, like the observer in a quantum experiment, influenced the result. Or perhaps this was what the island's lack of entertainment had led them to—a sort of conversational dance, banter acrobatics.

"Well, I can name almost every family, genus, and species in the Urticales and Magnoliales orders. Backward alphabetically," she said. "Or forward, if you prefer. Though that gets dull pretty soon. You could put it to music, I suppose. But its main value is in curing insomnia. Like counting sheep, but for the very compulsive and detail-oriented."

"Taxonomy!" Sven's eyes flickered. "Definitely something to work with."

Greer noticed that Burke-Jones, behind his thick bifocals, was studying her.

"Impressive stare," she said. "A good old-fashioned inquisition stare. But I'm afraid I've nothing to confess."

"This is Randolph Burke-Jones," Vicente said. "He is our engineer. Our architect. He is going to tell us how the Rapa Nui moved the *moai*."

Burke-Jones again lowered his eyes to the table. Before him stood the ruins of three tropical drinks—smashed pineapple chunks and wilted orange rings buried beneath a campfire of colored toothpicks. Where, Greer wondered, when they sat pouring drinks from a bucket, did he get all those colored toothpicks?

"You're British?" asked Greer.

He looked up briefly. The torchlight played across his face. "Indeed."

"Don't let him fool you," Sven said. "Brits try to pretend they're all poise and propriety. Not Burke-Jones. He's a wild card. Though he hides it well."

Burke-Jones slowly pulled the slender straws from his empty drinks, arranged them in a tidy row, then gathered the toothpicks and began piling them. Greer felt a sudden surge of warmth toward him—a man who indulged his eccentricities.

Vicente tapped Greer's shoulder. "So, you have taken your core?"

"Six meters of very wet, very fibrous peat. It should correlate to at least six centuries."

"And you'll be able to see the pollen for each time period?"

"Yes. But it'll take quite some time. The whole core needs to be sampled, cleaned, and treated. Extracting pollen grains is painstaking. Then counting them all. Just identifying what those grains are can take weeks." Saying it now brought back her sense of exhaustion.

How had she not realized the difficulty of doing this all alone? How had she gone from years of working in a lab with a team to collecting samples by herself on an island thousands of miles from anything? "But it's all in the service of getting an accurate picture of the island's early biota."

"Splendid!" said Sven. "Or, as they say in Spanish, *espléndido*."

"There!" announced Burke-Jones, and when Greer looked over, she saw on the table before him a miniature tepee of straws and toothpicks.

"Masterly, my friend!" said Sven, clapping him on the back. "Ah, look, here comes Don Juan." Sven closed his eyes, tipped his chin to the moon, and began to hum "*Che gelida manina.*"

An old man was walking by. He was narrow-shouldered, and the cuffs of his sweater had been rolled thickly to his wrists. He bent forward slightly, which gave him a look of pensiveness. Almost certainly this was the man she'd seen leaving the plate by the cave.

"Who is that?" asked Greer.

"Luka Tepano," answered Vicente.

"That," said Sven, " is Don Juan."

"Luka is the devoted caretaker of the island's hermit."

"Okay," said Sven. "Lancelot."

"The old woman in the cave?" asked Greer.

"Guinevere," said Sven. "Further along in life."

"You've been exploring!" said Vicente. "Yes. Ana has lived in that cave as far back as anyone can remember. The islanders say she is one of the forgotten Neru virgins—the girls who were confined in caves to become pale for religious festivals. Specially appointed women pushed food into the cave. When the enslaved islanders were returned by the Peruvians, they brought smallpox. Eighty percent of the population died within weeks. The Neru virgins did not know what had happened. The women who brought the food died, and the girls died of starvation."

"But this was in . . . ?"

"Eighteen seventy-seven."

"She can't be that old," said Greer.

"Don't forget," said Sven, smiling, "she *has* been keeping out of the sun."

"She's British," said Burke-Jones.

"Yes," said Vicente. "Some Rapa Nui believe she is British. Some say German even, left here by the fleet. Some believe she is a *tatane—*

the spirits that live in the caves. Of course, since ancient times the caves were homes for the islanders. There is also a long tradition of eccentrics and prophets living apart from the village."

"What," said Greer, pulling her notebook from her bag and searching for the page where she'd written about the old woman, "does *vai kava nehe nehe* mean? That's Rapa Nui?"

"Yes," said Vicente, "it means 'beautiful ocean.' "

"Oh." This didn't reveal much. "And the man? He brings her food?"

"Luka takes care of her. Some say he is her son. That he was born out of wedlock and she was sent in shame by her family to live away from the village. We have many incidents here of shameful unions, children separated from their parents. So many people are related, it makes courtship difficult."

"Luka's in love with her," said Sven.

"Sven, you see, has a fondness for older women. And therefore believes all men do."

"How many are still used?" asked Greer. "Caves, I mean."

"Difficult to say," said Vicente. "Many are extremely well hidden. Many, I think, have never been explored. But Ana's is the only inhabited one we know of right now. The caves, you realize, can be quite dangerous. There are scorpions and black widow spiders. You must be very careful. If you go inside, leave a piece of clothing by the entrance so that people can find you."

"If the islanders lived in them there are probably traces of their food, their garbage. There might be fossils in them."

"Bones," said Sven. "Piles of bones. Human bones. Men, women, children."

"Doctor Farraday needs plant fossils, Sven. Her main focus is pollen."

"That's my specialty."

Sven took a sip of his drink. "And for your husband too?"

"Yes," said Greer.

Something in the pause that followed told her they had spoken of this, her husband, earlier.

"I'd like to again give my apologies for not knowing the situation," said Vicente. "It is hard for us here to keep track of what is happening in the real world. My regrets."

"Thank you," she said.

"Yes," said Sven, "a devastating piece of news."

"For him, especially," said Greer, and as soon as she'd said this she realized they hadn't been talking about Thomas's disgrace. They'd simply been offering condolences about his death. Perhaps none of them recalled the details of the scandal. People outside palynology rarely did. They remembered only that the eminent Thomas Farraday had been dismissed from Harvard for something involving data, and their only real curiosity, the question asked of her too many times, was, simply: Did *Greer* know?

"I should get back," Greer said, rising. Vicente and Sven stood; Burke-Jones removed his glasses, wiped them clean with a handkerchief, put them on again, and examined his tepee.

"So soon?" Vicente asked.

"I need a shower and a good night's sleep. Tomorrow is another day in the field. And the next day. And the day after that."

"Please let us know how your research goes," said Vicente. "As I said, we must help each other whenever we can. All of our work is interconnected. We mustn't forget that. We will see you around." He touched her elbow and whispered, "So, the iris? It really means nothing?"

"It could mean a great deal," she said. "To the right person."

"Ah, I will consider that. Well, good night, Doctor Farraday."

"Good night," she said, lifting her backpack.

It was a short walk to the *residencial.* The streets were quiet, the small blue and white cement buildings, separated by trenches of shadow, tucked in for the night. The only sound was the soft flap of Greer's sandals against the street. Then, from one of the houses, came a young couple, islanders, their arms linked. The girl stroked a white shell necklace as she spoke, and the boy listened intently. They looked blissful, Greer thought. Trusting. They smiled as Greer passed.

Back at Ao Popohanga, Mahina was at her desk in the main office, making notes in a ledger book.

"*Buenas noches, Doctora!* How was your work? Ramon said you were happy with your piece."

It was hard to imagine Ramon saying much to anyone. "Yes," said Greer. "I took a good core, I think."

"You work all day at Rano Aroi, he says. Very near you was Terevaka. The most high point on the island. Someday, you take the time to go there. I will bring you to see. But now you have more work, *Doctora.* You have been given many, many books!" From behind the desk, Mahina pulled a stack of worn texts.

"For me?"

"Yes, yes. From Señor Portales."

"Thank you." Greer felt her spirits lighten. Work—good. Perhaps she wasn't yet ready for sleep. A little reading before she drifted off would remind her it wasn't all physical labor ahead. "Many thanks, Mahina."

"I have books too, you see." Mahina pointed above her to a glass-doored bookcase with a shelf of old leather volumes. The lettering on their spines had faded. "If you need, for the research, you ask. They come from my father."

"Thank you. Well, good night, then."

Back in her room, Greer took a long, hot shower and settled herself in bed, buttressed by a semicircle of texts: Roggeveen's journal, translated into English; a hand-bound copy of Captain Cook's log; Jean-François de Galaup, Comte de La Pérouse's *Voyage Round the World*; the document in which Don Felipe González y Haedo declared the island a territory of Spain; Pierre Loti's travel records; the diary of Paymaster Thomson of the USS *Mohican*. A sheet of paper had been inserted in Roggeveen's book:

> *You will, I think, find some helpful passages buried in these. You may now converse with all the early visitors, except the British who went missing with their journals and can be of no help. Do you speak French and Spanish? I should have asked. I can translate Loti and La Pérouse and González if it would be of help.*
>
> Vicente

Well, she thought as she propped the lumpy pillows against the headboard, Vicente certainly was kind. But there was something odd in him not mentioning the books earlier in front of the others, as though it were a private matter.

A cool draft billowed the curtain, and Greer pulled the quilt tightly to her chest. She thumbed through Jacob Roggeveen's expedition log, which detailed everything from his first sighting of the island to his departure. He had come upon Rapa Nui in 1722 on a mission for the Dutch East India Company. It was Easter Day, and from his ship Roggeveen at first thought the island composed entirely of sand:

> *. . . we mistook the parched-up grass, and hay or other scorched and charred brushwood for a soil of that arid nature, because from its out-*

ward appearance it suggested no other idea than that of an extraordinarily sparse and meager vegetation.

Nothing more, however, in Roggeveen's log mentioned the landscape. But this was useful: parched-up grass, sparse and meager vegetation. An island so barren it was thought covered by sand. It meant that in 1722 the island hosted little more flora than it did at present. Any mass extinction must have happened before he arrived.

Greer read on, and another section drew her attention:

During the forenoon Captain Bouman brought an Easter Islander on board, together with his craft, in which he had come off close to the ship from the land; he was quite nude, without the slightest covering for that which modesty shrinks from revealing. This hapless creature seemed to be very glad to behold us, and showed the greatest wonder at the build of our ship. He took special notice of the tautness of our spars, the stoutness of our rigging and running gear, the sails, the guns—which he felt all over with minute attention—and with everything else that he saw. . . .

A great many canoes came off to the ships; these people showed us at that time their great cupidity for every thing they saw; and were so daring that they took the seamen's hats and caps from off their heads, and sprang overboard with the spoil; for they are surpassingly good swimmers as would seem from the great numbers of them who came swimming off from the shore to the ships. . . .

As to their seagoing craft, they are of poor and flimsy construction; for their canoes are fitted together of a number of small boards and light frames, which they skillfully lace together with very fine laid twine. . . . But as they lack the knowledge, and especially the material, for caulking the great number of seams for their canoes, and making them tight, they consequently leak a great deal.

In the morning we proceeded with three boats and two shallops, manned by 134 persons, all armed with musket, pistols, and cutlass . . . we proceeded in open order, but keeping well together, and clambered over the rocks, which are very numerous on the sea margin, as far as the level land or flat, making signs with the hand that the natives, who pressed round us in great numbers, should stand out of our way and make room for us . . . we marched forward a little, to make room for some of our people who were behind, that they might fall in with the ranks, who were accordingly halted to allow the hindmost to come up, when, quite unexpectedly and to our great astonishment, four or five shots were heard in our rear, together with a vigorous shout of "'t is tyd, 't is tyd, geeft vuur" [It's time, it's time, fire!]. On this, as in a moment, more than thirty shots were fired, and the Indians, being thereby amazed and scared, took to flight, leaving 10 or 12 dead, besides the wounded. . . .

Roggeveen, it seemed, had no further explanation for the violence. Greer closed the book and set it down. How often in the history of the world, she wondered, had the same story unfolded? An armed exploring party goes ashore and opens fire. The *moai*, the *rongorongo*, the floral extinction: None of it really mattered. Easter Island was like every other landmass in the world—when after centuries of isolation it met the rest of the world, the world struck it down. But what could be done? Wasn't all prehistory and history—speciation, human migration, exploration—just an elaborate game of musical chairs? A border was crossed, a colony taken, an island explored. A snake stowing away on flotsam made it to a new shore, a breadfruit tree in the arms of a naturalist crossed the ocean, a prehistoric mammoth traversed a continental land bridge. The music played, positions changed, and in the end, a chair was taken away. A resource was removed and somebody was left standing. Extinction, genocide, survival of the fittest. Someone always had to leave the game.

Greer felt a familiar gloominess coming over her. She usually shook it away with a walk on the beach or a trip to the movies, but now she had to try to sleep it off. She shoved the books to the foot of the bed, turned off the light, and closed her eyes. The sounds of the night—moth wings batting her window, laughter from somewhere down the street—intensified. Turning onto her stomach, Greer held one of the pillows over her head to muffle the sounds, but still her mind prowled.

She directed her thoughts to Roggeveen and retraced his narrative. With what had the islanders constructed their canoes? What had been the effect of the exchange of goods on the isolated population? Would a population capable of building and transporting giant statues"lack"the knowledge of caulking a canoe? What was the psychological effect of the violence of Roggeveen's men?

A rustling of leaves from the courtyard distracted her, and once more Greer turned over, adjusted the quilt, and settled on her side with the pillow held against her ear. For the past few months, it was either insomnia or utter exhaustion. And after a day in the crater and drinks with the researchers, she should have been exhausted.

She began whispering the families in Urticales.

Urticaceae, nettle. *Urtica dioica,* stinging nettle. *Boehmeria nivea,* China grass.

Ulmaceae, elm. *Ulmus americana. Ulmus parvifolia. Ulmus rubra. Ulmus alata. Ulmus procera.*

Moraceae, mulberry . . .

Mulberry. Greer stopped. Mulberry included the famous strangler fig of the Amazonian rain forest. As a small sprout, it would climb the trunk of a nearby tree, leeching water and minerals from the bark, struggling to reach sunlight. Once the roots of the fig took hold, they thickened and hardened, grew branches and leaves, enmeshing the host tree, strangling it to death. In the end, the fig looked monstrous—bulbous, contorted—its roots fused like tumors onto its lifeless host. If you cut through the trunk, which Thomas had done in the front of his classroom the first time she'd ever seen one, you could see the victim within.

"And there it is. Nature isn't always beautiful," Thomas had announced as he pointed to a cross section of tangled roots. His eyes scanned the class. "One must never romanticize the natural world. What's important is to see it clearly, to see what's there, not what you would like to see. Plants have no inherent beauty, no inherent innocence. The *Artemisia absinthium* releases poison from its leaves—one rainfall and all other neighboring plants are dead. This is neither an act of goodness nor of evil. It's simply a mechanism developed by a particular organism to ensure its survival. The world's largest flower is produced by *Rafflesia arnoldii,* a parasitic plant of the Malay Archipelago. It lives inside climbing vines, then breaks through the bark of the host, expanding into a twenty-pound, three-foot flower that smells, quite unbeautifully, like rotting flesh. This is and will always be the difference between botanists and the rest of the populace, and you must remember it—we will look at a plant and we will see a complex narrative of need and fulfillment, of adaptation and mutation. Everybody else—your parents, your friends, your roommates—will see just something colorful. Something for the garden or a window box. They will see something that their dear benevolent Judeo-Christian God placed before them for their delight."

Thomas had perfected the pragmatic-scientist role, and liked to make a strong impression on first-year botany students. But Greer, when she watched him that day, didn't yet understand the drama of it, of him. He simply seemed an impossible cynic, a man who had looked in microscopes so long he could no longer see the beauty of the natural world. Never, she told herself, would she become like him: a hardened scientist. But something in his cynicism had challenged her, made her want to show him the world was, in fact, beautiful. And the day after the lecture, in a gesture that began their courtship, she slipped beneath his office door a passage from Whitman's *Song of Myself,* a poem she had always loved.

As she lay in bed, what Thomas said about the strangler fig now struck Greer as eerie. She'd heard him say it a dozen times, he said it to every intro class he'd taught while they were married. It was his favorite speech. But she'd never imagined his beliefs went beyond the natural world, that they could seep into his life, their marriage.

Greer felt a strange sickness rise in her stomach. She threw the covers back and stepped out of bed. On the desk sat the small seed stranded in its liquid universe. Eight years. She shouldn't have brought it here.

She slipped on her sandals, pulled a skirt over her nightdress, then grabbed a flashlight and left her room. The porch was silent, but as she moved quietly across the courtyard, she noticed, among the foliage, a flash of white: There, before the Virgin Mary statue, Mahina was kneeling in prayer. Her eyes were closed, her hands clasping what seemed to be a photograph.

This was where Mahina found peace. Prayer was how people made sense of the past. But Greer belonged to no church, no faith, and on nights like this, when she couldn't sleep, she was simply left with a sense of aloneness.

Greer tugged open the door to the main building, and walked into the night toward the lab.

10

In the shadow of the ancient Polynesians, the Germans made their way across the Pacific: Eniwetok, Fanning Island, Samoa, Bora Bora, Tahiti.

They took coal where they could, feeding the ships' bunkers at anchor beneath the blazing sun. At night, they lived in the pitch black of their cruisers—a single lantern could reveal them to a passing boat. Without activity or diversion, they were left only to thoughts of those who pursued them.

The ships of the British and French navies far outnumbered theirs; and the Allies had endless secure harbors for provisioning. With Japan now in the war, the odds against them became impossible.

At the Admiralty in Berlin, hope for von Spee's survival was waning. Kaiser Wilhelm, his sympathy ignited for this lonely commander, tried to send words of encouragement: "God be with you in the impending stern struggle." But von Spee, beyond range of the radio transmitter at Tsingtao, never received the message. He was operating in solitude, without the means to contact his country, his supply ships, or the other German warships in his squadron.

He needed to find a rendezvous point, a spot in the Pacific where he could try to bring the squadron together. He would have to break radio silence for this, risk the interception of the message in the hope of uniting his forces. But it was necessary.

The only question was where. Studying the map, searching for a safe harbor, he soon found the perfect place, a place he had once read about, where Captain Cook had voyaged, where strange giant statues lined the shore. A place that was the farthest one could get from the rest of the world: Easter Island.

—*Fleet of Misfortune: Graf von Spee*
and the Impossible Journey Home

11

On a thin strip of sand on the island's northern coast they make their camp.

Everything stowed in the hold must be rowed ashore through the rough surf. As the schooner heaves above the ocean, Elsa steadies herself and drowsily unties the crates and bags and buckets.

The previous night has drained her. The native visitors—forty of them, she finally counted—refused to disembark until they tired of their ceremony of welcome. This involved an elaborate exchange of wood carvings and sweets, bananas and tobacco, taro and tea. In the flurry of excitement, Edward's hat was swapped for a frantic chicken; then, moments later, the chicken's forlorn owner snatched it back. But when Alice carried Pudding's cage on deck, when a wave of awed whispers swept the visitors, the owner of the chicken came forward, suggesting, through a series of arm-flapping gestures, an exchange of chicken for parrot. Then Edward stepped in. "Not for eating. It is a pet. A friend. *Un amigo.*" His refusal clearly offended the group, but soon Alice began blowing kisses to Pudding, who said *superior bird,* and the affront was lost in their amazement. One of the men, his arms covered thickly with tattoos, wearing a red hat with brass buttons, then began to conduct a song. But he cut it short with a grunt of disdain when the younger boys, sidetracked by the discovery of Elsa's corset, garbled the words.

In a mixture of Spanish and Tahitian, Edward tried to rally workers for the next day. "*Carry? Llevar?*" As the islanders stared, he dramatically lifted a box full of tinned meats. "See: *Ca-rry. Work. Anga?*"

"*Tangata rava-anga,*" said Elsa.

A young boy with thick, cowlicked hair stepped forward and took the box from Edward.

"*Maururu*," somebody mumbled. *Thank you.*

"Well, it is to be expected," Edward said, near dawn, when the islanders slipped gracefully over the gunwale and into their canoes, calling *iorana* as they studied their lapfuls of biscuits and beans and cigarettes, the slim daggers of their boats stabbing toward the coast. A month's supplies had been lost in the greeting. "It is the best way to gain their trust. You'll see. They will no doubt extend the traditional courtesy of hosts. It was the same, at first, with the Kikuyu."

Now it is morning and Kierney and Eamonn have to make off quickly in search of the Chilean Company ship, which anchors by the village at the island's opposite side. Exhausted, nervous, Elsa stands on the schooner's deck and bids them good-bye. She does wish they could stay, if only for a few days. As they lob their bags into the dinghy, she gives them extra stores of tea and coffee. "Are you sure you'll be able to find the ship? Maybe you should wait and we can all find it together. To be safe."

"If there's one thing I know how to find, Mrs. Beazley," Eamonn says, climbing down into the dinghy, "it's a boat I'm suppos'd to be on."

A duffel then comes hurling over the gunwale and thumps into the dinghy. "To the sea, again!" Kierney hollers from behind. He jogs along the deck, clutches the gunwale, and vaults himself onto the ladder. Pausing, he looks past Elsa to where Edward and Alice, belowdecks, are unpacking a crate. He grins and whispers, "It ain't too late to sneak off with us."

"Are you suggesting," she laughs, "that I just traveled twenty-three hundred miles to head right back to Valparaíso?"

"We could have some fun." He winks. "You need some fun."

"Kierney, after all these months, have you still no sense of propriety?"

As he stares at her, she feels a blush crawl down her face. "Seems not," he says, snatching the tins of tea and coffee at her feet. "But I got first-rate vision." He laughs and leaps into the dinghy. "Best o' luck to Captain Beazley and the two Mrs. Beazleys!"

Edward appears on deck. "Ah, the men are ready? Excellent." He eases himself down the ladder, pushes the dinghy off, and rows toward the shore. Elsa watches the two men jump onto the beach and dart up the embankment, duffels slung over their shoulders, arms spilling with tins. At the top of the hill, a half-dozen islanders mounted on horses are monitoring the activity. Kierney and Eamonn, gesturing and pointing to the sea, approach them. Soon they each hand over the tins she has just given them, and mount the horses behind the islanders, wedging their duffels in their laps. The over-weighted animals plod along the coast, receding in the distance, and then out of sight.

The few remaining islanders watch the activity of the boat and Edward's efforts to row back to the schooner, but make no move to help. They do, however, wave.

"Work may not be an ethic indigenous to the Rapa Nui," says Edward as he climbs out of the dinghy, his face sunburned and glistening with sweat. He pulls out his monogrammed handkerchief and mops his forehead. "But at least they seem to be quite sociable." From the stale crumbs of their predicament, he is clearly trying to paste together a bit of cake. He did not, to be fair, expect Elsa and Alice to haul everything ashore. But now they have no choice.

The day is hot and windless. It is March, almost one year since they left England, but it is a different March from the one they left. Here, it is summer's end.

The only one not tired, Alice revels in the landing. She flings the blankets and buckets and tins of tea to the dinghy below, where Edward arranges them and then paddles ashore to unload. This endless chain of loading, rowing ashore, and unloading fills the day. They break only at noon to take shade belowdecks.

By sunset, they have pitched two makeshift tents on the beach and piled most of their equipment on the grass. The dinghy has been pulled onto the sand. And whether by habit or desire, when they agree it is finally time to retire, Elsa retreats to the tent with Alice. Even in his exhaustion, Edward comments: "Don't you think it's time Alice had some space to herself?"

Elsa pauses beneath the loose web of mosquito netting. She raises her lantern and studies him—his tall form, his broad shoulders, his look of need. After months on the boat, sleeping separately, after hours of setting up camp, how can this possibly matter to him now? If only he had some sense of timing, of the natural rhythms of these things. If only he could understand that she did not, tonight, of all nights, want to begin their intimacy. "Edward, please."

"Never mind," he says. "Never mind."

But he remains in the sand, in his wrinkled white captain's suit, his eyes glowing with indignation. Fatigue, it seems, has intoxicated him.

"Oh, just a minute," Elsa spits out. And in that one phrase the mounting pressure of all her former delicacy erupts. The journey is now over; the adversity of weather and rations is gone; the challenge that has for the past year forged their friendship, their union, has vanished. They've made it. And with their lives no longer in danger, it seems to Elsa as though the right to feel bothered, the liberty to be annoyed—suspended during those months of hardship—has been granted once again.

It is clear Edward senses this. He stands in the moonlight, surprised and bewildered.

But how can she resent him when she has *chosen* to marry him, *chosen* to come on this voyage? His solitary crime has been offering her her only viable choice, a compromised salvation that circumstances forced her to accept. He has, in fact, been good to her.

"Just one minute, dear," she calls. "I'm going to say good night to Alice." Elsa ducks into the green glow of the tent, and kisses her.

"Pudding too."

Pudding's cage is on the floor. Elsa blows the bird a kiss. "Good night, Pudding."

Alice giggles. "You're so mad at Beazley."

"We're just tired. That's all. Tired. We'll be right outside in the next tent."

"You're sleeping there?"

"Yes, Allie."

"What about us?"

"You and Pudding will be fine. If you need anything, call for me. All right?"

"Don't forget to come back in the morning."

"You'll call for me if you need anything?"

"If bats come, I will call for you."

"Allie."

"Or those mosquitoes." Already Alice has mummified herself in the sheets.

"I'll be just outside. Stick your head out of the tent and you can see where I am."

"I'm hot."

"That's because you've the sheets all wrapped round you, silly."

"Cool me off, Elsa."

Elsa blows on Alice's forehead. "I'm going to be right next to you. Now, good night."

It feels odd to leave Alice, but what choice does she have? This is merely fulfilling a new duty. Elsa zips the screen shut behind her and slowly, through the thick and heavy sand, makes her way to Edward's tent. He is seated on a stool in a white nightshirt.

"Elsa, we are married, after all."

"Yes," she says, trying to sound kind. "We're husband and wife. I know. But it's not a habit yet. I'm used to Alice. It has nothing to do with you. With us."

She unbuttons her blouse and skirt quickly. "It was quite a grueling day, Edward, wasn't it? All those crates. I'd stay here forever if only to avoid moving them all again. I hope tomorrow we can relax some."

"Tomorrow, I promise you, we will be nothing but tourists. We will explore."

"Good," she says. "I've never been a tourist."

As she seats herself on the edge of her cot, a silence falls between them. The surf outside roars. Wind ripples the tent. And Elsa can't help but think that in a moment Kierney will begin hollering from above deck or Eamonn will ask her to cleat a line or Alice will shout to an albatross. But there is only she and Edward, and what, now, do they have to say to each other? There is nothing that needs to be done, no tasks, no tending.

"Elsa . . . do I . . . *frighten* you?"

"Edward, that's mad."

"I realize I am much older than you. I am, well, old. I am surely not what a young woman your age dreams of."

At this, Elsa wants to move toward him, wants to kiss him, but is afraid this kindness will be misread. She cannot be with him now; it's too soon, too strange. "I've just been concerned about Alice," she says. "The rowing off—*that* was frightening. And the trip has been so tiring."

"Of course."

"I'd just like to adjust to this place. To settle in."

"Elsa, it is fine. We each have our own cot."

"Edward—"

"The most important thing is to get a proper dosage of good rest." He rises from the stool and slides himself beneath the loose sheet of his cot. He blows out his lantern.

"It *is* important for us to rejuvenate," says Elsa.

His back now turned to her, he whispers: "Don't forget to stuff some cotton in your ears. They're sure to have a variety of earwig."

"I will, Edward. Good night."

As soon as Elsa settles herself on the cot, plugs her ears with cotton, and blows out her own lantern, she tumbles headlong into a swamp of sleep. She dreams, as she will for weeks to follow, that she is still on the boat, gliding through the water. Sleek white seabirds circle overhead as she stares at the endless horizon. When finally she sights land, it is thick with moss and ferns, a slender plume of smoke rising from its center. But as she nears the shore, it vanishes.

Hours later, Elsa awakens in the pitch dark, in a strange and hollow silence, to a body weighted against hers. She freezes, suppresses a gasp. From her ears she pulls the coils of cotton. Would he *really*? Then a long lock of hair tumbles over her face. Soft, measured breaths fill the tent. Elsa relaxes, eases herself back into slumber. It is only Alice.

⚘

Surveying and photographing consume their first month. The distances are considerable, the terrain rocky, and for transportation they procure three horses in exchange for tobacco. After several days of coaxing—*Allie, it's far simpler than riding a bicycle*—Alice is finally persuaded to mount her animal, and together they ride across the island, evading the hundreds of sheep that roam the grassy slopes. They note on their map important distances, landmarks, and the locations of fallen statues. Every few days they ride to the crater lake for fresh water, filling their buckets and basins, hauling them back to the campsite. Once a week they ride ten miles across the island to Hanga Roa, the island's town, to barter for fruits and vegetables and meat, and to reclaim their belongings.

Cooking pots, petticoats, soap, tea, twine—every morning a new item is missing from their camp. As they step out of their tents the rising sun reveals on the sand a crate pried open, a bucket upturned, a steamer trunk ransacked. But it isn't long before they learn the simple method of retrieval: to ask. Riding to town one day, they pass an elderly islander with one of Edward's neckties knotted around his head like a bandana. When Edward points, the man simply unfastens the tie, hands it back, and rides off. They realize theft, though ram-

pant on the island, is balanced by the frequent, peaceful, and un-
eventful return of the stolen goods.

"You see, the island is a closed community," Edward says over
breakfast one morning after another of Elsa's sun helmets has disappeared. "Thievery, in the traditional sense, completely deprives the
owner of his property. But on the island, nothing can really be removed, it can only be transplanted. Ergo: *not—actually—theft.* Things
are merely, shall we say, *borrowed without asking.*"

On the beach they have set up a simple square table where they
take meals. For seats they have covered three crates with bedsheets.

"Well, it isn't cricket to *borrow* tea and then go ahead and brew it,"
says Elsa, spreading preserves on a biscuit. She doesn't much care
about the tea, but her copy of *The Voyage of the Beagle* is gone and
she doesn't know how to tell Edward. It is bad luck to lose a present,
she thinks. Especially a wedding present. Alice's leather satchel has
also vanished.

"Nolo contendere," he says. "Edibles do, in fact, defy my hypothesis."

From his tone she can tell she has come across as pugnacious. "But
it's a good hypothesis. Such extreme isolation seems to affect societal
rules."

"Well . . . Elsa," he continues, cutting into a piece of guava, "we
present an unusual situation for them. We could abscond from the island at any moment, take our possessions with us, take theirs, too, if
we had the same slippery notion of property. Do not forget: We have
the schooner."

"Let's hope it remains that way." Because of the strength of the current, they have had to move the schooner to the island's opposite side.

"Well, there must be a system to these exchanges, or there was before we arrived. I believe we might have opened their system, so to
speak. Sent them into a bit of a dither."

Dither. Yes. What else, she wonders, should they call it? One of her
volumes of Darwin has been stolen by someone who can't read English. Crates, once emptied, disappear. Women roam Hanga Roa in
her hats and petticoats, in Alice's lace-trimmed jackets; young girls
belt their smocks with Edward's neckties.

Before long the spirit catches Alice. One morning, she emerges
from her tent in a Rapa Nui white smock.

"Alice, where did that come from?"

"I borrowed it. I'm a Rapa Nui."

"Allie."

"See? I'm Rapa Nui Alice." And she begins an elaborate pan-tomime through the sand: She crouches, then pushes back the sleeves of her smock and pretends to pull taro from the ground. She digs a hole, carries invisible stones one by one and places them in her earth oven, then stands and proudly examines her imagined handi-work. How beautiful, thinks Elsa, this ability, this desire to imagine herself as other people. Alice can believe she is Rodney Blackwell or Elsa or anyone. But Elsa wonders if Alice understands the boundaries of herself, where the edges of her being end, and where those of others begin.

Several days later, when they are in Hanga Roa buying produce, the owner of the smock catches up with them. A pale woman ap-proaches Alice, still in the smock, and taps her on the shoulder. But there seem no hurt feelings. The woman produces Alice's leather satchel, and the proposed exchange of the goods elicits smiles from both women, as though it is Christmas and each gift a most thought-ful and generous surprise. Flinging off her smock and handing it to the woman, Alice is left in her camisole and bloomers. When the woman sees Alice open the satchel, stroke the soft leather of its sides, then close her eyes and hum, she freezes. With concern she looks to Elsa, then Edward. Finally the woman steps forward and returns the smock to Alice. She lifts Alice's hand, kisses it, then presses her own palm to Alice's forehead.

Alice then begins to laugh, to squirm, and soon the attention of the entire street is on her. A young boy, the boy who snatched the box of tinned meats from Edward's arms the first night on the boat, watches her in silent amazement.

At the end of the day, when they mount their horses, weighed down with bags of avocados and guavas and bananas, the same boy follows them on his pony out of the town.

This is Biscuit Tin.

The rest of the village takes distinctly less interest in their move-ments than in their tinned meats and tobacco. But whenever they come to Hanga Roa, this boy follows them from town all the way to Anakena, a silent and curious sentinel. And when finally they arrive at the beach, dismount, and tie their ponies, he sits on the sand and watches them check their equipment, build their fire, prepare their supper. His hair is a dense black meadow of cowlicks, disarrayed and gleaming, as though he has just come from the ocean. His eyes are a shiny brown, his nose broad, and his lips full and supple, so that when he smiles, both rows of bright white teeth are fully exposed. He studies the campsite intently, and with each visit moves closer to the activity, so that after several weeks he is seated against Alice's tent, gazing at her through the netted door-flap. He watches her carry Pudding's cage back and forth; he tries to tickle the bird through the bars of its cage. But the boy refuses to speak, refuses even to offer his name. Alice begins calling him Biscuit Tin, for he can be persuaded to return to the village in the evenings only if Alice gives him his choice of biscuits. (To Elsa's dismay, he places his hand on each one before making up his mind.) But playing with him delights Alice. She has tired of being the source of the fussing. Now *she* can fuss. Gleefully domineering, she repeats all of Elsa's warnings and cautions to Biscuit Tin: *Are you sure you don't need a jacket, Biscuit Tin? Biscuit Tin, you stay away from the ocean. There are nasty sharks in there. Watch where you step, those rocks are very, very sharp.* Like a mother, Elsa thinks as she watches them together. And something in the boy loves Alice's admonitions. She can grab his thin arm firmly, shake him; she can drag him by the neck of his tattered shirt away from a cliff's edge, and he beams. Only, he is reticent to touch her, or any of them. He remains at a distance, politely reserved.

But he develops a habit of borrowing Alice's nightgowns, bursting from her tent in a flutter of white, skipping and twirling like a silent banshee, cheered and frenzied by their campfire laughter, his ankles eventually swallowed by the spirals of his white cotton wake, plunging him headlong into the sand. Elsa wonders some nights if they should be more concerned about the boy—what would his parents think? Is it safe for him to ride his pony alone in the dark? Why does he seem so free to roam about? But she has no way of asking what is proper, and the boy seems determined not to speak. So she lets the questions slide to the back of her mind. For now he delights them. And in this new place so far from home, Biscuit Tin, though probably no more than nine, is their only friend.

❁

In their second month Edward decides to begin work at Rano Raraku, the *moai* quarry four miles southeast of their camp. This, the volcanic crater from which the statues were carved, holds the greatest interest for him. Scores of unfinished *moai* are stuck in the rock inside the crater; on the outer grassy slope, dozens more stand at all angles, frozen, it seems, on their way somewhere else. First he wants to measure and catalogue each statue. After that, he intends to excavate.

Throughout the day, Elsa lies in the long grass, a parasol pitched by her side, drawing the elongated profile of each stone face—the sloping noses, the square chins, the dangling earlobes. Edward walks the hillside numbering the base of each *moai* with chalk and entering it in his log. "Thirty-five feet, Elsa! It must weigh over fifty tons!" Sometimes he calls out more elaborate descriptions—*Oval carving, suggestive of an egg, on the posterior of 87A*—which she notes in her log.

It is convenient, while he and Elsa examine the statues, to leave Alice and the boy to play. At the base of the crater, beneath a makeshift canopy, Alice spends days on end trying to teach him bezique, then tries to teach him about birds. But there are no hawks and terns to show him—of this Alice complains endlessly.

The *moai* are more numerous than expected. Some lie tucked away in the rock, overgrown with pale grass. Some sprout like wild shoots of stone. Others are buried almost to their heads. "I'd guess there are over two hundred," says Edward.

"It's eerie," says Elsa. "Them abandoned like that. And all the statues around the coast. Fallen."

"There must have been a tremendous seismic event here," says Edward. "Not a single statue remains upright."

"It would be devastating to work so hard to build these things and then have them all collapse."

"An event strong enough to tumble these statues must have ravaged the island. A tidal wave? It would have wiped out all crops, all livestock. Any volcanic activity would have ruined the soil. And then there is, of course, the secondary emotional and mental response. Events like that, natural disasters, become omens to primitive societies. When one lacks a scientific explanation or understanding, a horrible event like that can seem like the anger of the gods, inter alia."

"I'd like to know what it would have been like to live here. To know only this island. To imagine us here, right now, without our memory of England."

"But we cannot imagine ourselves without certain memories. The 'we' imagining will always have the memory."

"Of course. But it's still possible to think of yourself as living in a different place, a different time. To simply imagine what it might be."

"Yes, I think I understand."

"I just wonder if our place and time is really a part of us, if it's attached to us. . . ."

They talk like this until sunset, measuring and sketching and conjecturing. Then they mount their horses and return to the camp, which is now fully arranged.

Cooking dinner is managed as quickly as possible. Flies and mosquitoes swarm the campfire, plunging dizzily into any open pot; soups and stews grow speckled with the small black bodies. Once, as she prepares a chicken for dinner, Elsa counts twenty flies on her arm. She is rapidly adjusting to this daily battle with insects. One night, a thumb-size red cockroach drops onto her face in the tent. After that, the drowsy black flies seem manageable.

At twilight, they all clamber into Alice's tent—if Biscuit Tin is still lurking, he is duly propped on his pony and given a treat for the way home—and read aloud for an hour—from *The Life and Voyages of Captain James Cook* or *Amurath to Amurath*, a book by the famous British adventurer Gertrude Bell about her journey through Mesopotamia.

"You see, my dear," says Edward, "a woman can often have extraordinary insights into foreign cultures. Who knows? You could be the very next Miss Bell!"

But there is no need for him to say it—the thought has already occurred to her, returning to her nightly as they read Bell's book. Could Elsa write about their trip? Their work? She is, after all, in a place where no other Western woman has set foot. But Bell went to Oxford, her fate spun from the silken threads of age-old aristocracy, while Elsa has spent her life with books borrowed from employers' shelves, lingering outside the doors of lecture halls at her father's university. But the possibility of a memoir fills her with new vigor. As they read in the lamplit tent, listening to moths clacking and fluttering at the light, to the distant rush of surf, her mind fastens on the idea of *her own* work on the island, *her* notebooks, what might someday be a book by Elsa Pendleton Beazley. But she must, then, find her own research. Something other than the quarry—that belongs to Edward.

The chapter finished, the book closed, the lantern's fast flame sacrificed to the moon's soft radiance, they say their good-nights. Elsa and Edward return to their tent—Elsa now spends every night there. Sometimes, Alice creeps in while they are asleep, collapsing on the floor beside Elsa's cot, or nestling beside her, whispering "stove, stove." And once or twice, Elsa awakens to find Alice clinging to Edward's half-naked form. On these occasions she nudges Alice and pries her off.

But one night, when Elsa can no longer shake from her mind what Edward said to her on the eve of their arrival—*I know I am not what a girl your age dreams of*—when the memory of his shame becomes too much for her, when his nightly assurances that she has her own separate cot and that he would be pleased to turn away as she undresses seem a generosity unearned by her, in the dark tent she tiptoes to his cot, seats herself on the edge, and quietly offers herself to him.

That Alice has heard or seen anything of the intimacy Elsa doesn't think possible. But Alice must sense something. Something, from the sour look on her face the next morning when Elsa ducks into her tent, she doesn't like.

After this, Alice's visits cease.

12

The day after she slid the Whitman poem beneath Professor Farraday's door, Greer arrived in class to find written on the chalkboard:

True or False?
I believe a leaf of grass is no less than the journey-work of the stars,
And the pismire is equally perfect, and a grain of sand, and the egg of
*   the wren,*
And the tree-toad is a chef-d'oeuvre for the highest . . .

"A question has been provoked by one Walt Whitman, poet of the people," Thomas said, his pointer tapping the board. "Is a leaf of grass the journey-work of the stars?"

He read the entire poem aloud, pausing between lines, and when he'd finished sat behind his desk, put his feet up, and clasped his hands behind his head. "I think it would be best if we composed our own little poem in response." Thomas appointed a student to transcribe what turned out to be six stanzas on grass species that produced toxic hydrocyanic acid, and on pismire colonies that took slaves. The students were amused; Thomas had a reputation for combativeness and to them this was a punch line they had long awaited. Here was the man who'd won Princeton's Linnaeus Prize as a freshman, had published three papers pioneering fossil pollen analysis before he'd even left graduate school. The man who in 1953, at thirty-three years old, organized the world's first palynology conference. This poem, the students knew, would enter Professor Farraday folklore, and they were happy to be part of it. But Greer sat silently in her chair, amazed anyone could so rigidly deny the possibility of a benevolent intent, or some cosmic perfection, behind nature. At the end of class, as she was midway up the steps, Thomas called to her.

"Miss Sandor, the poem, of course, displays excellent command of language—even I am not immune to lyricism—but little command of, well, the nuance of science. After all, if we don't defend science, who will? I thank you for the challenge."

She turned to face him. His nose was large, almost beaklike, but it balanced, in a pleasing way, his wide-set eyes. He was forty-two, and a hint of silver dusted his thick sideburns. Otherwise his hair was dark brown, and noticeably uncombed. He wasn't handsome in the traditional sense, but his face seemed the natural expression of inner intelligence, as though each feature had risen like a mountain from his mind, the nose, the eyes, the wide forehead all manifestations of his internal energy.

"Professor Farraday. What makes you think I have any interest in that poem?"

"I don't believe in a grand design, but I am fully aware of the patterns of daily life. Only women," he said, twirling a piece of chalk like a miniature baton, "slip poems under doors. And you've noticed, I'm sure, that you're the only woman in my class."

"Oh, I've noticed."

He was clearly waiting for more, but Greer turned away without anything further. As she pulled open the door of the lecture hall, she could feel his stare pursue her, the footsteps of his curiosity.

Greer had of course realized, from the very first lecture, she was the only woman. And, further, that she was one of only six women getting a Ph.D. in botany at the University of Wisconsin. This fact had been recognized by everyone—the women, the men, the faculty. And in response to this situation, the loudest and most outgoing of the group—Mildred Ravener—had called a meeting of the women. On a crisp September day, Greer sat on the Union Terrace with Alice Beemer, Gerty Smith, Elaine Ferguson, and Jo Banks, eating bowls of the university's homemade ice cream. They talked about their interest in botany, their childhoods, and the difficulties they had faced as woman scientists. Greer listened to each one, and, when her turn came, offered the only anecdote that sprang to mind.

"I was proving that bees were attracted to violets by virtue of their color, not smell, by placing an inverted test tube over the violet, and then monitoring the flight path of the bee. Of course, the bees flew straight into the tip of the test tube, where the color dominated, not to the base, where smell escaped. But my teacher got stung trying to judge the experiment, and Joshua Kleimer won for taking apart his mother's refrigerator. And labeling all the parts. The end. Five dollars if you can guess what he was doing last time I saw him."

"Professionally, you mean? Or what he was actually doing?" asked Gerty Smith. Gerty Smith was married to a dentist.

Greer sighed. "Appliance repair."

"So what grade was this?" asked Mildred Ravener.

"Third," said Greer.

Greer knew this wasn't the sort of anecdote they were looking for—the others had been pawed by teachers in dark corridors, had been told by their parents that science would ruin their hearts and their wombs. Mildred Ravener described the time her father shoved all her science books in the stove, set them aflame, then replaced them with a gift-wrapped pile of cookbooks. ("You see, ladies, he considered this an act of love.") Two months later, he replaced the microscope she'd saved for years to buy with a Singer sewing machine. Mildred had, by her own account, many "feelings of resentment toward the other members in her family unit." She was an obsessively articulate, deeply religious woman who believed communication could resolve all conflicts. Each week she wrote her parents a letter—the same one, it seemed—explaining her love of science. And each week, no reply. Still, she had faith she would be understood, that one day, in her mailbox, she'd find the long-awaited envelope.

Greer's father, however, had always been encouraging; he was the reason she'd become a scientist. So she felt she had little in common with the group. The only woman Greer really liked was Jo Banks— she was a few years older than the rest, had a quick mind and a knack for identifying pollen. Jo never seemed to lose the bronze sheen she had acquired in the Caribbean, where she had lived for several years working as a scuba-diving instructor, and where she had had some kind of life-altering spiritual experience with a barracuda, which she alluded to often but never explained. She had six brothers—Jeb, John, Jack, Judd, Jessie, and Jeremiah—whom she referred to as though everyone else knew them ("Judd hates vanilla too"). But she spoke of her parents only once, and that was to say that her parents never spoke of her. "They don't like you in science?" asked Mildred. "No," said Jo. "They like me in science." And that was the end of it. Jo Banks was unnervingly comfortable with the act of silence. She sat, she watched, she nodded; and when she talked, she spoke her mind, concisely. But she was extremely good-humored. She was the one who came up with the nickname for Professor Farraday's lab: The Philodendron. And then for him: Jackass in the Pulpit. Both plants produced exclusively male flowers in their first season, and only after several seasons produced a small number of female flowers confined to the bottom of the stalk. Jo had taken Thomas's class the year before Greer, and warned her:

"Nod, smile, tell him you like his ties. He can be a prick, but he's the hotshot of the department. His angiosperm research is ground-breaking. Just remember, when he starts in on atheism, look really interested." Jo widened her eyes, arched her eyebrows, let her mouth hang open—her parody of interest. She had thick brown bangs and always wore her hair in a ponytail, which she now tightened. "Remember. This guy doesn't need to be lecturing first-years. He teaches because he *enjoys* it. Sick, huh? So play along. Try to lean forward in your seat—he loves that shit. You want him on your team."

But Greer had wondered if she had cut him from her team with her poem.

"Holy shit," Jo said when Greer told her what had happened. They were drinking beer at Jo's apartment, and Jo had just pulled out two cigars. "Last year, a guy tried a deistic stunt like that and right in the middle of the lecture Jackass told him to gather his stuff, to leave and go sit in church instead. You left him a Whitman poem and he didn't seem pissed?"

"He seemed amused."

"Here, take the end off, like this." Jo bit off the tip.

"Yum," Greer said, spitting the end into the conch shell Jo held out.

"Amused. Uh-oh. Call the papers. I think Jackass in the Pulpit is interested."

Greer paused; this had already occurred to her.

"Oh, shit. *You're* interested."

"I shouldn't be."

"Well, he is an ass."

"An intelligent ass."

"A mildly accomplished ass. I'll concede that."

"At least he's not married."

"He sounds pure dreamy now. Stop before I fall in love."

"Well, he's almost twice my age."

"And that never happens."

"I know it happens. It happens all the time. That's why it's less interesting. It's a cliché."

"Are you really looking for something non-cliché?"

"I don't know."

Jo settled into her couch and considered her cigar. "Cuba. We could go to Cuba and get real cigars. I've always wanted to live abroad. And what we really need is to get involved with some kind of revolution. We could be generalissimos. God, we would make great generalissimos. Or at least I would, but you're a pretty fast learner. We could wear fatigues. Berets. Maybe keep the earrings and the curls. Now, *that's* not cliché."

Greer stretched out on the carpet, staring at the mildew stains on the ceiling. "Well, Castro's not half bad-looking."

"My God, you have odd taste. Number one rule of being a generalissimo, Greer, you cannot have the hots for the head guerrilla generalissimo."

"Fidel happens to be prime minister now. That's very respectable. And in my communist dictatorship, there will be special adjustments made for romantic relationships."

"That's not a communist dictatorship, that's a commune."

Greer laughed, and tucked one arm beneath her head.

"Well," said Jo from the couch above. "Living a cliché is a lot better than living a deviance."

"We'll see."

"Just remember, sometimes an older professor," Jo said, waving her cigar before Greer, "is just an older professor."

But, when Greer returned to Professor Farraday's class the following week, it was as if nothing had happened. She arrived early in a yellow skirt and white blouse. She'd even put on makeup. In the front row, as she took her seat, she slowly tucked her skirt beneath her, but Thomas, reading through a paper on his desk, didn't look up. Only as the last students filed in did he stand and make his way to the board. He was wearing his usual blue suit, wrinkled across the back; the sleeves fell an inch too long and when he wanted to write on the blackboard he had to shove them up his arms, although they promptly tumbled down again. His disarray perplexed her. Why didn't this man have a suit that fit properly? A well-known scientist, the department's darling—certainly he could afford it.

She knew he was unmarried, but now recalled hearing about his solitary habits. People spoke of his monastic existence, occasionally speculating about his love life, linking him to the department secretary, and to an assistant at the university greenhouse. So rarely was he seen in the presence of women, he was assumed attached to any woman he spoke with. Anything he did outside the classroom was cause for conversation. Mildred Ravener had once seen him at the grocery store, and when she mentioned it to other students, they wanted to know what he'd been buying. Something in the way Thomas carried himself implied he had no time for trivialities; he turned his attention only to what was essential, to things with the density of fact. And clothing must have seemed to him an inconvenience. Or perhaps Greer was wrong; his disorder might be the result of nothing more than simple arrogance. As if his intelligence were handsome enough.

When class ended, Greer was slow to gather her books—allowing him time for a hello, allowing them a moment when the room was less crowded—but he didn't once look over. When another student approached him, however, with a question about writing grant proposals, he said: "Simple. State your credentials and your proposal. Don't try to be charming, don't try to be funny. And whatever you do"—his voice suddenly amplified—"for science's sake, don't quote Whitman."

It wasn't until a week later, when she was working alone in the lab late at night, that she knew she had his attention. Greer had gotten stuck with the two A.M. to four A.M. slot for lab time, which she didn't mind—she liked staying up late. But the temperature had fallen early that year, the lakes were already freezing over, and the university hadn't yet begun heating the buildings. With a rough wool blanket around her shoulders, two pairs of socks over her panty hose, and Elgar's Cello Concerto playing on her radio, Greer was looking at unidentified pollen types, when the door creaked open. She wasn't alarmed. She had a feeling it was him. Something had passed between them, a current, and it was as if for the past week she'd been awaiting this moment. His footsteps moved toward her, but she didn't look up—she didn't want to appear eager. A hand wrapped itself around hers and guided it to a warm metal cylinder.

"Fuel," he said.

Greer kept her eyes pressed firmly to the ocular. A grain of black willow pollen loomed beneath her.

"It's cold, Miss Sandor."

"I have a blanket."

"And it's late. This building is deserted." He cleared his throat. "I don't think it's safe."

"I have heard rumors of professors who prowl the halls late at night."

He chuckled. She could sense him exploring her work space, looking at her notebook, her taxonomy books, her pile of broken pencils, her radio.

"You like your work?"

"I love it."

He adjusted the blanket over her shoulders, then retreated. When the door clicked closed, on the table she found a thermos of hot coffee and a ceramic mug.

The next night, he returned with a space heater. He said nothing as he carried the small machine across the lab. Greer sat at her microscope, watching as he plugged the black box into the socket.

"I liked your lecture on seed dispersal," she said.

"Good."

"I'm interested in cross-water dispersal patterns."

He smiled.

He angled the heater toward her, flipped on the switch, and waited as the machine whirred to life. "There," he said. "The dial in the back adjusts the setting. It sticks a little, so twist it hard."

"Thank you."

"Well, good night, then, Miss Sandor."

"Good night, Professor Farraday."

"Ah, Professor Farraday," he mumbled, as though speaking of someone he had known once, and forgotten.

Thermoses of coffee, cookies and muffins, naturalist notebooks, lithographs, photographs. For months this went on; he arrived once or twice a week, in the middle of the night, always leaving something on the table. At times he must have found her asleep, her face pressed into the pages of a book, because she would awaken, bleary-eyed, to a gift beside her. Few words were exchanged—"You should eat" or "Get some rest," always the admonitions of "It's cold" and "It's late"— as if the offering were conversation enough, as if the visits were the most natural thing in the world. It was as if they were a couple with their own linguistic shorthand: *Honey, lights. Door. The dog.* But she felt a slow seduction developing between them. As she sat examining grains of pollen, in he walked, a pioneer of palynology, her teacher, and yet, even when they spoke of science, the conversation inevitably became physical—it focused on the body, her body's needs.

Greer now seated herself in the back of the classroom and avoided eye contact, yet she felt his attention even more powerfully. Had she discovered a mathematic principle: For each outward display of interest eliminated, inward interest was squared? Sometimes, during department talks, she would watch him onstage, beside Professor Jenks, Professor Mitzger, and Doctor Hawthorne, arguing and gesticulating with his usual bravado. Her thoughts would drift miles from the topic—the destruction of tropical forests, the extinction of the Mauritius dodo—toward him, Professor Farraday, or Thomas, as she now thought of him. In public he held himself with such authority, people treated him with such deference, it was sometimes hard to believe this was the same man who visited her at night with slices of apple pie. But this was part of what attracted her. The dichotomy. The knowledge that beneath his public self there lived a private, flirtatious self he shared only with her. And for now Thomas wanted the whole matter kept quiet. So did Greer, who never for a moment forgot she was the only woman in the class.

"Well, he's either in love with you or he's trying to fatten you up," said Jo, when, toward the semester's end, Greer finally confessed to the late-night trysts.

"I don't know what it is."

"But you like it."

They were having lunch in a diner, sipping milk shakes.

"I guess I like it a lot," said Greer.

"I don't need to tell you that it's going to make your status as a woman around here even weirder."

"I know."

"It's worth thinking about."

"You don't think it's a good idea?"

"Greer, I'm not the person to ask."

They opened their books and began to review the material for their next lab assignment. "Sample purification," said Greer. "I'm trying to get a handle on it. It's taking up too much of my time."

"It's all about centrifuging. Watch each step, decant, centrifuge. It helps if you don't daydream about professors between each step."

"Ha-ha."

"I'll go through it with you if you want."

"That's all right," said Greer. "I need to do it on my own."

"I figured."

"And what about the Wichita outcrop samples? Apparently there are some strange grains with echinae."

"I looked at them on Tuesday. They almost have that weird pear shape of sedge pollen, and a definite echinate sculpturing. They're late Miocene. The plant, whatever it is, has been extinct for a long time. I'll get you a sample."

"Thanks, Jo." Greer flipped through her notebook, drew one last sip through her straw, and slid the glass to the side. "All right. Listen. If I deny myself an attraction because I'm afraid it will compromise my status around here . . ."

"Uh-oh."

"I'm serious. If I deny myself something I want because I'm afraid it will compromise my status, what have I won? It still means I'm allowing myself to be trapped, to be dominated by the system that I'm not a part of."

"That's a positive way to think about it."

"You think I'm deluding myself?"

"I think you're in love and that feminist politics or anything else doesn't mean shit to you right now."

"He respects me, you know. He respects my work."

Jo set her palms on the table and looked at Greer. "That should be a given, Greer. Not a privilege. You're the smartest one in the whole goddamned program. You're just a little preoccupied right now."

"Don't worry, Jo. I'm going to give it some time."

"Good."

"I'm going to take this slow."

"Excellent."

"There's no reason to rush."

"I'm totally convinced. Are you?"

"Barely."

"Remember the barracuda."

Greer laughed. "Jo, what exactly *is* the story with the barracuda?"

"I'll tell you someday. But the details are irrelevant. The point is, you look into the face of death and you stay calm, you collect your own strength, and you tell yourself that life and death are in your own hands. They're not outside you."

Greer nodded. "Inspiring. Of course, I have no idea what you're talking about, but it's inspiring nonetheless. Hey, someday, Jo, take me scuba diving?"

Jo turned the page in her book. "Anytime you want."

※

At the semester's end, when Professor Farraday's class was over, Greer went to his office. It was December, the lakes were frozen thick with ice, and the city was dusted in white. From his window she could see people skating on Lake Mendota.

"I think it's time we went out to dinner, or to a show, or for drinks. Something real." She was in mid-sentence as she walked through the door, afraid of losing her nerve. "A date." She lobbed the word at him.

"I was beginning to wonder what a man had to do around here to get asked out."

"Is that a yes?"

"I was running out of baked goods. I figured if I had to wait until spring, I could bring fresh fruit."

"Yes, no. True, false. Are we going on a date, Professor Farraday?"

"All right. What are your plans for the holidays?"

"I was going to put in some extra lab time. With everybody gone I might actually get sunlight through a window."

"No trips home?"

"No."

"No family visits?"

"No family," said Greer, hating how final this sounded. Her father had died just before she'd been accepted to graduate school, a blow that had knocked the wind out of her. School gave her something to occupy her mind, but she missed talking to him about classes, about lab, and she now wished she could talk to him about the man standing before her. Greer didn't know what her father would think of her romantic life—her relationships in college hadn't been significant enough to mention. Once, when she was home for the holidays, he had asked, "You have friends at school?" "Some," she answered. "Special friends? Those can be as important as your studies." "When I meet a man as interesting as botany, you'll be the first to know," she replied. After his death, she'd sold the house to finance her degree, and now there was no home she could go back to. Greer felt the weight of her admission hanging between her and Thomas. This was the first personal information they'd exchanged, the first hint that behind their late-night meetings, their banter and flirtation, lay real life, the past.

Thomas adjusted his mood accordingly. "Well, certainly you should have some plans for Christmas. That's no day to be alone."

"I didn't exactly imagine *you* celebrating the birth of Christ."

"I'm using the day to core on Lake Mendota."

"Much better."

"Would you like to come?"

"At last, a date."

"A working date. If you do a good job, I'll take you to dinner afterward."

Greer considered this, letting her attention drift over the walls of his office: certificates, awards, more Latin calligraphy in this one room than she'd seen in a lifetime. She knew he liked her—he had, after all, pursued her—but it was still hard not to feel overwhelmed by who he was. She could think of only one way to shake her intimidation. "How about you take me to dinner Christmas Eve, and if you do a good job, I'll consider helping you take samples the next day."

"The next day?"

"We can arrange something," said Greer. She scribbled her address on a sheet of paper and tore it from her notebook. "You have to hold the doorbell down hard," she said. "If that doesn't work, throw a snowball at the second-floor window."

For the next two weeks they didn't see each other. Greer heard from another student that Professor Farraday was lecturing at a symposium at the University of Iowa, and the shades on his office door were drawn. The campus buildings quieted, the crowds on State Street dissolved. Jo left to spend Christmas with Jeb and Jeremiah in Minneapolis, and for the first time, Greer, in her small apartment, looking at the rows of dark windows across the street, experienced the full realization of her solitude. When she was young she had gone on long horseback rides through the countryside by herself, watching birds or bullfrogs for hours on end—a kind of loneliness, but chosen. This was a sense of people vanishing, of empty rooms, and it unsettled her. She called Jo a few times but never reached her. She ate dinner out for the noise and the company. Mainly, Greer missed her father—it was her first winter without him, and even though she kept herself busy in the lab, working late into the night, shuffling endless slides beneath her microscope, it only reminded her how much she wanted to talk to him.

By Christmas Eve, her sadness had turned to numbness. Greer had simply tired herself with feeling lonely. She managed to put on a red cardigan Jo had told her looked good; she barretted her hair, rubbed some rouge on her face. But when he rang her doorbell, and she met him downstairs, her smile was strained.

"I should let you know I was entirely prepared to throw a snowball. Oh, no."He was standing on the walkway."I'm too late. The holiday blues have gotten hold of you."

"I'm just tired," said Greer, examining his face, recently shaven, and the sharp line of his jaw against the collar of his coat. She couldn't believe he was there. And she couldn't believe how much she had wanted to see him, what need she harbored in herself.

"Trust me, I know the look. It took me fifteen years to devise a way to avoid the holiday blues. And now, for the price of your charming company, I will share it with you. I'll save you years of despair. Trust me."

"*You* know the holiday blues?"

"Miss Sandor, I've spent most of my life alone. Holidays. Birthdays. Symposiums. Even football games. You are dealing with an expert in solitude. I'm an award-winning solitarian."

There must have been women, thought Greer. Perhaps on other holidays, perhaps other students. But she had no desire to ask about that now. She was simply glad that he was here. Beneath his overcoat he wore a blue sweater over a plaid shirt—the shirt's collar was crooked, one side tucked beneath the sweater's neck, the other side flipped upside down, a plaid arrow at his chin. It was the first time she'd seen him in anything other than a suit. His cologne floated toward her on an icy breeze.

"But you'd rather not be alone," she said.

"I'd rather you not be alone."

"Well," said Greer. "Ditto, then."

They let a pleasant silence spread between them.

"Hungry?" he asked.

"Ravenous."

"Good. Me too." He linked his arm in hers and they stepped slowly down the icy path."Button up,"he said."It's cold."

"You too," she said. They buttoned their coats, adjusted their scarves, watched their breath steam into the night. He then pulled up her collar and wrapped her scarf in one more loop around her neck. "There,"he said.

Greer suddenly felt happiness, in all its perfect confusion, rise like tears. She leaned forward and kissed him—a burst of heat in the cold. "Merry Christmas," she said.

He smiled.

And she felt the numbness begin to slip from her. She felt it would be a good evening, that they would enjoy each other, that this—his arm threading itself through hers—was the period put on a sentence begun months earlier. They began to walk, and Greer looked at his face. There is great beauty in this man, she thought.

"All good?" he asked.

"Very good," she said. He steadied her as they made their way slowly along the icy path. A cold wind battered their faces, and as they leaned into each other she felt the weight and the warmth of him all at once.

13

After their ten-thousand-mile journey across the Pacific, after their eight-day rendezvous at Easter Island, the German squadron experienced a small victory at the Battle of Coronel.

On November 1, off the coast of Chile, Admiral von Spee detected the British *Glasgow* nearby. Von Spee, who had received reports of a single enemy cruiser in the area, ordered his fleet to overtake the ship.

The *Glasgow,* however, was part of Rear Admiral Sir Christopher Cradock's squadron, which lay nearby, unseen.

Admiral Cradock was equally misled. Reports had reached him of a single German cruiser, *Leipzig,* in the area, and by chance this was the first of von Spee's ships he spotted. He, too, ordered his squadron into rapid combat against the single cruiser.

Each side believed it had the superior force, and by the time the situation was clear, action was under way.

The German ships carried more big-caliber guns and the weight of their fire was nearly double that of the British. Within two hours the Royal Navy lost two cruisers and nearly sixteen hundred men beside the Chilean town of Coronel.

Von Spee, from his lookout, was surveying the British cruisers, when suddenly flecks of red and green and yellow burst from one of the flaming ships, like bright scarves in the sky. They swirled in odd circles, then began to flutter—they were parrots. The British officers had released parrots bought in Brazil as gifts. The birds, however, were too stunned by the explosions to accept their freedom. Swooping about the smoky forecastle, they collided with the cannons; they perched on the gunwale as fires erupted around them. It was noted by a young German officer that almost one hundred birds soon bobbed lifelessly on the sea. "This seemed to all of us," the young officer wrote in the last letter his mother would receive, "a most eerie omen."

The Battle of Coronel was the first defeat suffered by the Royal Navy in over a century, and prompted First Lord of the Admiralty Winston Churchill to send almost the entire British Fleet after von Spee. Churchill's orders were unequivocal: "Your main and most important duty is to search for the German armored cruisers. . . . All other considerations are to be subordinated to this end." Von Spee was in immense danger. The battle had expended nearly half his ships' ammunition, depleting the only resources that might have saved his fleet and returned him home.

Also, the sinking of Admiral Cradock's ship, *Good Hope*, contributed to von Spee's growing tension. Von Spee had known Sir Christopher Cradock since his first posting to Tsingtao; he had sent a man with whom he'd been friends for fourteen years to the bottom of the sea.

Days later, at a dinner to celebrate their victory, an officer made a toast: "To the damnation of the British navy." Von Spee then stood and raised his own glass, proclaiming: "I drink to the memory of a gallant and honorable foe!" Without waiting for support, he drained his glass, gathered his hat, and departed.

The portentousness of such a victory on November 1st would not have been lost on von Spee, a Catholic. It was All Saints' Day.

—*Fleet of Misfortune: Graf von Spee*
and the Impossible Journey Home

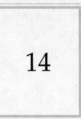

14

The island is honeycombed, a lattice of caves. In some distant past, these were homes, shelters, hideouts for women and children. Now they house only relics, scattered bones, and, according to legend, the spirit *tatane.*

Two female *tatane*—Kava-ara and Kava-tua—are said to live in a cliffside cave on the northeast coast, keeping watch over the sleeping figure of the man they fell in love with centuries earlier and kidnapped from Hanga Roa. It is said that from the cliff's edge you can hear the man gurgling in deep, silken sleep, and above that the singing of his *tatane* captors as they try—for if his spirit awakens it will take flight—to prolong his slumber.

This is the only cave Biscuit Tin avoids. He knows them all, the caves strangled by grassy overgrowth, the caves clogged with lava rocks, the ones beneath the sharp cliffs splashed by surf, as though his short life has been spent exploring every inch of this island. Small and lithe, he can wiggle into the smallest of holes, emerging with a bone, a dusty tooth, a wooden figurine. He gives everything he retrieves to Alice, but she cares only for the strange tablet he presents one day: a three-foot-long piece of wood, oiled and worn, covered with pictorial engravings. As if reading braille, Alice runs her small hands across the mysterious script.

Alice then hands the tablet to Elsa. "Squiggles," she says.

The moment Elsa touches it, she knows this is what she has been looking for. This is the script González noticed on his voyage almost one hundred and fifty years earlier, and deciphering it will be her project. The *moai* fascinate her, but their story belongs to Edward, and though she is glad to assist him, Elsa needs something of her own.

She wants to secure a balance between them, even a distance. The tablet could record a genealogy, a legend, a codification of ancient law. It might help unravel the story of this island. If she can learn to read it, or grasp some small part of it, it will mean all her choices have served some higher purpose.

Her first task is to see if they can find more tablets. For weeks, led by Biscuit Tin, Elsa searches scores of caves, upturning skeletons, swatting at cobwebs, moving, one by one, the stones blocking secret chambers. Alice refuses to enter, so Edward waits with her outside while Elsa and Biscuit Tin survey the chambers. Edward has offered to go in, to let Elsa sit with Alice, but she has politely declined. If the tablets are her study, she should retrieve them. And, for practical purposes, she knows she is more agile than he is.

Soon they have amassed over twenty tablets and several inscribed staffs, the likes of which Elsa has never seen. The writing is an endless stream of small bulbous figures, hundreds squeezed onto each line. She has no immediate sense of whether the script is logographic, syllabic, or alphabetic. Some combinations of images appear over and over again, and some are unique. As she lays them side by side in the tent at night, the ambition of her task begins to overwhelm her. Where on earth does one begin to understand the markings? What she desperately needs is a key, her own Rosetta stone or Behistun rock, but the tablets seem filled with the hieroglyphics of one language alone.

She is thankful, now, for the distance from England, from scholars, from those qualified to take on this job. She knows it's not the kind of project for a former governess, even the daughter of a professor. But she is here. And what, after all, is better than opportunity and desire?

First she decides to have Alice copy the figures, so they will at least have an accurate record. Also, Alice will be kept out of trouble.

For several weeks, Elsa sits on the hill above their campsite and reads Sir Henry Creswicke Rawlinson's *A Commentary on the Cuneiform Inscriptions of Babylon and Assyria* and Champollion's *Summary of the Hieroglyphic System of Ancient Egyptians.* Alice, beside her, sketches near-perfect reproductions of portions of each tablet.

As each series is completed, she shows Elsa. "Here, look."

"They look like birds," says Alice. "Angry birds. And trees. My drawings are better, don't you think?"

"Much better," says Elsa.

Alice's renditions allow Elsa to examine each image individually. She sorts Alice's copies, and assigns a number to each character. Soon she has almost one thousand unique figures, which suggests the script is not alphabetic. But it is difficult—some figures look very similar. Day after day Elsa stares at them; at night they dance across her dreams. So many seem to be birds and plants and animals—the very things lacking on the island. If the script is indigenous, it should use representations the islanders would have known. But perhaps the figures are not what they seem—perhaps she is seeing only what *she* has seen before.

As Alice begins copying the larger tablets, the task seems to bother her. Occasionally she hurls her notebook down and stomps off across the grass. She chucks pebbles at her pony, tugs at her own hair.

"What's wrong, Allie?"

"They're ugly. That tablet is ugly. All the faces are angry. I don't want to look at it anymore."

"Then we'll just tuck it aside. You don't have to look at it." Elsa wraps the tablet in canvas. "Why don't you take a break from all that and do some nice portraits? That always makes you happy. How about a drawing of Biscuit Tin?"

So for several days Alice makes a portrait of Biscuit Tin, though he can't stop giggling for more than a few seconds at a time, and this only when Alice looks away to grab a new charcoal or a rubbing cloth. As soon as she studies him, he plants his palms on his cheeks and laughs. Then Alice scolds him, tosses grass at his face. It is only in the brief moments when Alice seems to disappear, when her eyes retreat, when the motion of her charcoal suddenly stops, that the boy's face becomes still and solemn. He composes himself and sits patiently, as though in the presence of one who is sick. And when she returns to the world, to him, her feet kicking at the sand, he is clearly relieved. After a week, when the portrait is finished, she presents it to him. He has not been permitted to see the work in progress, and when finally he does see it, Biscuit Tin nearly bursts into tears. It has, thinks Elsa, captured his spirit: the disarray of his hair, the loyal eyes, the mischievous grin, the narrow neck suspending the full moon of his face. Snatching it from her, Biscuit Tin darts off across the sand, then through the tall grass, the paper flapping beside him.

The next day Alice draws a picture of their father's house in spring, surrounded by thick hibiscus and wild roses, the trees shading the front path, the hills in the distance blanketed with clover and thyme. But the likeness is too good, and Elsa cannot bear to look at it—this reminder of home, of the past.

When Alice hands the picture to the boy, his eyes widen.

"Home," Alice tells him. "That is where Pudding and Father and Elsa and I live. I share a room with Elsa."

The boy's finger traces the flowers, the bushes, the tall trees.

"That is home. Far from here. In Europe."

Gesturing at the tree, the boy hands Alice a blank sheet of paper.

"Just a tree?"

The boy squints, as though trying to figure out what she has said. As she draws two sweeping lines of trunk, he nods.

"I'm going to put birds in it. A tree without birds is no good."

Elsa is happy that Alice is enjoying drawing, but when Alice returns to work on the tablets, they again upset her. One afternoon, returning from a visit with Edward, Elsa finds Alice crying over her notebook.

"I don't like them," Alice shrieks. "I don't want to do this anymore."

"Very well, Allie. You can do whatever you like. Do you want to go for a ride with me? We can go fetch Biscuit Tin for you."

"I miss the boat," Alice huffs. "I liked the water, going fast on the water. Beazley was funny on the boat."

"I know." Elsa rubs Alice's back. "I promised you that if you were unhappy, we would go home. Didn't I?"

"Yes."

"And we don't have to stay here. We can go back on the water, back to London, whenever you like. . . . Do you want me to braid your hair? Here. Turn around. Let's give you some braids."

Elsa runs her fingers through Alice's heavy hair. Yes. She *has* promised Alice they would go home the moment she wanted to. But what good will come of leaving now? Before they've even made a full survey of the *moai*? They can't just abandon the expedition. The voyage took nearly a year, and now that they are here and have finally grown accustomed to the wind and the rocks and the strange language, they are making real progress. This isn't, after all, just a honeymoon. Their work—the measurements, the copying of the tablets—is unprecedented. Besides, returning to England will take at the very least eleven months, and in that time Alice will likely change her mind. Elsa's promise to Alice was made before they reached the island, before they even left England. At that point she had imagined the worst; she feared being stranded, friendless, in the farthest reaches of civilization. She had wanted the trip, but had also imagined it as a necessary part of her arrangement with Edward, something she would endure for the sake of Alice, perhaps for her benefit—was it wrong to imagine Alice would flourish away from the scorn of Europeans? But the promise, she now realizes, was really meant for herself. She made sure she could escape if *she* needed to. How could she know this sacrifice would become her greatest pleasure?

Of course, her hands still blister from washing their bloomers and blouses each morning, Edward's shirts and socks; her face warms uncomfortably as she stirs chowder over the fire, though she is learning to make the Kanaka-style earth oven; she still hikes down to the shore in the moonlight to plunge greasy pots into the surf. And, as always, she has to look after Alice, and now Edward. She is still pinned like a butterfly to the frame of her circumstances, but here she can, for a few hours each day, at least imagine herself free.

Riding her pony up the slope of the quarry, she likes to gaze at the *moai*, the vast stone spirits, the work of strangers who lived centuries before. She remembers reading about the Egyptian pyramids, that tens of thousands were conscripted to build the great limestone tombs. Well, the *moai*, too, must have been the work of hundreds of men, carving and chiseling in the sun day after day. And the scale of it all—the ages of labor, the tons of stone, the decay of abandon—astounds her. She feels small, irrelevant, and utterly safe. What comfort there is knowing she is a part of something old, something larger than herself. Elsa, when she looks in the quarry, thinks to herself: *God*. It is the only name she can think of for the feeling the place gives her. Is God, she wonders, simply a sense of history? A sense of others having stood on the exact same patch of earth, years before, of strangers filled with the same fears and regrets?

Being on the island gives Elsa a sense of peace she has never before known, and with this comes purpose. The past lurks around her like a mystery demanding to be unraveled. Why shouldn't they unravel some of the mysteries? Perhaps they will decipher the native script, and they will—*she* will—be a part of something important. Her life, despite the compromises, might at least have larger meaning.

"Ouuch!"

"Sorry, Allie." She has pulled Alice's braid too tightly. "Let me loosen it. You know what, Allie? I think we should give the island time."

Alice clutches at her braid, feeling the uneven bumps and ridges.

"Do you love Beazley?"

"Allie, you know Edward and I are married. We're husband and wife. Just like Father was with Mother. But I don't love him as much as I love you. You know that. Don't you, Allie? You are my true and absolute love."

"Does Beazley love you?"

"Of course he does. But not as much as our little Mr. Biscuit Tin adores you! Allie, just think how it would break Biscuit Tin's heart if you left. You must stay for him. And for now, you don't have to look at another tablet, ever. I'll put my poor artistry to work."

For the time being, Elsa is busy learning the native language, since fluency seems the natural step toward unraveling the script. Gertrude Bell knew Arabic well before making her journey through Mesopotamia. Elsa's initial phrase book can get them directions to fresh water and fig trees, but she wants to talk to the islanders about their culture. Where did they come from? What kind of a society did they create? What might they have wanted, or needed, to write on the wood? And now that sheep shearing has ended, the islanders are taking an interest in the expedition. Several children come by the quarry one day to watch as Elsa helps Edward measure the *moai*. On their ponies, the children laugh and sway, hollering in a fusion of Rapa Nui and Spanish, "*Amor los moai?*" But when they see Biscuit Tin emerging from behind a *moai*, they begin to hiss. With his chubby forefinger, one boy smashes his own nose and emits a series of grunts. Another tugs wildly at his own cheeks. A freckled girl with red hair flips back her eyelids and juts out her tongue. Then a dirt-smeared boy jumps from his pony and lobs a large stone at Biscuit Tin, who ducks behind the statues. In a flash Alice lunges forward with her parasol, shrieking wildly. As though it is some mystical weapon, she rhythmically opens and closes the parasol. Alarm spreads among the children and they scream, "*Tatane! Tatane!*" The boy who lobbed the stone fumbles back onto his pony as Alice continues her charge up the grassy slope. He trots off, his small body convulsing with sobs, just as Alice reaches the rise. Edward says to Elsa, shaking his head, "My goodness, I'll have to be careful never to incite her wrath." When Alice comes back down the slope, Biscuit Tin finally emerges from behind the *moai*. For the rest of the day, he does not leave her side.

"I like the boy," Elsa whispers to Edward in the tent one night. "Very much. But I wonder why he's alone."

"Alice likes him too. I think you'll have to let Alice have him. She seems to have won his heart."

"I know."

"Do you want . . . Elsa? I didn't think you wanted children. . . ."

"No. Of course. I can't."

"You have Alice to take care of," he says. "And you think of her . . . as your child."

"No," she says. "But I think of myself as her mother. It isn't quite the same."

Elsa closes her eyes. It is true. She cannot imagine looking after Alice *and* a child of her own. But it is more than that. It is the memory of the midwife clutching Alice to her chest, of her father forbidding Elsa to open her mother's door. "Your mother gave her life for our little Alice," he had said, trying to mask his despair. "She sacrificed herself for a new child." But this version of events wasn't shared by Elsa. Behind that door Alice had *done* something to their mother, and for this Elsa felt hate. For an entire year she cursed her sister, whispered angry words when her father was asleep. So when they began to notice the strange roaming of Alice's eyes, the tantrums and the silences, Elsa believed her hate was the cause. That the curses, the prayers, and the whispered accusations had harmed her.

"Are you asleep?" she whispers.

"Not yet," says Edward.

"Sometimes, I've thought, well, that Alice was my fault. I'm sure it sounds mad. But why should a thing like that happen to a child? To anyone? There must be . . . a reason."

"Elsa."

"My whole life I've wondered if . . ."

"Alice is a blessing."

"I know that."

"You mustn't ever let yourself think it would be better if she were different."

"Sometimes, Edward, you sound so very much like my father."

"Your father," says Edward, "was a wise man."

For weeks afterward, there are no visitors to the quarry, and Elsa suspects that the story of the English *tatane* with her parasol has been tearfully recounted and embellished. But soon a man on horseback arrives on the crater's rim. Elsa recognizes him as the man who led the islanders in song that first night on the schooner, his arms thickly tattooed, wearing the same hat he did then: a faded red velvet tricorn with a row of brass buttons. He looks to be in his forties. Thin brown curls, with a few streaks of gray, fall to his shoulder. He introduces himself as Te Haha Huke.

It appears he wants to make his services available, but what exactly these are it is difficult to discern. At first he seats himself atop a *moai,* his bony legs crossed, and begins to sing. His curls shift in the breeze; his eyes close as he loses himself in his song. But his voice, an unsteady flux of gravelly bass and bursts of soprano, distracts Edward. "Really, Elsa, I shouldn't like him to think I'm declining his kind offering. However, I've a suspicion he's inebriated. I should hope nobody would sing like that if he were sober enough to hear himself."

Sensing their disappointment, the next day Te Haha returns with a guitar, strumming pleasantly atop the *moai.* They enjoy this, and attempt to show their gratitude by stopping work and sitting in the grass below his perch, but Te Haha soon tires of his own performance, shaking his head and muttering what seem to be admonishments.

"Nota bene," Edward whispers to Elsa, "the so-called artistic temperament is not restricted to the European continent."

When Te Haha next returns he sits for hours carving their likenesses in wood, a craft at which he is exceptionally skilled. Edward suggests to Te Haha that he could be of great use in other ways—could he help bring a bucket of water up the hill? Could he help move this pile of rocks? Could he hold this end of the measuring tape? Te Haha assists with a few of these tasks, but he is clearly bored—and Elsa can't blame him. He sets his finger on his forehead to indicate for Elsa and Edward the source of his real strength—he is not a physical laborer; he is a man of the mind.

Well, thinks Elsa, perhaps he can help with my project. She tries to explain that she wants to learn the language.

"*Arero!*" he shouts and runs off.

The next day Te Haha appears on his horse with a large sack on his lap. He dismounts hurriedly, and tugs his sack up the hill, zigzagging through the *moai*. As Elsa greets him, he drops the bag and quickly pulls off his hat.

"*Hau,*" he says to Elsa, rounding his lips. "*Hau.*" This is the first time she has seen him without his hat, and a large bald spot crowns his head. "*Hau,*" he says, setting the hat back on his head. From the sack, he pulls a dried fish and holds it in front of her face, making it swim through the air. "*Ika,*" he chants. "*I-ka.*"

Hau. Ika. Miro Toki. Mamari. Auke. Karu. One by one, he waves before her familiar objects, and when his sack is emptied, he points to the crater and says, "*Rano.*"

"Crater?" Her arms form a basin and she makes the roar of an explosion. "Volcanic crater?"

He nods and pats her proudly on the shoulder.

It soon becomes clear Te Haha is a born teacher, and Elsa guesses she is his first pupil. He is thorough, rigorous, demanding. He shows her every subtlety of the language.

He greets her at sunrise at the campsite, instructs her to sit beside him with her journal open while he slowly names nouns, verbs, prepositions.

And this is how Elsa begins her dictionary, and finally learns the name of the hieroglyphics she is trying to decipher.

They are called *rongorongo*.

5th March 1914

I have apparently generated much amusement among Te Haha and his friends through my inquiries into the relations between the sexes. For the purposes of the RGS, it seemed best to determine the preponderance of polygamy on the island and to attain some sense of the general position of women, concerning property & marital rights, etc. I therefore asked the men gathered round our circle how many wives each had, or hoped to have. "O te aha?" (why) they all asked with broad smiles. They could not understand why this was of interest. They pointed to my notebook. Why was I writing this down? (They have had the same reaction to our study of the moai, a general disbelief that anyone would be so interested in the statues they have been looking at every day since infancy.) I therefore thought it best to attempt an explanation, in my still awkward Rapa Nui, of the monogamous habits of our western world, with more than a little suggestion that our arrangements were of a more civilized nature. Well, I might as well have told them I was part monkey! The men all shook with hearty laughter. On pressing the source of this riotous kata, I found *myself* the sudden object of inquiry. Was I not uha to matu'a Edward? Of course, I responded. And was not vi'e Alice also uha to matu'a Edward? The source of their confusion suddenly evident, I set them to a correct understanding of our familial relations. Edward, I explained, had only one wife, and one sister-in-law. They were very disappointed, and a bit confused.

I have decided, however, to postpone further anthropological inquiries and focus primarily on the rongorongo. This is the most important task, as the most reliable information about the tablets is stored within the minds of the island's elders. Thus far, I have determined that the Rapa Nui believe the original rongorongo symbols were brought to the island by the first settlers, and that they were on some form of paper (probably bark). When the paper was exhausted, they began inscribing on banana plants, and then, finally, wood. It is believed the inscriptions were made with a shark's tooth. It seems, however, that most of these tablets were burned with the houses during tribal warfare. (There seems to have been a prolonged war between the island's two main clans—the Hotu Iti and Kotuu—of which I plan to make further inquiries.) As for the inscriptions on the tablets, several middle-aged islanders offered quite eagerly to "read" them for me, but after ten such episodes of entirely different readings, it is clear they are holding the tablets in front of them and reciting random stories. I have not yet made much contact with the eldest members of the population (some are believed to live at the leper colony just outside Hanga Roa), whom I hope will offer the much-needed knowledge of the script.

I have asked what is known of how the island was settled, where the people came from, and when. They have no numerical dates, but they say there have been twenty-seven kings. The first was Hotu Matua, who landed his canoe on the beach at Anakena, the site of our very own camp. They say he came from a group of islands in the direction of the setting sun, and the name of that island was "Marae-toe-hau," which seems to translate as "the burial place." They say that Hau Maka, *advisor to Hotu Matua, had a dream, and that Hau Maka's dream soul visited the island, found it to be beautiful and bountiful, and that is why they searched for the new land. If the legend is true, one must wonder if the king Hotu Matua was disappointed in the barren land that he found, if he must not have wondered if he had found the wrong one.*

❁

Edward is on the verge of deciding which statue he will first excavate. Each evening, with several lamps burning their new stores of porpoise oil, he sifts through his data. Elsa tries to tempt him with the tablets, holding the wooden slabs before him in their tent, rattling off information—*Now, this one is the only Kohau we've found from the caves near Puna Pau, and it's markedly different from the others. See the repetition of the hunched figure followed by the tree? Quite lovely, I think.*

But for the moment the shadow of Edward's interest falls only on the statues.

"We should begin digging soon," he says, peeling off another page of notes. "Whatever we find at the base will be essential in understanding the method of transport. That, it seems, should be the thrust of my inquiry."

When he decides which *moai* to excavate, the logistics consume him. With sufficient barter incentives, he finds a group of islanders willing to help. But preparing the site proves difficult because of the lack of wood.

"There isn't a single branch on this whole island that could be used for construction," Edward complains. "It's amazing, really, that the people here ever managed to make a life."

Eventually, he decides to dismantle some of their crates for scaffolding.

Once the excavation begins, Edward relaxes again. Each afternoon when he returns from the quarry, and Elsa from her interviews, they share the details of their day, blurry with an invigorating fatigue, already imagining what the next day's work might hold.

"I think," Edward says one night after she's described a particular series of bird images, "you may have found your true calling."

Between them a kindness, a mutual respect, has arisen. They have become like business partners, talking excitedly over dinner about their work. Their routine is fixed, comfortable, and forged entirely by common interest.

Still, she finds her true companionship in the pages of her books.

Her copy of *The Voyage of the Beagle* seems to be gone for good, and she has finished *The Different Forms of Flowers on Plants of the Same Species,* so she returns once again to *On the Origin of Species,* where she finds what seems to be a confession by Darwin:

> My work is now nearly finished; but as it will take me two or three more years to complete it, and as my health is far from strong, I have been urged to publish this Abstract. I have more especially been induced to do this, as Mr. Wallace, who is now studying the natural history of the Malay archipelago, has arrived at almost exactly the same general conclusions that I have on the origin of species. Last year he sent to me a memoir on this subject, with a request that I would forward it to Sir Charles Lyell, who sent it to the Linnaean Society, and it is published in the third volume of the Journal of that Society. Sir C. Lyell and Dr. Hooker, who both knew of my work—the latter having read my sketch of 1844—honoured me by thinking it advisable to publish, with Mr. Wallace's excellent memoir, some brief extracts from my manuscripts.

"Edward," she says across the tent, "do you know the work of Alfred Wallace?"

"The Malay Archipelago man."

"Was he working on a theory of evolution at the same time as Darwin?"

"He was, but it's hard to say whose came first. The Linnaean Society presented their papers at the same time, but Wallace's got no attention. Darwin was a Cambridge man and Wallace was self-taught, had to finance all his travels by sending insects and stuffed snakes back to England. I suppose he didn't have much of a chance at being taken as seriously. Then Darwin published his book before Wallace's, and, of course, Darwin is credited with the theory."

"Did Wallace need a degree from Cambridge in order to have a theory?"

"Of course not."

"With that thinking, thousands of England's best should have discovered evolution."

"It's just how these things work, Elsa. Darwin was a man of the establishment, you can't blame him for that."

"No blame, I just feel sorry for Wallace."

"Well, Wallace accepted it. He called his own book on natural selection *Darwinism*. That certainly concedes the discovery."

"Perhaps he didn't think he could win the fight."

"Well, don't be too hard on either of them. They were both, after all, in search of the truth."

In these words she hears an echo of her father's admonitions against her hasty judgments. Edward has, in fact, become very much like her father, or her ease with him has become the same. Even the arrangements of watching Alice take on new simplicity. After Alice's fits bring one of Elsa's interviews to a hasty end, Edward offers to take her along to the excavation.

"You must be able to work without interruption, Elsa. It's simply too important. And at least we know for certain she won't frighten the statues. I hope you trust that I'm able to look after her."

She does trust him, after all these months. He is attentive with Alice, has grown accustomed to her outbursts, and Alice seems comfortable with him.

"Of course," says Elsa. "Of course I trust you."

One more leash untethered. Now Elsa can move about the island freely—a true explorer, a true scientist—with nothing to divert her from her work.

Elsa throws herself into the island, the language, the *rongorongo*. She can now converse comfortably in Rapa Nui, and Edward even uses her as a translator. She takes copious notes as the islanders share their legends and myths, but they seem to lack an oral history of the *moai* building and their collapse. Elsa suspects the wooden boards might record such history. An account of major events must have been stored somewhere, and if not in the memories of the people, then perhaps on the tablets. But each time the strange glyphs begin to hint at a meaning, they pull back, as though teasing her. And she is beginning to wonder about the wood itself. The tablets are made of a dark and dense wood she has not seen anywhere on the island. Where did it come from? Could the tablets have arrived here from somewhere else? Could they all have been carried in that first canoe with Hotu Matua?

She thinks of Hotu Matua's long journey, and of their own journey from England. Neither the Polynesian king, nor Edward, nor she, could have known what awaited them on this new shore. It was a place of myth until they arrived. But now her past has become the myth; Max, her father, their house in England—all of it seems an island once dreamed of.

And when Elsa lies in the tent at night, her books piled beside her cot, listening to waves break against the shore, she feels she has done the right thing. She is supposed to be here, on this island. Even now when she sleeps beside Edward, she is content. The languorous weight of his heavy arms, the smell of soap and tobacco rising from his chest—it helps her drift into a delicate sleep. She is growing used to him. And caring for him, being comfortable with him, helps ease her guilt. No longer does she see him as an opportunity to help Alice and herself. She sees him as her husband. Is it really, she thinks, so awful to be loved by this man? He is Edward, dear, sweet Edward. And this—Edward, Alice, this windswept land in the middle of nowhere— is now her life.

15

In her second year of graduate school, after much discussion and debate, Greer chose Thomas as her advisor. They had already made their relationship public, an event that Greer had dreaded—anticipating scorn, distrust, even jealousy—but which, in the end, elicited little more than shrugs from her classmates. Everybody had guessed long ago.

Without question, Thomas was her top choice for advisor. His work was the most interesting in the department; his lab had access to the best equipment and the largest funds. He'd recently been awarded a grant from the American Institute of Biological Sciences, had been honored by the university at a black-tie dinner to which he'd taken Greer, and had been featured in an article in *Life* magazine, "The Science of Today and Tomorrow," complete with a photograph of him standing in his lab over a two-meter core he and Greer had taken that February from the banks of the Mississippi. But the article bothered Thomas because it divided scientists into two categories—traditionalists and renegades. Thomas, who had just turned forty-three, was put in the traditionalist category, and mention was made of the phenomenon in science of great discoveries being made by the young, alluding to his own early successes: the Linnaeus Prize, the First Palynology Conference. But there was no denying the attention the article brought—the university even added his lab to the campus tour, and sometimes, from his office window, he and Greer would notice a dozen teenagers with their parents gazing up at the building. "They can't see anything from there," Greer would complain as she lowered and raised the blinds. "Why not show them some fossil pollen? That's interesting." "Because," said Thomas, "they don't want to see science, they want to see what they think is celebrity."He seemed quite pleased with that label, though. Now everybody wanted to work in his lab. Even Jo, who had joined his team that semester. But Greer was conflicted.

"The only question in your mind, Greer, should be whether or not you want to spend that much time with your boyfriend. Day and night,"Jo said.

"What about working *for* him? It seems odd."

"Well, you can work for Professor Jenks. Or dipshit Doctor Hawthorne. No matter which way you cut it, you're working for somebody. Just pick somebody you want to work for. Somebody whose work you're interested in."

"Well, Thomas's work is, really . . ."

"The hottest ticket in town?"

Greer shrugged, helpless."It's true."

"It would be a hard opportunity to pass up."

"We could be like Marie and Pierre Curie. Carl and Gerty Cori."

"Listen. There's no guaranteed answer here, Greer. Do what you need to do for your own work, your own development. And if that means working in Jackass in the Pulpit's lab—"

"Jo."

"—in *Thomas's* lab, then do it. Besides, it means we'd be working together too. Side by side. Like the Bobbsey twins."

"True."

"And how can you pass that up?" Jo blew the bangs from her eyes.

"How can I?"

Thomas himself had no objections.

"Lily, I can't imagine someone better to have in the lab," he said. "You're fast, you're accurate. And you're committed to the project."

The project was researching the evolution of angiosperms: flowering plants. This included most trees, shrubs, wildflowers, edible fruits, berries, nuts, grains, and vegetables: 235,000 different species that accounted for about ninety percent of the world's plants. And yet, the planet had once known only gymnosperms—*gymnos sperma*, naked seeds—the pine and cypress and fir and cedar trees. Ginkgos and the cycads, whose seeds formed on the edges of cones and waited to be carried by wind. Theirs was a primitive and passive reproduction. But with angiosperms came pistils and stamens and carpels; red and purple and white ruffled petals; nectar and perfume. Enticements. Greer thought of it as the plant kingdom hitting puberty, all the naive firs and drab pines suddenly putting on makeup and party dresses. Angiosperms brought desire into nature, they started the courtship waltz between stamen and pistil, petal and pollinator, a dance that had spread across the world and lasted millions of years. Eventually pairs of flora and fauna coupled off, coevolved, so that each flower now had its very own pollinator, each fruit a bird to eat it.

The evolutionary shift from the gymnosperm to the angiosperm fascinated Thomas, represented, for him, an advance far more significant than that of ape to man. Flowers brought fruits and nuts, producing food that had allowed the rise of large mammals, and eventually Homo sapiens. And mankind had become the flower's greatest fan. "It was the poppy, after all, like a floral Helen of Troy, that launched a thousand opium warships." Human migrations, trade routes, invasions, wars—they all came down to angiosperms. Tea, spices, tulips. Man had joined the dance, seduced, like all other creatures, by nature's greatest invention—the flower.

But how had this transition come about? Exactly when, and where? Darwin, a century earlier, had noted it as "an abominable mystery," and since then, nobody had come up with an answer. The mystery was too ancient, the evidence buried deep in the earth. Thorough investigation would require extensive paleobotanical evidence—Thomas's expertise.

Thomas's project had started the year before Greer entered graduate school. He began gathering Cretaceous rocks from various sites within the United States and set a small team of Ph.D. candidates to look for fossil pollen. Their task: Find the first flower, the oldest angiosperm known on earth. Thus far, they'd come up with a likely suspect: the magnolia. In several rocks dating back to the mid-Cretaceous era, 120 million years before the present, they'd found traces of magnolia pollen. But this was just the beginning. The lab's next and most important step was to eliminate the magnolia's competition.

To do this, they needed to examine sedimentary rocks from all over the world. At the time Greer joined his lab, Thomas had received a new grant, and was arranging to get samples from South America and Europe. There was also talk of trying to get samples from Greenland and Australia. The lab would examine these international rocks and verify that there was no mid-Cretaceous angiosperm pollen *other* than magnolia.

If Thomas could definitively prove the magnolia was the first flowering plant, it meant the magnolia's structure represented the significant evolutionary shift from gymnosperm to angiosperm, the first domino to fall in the world's greatest ecological evolution. And it meant that Thomas Farraday would once again win the scientific gold. The first, the largest, the smallest—in any discovery, preeminence in size or age was crucial.

Greer also had to settle on a dissertation topic related to Thomas's project and the work she would do in his lab. Finally she decided on the cross-water dispersal patterns of magnolias. If the magnolia emerged in the mid-Cretaceous period, it was after Pangaea, the landmass that had once held all seven continents, and the supercontinent of Gondwanaland had broken apart. The magnolia appeared in a world where water divided lands; therefore for angiosperms to have spread, they had to cross the ocean. While Thomas determined when the magnolia first appeared, she would track its movements.

The bulk of the lab work was the scientific equivalent of typing or filing. Thomas was a demanding advisor, and weeks passed when Greer did nothing but purify samples, walking between the centrifuge and the sink. Then she had to determine which pollen came from gymnosperms, which from angiosperms. At her microscope for hours, she counted the known and unknown grains, examining the structure of each—their bulbous forms, the lines mapped like veins along their exines, the blemishes and beauty marks. Their variety and resilience impressed her. Here was pollen blown across meadows and valleys millions of years ago, buried in the earth, perfectly fossilized, waiting to be explored. When she looked into the microscope, it felt like coming upon a hidden landscape, like glimpsing a distant, unnamed moon.

That first year, she and Thomas worked together constantly. His office was just down the hall from the lab, and he would stop by every few hours to see the team, always checking in with her. At lunchtime, she brought sandwiches to his office and they talked about the project's status. Often, before she returned to the lab, they pulled the shade on his door and kissed. They enjoyed the temptation of working nearby, had fun sneaking small touches, lingering in the building at the end of the day after everyone had left. Thomas would be sitting in his office with his books open, and Greer would begin unbuttoning his shirt, unbuckling his belt, while he feigned trying to read. Or Thomas would find her in the quiet lab, and slowly remove her white coat while she looked in her microscope.

Often, they traveled together for sample collecting. Her first year in his lab they went to Brazil and Belize. In her second year, they took a two-week trip to Nova Scotia, then Greenland. She loved the travel—it was on these trips, watching Thomas out-of-doors, away from colleagues and admirers, shedding his classroom bravado, that Greer realized how deeply she had fallen in love with him. Watching him collect samples was like watching a boy swipe a twig across an anthill, amazement brightening his face as life emerged beneath his touch. Thomas could insist all he wanted that nature wasn't beautiful, but he was speechless in the face of its intricacy.

Without rest, without reservation, they both threw themselves headlong into the project, lured by the idea of the world's first blossom. The magnolia was a white-petaled dream they were chasing, a ghost they wanted to touch. Some nights, when she fell asleep in the lab, Greer dreamed she was floating above an ancient landscape thick with dark-needled trees, searching for one white flower. Once she even saw the bloom in the distance, winking from a shadowy forest.

When Thomas found her and roused her from her workstation, she described her dream.

"And you didn't bother to ask what continent the bloom was on? I'll believe in the psychic relevance of any dream that answers a question."

"Mags doesn't like questions," said Greer.

"*Mags?*"

"With this many people pursuing her, I think she deserves a name."

In the afternoons, they would take a break from the lab and wander through the university greenhouse, talking over the research.

"Some of the samples simply don't date back far enough to be relevant."

"Mags is just being coy," said Greer. "Give her time."

"You know, in the end, it'll come down to examining enough rocks from enough regions. Quantity and variety, that's all. We'll probably never find magnolia pollen that predates mid-Cretaceous. All we can do is make sure that we don't find any other angiosperm pollen in that era."

"And hope that nobody else does."

"You know, Lily, that's precisely it."

"Don't worry," said Greer. "You've devoted yourself to Mags. She won't let you down."

"I hope not," he said.

"Just think, Thomas, we're on the trail of the earth's first flower." They had waded through the tropics, the glass-enclosed sanctuary of misted ferns and guavas, and now crossed into the Orchid House. Greer looked around her at the sea of purple and red petals. "Before there was a human to smell it," she said, "to touch it, to know it was beautiful, before a pollinator knew what to make of it, somewhere there was one spectacular flower, waiting for the world to catch up with it."

"Ah, Lily."

"What?"

"Well, you're a woman, aren't you."

"So they tell me."

"Just don't let your imagination distract you from the science. Don't search for what's beautiful to you. Remember, search for what's true."

"Distract me? I'm in there, doing science longer than anyone else. I acid-wash, I count, I analyze. It's just nice once in a while to remind myself of what it all means."

"You're right. I know. You work like a machine. I'm sorry. I'm just worried about this project, about all the work ahead."

She looped her arm around his waist. "Let's just remember to enjoy it."

He kissed her. "My sediments exactly."

❁

The next two years Thomas was often gone, giving lectures at symposia in Missouri or Iowa or Ohio. Greer didn't like these separations but learned to live with them. Several times he was invited to Harvard, to guest-lecture. News of his study kept him in the scientific spotlight but left little time for work. When he visited the lab, it was usually to collect data sheets from Greer and Jo and Bruce Hodges, a new research assistant who had just transferred from Harvard to join Thomas's project. Bruce was a former all-American linebacker who liked nothing more than to brag about the game in which he had three sacks, two fumble recoveries, and an interception.

"But you can't top that, so in the end I junked the pads and the helmet for a lab coat," he would say theatrically, the epilogue of his athletic saga. But he certainly had a knack for science, even if he did lack the passion. He could rattle off pollen classifications like sports statistics.

"And here we have a Magnoliaceous dicot, a May-Juner, making a strong dash for the mid-Cretaceous! Our little *clavatipollenites* is holding tight to the reticulate veins and dual cotyledons!" He would then cup his hands to his mouth, hooting and whistling, the sound of a hundred fans cheering his taxonomical victory.

Jo found him tedious, and gave him the finger when he wasn't looking. But Greer thought he was mildly charming, and was glad for the extra company in the lab; it felt empty with Thomas gone.

Returning from his conferences, fatigued, hoarse, Thomas would sit with Greer late into the night, reviewing the data. She told him what samples should be looked at next, or where they needed to collect their next batch of sedimentary rocks. He was always sure to ask, at the end of it all, about her dissertation. His interest in her work never waned. And they would chat for several minutes about magnolia seed and pollen dispersal patterns, and he would give her research leads, sometimes suggesting biogeographical studies to read.

"What's interesting is to correlate the magnolia dispersal with pollinator dispersal."

"Exactly," said Greer.

"Because even if you have cross-water movement of pollen and seeds, the plant can't colonize without pollinators."

"I've been poring over the data and I think I'm coming up with some interesting numerical relationships. It involves the delay factor—the time lapse between the arrival of the flower and the beetle. I think it might turn out to be a significant equation."

"The equation should account for the threshold. The number of plants required to permanently install a community." Thomas would rub the sleep from his eyes, then take her hands. "I missed you."

"You too," she said, resting her forehead on his chest. "You're gone a lot."

"Work calls."

"I know." She listened to the beat of his heart, that soothing rhythm of life, then lifted her head. "The numbers will differ, of course, from plant to plant. Flowering period, gestation, et cetera."

Thomas laughed. "Work calls you too."

Greer smiled. They understood this in each other, what they were driven by.

"You know," said Greer, "the magnolia had something no other plant had."

"What's that?" asked Thomas.

Greer couldn't help but smile at the thought. "A yearning to exist."

✿

They were married in a small ceremony at the university's arboretum. Bruce Hodges and Jo Banks and Professor Jenks were in attendance.

For a wedding present, Thomas gave Greer the seed of a magnolia in a Venetian apothecary jar.

"For your work," he said. "You'll be just like Darwin now. He tested all sorts of seeds in jars of salt water to see how long they could survive in the ocean. It's perfect for you."

Greer gave Thomas her father's microscope, the one he had kept in his basement lab for years, the first microscope she had ever used.

Thomas examined the brass knobs, the thick ocular. "Thank you for trusting me with this."

On their honeymoon in Tuscany, they spent two weeks driving through the Apennine Mountains to collect sandstones and marls. The Magnolia Project was stalled, and needed samples of greater geographical diversity. Greer and Thomas managed a few elegant dinners in Florence, a brisk walk through the main galleries of the Uffizi; they had their photograph taken on the Ponte Vecchio, but the rest of the trip was work, hunting down Cretaceous and Jurassic outcrops. They tried to make the most of it, stealing kisses between procedures, calling each other "Husband" and "Wife" as they hammered at the rocks and lugged their heavy packs from site to site. In the evenings, when they returned to their hotel room, they peeled off their soiled clothes, climbed into the bathtub, and scrubbed each other's back and arms, shampooed mountain dust from each other's hair. And when they were both pink-skinned from the bath, they climbed into bed and made love.

Shortly after they returned from Italy, Greer developed a bad neck cramp and had to see a chiropractor, who told her to limit microscope work to five hours a day.

"We'll get you a nice cot so you can lie down when you start to cramp," Thomas said in bed one night. They had just moved into an apartment on Madison's West Side, on the edges of the arboretum. He was massaging her neck. "And one of those special neck pillows."

"Why don't we just get someone else to do some of the counting? Another grad student. Then I can do some unknown IDs. Or help with the analysis. You're gone too often now. You're overextended. Someone needs to check the results, the math."

His hands stilled. "Listen, don't be angry, Lily . . ."

"Uh-oh."

"Bruce is going to help with the analysis."

"Bruce?"

"He's sharp."

Greer flipped on the light and turned to face him. "So am I. Why not have him keep counting? He doesn't have any neck problems."

"Lily, I'm not asking you to aggravate your injury. Take a rest. I'm just saying that Bruce is going to help with the analysis."

"What about me? Or Jo? We've both been in that lab longer than Bruce. Jo, the longest. *She's* sharp."

"Bruce was the top of his class at Harvard. Listen," he sighed. "I can't have him transfer here to work in a lab under my wife. Or under Jo. I'm sorry, Lily. It has nothing to do with my feelings. He wouldn't stay and you know it."

"I don't know it."

"Lily, please, don't be naive."

"Fair isn't naive."

Thomas looked helpless. "It's just not the way things work."

"One year, Thomas. He's been here one goddamned year."

"Please. If you care about the project, and if you care about me, you'll understand. Besides, you still have your dissertation. There's no way for you to do a good job on that and work on my analysis."

"There's no way for me to do a good job on that and spend eighty hours a week here at a microscope trying to help you count pollen faster than anyone else in the world!" She could feel anger heating her face.

"I never asked you to neglect your own work."

"But what did you think would happen? When exactly do you think I work on my research?"

"You know what I think of your abilities. I wouldn't have you in my lab if I didn't think you were capable."

"*Capable?*"

"Lily."

She turned out the light.

"Lily." His hand touched her shoulder. "Please."

"Bruce? I'm sorry, Thomas. I just can't believe it."

"Don't think about Bruce. Focus on your dissertation. *Your* work. Think of your career. You're going to have a great career, Lil. This is nothing in the scheme of things."

Perhaps it was nothing. Greer wasn't, after all, interested in fame. The spotlight in which Thomas basked held little appeal for her. The attention no longer seemed to flatter him, but had become an awkward weight he had to carry, a strain that slowly drew his attention from the work.

So Greer did focus on her dissertation. She spent less time at the microscope, and more time reading about biogeography, dispersal patterns, islands, and continents. What she liked were the patterns; over and over again, nature displayed the same urge. The story never changed. Each species was just a variation in the king's name, or the color of the princess's hair. The moral was always motion, and life.

She used the magnolia data she'd gotten in Thomas's lab and applied it to her dissertation. How had the magnolia gone from a solitary bloom in the middle of nowhere to a tree that grew on all continents? Working in a small library carrel, she studied numbers, graphs, and curves. She liked her research, but missed the camaraderie of the lab. To work there, though, or to stop by while Bruce was in charge would seem like surrendering. Thomas was still traveling and lecturing, preparing his next paper. So Jo was her ambassador; Jo found Greer in the library a few times each week and let her know what was happening in the lab.

"If I have to listen to one more touchdown metaphor, I'm going to ram a football down that guy's throat."

"He's that bad?"

"Worse."

"I'm sorry, Jo. I'm sorry I haven't been around."

"Hey, I'm sorrier for you. . . . The lab needs you."

"Well, I need to be working on my dissertation."

Greer hadn't told Jo about her discussion with Thomas. She had pretended Bruce's new role was a joint decision, but wasn't sure if her misrepresentation had been out of loyalty to Thomas, or to simply save face. From Jo's expression, it was clear she knew Greer was unhappy. But Jo played along.

"And how *is* the opus coming?" Jo asked.

"Not to pollinate my own stigma—"

"Oh, jeez."

"But I'm pretty happy with it," said Greer.

"You'll let me read it?"

"I'll force you to."

"I'm sure it's brilliant."

"Blossoms. Beetles. Something for everyone."

Jo gave Greer's shoulder a slight squeeze. "I can't wait."

By February, Greer had completed a first draft she was happy with. It focused more on theory than data, but the data had been gathered in Thomas's lab, under Thomas's direction, and she felt it was important to step back from his project. Her paper was thick with evolution and dispersal theory, graphs relating populations of flowers to pollinators, the time lapse between plant dispersal and pollinator dispersal. It was nontraditional, something at which she knew her committee would raise their eyebrows, but it was a risk she was willing and eager to take.

She gave a copy to Jo and a copy to Thomas, who had already removed himself from her committee. Both said the paper was wonderful, each recommending a set of revisions and adjustments, Jo, in the end, taking more time than Thomas, because Thomas was busy finishing his own paper, and was gone for weeks at a time with Bruce Hodges.

She went back to her carrel and spent another month reworking her material. In March, Thomas concluded the final revisions on his own paper, and offered—a late concession—to let Greer read it before publication. But if he hadn't wanted her help in the beginning, she wasn't going to offer it now. She said she was busy. Marriage, she had decided, was more important than professional collaboration.

It was May when she finally submitted her dissertation to the committee, and after a few weeks of waiting around the house, Greer decided to distract herself with a short trip back to Mercer. She wasn't sure why then, of all times, after six years, she wanted to see her hometown. She and Thomas had spoken of visiting; perhaps she was tired of putting it off, waiting for a break in his schedule. Thomas was once again traveling, this time presenting the paper about to be published, with Bruce Hodges coauthoring. It was a warm day, and she drove slowly through the town, looking at the familiar names on the mailboxes—Feyenbacher, Simpson, Gertz. When she finally made her way down the road to her parents' old house, it was smaller than she remembered, but the same shade of yellow, with the same wraparound porch. She parked the car and knocked on the door. A woman appeared, her hair in a loose bun, wiping her hands on the fraying hem of a pale blue apron.

"You must be Maria Compton. I'm Lillian Greer. I grew up here."

"Ah, yes, Miss Greer. Please, come on in now. I've some lemonade if you'd like. And there's a cake in the oven. Double fudge."

"No, thanks. I was just wondering if it would be all right if I wandered up the hill to where my parents are buried. It's been a while."

"Sure thing, you go right on ahead. We ain't touched a thing. The stones are still there, and Harold trims the grass 'round them quite regular. Our girl Becky asks who's there, 'cause she likes to sit on that hill, and we just tell her it's nice folk."

Greer smiled. "I won't be long."

"Long? Nonsense. Take your time. I got tissue if you want."

"No, thank you."

Greer walked up the hill and lay down between the two simple headstones, staring at the slightly overcast sky. The ground was cold and moist beneath her and soaked the back of her blouse. She let her hands wander the grass, remembering how years before she'd come up here to pluck wildflowers, carrying them back to the house in the bib of her shirt, hoping that under the microscope she would find something that would explain where her mother had gone. Greer wondered if it was really any different from what she was doing now, lying by their graves, because she believed, or wanted to believe, that life was somehow bound to matter, that spirit lodged itself in land.

She felt a spider inch across her ankle, and she sat up and let it walk onto her hand, examining it closely. Whitman's verse came back to her: *I believe a leaf of grass is no less than the journey-work of the stars / And the pismire is equally perfect, and a grain of sand, and the egg of the wren / And the tree-toad is a chef-d'oeuvre for the highest . . .* The spider, too, should have been equally perfect. It roamed her skin, wandering the peninsula of each finger, until she set it gently back in the grass.

But Greer worried she was losing her belief in the journey-work, that nature was becoming a speck on a glass slide in a sanitized room. Investigating to produce publishable answers—this was what had filled her days for the past six years. Was she now less moved by science? Or was she simply feeling the exhaustion of finishing her dissertation, years of work officially surrendered. She got up, brushed the dirt off her back, and walked down the hill.

"Thanks," she called out to Maria Compton, who was just then stepping onto the porch with a cake in hand.

"Double fudge!" she sang. "That's fudge plus fudge."

"I want to make it back before dark."

Greer had plenty of time, but the sight of the house depressed her. Its memories seemed out of reach.

"I have a big meeting tomorrow," Greer said.

"Well, you stop by anytime. Hear me? Anytime. We'll keep them stones clean."

"Thank you," she said, and drove down the dirt road that once seemed the longest road in the world.

The next day, Greer awoke early and dressed for her committee meeting. She had bought a black suit for the occasion and looked, as she glanced in the mirror, surprisingly professional. She fastened her hair with two tortoiseshell combs; she applied some lipstick. She fixed herself coffee, a bowl of cereal, and opened the sealed envelope Thomas had left her:

> *Remember. No fear, my love. You'll be great. I miss you.*
> *Home soon.*
>
> > *Your husband*

She was disappointed he wasn't there; this day was the culmination of all her work in the lab. But she knew he couldn't get out of this conference, or at least felt he couldn't.

As Greer walked slowly over to Birge Hall, she reviewed in her mind the details of her paper. They could ask about anything, try to trip her up on the smallest of details, though she had a feeling they would be less aggressive than normal. After all, she'd been to cocktail parties at all their houses, had helped their wives clear plates from the dinner table, had sat with them into the night, sipping port and brandy to the sounds of Bach. It would be difficult for them to attack her, and in a strange way, this was disappointing. Greer felt good about her work, and didn't mind a scuffle.

It was a beautiful spring day—a loose net of cirrus clouds caught the bright sun at brief intervals—and she promised herself she would take a long walk after the meeting and try to bask in the end of this rite of passage. She was meeting Jo later, to celebrate, and thought they should have dinner outside on State Street.

She arrived at the lecture hall—the same hall where she had taken Thomas's class years before—and sat in the front row. There was a bustle among the five members of the panel as they opened their folders and files, and then Professor Jenks, whom she'd last seen at Thomas's birthday party, called her name. She stepped up to the podium, her folder in hand.

"Mrs. Farraday," began Professor Jenks. He looked surprisingly tired, disheveled, almost annoyed. The green plaid bow tie he was famous for wearing daily appeared hastily tied. For a moment she was tempted to ask him if he was all right, but thought this would compromise the meeting's decorum. His wife had been recently diagnosed with cancer; it seemed to be taking a large toll on him. She'd heard complaints that he'd been neglecting his chair responsibilities. In fact, he hadn't met with Greer about her paper in months.

"Good morning, Professor Jenks." She tried to lend kindness, of the professional sort, to her voice.

"Yes, yes. Please, Mrs. Farraday." Professor Jenks stood. "You have of course placed the committee in a most uncomfortable position. And before we go any further we would like to tell you that you will, of course, have the opportunity to submit a new paper. We do not intend for this incident to ever go beyond these halls." He returned hastily to his chair. "That is the end of it. Take whatever time you need."

"I don't understand."

"Please, Mrs. Farraday. This is awkward for all of us."

"Me, especially. What, pardon my language, in hell is going on here?"

Professor Jenks let his forehead fall into his palms. "We've read Thomas's paper. Did you really think we wouldn't?" He looked up and ran his hand through his hair. "Well, anyway, that isn't the point here. It's done. Done. And we don't need to deal with that. Again, Mrs. Farraday, let me assure you, you have our word that this will never leave this hall. It's of no advantage to any of us, as individuals, or, for that matter, as a department with a reputation to uphold. You have been working very hard in the lab, we know. It's a tiring job. A thankless job. It can easily exhaust a person. Blur a person's normal judgment. There is no accusation, you understand, in any of this."

Greer's mind was trying to sift the data: Thomas's paper, her dissertation, no accusation.

"Of course," Greer finally managed to say, then closed her folder. "I need to review some materials." She gathered her purse, pens and paper clips spilling as she slung the strap over her shoulder, and hurried from the room. In the hallway, with the door sealed behind her, she took a deep breath and let the eerie silence of the corridor surround her. She walked quickly to the library, fumbling in her heels, soon breaking into a run in front of the periodical shelves. She peeled off her blazer and let it fall to the ground. The man at the circulation desk called out, "Ma'am, are you all right over there?"

She felt along the shelves until she found it: *Nature.* Spring 1967, Vol. III. In the index she saw the title: *A Preliminary Study in the Evolution of the Magnolia Flower* by Thomas Farraday, Ph.D., and Bruce Hodges.

She skimmed the first few pages: descriptions of sample collection techniques, location, data—what she would have expected—and then, at the end, a sidebar: *Magnolia Dispersal: A Mathematical Theory.* She read every word. In it was the same data she had used, the same analysis, and the same equation she had presented to the committee. *Her* equation. Greer closed the journal, set it back on the shelf. She began to walk away, her jacket abandoned.

The man at the circulation desk called out, "Ma'am, would you like some water? Or a chair?"

But Greer said nothing as she pushed open the heavy glass library door, and felt the warm air shock her lungs.

16

Von Spee must have felt the strain of his predicament. Ammunition and coal supplies were low; the journey across the Pacific had been long and lonely. Would those dusty orders issued by the Kaiser have started to haunt him? *He must never show one moment of weakness.* How, in the knowing approach to doom, would that have been possible? Even for a man known for unwavering confidence, for unflinching calm?

Now that the squadron was off the coast of South America, cables and telegrams once again reached him on the ship's radio. Despite the clear impossibility of the fleet reaching Germany, Berlin advised: "Break through for home." At the same time, von Spee learned that Japan, France, and Britain were concentrating their entire naval efforts on his squadron. ("Thus," Churchill would later write of the hunt for von Spee, "to compass the destruction of five warships, only two of which were armoured, it was necessary to employ nearly thirty, including twenty-one armoured ships, for the most part of superior metal, and this took no account of the powerful Japanese squadrons, and of French ships or of armed merchant cruisers.") But information as to the enemy's position reached von Spee only weeks after dispatch, when it was no longer useful. As he was rounding the coast of South America, the enemy, larger, more powerful, and invisible to von Spee, was closing in.

Von Spee knew he could not lead the squadron's two thousand men safely home. Is it not likely this plunged him into despair? Despair so great it caused him to miscalculate at the

Falkland Islands, an error, in the end, that would cost him the
fleet?

Shortly before leaving for the Falklands, at Valparaíso, von
Spee sent this message to his Kaiser: "I am quite homeless.
I cannot reach Germany. We possess no other secure harbor. I
must plough the seas of the world doing as much mischief as
I can, until my ammunition is exhausted or a foe far superior
succeeds in catching me."

When a visitor aboard the ship handed him a bouquet of
purple irises, von Spee is reported to have said: "Thank you,
thank you, indeed. They will do very nicely for my grave."

—*Fleet of Misfortune: Graf von Spee*
and the Impossible Journey Home

17

The small beans, shaped like hearts, arrive in the middle of the night.

At dawn, when Elsa walks down to the ocean to splash her face, there they lie: small black hearts, wet and glistening, scattered like pebbles along the beach's rim. They have come, she knows, from somewhere far. She tries to calculate how long they've been at sea. If it was three weeks by boat from the mainland, then drifting on the current alone would take at least two months. Two months—assuming they left the nearest landfall. But they could come from anywhere—Argentina, Brazil, Indonesia. And this reminds her, as nothing for the past year has, of lands beyond this one, each bean like a bottle with a distant greeting. Plucking them from the sand, Elsa wipes each one on her skirt, and then cups them in her hand. She is collecting them to make a necklace for Alice's birthday.

It is October and the weather is getting warmer. A party will be held on the beach—Elsa making the traditional taro cake as she has learned from the islanders, Te Haha singing. Too many birthdays have passed without event. Christmas and New Year's marked only by sips from the small remaining store of brandy. But now, Elsa has decided, they will return to tradition, will pretend, if they can, that their lives are proceeding normally. And so seaweed is strung like tinsel from the tents. A white lace cloth sewn from Elsa's old petticoats is laid across the small table. When they are all seated on their linen-covered crates, the coconut that miraculously washed up the week before is cracked open, its white flesh sparkling like ice, and is admired from all angles before Alice lifts the first crescent to her mouth.

She gnaws at the meat of the nut, sucks the inside of the shell."Try it, Beazley," she says. *"Co-co-nut."*

Edward takes his share, then Elsa, then Biscuit Tin and Te Haha. They all nibble slowly at their slivers of the white nut. It could be months before another washes ashore.

Elsa lifts the necklace of hearts from her lap and hands it to Alice.

"Twenty-two hearts, Allie. For the twenty-two years my heart has belonged to you."

Alice fingers the necklace."Beans!"

"It's for your neck. To wear."

But Alice simply sets it beside the ruins of her coconut.

"And, Alice," begins Edward, lifting from his lap a bundle swathed like a mummy in silk handkerchiefs."For the birthday of my most excellent assistant."

She unfurls each cloth until she is holding the small figure of a *moai.*

"You see." Edward reaches forward to touch the statue. "It is made from the same volcanic tuff the real *moai* are carved from. From the quarry. The proportions are identical to those of the one we are excavating."

"My own *moai*! Alice's *moai*!"

"Yes, Alice. Your own *moai.*"

"Edward, that's wonderful," says Elsa. Alice has been helping Edward at the quarry. As the pit around the *moai*'s base grows deeper, Alice can climb to the subterranean level to make sure the workers don't damage the statue. She describes to Edward any marking she notices, makes drawings of any petroglyphs. Alice has loved working there, her happiness awakened from a long sleep. The gift is perfect, thinks Elsa.

"*Moai iti,*" says Te Haha. *Little moai.* He examines it, clearly unimpressed by its artistry."Humph." He is, after all, a wood-carver. He is the artist among them.

Alice snatches the *moai* and clutches it to her chest."*Moai iti,*" she whispers.

Soon the taro cake is presented. Te Haha rises from the table, sits cross-legged in the sand, and begins one of his warbling songs. Elsa feels herself relax. She is grateful to Te Haha, her teacher, their friend. She is grateful for this small family they have forged. Biscuit Tin, who has grown two inches in the past months, sits beside the birdcage. As Alice sways with Te Haha's chant, losing herself in the music, he watches with fright as she seems to disappear.

Elsa lifts the necklace from the table and strokes the hearts. These beans washing ashore, the coconut on the sand, they make her wonder—could the tablets be made from driftwood? Where else would the pieces have come from?

"Elsa." Alice's eyes are on her. "That's my necklace."

"It is, Allie. Do you want to wear it?"

"Yes." Alice leans across the table and Elsa places it around her neck.

"My necklace," Alice says, squinting. "Mine."

Several nights later they are having dinner on the beach. To the west, the sky is primrose, the clouds like melting pearls of sunset. The scent of smoke and sweet potatoes and roast mutton fills the air.

"I've been thinking," Elsa says as she pries a pile of steaming banana leaves from the earth oven, "of paying a visit to the leper colony."

"Elders?" Edward is seated on his crate, leafing through his notebook. He has been excavating eight hours a day; drained, he now speaks only in the most efficient shorthand.

"If rumor is correct, there are at least three people there old enough to remember the Peruvian slavers." She forks a sweet potato and shakes it onto a metal plate. "And Te Haha says there is a man there who can write *rongorongo.*"

"The lepers? Write?"

"Well, I have to see, don't I? I can't pass up what might be a conversation with the only islander left who can read the script." After all her interviews, her extensive records of the island's folklore, Elsa feels she is close, on the verge of at least a partial decipherment. "Given the age of some of these people, it would not be wise to put it off."

"Yes. Quite right, dear. Do go."

Alice is perched on the sand beside Edward's crate. "Quite right, dear," she says. "Do go."

Edward pats her head and Alice grins. From in front of Alice's tent, Biscuit Tin kicks at the sand; it drifts into Elsa's oven.

"You quit that, Biscuit Tin," Alice says. "He's misbehaving. See? Biscuit Tin is being nothing but naughty. Go play with Pudding."

The boy dislikes Alice's attention drawn from him. Biscuit Tin hasn't been allowed near the excavation, directed instead to keep watch over Pudding. "Biscuit Tin is just a child," Alice has said, "and

archaeology is for professionals. Only grown-ups are professionals."
This leaves the boy bored—even, Elsa thinks, slightly angry. He now
refuses to perform his nightly dances no matter how much they beg.
But like a determined sentinel, he stays with them, slumped by the
side of a tent or a rock, chewing on a biscuit or a banana. Sometimes
he unrolls the portrait Alice made of him, holds it up to her, a reminder of her former affection. Elsa feels sorry for the boy; his heart
must be broken. "Perhaps," she says, turning to him, "Biscuit Tin
would like to come with me."

"Fine,"says Edward without looking up. He says this flatly, his lack
of concern—leprosy is, after all, a contagious disease—taking Elsa
aback. She knows he trusts her judgment in risking a visit for the investigation, but has he no concerns about the boy?

"Edward, are you well?"

"Yes, fine, Elsa."

Excavation is clearly sapping every last bit of energy from him.
Perhaps he is too old for this, for digging each day beneath the hot
sun. When he began in winter, the air was crisp, the days short. Now
humidity blankets the island. But he will not complain, he will still
not, after all this time, admit to the possibility that this work is too
strenuous for him. He has even given up reclaiming their lost items
in Hanga Roa. A pair of his boots and another of her Darwin volumes
have disappeared, but he has simply said,"The cycle is endless, Elsa.
We could do nothing but search for our belongings. Let's concentrate
our efforts on the studies."

"Good, then,"Elsa says, handing the dinner plates to Edward and
Alice and Biscuit Tin.

"You'll take the necessary precautions?"

"Of course."

"No physical contact. No contact with objects they've touched."

"We'll be careful," says Elsa. "He'll be my assistant for a change.
But I won't let him near the people."

"Your assistant," mumbles Alice. But there is something sharp in
her tone. Some new testiness. It sounds like anger withheld, an out-
burst reined in.

Can Alice be angry with poor little Biscuit Tin?

❈

At sunrise, they set out on their ponies along the southern coast. Elsa
has offered her morning kisses to Edward and Alice, and has prom-

ised to be back at the campsite by dinnertime. This is Elsa's first out-
ing alone with the boy, and she watches him sway on his saddle, his
bare legs straddling the horse, his hands clutching the reins. He has
changed much since that first day he followed them from Hanga
Roa—his neck, always narrow for his head, looks giraffelike since his
last growth spurt, his shoulders have sharpened, as though his bones
are growing too fast for his skin, and his eyes have taken on a gloss of
solemnity, of something that looks, to Elsa, like wisdom. He is a playful child, but beneath it all there is a seriousness. He is an observer, a
small and silent witness of the inexplicable. It strikes her that seeing
him each day has let this change slip by her. He must be almost
eleven now.

In Rapa Nui, she says: "You're a good friend, *poki."* *Poki* is Rapa Nui
for child.

He laughs. Biscuit Tin seems unusually energetic today. He bal-
ances the two-foot *kohau* in his lap, and Elsa constantly glances over
to make sure he holds it steady. This seems to make him giggle even
more.

"You'll have to wait outside, you know," Elsa says. "The people we
are going to visit have a contagious condition, *aau,* you know, *mamae,
e? Papaku.* And you don't want to go near them. That's why they've
put them away from everybody else. You understand? Don't touch
anybody or anything or I will drop you in a bucket of borax. *Beha! E!"*
She shakes her head, dangling her tongue like a ghoul.

The boy smiles, as he always does when spoken to. Elsa has come
to suspect he understands most of what is said to him, especially the
admonitions in English. But for some reason he is unwilling to speak.
As if there is an intelligence in him that does not want to be troubled
with the facade of words.

Just past Hanga Roa, they cut inland and follow an overgrown
path—nobody visits the colony. At the top of a hill sits a cluster of
small huts. Silence reigns. Elsa scans the area for a rock or piece of
wood on which to tether the ponies, but Biscuit Tin has already dismounted and is leading his pony to a small metal post nearby. Elsa
follows. As she ties the rope and blows the sand off the *kohau,* she
hears the fast flapping footsteps of Biscuit Tin running uphill.

"Poki! Ka noho!"

The boy looks back with an excited, innocent grin, and Elsa races
after him, but not before he rolls a stone into the entranceway of one
of the huts. Elsa grabs him back.

"*He aha koe, poki!* You must listen to me!"

But the boy's smile persists, and he wriggles his arm free, plunges two fingers into his mouth, producing a dry, sharp whistle.

"*Poki!*"

Elsa is about to drag him back down the hill, when a woman's voice calls, "*Luka?*"

A bony woman in a man's coat and felt hat emerges from the darkened doorway. Her small, piercing eyes fall on Biscuit Tin. Behind her, a man appears, wrapped in a thick wool blanket, his black hair a field of cowlicks. He limps up to the woman's side. Together they stand in front of their hut, smiling, their sides touching, and each raises an outer arm in a semicircle, so that one's fingertips reach for the other's, and then Biscuit Tin, several yards away, begins to spin giddily, a tornado of excitement, and as he twirls and twirls, the couple close their eyes and bring their circle tighter, their arms trembling, rapt by the embrace of their invisible dearest, Biscuit Tin, who spins wildly in the love of their imagined arms.

Of course, thinks Elsa. Of course.

Maria and Ngaara Tepano know the *rongorongo* man, and point out his hut at the far edge of the colony. As they lead her toward this man—Kasimiro—Elsa trails several yards behind with Biscuit Tin beside her. It seems the boy wants his parents to think he has brought her, Elsa, his new friend, there to meet everybody. He points at her, nods in approval. He is showing her off.

Elsa looks at him, the pink flush of his cheeks, the brilliance of his eyes. A strange jealousy pricks her as she realizes that the boy belongs to others, that he has always wanted to be here, not at the campsite. But she must now play the complimentary teacher: "*Poki . . . riva riva,*" she yells to the parents. "Clever. Funny. Big help to our study." Yards ahead, the couple turns and beams. When they arrive at Kasimiro's hut, they gesture for her to wait outside. A moment later, Maria returns.

"Have you any tobacco?" she asks in Rapa Nui.

"Not with me," Elsa says, angry with herself for forgetting the island's system of gift giving. This man might hold the key to all the tablets; she needs to tread carefully. "But I can get some. I could bring it back another time."

Maria disappears again into the hut, and when she reemerges she is guiding Kasimiro, with Ngaara on the other side. One of the man's legs, thinner than the other, dangles lifelessly as they help him forward. Maria takes Ngaara's wool blanket and spreads it on the grass. Kasimiro, his arm around Ngaara's neck, allows his limp leg to collapse on the blanket, then arranges his other limbs around it. His skin is dark brown and loose. Wisps of gray hair sprout from his scalp. He looks up at Elsa, sees the tablet in Biscuit Tin's arm.

"Ahh! The *rongorongo*. Of course, of course. You want to read it. That is not a problem. But I have stories, you know. Good stories." He offers a dramatic wink. "I had two wives who both tried to kill me!" The Tepanos shake their heads. It is clear they have heard this story many times. They settle themselves on opposite sides of Kasimiro, crossing their legs, planting their palms on the ground. There is a unison to their motions, a symmetry, as though living for so long together in seclusion they have blended into one being.

Kasimiro continues. "At first they tried to get me on their own, and then together. But I outwitted them!"

Elsa lingers several yards away, well beyond the blanket's edge. She is unsure how she is going to manage this. If she gives him the tablet to translate, it won't be safe to handle again. And what if he can't really translate it? She can't afford to sacrifice this *kohau* to a charlatan. Perhaps she can hold it in front of him.

Kasimiro looks at her. "No stories?" But before she can answer, his hands are in the air. "Ahh! Fine! Luka will hold the *kohau* there, and you will give me paper and pen to write, and you will stand there, just above me, and make your own copy of what I write. Yes? Fine. Be very careful not to touch me."

"I just . . ." A blush rushes to Elsa's face.

"*Mâtake,*" Kasimiro pronounces, "*riva riva.*" And he offers her a wide, crooked grin. *Fear is fine.*

She signals Biscuit Tin to hold the *kohau*. She pulls several sheets of paper from her bag and slides them to Kasimiro, then a pen, and, as carefully as she can, she offers him a bottle of ink. As he reaches for it, she notices his fingers are twisted and curled. She flinches, but nothing in her movements seems to upset or surprise him.

He smiles again.

"Kasimiro, how long have you been here?"

"Ten years. Ten years with these crazies." He gestures to the Tepanos, who simultaneously grin. As he begins scribbling, Elsa hovers a few feet away, her eyes straining to read. A dozen or so people come forth from the surrounding huts. They spread blankets nearby to watch. Their legs are marbled with blisters; behind a mesh of stringy brown hair, one woman's nose has collapsed.

Elsa begins her writing. As Kasimiro scrawls, she too scrawls. *He ngae-ngae te tumu i te tokerau:* The trees sway in the wind. After several minutes, he says to Biscuit Tin, *"Harui,"* and the boy pivots the tablet so that the opposite end is now on top. With that movement, Kasimiro continues to scrawl. *E ai no a te tumu toe:* Are there any trees left? Every few minutes, he repeats the *harui* command, then falls again into the trance of writing. *Ko ngaro'a ana e au e tu'u ro mai te pahi:* I heard that a boat would come.

Elsa suddenly recalls a word from the recesses of her memory: boustrophedon, scripts written in alternating directions. Could the *rongorongo* be the same?

Kasimiro continues feverishly, pausing only to look up at the tablet, or to exorcise a stubborn cough. He is the first islander to suggest a particular spatial reading of the *kohau.* In less than an hour, she has a copy of his translation. But her delight is tempered by the need to verify its authenticity.

"Kasimiro, I was wondering if you could also make me a dictionary. On one side the *rongorongo* sign and on the other side the Rapa Nui word."

He looks at her wearily. It is midday and the sun is hot. His curled fingers scratch at his chin. "This is not enough? This is no good?"

"We have dozens of *kohau,*" Elsa says. "Too many to bring them all here."

"Aggh," he spits out. "You must bring them here, one by one, to Kasimiro. We will all sit down for each one. Yes. All of us together with our English friend." He flashes a smile and sweeps his arm to indicate his neighbors. "We will have tea! Yes! And tobacco!"

"Perhaps I can bring some more *kohau.* But it would still be best to try for some kind of key." It seems unwise to wager her translations on his health. Still, she must promise another visit—she can see his sunken eyes beseeching. "Of course I will come back. Even just to say hello."

But suspicion tightens his stare. "I'll make you a key, but not today. Too hot. Come back tomorrow. We begin it then."

"Very well," Elsa says. What can she do? "Tomorrow."

Biscuit Tin offers a flurry of distant good-byes, the pantomiming host of this unusual party. They ride back along the coast at a rapid trot, Elsa appraising the day's discoveries. Finally, a translation—one brief chapter in the island's history. The story of the land itself, of trees and birds and flowers. *He ngae-ngae te tumu i te tokerau:* The trees sway in the wind. Hotu Matua did find the luxuriant island of Hau Maka's dream, but then the *moai* made war against the land—it is some sort of riddle. And there is more to come. The other *kohau* must tell other stories because their combinations of glyphs are different. Tomorrow she will begin her key, and then she will be able to decipher the *rongorongo*—this alone could put their expedition on the front page of the *Spectator*. This alone could be her very own book! No. She pushes the thought back. There is too much work to be done, too much needing verification. Still, she wants at least to share the news with Edward. They will be at the quarry.

She and Biscuit Tin cut inland toward Rano Raraku. The sun, directly above them, beats steadily. It has been weeks since Elsa has visited Edward's site, weeks since she has allowed herself to sit amid the *moai,* imagining their past. Now, with this small translation, she is beginning to know them better. She suspects the tale of their creation, their transport, perhaps their demise. She cannot wait to tell Edward what fools they've been, wondering how the statues were moved without timber. The tablet holds the answer: There were trees on the island.

Approaching the base of the quarry, Elsa hears Alice squealing from above.

"You've got quite a difficult girl on your hands," Elsa teases Biscuit Tin as they halt their horses. But the boy's face, as he looks up at the crater's rim, is grave.

Elsa gestures to a rock where they can tie their ponies. As they begin the climb, winding through the maze of *moai,* Biscuit Tin trailing hesitantly, she hears Edward let out a sharp shout, something like the word no. Whipping up her skirt, Elsa breaks into a run. The tall grass scratches at her legs, her feet loosen several rocks, and as she reaches the top she is nearly knocked down by a darting Alice. Elsa steadies herself and sees Edward below, his arm braced against a *moai,* heaving in exhaustion.

"Have you hurt yourself?"

"I'm fine," he says, "just fine."

"You look exhausted! Have you been running? Sit, Edward. You should really be in the shade at this hour, you know that. You can't do this to yourself. You can't exert yourself like this. It's ridiculous. I've some fresh water down at the horse."

"I'm fine," he says, catching his breath.

Elsa now notices the stillness of the quarry. "Where are the workers? Please tell me you haven't been trying to excavate alone."

"They went back to Hanga Roa early," he says, searching the landscape. His eyes fall on Alice, now crouching on the crater's rim. "Please," he calls to her.

"Alice shouldn't be running around at this time of day, she'll have heatstroke. You know that. Allie dear, come here and sit."

But Alice's head sways, her shoulders tense, and a blush spreads across her forehead.

"Allie?"

Alice stands and begins to walk down the outer side of the crater, dragging her feet, shedding whispers and snatches of sentences like petals that catch in the breeze and float back to Elsa. *Beazley . . . I help . . . oh, no, too much all alone for Alice . . .*

"What on earth's upset her?" asks Elsa.

"How should I know? Maybe you startled her? You said you were going to meet us back at—"

"Why is she running off? Allie! And what on earth is wrong with you, Edward? Why are you looking at me like that? Al-*ice!*" Elsa stands on the rim, looking down at her sister. Alice is almost at the bottom of the hill, at the post where her pony is tied. "I'm going to get her."

"Have you gone mad, Elsa?" Edward asks, his face red and belligerent. "For goodness' sake, you've just come from a leper colony. Go disinfect yourself!" Something violent has risen in his tone. "Go!" he says, and then he, too, strides away, down the hill, without looking back, after Alice.

18

In May of 1968 Thomas and Greer packed up their Madison apartment, their lab, said good-bye to their friends and colleagues, and moved to Massachusetts. Harvard had given Thomas the Asa Gray Chair in the Department of Biology. But he still wanted to teach the same intro lecture he'd taught at Wisconsin, believing ardently in the need, and his own unique ability, to free students of scientific romanticism. He still sliced open the section of strangler fig in the second week of class and gave the speech Greer could recite in her sleep. *(Nature isn't always beautiful . . .)* His Magnolia Project was now known worldwide, and Harvard was paying good money for his scientific celebrity. He and Greer bought a duplex in Cambridge, walking distance to his lab, and a house in Marblehead, where they spent weekends, holidays, and summers when they could. But true vacations were rare for them. Work was too much a part of their life, so they assembled a makeshift lab in the basement of their house, with a refrigerator, centrifuge, microscope, and acids. Greer, who had been given only a research assistantship, found most of her work could be done there. She preferred this to the university's cold halls and the endless buzz around Thomas's new lab. *Professor Farraday, I'd love to hear about the conference in 'fifty-three, what it was like to pioneer this field. Professor, I remember reading about your work when I was an undergraduate. I never dreamed I'd meet you, let alone work for you.* Thomas's celebrity generated an anxious energy in the lab, the new post-docs and grad students competing for his attention. The camaraderie of Madison had vanished, so when Thomas drove back to Cambridge, Greer often stayed in Marblehead to work.

Jo had taken a research assistantship at the University of

Minnesota (*It's not Cuba,* she wrote, *but at least it's far from Madison*), but Bruce Hodges had moved east with them, installed as an assistant professor and research partner in Thomas's lab. Bruce was thrilled to be back at Harvard, where many of his old friends had settled.

Greer missed Jo, and felt, at times, a sense of abandonment in Jo's disappearance from her life. She had few friends in the new department. There were no women, and the men primarily saw her as a conduit to Thomas, hoping she'd put in a good word. Her only pal was Constance McAllister, a marine biology post-doc whom she'd met one day in the ladies' room. They developed a nice hallway friendship, arranging a few coffee breaks in the lounge, leaving each other jokes taped to the bathroom mirror—*If you're not part of the solution, you're part of the precipitate,* or: *How many evolutionists does it take to screw in a lightbulb? One, but it takes six million years.* Constance was from Boston, however, and spent most of her free time with her mother and the eccentric aunt for whom she'd been named. Or else she disappeared to Woods Hole for weeks at a time, allowing little opportunity to take the friendship further.

Greer was content to work primarily in Marblehead; she had her books, her pollen, her radio, and when Thomas returned from Cambridge, she had him all to herself.

Just before they left Wisconsin she'd completed her dissertation, and now had her Ph.D. The department, as promised, made no mention of the incident, and she was able, without any trouble, to change her topic to the broader field: the floral biogeography of isolated landmasses. If she wanted her degree, she had no choice. The only trouble was with Jo, who had read Thomas's paper within hours of Greer's committee meeting. When they had met for dinner that night outside on State Street, Jo stared at her across the red-checkered tablecloth, tapping her fork, waiting for Greer to speak.

"Look, it's only appropriate that I let you be the first to tell me what you think," Jo said. "But if you don't say something soon, I'll be forced to give you my opinion."

Greer took a deep breath. "I don't know what to think."

"All right, then." Jo set the fork down. "Do you want to know what I think? Do I have your permission to speak freely?"

"Jo, you can always speak freely."

"Well, then, get ready, 'cause I've got shit to say. You understand, don't you, that your sweet old husband, your dearest Jackass in the Pulpit, has used your work and passed it off as his own in a national journal. He's ruined your dissertation, humiliated you in front of your colleagues, and has gotten you to do his grunt work, impeccably, for five years while he flew all over the country playing big-shot scientist."

Greer steadied her hands on the table. "No one in his position does the grunt work. They all get lab assistants." She knew she sounded defensive.

"They don't all get you for a lab assistant. They don't all get your work. Jesus, Greer. Please, tell me you're angry, tell me you're fucking furious, or I'm going . . . well, I'm going to have to smack you."

But there was something good in Jo's anger. With each step Jo climbed toward rage, Greer felt herself descend toward composure. "I'm upset," she said.

"Upset?" Jo's eyes traveled the neighboring tables in desperation. "Somebody get me some smelling salts. You," she said, eyebrows arched, "are unconscious."

"It's not as simple as you think. I've been over this for hours in my head. It's complicated."

"I'm ignorant, then. I don't see any complications."

"Jo, Thomas and I have been working together for five years. I've been gathering data for him, in *his* lab, for five years. I used that data for my dissertation, the same data I knew he was using. I should have realized."

"The data doesn't matter. It's the analysis. The equation. That's not shared property."

"I know. But we talked about this stuff. Cross-water dispersal. Magnolia population thresholds, beetle populations, the time lapse. All of it."

"So you talked with him about your dissertation."

"It's just that it's hard to know what was mine and what was his. He had ideas, I had ideas, we talked about them. For God's sake, he asked me to read his paper. How do I know who borrowed from whom?"

"Are you really asking yourself that?"

Greer suddenly felt tired. She had used up her small store of arguments and clearly could not subdue Jo's anger. She wished now that Jo had been there for all those talks. Then she would understand why it wasn't easy. Greer thought of asking Jo simply to leave her be, but knew she would take that as an admission. Finally, she said: "Yes, I really am asking myself that."

"I'm sorry, but you seem to be stuck in a goddamned swamp of denial here."

"I'm sure it looks that way to you."

"You're forgetting that I work in that lab, that I know Thomas's research, and that I read your dissertation. I'll tell you this much, you can deny what happened all you want, but I know, and I'm not going to keep quiet."

"Jo, this is for me to deal with."

"You're not dealing with it."

"You weren't there. You weren't there for our conversations. I know you're trying to protect me, but you . . ." Greer looked at Jo, who was leaning toward her across the table, her eyes red. What was it in her face? Greer didn't want to move toward something she could never retreat from, but hadn't Jo always been waiting for Thomas to mess up? She had never liked him, she refused to. "Jo, you have your own bias here."

"So let a committee decide. Let an objective group of outsiders evaluate the situation."

Greer's hands flew up at this and knocked over her water glass. "What objective group of outsiders? Professor Jenks? Is it not already completely clear to you that nobody would believe in a million years Thomas borrowed even a punctuation mark from me?" She let the glass remain on its side, water spilling across the table and dripping onto her lap. "It wasn't for a moment a question in anyone's mind that *I* used *his* ideas."

"That doesn't mean it shouldn't be a question in your mind. Or a certainty. Jesus, Greer."

The waiter appeared at that moment, slow and cautious, clearly aware his customers were engaged in a heated debate. He quietly righted Greer's glass and swept a thick towel across the table. He asked if they had decided on their dinner.

"Lasagna," said Greer without looking up.

"Same," said Jo. "And a bottle of red wine."

"We have a Chianti . . ."

"Anything," said Greer. She unfolded her napkin and attempted to dry herself. She rubbed at her skirt, her hands happy to be occupied, and tried to avoid Jo's stare.

"You know, we should have been celebrating tonight." Jo's voice sounded far away, like a voice struggling over a tangle of telephone lines. "We should have been ordering champagne. You deserve champagne, Greer. The best champagne in the world. You really do." Greer dropped the napkin and looked up. Jo's eyes had filled with tears and now fixed themselves on the tablecloth. "Fuck."

"Please don't, Jo."

"I'm sorry." Jo wiped roughly at her eyes with the back of her hand. "You just don't know how much I care about you. How much this kills me."

"I know," said Greer. And then, tentatively, "I think I know how you feel."

"Do you?" Jo said. "Do you really know?"

"I know, Jo. I guess I've always known. But . . ."

"You love a man who steals your dissertation. And here I am, ready to do anything for you, and . . . well, what a fucking world."

"He didn't plagiarize, Jo. You've got to understand." Saying it felt good. It calmed her. "He didn't plagiarize."

Jo shook her head. "I just want to know what you're going to say to him when he gets back. 'Congratulations on your paper, honey'? Yeah. Congratulations," she spit out, "let me give you a big wet kiss."

"Jo."

"Let me see if I can't give you five more years of my life and work so that you can have your name in *Nature*." Jo was looking into the distance, talking to herself now.

"Stop it, Jo, I don't—"

"Because I'll do anything my husband asks? Because I'm just a stupid little woman?"

"Jo!" Greer nearly screamed this. People at nearby tables turned to stare at the two of them, dressed for celebration, disheveled by anger.

Jo stood. "I'm sorry, Greer. I can't help you right now. I'm going to go."

"You've got to trust me."

"I know."

"I'll talk to him."

"Good," said Jo, folding her napkin into smaller and smaller squares and setting it neatly on the table. She straightened her fork, slid her water glass to its original position, and pushed in her chair. She then looked at the spot where she'd been sitting and nodded slowly, as though satisfied, or saddened, by how easily she'd managed to erase all traces of herself. In the blue light of the streetlamp Jo seemed paler than usual, almost ill. "You'd have been better off with Castro," she said.

Greer couldn't look at her. "I'd have gone to Cuba with you." She wanted her words to be sweet, but she knew they sounded like an ending. "Jo," she said, as if she were calling to a ship on the horizon, so far-off she only thought to whisper.

Then Jo turned and walked slowly up State Street, and Greer watched her best friend disappear into a sea of strangers.

❀

The truth was Greer didn't exactly believe everything she had told Jo. It wasn't that she had tried to lie, but she had needed to play devil's advocate and to see how well the devil fared. The committee meeting still seemed a nightmare from which she was waiting to awaken. She reread her paper, she reread Thomas's, she wandered through the lab replaying their conversations—too many to keep straight—and in the end came up with only this: Thomas couldn't have *stolen* her equation. He wouldn't have offered to let her read his paper if he'd been *hiding* anything. The whole thing was simply an awful coincidence.

"Good God, Lily. I can't believe Jenks said that, implied that. I'm going to phone him right now."

"Thomas, talking to him won't matter. I don't want him to take it back. It's perfectly clear what Jenks and the committee as a whole think, whether or not you muscle them into recanting."

He had returned from his conference at Harvard, put his suitcase in the bedroom, and immediately pulled champagne from the refrigerator. "Only the best twice-fermented carbon dioxide bubbly for my wife."

Greer took the bottle from his hand, settled into the couch, and told the story of the meeting.

Now Thomas was pacing the living room. "They obviously don't understand what happens when two people are working with the same data. There are a limited number of paths the mind can follow."

"Is that what happened?"

"For God's sake, I trust you, Lily."

"Is *that* the question?"

"I know you'd never intentionally borrow my work, or anyone's. That's what I want to tell Jenks."

"That's not what I'm asking."

He stopped pacing. "What *are* you asking?"

"What do you think I'm asking, Thomas?" She had practiced this a thousand times. Be calm, she told herself, unaccusing. Of course he hadn't stolen her work; but she needed some sort of explanation. The words came slowly. "You know, you did read my dissertation."

"Jesus, Lily! You're not even for a moment thinking . . . Talk to Bruce, look at my notebooks! We've been toying around with equations for over a year, well before I even looked at your paper."

"Excellent," said Greer. "I'll talk to Bruce. Problem"—she raised her hands dramatically in the air—"solved!"

"Lily, let's stay focused."

"All right, then, focus." She turned to him. "Were you working on dispersal equations before I told you what I was working on?"

"Lily, don't you remember? I was the one who told *you* what to look at. I was and still am your teacher, for God's sake. Your advisor. That was your choice. You came to me, you needed direction, and I gave it to you."

"I didn't *need* direction, Thomas. I turned to you, and not as my teacher or as my colleague, but as my husband, to share my work with you."

"Your work?" The words were pitched too high, and each one rang like a bell of disdain. "Lily, I love you dearly, you know that, but please. The Magnolia Project was and is mine. And I couldn't be more pleased to have you in the lab, but it's not exactly your work."

Then why was she working longer and harder than he was, than Bruce was, to get results? "I can't believe you."

"Lily, I'm telling you the truth. I respect you enough to be honest with you. Do you want me to humor you? Do you want me to condescend and pretend you've got your own project? Your very own lab?"

She had heard him take this tone with colleagues, at conferences, but never before with her. She was stunned.

"I'm a fucking Ph.D. candidate, Thomas. I'm not supposed to have my own lab." She hadn't realized, until this moment, as her body shook with rage, how very badly she wanted his approval, had wanted it from the beginning. "But yes, I do have my own work. Or I would if I hadn't spent so much goddamned time trying to make sure no one in the world finds a speck of pollen predating yours."

"Lily." He came toward her now, put his hand on her head.

"What?" she snapped.

"Lil, please. You have it in your mind that I don't know how much work you've done, or that I don't appreciate it, and you're wrong. I appreciate what you've done. But, more important than that, than the lab and the data, I love you. You're my wife, my family. You are the only life I have or have ever had. You can't forget that. You know what that means to me."

There. Finally. The words were like an incantation, an ancient chant that would always, for Greer, end even the longest trance of anger. "You're my life too, Thomas. Which is why something like this isn't just a professional nightmare." She felt her posture relax. They had traveled to rage and were returning, after a long drive, to home, to kindness. "It rattles the ground beneath everything."

"Look. This will all be all right." He sat beside her and took her in his arms. "We'll take care of this." He began to rock her. "It'll all be fine."

"I just don't understand how you didn't see this coming. You read my paper."

"It was a busy time."

Perhaps she was simply going mad. Greer rubbed her face and tried to stir some memory of herself. Was she, after all, the thief? Could she have fallen so strongly under the spell of his work, his ideas, that they permeated her own?

Greer sank deeper into the sofa, into the yielding cushions; she felt she could stay there forever. "I can't believe this happened. I can't believe I have to walk these halls, passing people who think I'm a plagiarist." She closed her eyes.

"Well, you don't have to stay in these halls if you don't want to."

Greer looked at him wearily.

"Harvard," he said. "They've offered me a chair."

✲

By winter of 1969, at Harvard, Thomas decided he had amassed enough evidence to formally announce a new discovery. After examining over five hundred shales, coals, and sandstones from around the world, the earliest angiosperm pollen was always a Cretaceous magnolia. The lab team assembled the seven years of data, and Thomas went public: Magnolias, he stated, were the very first flowers.

But around this time, several other scientists joined the early angiosperm search. A botanist at the University of California and a geologist at Oxford both began to research ancient magnolias, taking Thomas's investigation one step further. They accepted Thomas's discovery that the magnolia family had come first. But they were asking a new question: Which *species* of magnolia came first, when, and where? Two names—Gerald Beckett Lewis and Jonathan Cartwright—were mentioned in almost all the press coverage of Thomas's announcement. If Thomas's photo was printed, so were theirs. Because the media had generated a question of its own: Which of these men would find the first flower?

Before Thomas could formally present his paper, the hunt for the oldest sample of magnolia pollen was under way. He had always suspected there might be angiosperm pollen in early Cretaceous or perhaps pre-Cretaceous rocks, and now it needed to be found. The entire lab's efforts were directed at this. For six months, the whole team examined even older rocks from North America, but to no avail.

And then, in November 1970, the situation worsened: Bruce Hodges returned from a trip to London with news that Jonathan Cartwright was rumored to have a pre-Cretaceous species and hoped to go public that spring. Panic seized Thomas; it seized the lab. He brought in three more Ph.D. candidates to analyze data. The last of the project's grant money was used to send the post-docs, Lars Van Delek and Preston Brooks, to Europe to get pre-Cretaceous rock samples.

Despite the new researchers, and the fervor of their quest, the atmosphere in the lab grew oddly dull. The more people, the more samples, the less enthusiasm there was. To Greer it felt like working on an assembly line. Hours of cleaning and analyzing each sample to ask a simple yes/no question—is there angiosperm pollen here? The answer, of course, was always no. Nothing learned, no assumptions redefined. On to the next sample.

Thomas no longer stopped by to glance in her microscope. There were no walks through the greenhouse. She lunched alone, or with Constance McAllister, when she was around, because Thomas was too harried to take more than a ten-minute break.

Greer tried to step away from it all, returning to the Marblehead lab and her own research. Whether her pollen was old or the oldest made little difference. She cared how pollen moved, why it moved, how the urge to live manifested itself in nature. And since Harvard's department offered her no room for promotion—women couldn't advance beyond research assistantships—Greer felt it was her right to offer Harvard, and Thomas, a little less of herself.

She used Harvard's restrictions on women to justify her retreat. After all, she couldn't tell Thomas the project was boring her, or that the frenzy in the lab was tainting everyone, including him.

"Lil, women still aren't even allowed to use the telescopes at Mount Wilson and Palomar," he reminded her. "Botany is years ahead of the other sciences. You have all the equipment you need for your work. You need something, tell me and I'll get it for you. Anything. Nobody is shutting doors on your ability to do what you love."

People would talk, she knew. They would complain about her "special" position in the lab, but Greer no longer cared. If she'd never become a full professor, or even an assistant professor, why not be the hermetic wife of the famous Thomas Farraday? All that mattered was that she could do science.

Greer had become intrigued by island biogeography, a new theory presented in a 1967 monograph by Robert MacArthur and Edward Wilson. Their book's preface stated what to Greer seemed an incontrovertible truth: *"By their very multiplicity, and variation in shape, size, degree of isolation, and ecology, islands provide the necessary replications in natural 'experiments' by which evolutionary hypotheses can be tested."*

Off the coast of Iceland, in 1963, a deep-sea volcanic eruption had formed the island of Surtsey. After the lava flow ceased, a preliminary expedition ventured there in '68, and, while Greer was packing up her life in Wisconsin, and unpacking in Massachusetts, she had looked eagerly for news from Surtsey. Eventually the team issued a report, documenting mosses, lichens, and four new plant species on the island. But the flora was still young, and there was talk in the scientific community of another expedition, to which Greer paid close attention. Exploring a newborn island would be ideal. Krakatoa, after all, had been invaluable to nineteenth-century botanists. But Surtsey was difficult to reach, and research depended on a formal, organized team. She would have to wait. And then one morning, Greer saw the ad in the travel section for Lan Chile's service to Easter Island. The match seemed perfect.

"Thomas, what do you know about Easter Island?"

"Big statues," he said, somewhat distracted. He was rereading a journal with a paper by Jonathan Cartwright. He took a bite of toast, turned a page. "Supposedly deposited on the island by aliens. They say it might even be the lost continent of Atlantis. A hotbed of scientific theory, as you can see."

"You can fly there now. From Santiago."

"It's far."

"About twenty-five hundred miles from Santiago. But that's what's interesting, I think. The distance. It would make a perfect biota study."

"It would," he said, though his mind was clearly elsewhere. Ever since the news about Jonathan Cartwright's pollen, Thomas had canceled most trips and symposia, spending all his time in the lab. And after one of the new grad students quit, opting for another advisor, Thomas grew even more tense. "What, he doesn't think we'll find it?" he ranted to Greer on the phone one evening. "You don't just walk away from an opportunity like this. After all, I practically founded the damned field!" Most of the week, Thomas now stayed in Cambridge, and on the few nights he spent in Marblehead, if they made love it was hurried and mechanical; afterward he was quickly in his robe, back at his desk, reviewing lab data. This was the first Sunday in over a month Thomas had been at the house.

"Easter Island would be great for fieldwork," said Greer.

"I'm sure," he said.

"But expensive."

Thomas set the journal down. "You're not really thinking of going?"

"Sure I am. Island biogeography? Easter Island? It's everything I've been working on with cross-water dispersal."

It appeared he was considering her question. "Well, when would you want to go?"

"I hadn't thought that far."

"I think it's a good idea. An excellent site for research. And no one is more qualified than you; no one could do a better job." He paused. "But is right now really the best time?"

"Do you mean because of the weather this time of year? The nonexistent political unrest? Or because of your work?"

"You're angry with me."

"I hardly ever see you, so it's not exactly anger. I'm frustrated, I guess. And I just want some clarification. You're hoping I won't go, not because you want my company, but because of *your* work, right? The magnolia. The lab. Thomas, if you need me there, or if you want me there, just say it. God, say anything so we can have a normal conversation without books open and slides in front of us."

"I always need you there, Lily. You're my best researcher."

"Don't tell Bruce."

"I *have* told Bruce, and you know what? He didn't like hearing it one goddamned bit. He's angry, but let him cope with it. Lil, there *are* gray areas in life. Complexities. Is Bruce number one in the lab? Yes. Is he the best? No. Is it fair? No. Is it my fault? No. And you can't keep holding me personally responsible for a societal system of sex discrimination."

"I hold you responsible only for your choices."

"Harvard's choices. Lil, we don't live in an ideal world, but it is getting better. Why not focus on the opportunities you have rather than those you don't?"

It was true. Her complaint, his exhaustion—they were reading an old script and they both knew its ending by heart. But this time she had a bargaining chip and was prepared to use it.

"A simple proposal, Thomas. If I do the work, and if I do more of the work, which you know I will, I want my name beside Bruce's as coauthor. That's all. You're the hotshot of the department; use your influence."

"Lily, I've never tried to hold you back. I've been your number-one champion."

"I don't need you to be my champion. I just want credit, on paper. Something I can use to try to get my own grants, my own work. Do we have a deal?"

"Deal," said Thomas. "We just need to find a grain of pre-Cretaceous angiosperm pollen."

"God, Thomas, we're really talking needles and haystacks."

"Not even haystacks. Pastures."

"I just want you to know I think your work is important, no matter who in the world finds the oldest grain of flowering plant pollen. This project is just too big, too meaningful, to come down to some hairsplitting interpretation of the argon-argon dates."

"Unfortunately, the rest of the scientific community doesn't think that way."

"I know." She put her hand on his. "Listen. Don't worry. We'll find it."

So her dream of Easter Island was set aside, and she returned to Cambridge for six months. Greer worked in the crowded lab ten hours a day, once again alongside Bruce Hodges, who was by that time aware she sought his position. Like a dormant giant, his football self awoke, resurrecting a rough competitiveness; he scowled, he teased, and every once in while, when he really wanted to bother her, he would say, "So how's that old friend of yours doing? What's her name, Jo? That's right. You two were pretty close. . . . Did you know, Greer, that ninety percent of all angiosperms have bisexual flowers?"

"Go to hell, Bruce."

Greer hadn't, in fact, heard anything from Jo, not since the post-card announcing her new job at the University of Minnesota. After their last dinner, Jo had left Thomas's lab to work briefly for Professor Jenks. Then she had gone to Minnesota, without a good-bye. From time to time, Greer thought of writing her about the house in Marblehead and the lab, but she didn't think Jo wanted to hear from her, and she knew Jo would be disappointed in her life with Thomas. When the new paper came out—with Greer as coauthor—then she would write. The thought made Greer smile. Jo's faith in her, which she had for so long taken for granted, might be reinstilled.

Greer returned to counting and examining grains. Beside her microscope she kept a bottle of aspirin, a hot water bottle, and a tube of Ben-Gay, which she rubbed into her neck every two hours. Despite Bruce's goading, despite the frenzy, a certain camaraderie eventually developed in the lab. They all spent so many hours together, performing such tedious tasks late into the night, that friendship eventually emerged from their pool of disenchantment.

Bruce was gaining weight because of the inactivity of lab life, and fatness seemed to make him friendlier—he had room, it seemed, for only one enemy at a time, and fat was now it. He then began what could be viewed only as a "project" of flirting with Greer, weaving through the lab with a mischievous smile to look at her samples. Greer found his new friendliness, though strained, at least preferable to antagonism. Then one night, when it was just the two of them left in the lab, he wandered over to her workstation.

"Hey, Greer."

"Hodges, I'm not even going to look up. I've got three more samples to count before I can get out of here and I'm tired as hell."

"You're like a Rosie the Riveter of palynology. Greer the Grain Counter."

"Two options: Help or shut up."

"You know, you've always worked hard. Even back in Wisconsin."

"Okay. Pass me the third test tube from the left. And put this slide in the case."

They exchanged items, and he pulled out the lab stool beside hers and sat down. "I read your dissertation, you know."

Greer looked up.

"The first one," he said, a look of earnestness on his face. "And I was wondering if you thought Thomas had been influenced—"

"No, Bruce. Not at all."

"Because it was weird."

"It was an unusual situation. We should have been more careful, that's all. You were there. You know how people stumble onto discoveries, how hard it is to determine the precise origin of an idea."

"Do I?"

❁

In March, three Ph.D. candidates returned with a dozen samples from Southeast Asia. It was like Christmas when they arrived, excitement throughout the lab, each rock unwrapped and admired. Thomas divided the samples among the assistants, and the next day everyone went to work. Greer had a pre-Cretaceous sample from the Malay Archipelago, which seemed a wonderful omen. Malaya— where Wallace, almost a century earlier, had struck upon natural selection. She dissolved, washed, centrifuged, and examined late into the night, and was usually the last to leave the lab. She found endless gymnosperm pollen—ginkgoes, cycads—she found fern spores, but nothing resembling magnolia pollen. Finally, one morning, hunched over the microscope, her neck began to spasm.

"Thomas," she called. The hum of slides shifting and counters ticking ceased. Everyone looked over. Thomas, however, hadn't moved. "Jesus, Thomas"—she could hear the pain in her voice, and he immediately stood—"I can't move my neck."

"Stay right there. Lars, get the cot from the lounge and some pillows. Okay," he said. He was beside her now. "I'm going to rest my hand on the back of your neck . . ."

"Oh, goddamned hell." The pain was awful, a live wire thrashing the branches of her body.

"Okay, I'm not going to touch you. Bruce, call an ambulance."

"I'm sure it'll be gone in a second," she said. "It just came on so fast. Everybody go back to what you were doing. Watching me moan isn't going to help."

"Well, it's helping me," said Bruce.

"Shut up, Hodges," she said.

"No, really, who thinks that Greer in pain is more interesting than pollen? Let's see a show of hands."

Greer couldn't help laughing—but even that hurt.

"Now, I know you can't actually see our hands, Greer, but let me tell you, it's a landslide."

"You dick," said Greer.

"Pain in the neck."

"You know, sometimes," sighed Thomas, "I feel like a grade-school teacher."

They tried to keep up the laughter until the ambulance came, and Greer was lifted onto a gurney. Thomas accompanied her to the hospital, where they had to wait an hour for a doctor. Thomas was irate. He was in his lab coat, hair disheveled, looking older in the glare of the exam room. "Is there an alternate meaning to the word *emergency?*"

"Doctor Farraday!" The examining doctor stared at Thomas. "Wow. I didn't realize. We're understaffed here, as always. Cambridge sees a surprising amount of—"

"Don't talk. Help. My wife can't move her neck. She has a shooting pain. Fix it."

"Yes, sir."

Greer was ordered to stay in bed in a neck brace for two weeks, was given two bottles of painkillers, and was instructed to avoid all microscopes for at least a month. "If you find yourself restless," said the doctor, "we have some nifty devices that will hold a book at the proper height for reading without moving your neck. They're very popular with our neck and back patients."

"Ingenious," said Greer, less than thrilled.

"You would think," said Thomas once she was comfortably installed in the bedroom in Marblehead and he had called to check on things at the lab, "that with a husband twenty years your senior, if one of us were going to start going kaput, it would be me. And here you are, my young, beautiful wife, all laid up like an invalid." He pulled the patchwork quilt to her chest, fastened it beneath her arms.

"Thanks for the reminder."

"Don't worry. I'll be your Florence Nightingale."

"This Florence needs to shave, I think."

"But devoted to only one patient, a prisoner in my bed."

"Quick, get me that reading device."

"My dear, I'll entertain you!"

"Thomas, you seem awfully giddy. Drugged, in fact." Greer lifted the bottle of painkillers and examined it in the light. "It frightens me to see how completely happy my incapacitation makes you. I can't imagine the jubilance I'd see with a terminal diagnosis."

"Cruel words." He kissed her on the forehead, the ears, then he landed one large, manic kiss on her neck brace.

"Really, Thomas." After months of sullenness, fatigue, and anxiety, his behavior was startling. "This isn't like you."

"A man can't adore his wife?"

"Of course he can," said Greer. "But I've a feeling that this man won't be doing much adoring tonight. I expect he'll be back in his lab by sundown."

"In spirit I will be adoring you."

"Of course."

"You're not angry?"

"No."

"Frustrated?"

"Resigned. Which isn't necessarily a bad thing."

"Remember, I love you," he said. "You're the love of my life."

"In Thomas-speak, I think that means 'I want to go to the lab right now.'"

"Lil."

"I'll be fine. Look, I've got a stack of books on islands and bio-geography. I won't miss you one bit. Now go find Mags."

Greer saw him only a few times over the next weeks. She didn't mind his absence and didn't mind the opportunity to catch up on reading; what she minded was her lost chance at coauthorship. She was out of commission at a crucial time—the bargain was clearly off. She followed the doctor's instructions, stayed in bed, took her painkillers, but toward the end of the third week, when she was feeling better, decided to drive into Cambridge and get back to the lab. If she couldn't do counting she could at least do washes and centrifuges. Maybe prepare samples for dating. With the neck brace, she had trouble seeing the rearview mirrors and drove slowly. The piles of gray snow that lined the streets for months were finally starting to melt, but a raw dampness still hung in the air.

She parked beside Thomas's car and slowly climbed up to the third floor. The lab door was locked, so she walked down the hall to the men's room, where Thomas kept an emergency key. The lights were on, but the lab was abandoned—beakers stood half-filled, acid jars were off the shelves, a slow drip fell from the faucet. It looked as if all work had stopped abruptly. Greer shook off her parka and draped it on a stool. She went over to Bruce's workstation, thought about looking in his microscope, but decided not to risk the neck pain. Instead, she flipped through the last few entries in his notebook. Dull stuff, like her own. Sketches of gymnosperm pollen types, numbers, percentages, and in the margins a few doodles of footballs. The analysis of the pre-Cretaceous sample he'd been testing—not a grain of angiosperm pollen in the whole thing. He'd wasted weeks on this sample, months on this whole race. Everyone seemed to be pouring energy into a search that was leading nowhere. Greer wondered if Jonathan Cartwright had been bluffing. A brilliant joke to play on your opponent, she had to admit. Maybe Cartwright was in Oxford right now, doing real research, while Thomas and the rest of them scurried like mice through an endless maze, never realizing the grain of pollen at the end was a mirror trick.

Thomas's desk was filled with the same clutter she'd seen for years. Notebooks, slides, note cards, books—but it was messier than she remembered, as though he had slipped into a new level of disarray. This race was too much for him; it would be too much for anybody. She flipped through his notebook, his argon-argon data for the interbedded tuffs—an assortment of pre-Cretaceous rocks from Australia—all free of angiosperm pollen. They all would be. That was the obvious answer.

She sifted through the case that held his slide collection, through rows of pre-Cretaceous samples from Greenland and China, the samples from Australia; she decided to grab a few slides and carried them to her microscope. Just one peek, she told herself. She unfastened her neck brace and flipped on the switch. She took an unlabeled slide, placed it under the microscope, and adjusted the ocular. Carefully, she bent forward. No angiosperm pollen, of course. Only an assortment of trilete and monolete spores, gymnosperm pollen from conifers and cycads, and several fern spores with distinct exine ornamentation, heavily ridged at the equator. They looked like a family known to have appeared in the mid-Cretaceous period, but the sample had to be pre-Cretaceous. Thomas examined only pre-Cretaceous rocks. She zoomed in, poked the cover slip to roll the grains over, then pulled her face away. She grabbed one of her manuals and began flipping through the pages of fern spores, looking for an image that matched the one on the slide, when the door opened.

It was Thomas, unkempt. "Lily?"

"I couldn't stay away any longer," she said. "I took one peek, that's it. I promise, my neck is much better."

"Oh, Lily," he said, his voice apologetic. "It's wonderful. It's ter-rific." He rubbed his eyes. "It's *all* over."

"What is?"

"I found it," he said. "I found *Mags*."

❄

Winter receded slowly, inching back the blankets of snow, cold winds slowing to warm breezes that carried the smell of wet earth and grass. Rooftop icicles dripped into shiny puddles. The first sprouts of spring pushed through the bald ground.

Greer watched from the house in Marblehead as the earth re-vived. She took long morning walks on the beach before setting her-self up for the day to read on the porch. It was a comfortable routine, but Greer missed research.

Thomas was shuttling between the lab and their apartment, meeting with Bruce, sending samples out for verification, dictating his paper to the department secretary. Greer's neck had gotten worse. The doctor scolded her for taking the brace off early, and she still had to wear it. Through all of the last-minute pollen counts and strata dating, she was unable to assist. And out of disappointment, and stubbornness, perhaps, she decided to resign from the project.

Only for the symposium in May did Greer muster the energy to attend. It was a bland hotel conference. They wore name tags, ate sandwiches and pretzels, wandered beneath the bright lights of the carpeted room, shaking hands with colleagues from distant universi-ties. It was like the few others she'd attended with Thomas, but Greer felt some sadness, and even jealousy, that after all her efforts she was still just a spectator.

This was only the paper's preliminary presentation—a penulti-mate draft before publication—but it would clock Thomas's dis-covery in before Cartwright's. Thomas was first on the program, and when everyone had been seated, and the lights dimmed, he ap-proached the stage. Greer sat away from the lab team, in the back row, with a few half-interested stragglers. Most didn't have name tags, and looked like guests of another convention, or a wedding, fed up with their own event, wondering what on earth a palynology symposium was all about.

Seeing Thomas behind the podium reminded Greer of sitting through his lectures so many years earlier. His voice filled the room with its old intensity. He was in a blue suit, though this one, which she'd picked out, fit him well. In the past year he'd become conscious of his appearance, picking out his clothing with greater deliberation. But the gray streaks in his hair had become more pronounced, and half-moons of darkness cradled his eyes. He had just turned fifty-two.

Thomas began with a slide presentation—the pollen, a photograph of the intact sedimentary unit, even a picture of Lars Van Delek and Preston Brooks, dust-covered and deeply tanned, extracting the samples in Australia. He spoke of the history of the magnolia, the genus that had been vying for the position of "original flower," and the final discovery of what he had decided to name *Magnolius farradius.* At the end of the talk, he thanked his coauthors, and asked them to come on-stage: Bruce Hodges, Lars Van Delek, and Preston Brooks.

She had been expecting this moment, but still, Greer held her hands in her lap as applause filled the room.

"You're not clapping" came a voice from a few seats down.

She looked over at a slight man, in his thirties. His face was long and pale, his mouth pinched. He wore no name tag and sat slouched with boredom. He had obviously picked the wrong conference to crash.

"I'm not clapping, either," he said.

"Self-awareness is important."

"It's all so impressive," he said. "All so unbelievable."

"Palynology can be that way."

"There aren't any women here," he said. "How'd you get in?"

"I said I was a man."

"Me too," he said. She noticed the smell of whiskey on his breath, that he was listing slightly. "Do you want to go for a walk? Or a drink? This conference is no place for a lady to spend her day." Greer couldn't tell if he was slurring his words or if he had an accent. "There's a wedding on the mezzanine. They've got a swing band. We'll sneak in. I'll say you're my wife."

People were standing now, moving toward the podium to shake Thomas's hand. Greer stood. People were also gathering around Bruce Hodges and Preston Brooks. Lars Van Delek had moved off to the side and was talking to a reporter.

"Come on. *Swing* band."

"Please buzz off."

"Quite right. Buzz off, Cartwright."

Greer turned fully to look at him—his eyes roaming the room, his shirt rumpled. He looked only vaguely like his photograph. Jonathan Cartwright.

"You," she said. "Tell me, did you really have your own pre-Cretaceous angiosperm sample?"

"You don't want to talk about that nonsense."

"You didn't have one?"

He seemed forlorn. "I don't think there is such a thing."

So maybe it had all been false rumor.

"You realize, of course, none of this means anything," Greer said. "This isn't science."

"Do you know how to dance to a swing band?"

"This is a number, this is breaking a record, but it doesn't *mean* anything."

Cartwright placed his hands on the seat in front of him and pushed himself up.

"They've got a whole table of those piña coladas. And you know what? We'll have fun because it doesn't matter. He's absolutely wrong. I've *seen* those sediments. From the same site. Nothing. How is *that* possible?"

"I don't know," she said, and walked slowly, uneasily, to meet her husband.

✿

June arrived, hot and dry, and droughts swept the country. The news showed pictures of distraught farmers, restless children. The month passed sluggishly.

Thomas was in Cambridge most of the time, commuting twice a week to Marblehead, basking in the recent attention. Greer's neck was finally better, the brace came off, and she returned to her own work in the basement. She was happy to be researching cross-water dispersal patterns again; she had put aside her disappointment about not being coauthor on Thomas's paper.

Occasionally, though, when she was in her lab, her mind returned to the image of the fern spores she'd seen that night in Thomas's lab—spores that shouldn't have been in a pre-Cretaceous sample. It was possible she'd been wrong about the species. But still, it was odd she'd heard nothing further about it—no mention of an unusual appearance. It begged analysis.

Then one afternoon, while she was working in the cellar, a telegram arrived. No sender was named. It said simply:

Finally you'll have to face the barracuda.

Greer held the strip of paper for several hours, sitting on the porch, wondering at its contents. Jo, of course. But why now?

And then another delivery followed, this one from a popular scientific weekly. She unwrapped the brown paper. The cover read:

ACCUSATIONS OF FRAUD. DATA FALSIFIED BY THOMAS FARRADAY, PH.D.

Thomas, it explained, had been accused of contaminating his samples, of allowing angiosperm pollen from a Cretaceous sample to make its way into a pre-Cretaceous sample. It said that in attempting to beat Jonathan Cartwright, he had generated fraudulent data in his lab.

The accusation had been made by Bruce Hodges.

19

On her way back to camp it begins to rain. The red soil churns to mud beneath her pony's hooves. Elsa flings her drenched skirt over the satchel and *kohau* on her lap, leaving her half-bare legs dangling beside the pony's flanks. A pungent heat rises from the beast. Her leather boots darken, her stockings freckle with mud under the battering raindrops. I will have to dry off, she thinks. I will have to get warm. And clean. Yes. There are necessities. And if the wind is strong, she will have to fasten the crates, then check the tent stakes. And if there are leaks—when did she last check the canvas tops?—she will have to patch them. It might even be a mounting storm, she thinks. Hopes. The needles of water, the brine-clogged air, the spray of mud, are disruptions she needs.

Good-bye to the two Mrs. Beazleys. . . .

She wipes the water from her face with her sleeves. As the pony lumbers along the path, Anakena comes into view. She dismounts at the bottom of the hill. With one hand she leads the animal, with the other holds the satchel and *kohau* wrapped in her skirt, so that she strides, half-hunched, through the rain over the rise. The camp below is empty.

I have first-rate vision.

Elsa tethers the pony and stumbles down the hill, taking refuge in the tent. The canvas shudders all around her. She towels off the *kohau* and her notebook. She lights the lantern, searches her mind for her tasks: *Check leaks, secure stakes, move crates inside.* Two cockroaches scurry toward her, and she stomps them with her boots.

She raises the lantern to the drooping canvas ceiling and searches for small tears. Impossible to hear the drip of a leak with the rumbling of this rain, she thinks. She will have to scrutinize every inch. But as her finger traces the long seams, silence descends. The rumbling has stopped. She steps outside to see that the sun has freed itself from the tatters of gray cloud. She now sits on the sand, watching the brightening sky, waiting for the rain to resume.

In the distance, through the mist, she can see where they first anchored the schooner. *Good-bye to the two Mrs. Beazleys.* That's what Kierney shouted from the dinghy. *I have first-rate vision.*

Elsa returns to the tent and sits on her cot. Opposite, draped across a piece of twine, is Edward's nightshirt. An image of Alice slung across Edward's sleeping form springs to her mind, and she tries to push it away. She still has work to do. From beneath her cot she pulls her stack of notebooks, locates the one with her notes on the *rongorongo,* and opens it. In a cup beside her, she finds her fountain pen, the one her father gave her when he fell ill. *Professor Beazley seems quite fond of our dear Alice.* Elsa pushes the pen firmly against the page:

> *I have determined a strong likelihood that the rongorongo is boustro-phedon. Alternate lines read upside down. Need confirmation.*

She sets the pen down. But is it possible her father meant—? No. The idea is ridiculous, the story too absurd. A professor who falls in love with the half-wit daughter of his colleague! She isn't well. Her forehead burns. She is shivering in her damp dress. Perhaps she has caught something from the lepers, something strange and feverish that tricks the mind, makes you see frightening things. She leans forward and her hands, fidgety, begin to untie the wet laces of her boots.

After all, it is insane. Falling in love with a girl he's not permitted to love. Marrying the girl's sister, the girl's caretaker, so that he can be near her. Elsa was the one to make the sacrifice, for *Alice.* If she hadn't had Alice to look after, she could have found a real husband, she might even have found a way to be with Max. She could not have been—the word rises up before her in the dark tent—*duped.* Was it possible she'd given up the life she wanted, not for Alice, but for *Edward*?

"Elsa!" From outside comes Edward's voice.

A moment later, his rain-slicked head appears in the tent, water dripping from his beard. He seems cautious. He is waiting for me to scold him, thinks Elsa. He is waiting to see what I know.

"Alice is drenched. Would you come help?"

Help, thinks Elsa. Of course. I'm always ready to help. I'm the governess again. The governess in his employ to take care of Alice.

"She'll catch pneumonia."

"Well," Elsa begins with unexpected sarcasm, "we must get her out of her wet clothes, then." And you are frightened to do it yourself, she thinks. Frightened of how it might seem.

Elsa grabs a blanket, wraps it around her shoulders, puts on a hat, and follows Edward to Alice's tent. Alice is facing away from the entrance. Her blouse, wet and translucent, clings to her skin, and Elsa can see the strong pulse of her back.

"Somebody's been parading about in the rain," says Elsa. "I wonder who could have been parading about in the rain? It couldn't have been Allie because she's been told over and over *not* to go running about in deluges."

Elsa steps behind her, resting her hands on Alice's shoulders. Beneath her palms the slim bones arch gently. She traces the cliff of Alice's back. It is strange: *This* is the body she knows best. Better than Edward's, better than her own. This is the body her hands always seek. This is the body she has watched grow, the body it has always been her duty to protect. She wishes now she could leave her hands here forever, nestle them against this warm skin, knead them into this flesh and forget the chasm of cold air between her and Alice. She would like to slip into this other being, blink her eyes and say: *I am Alice.* Instead, she begins the only thing she does know how to do—tending. She unfastens the top button of Alice's blouse.

"I'll check the equipment," says Edward, slipping out of the tent.

His delicacy is too overstated.

"Allie." Elsa's fingers inch toward Alice's jaw. "Allie, look at me. What's wrong?"

But Alice only sways.

"We must get you out of these wet clothes." Elsa continues to unbutton the blouse, then unclasps the skirt. In the steamer trunk, she finds a fresh towel and rubs it over Alice's head, works it around her neck and arms. When Alice is dry and blanket-wrapped, Elsa crouches before her, takes her hands. "Allie, has anything . . . happened?"

Alice's eyes return from their inward stare, taking in the room, taking in Elsa.

"I mean, with Beazley . . ."

Alice's eyes flash to full alertness. "Beazley does not *does not* love you!"

Elsa nearly falls back from the anger in Alice's voice. But her fingertips, by instinct, reach for Alice's cheek. "Allie."

Alice flinches, then swats at Elsa, her nails scratching Elsa's neck.
"He loves Alice! Do you hear me?" A bitter sadness rings through her
voice. "He loves Alice!"

Elsa sits at the table by the beach. Across from her is Edward, who
has wiped all traces of rain from his face, but now sweats. Several red
splotches have erupted beneath his skin, spilling over his cheeks.
Alice is asleep now, in her tent.

"I am not a sick man," he says. "Please do not look at me like that.
I am not a sick man."

Elsa is silent.

"You asked me to care for your sister and I have cared for her. I
have watched her and waited on her. You wanted me to love her and
I loved her. I've never . . . never *done* anything . . ." He produces a
handkerchief from his pocket and pats his forehead. "She plays
around, you know her games. She grabs and kisses. Play, Elsa. Just
play. You mustn't think I would do anything inappropriate."

Elsa does, in fact, believe what he is saying; but something larger,
something she can't place, disturbs her.

He crumples his handkerchief into a ball. "I have always tried to be
a good man, Elsa. I am not an exciting man, not an entertaining man,
not a passionate man, but I am a good man. After all this time, I'd
think you would know that. Please allow me that one credit."

Elsa looks up at the sky—a dim blue dome above them. A good
man. Yes, and what of it? Does he want her to soothe *him* now? To
make *him* feel better?

Edward's eyes follow the path of her own. He looks at the sky, the
grass, then finally at her.

"Elsa, I harbor no delusions. It is the benefit of being a perpetual
scholar. I do not daydream, and I do not let desire deceive me. Let us
at least admit to each other that you never wanted to marry me. That
has always been clear. You never would have married me if you
hadn't had Alice to look after."

Elsa holds her hand in front of her face, spreads her fingers, and
examines the web of lines and grooves in her skin.

"I am old, but not a fool, Elsa. I know where you stand. I've known
from the beginning."

Yes. She asked them to tolerate each other, to be kind to each other, but nothing more.

"What would you like? Would you like me to apologize? Because I care for Alice, just as you asked? Well, I refuse to. You cannot control us. You cannot dictate the terms of lives for three people. Do you insist that she show me the same polite indifference as you? You cannot decide that for her." He stops as if to gather the scraps of disparate thoughts. "Elsa, I have never been loved. I know you care for me, but I am not the kind of man people fall in love with. But Alice loves me, is in love with me, and I refuse to disdain that simply because she's different, or because you didn't factor that into your arrangement. How could Alice's affections come between us when you have seen to it, from the beginning, that there is nothing between us . . . ? Are you hearing any of this? Elsa?"

Elsa recalls what her father said years before: *Old Beazley has suffered his fair share of amorous afflictions. Enough to send him all the way to the African continent.* Afflictions so great he could find comfort only in a girl incapable of hurting him?

"Well," says Elsa. Her lips feel rigid, her tongue swollen. Each word is a stone. "Alice—does—love—you." She looks at Edward's furrowed brow, his sunken cheeks. He is like a man awaiting absolution. Is *she* supposed to absolve him? Is she once again supposed to attend to someone else? But how *easy* it would be to give it all up, to walk away, from Edward, from Alice, from herself. What, in the end, binds her to goodness, to love, to anything, but her own will to be bound? Duties are not facts; they are feelings. She takes a deep breath. It seems so frightening, so simple. She can sense her lips curling into a nervous smile: "But Alice has the mind of a *child*."

"Elsa—"

"She cannot love you. Really. You mustn't fool yourself, Edward."

"You yourself have always said she comprehends more—"

"Amentia, madness, stupidity. Call it what you like. It doesn't change—"

"Please, Elsa—"

"Don't you understand? After all this time? With all your degrees and books and your anthropological studies you can't see what she really is? Why don't you study *her*? Interview her and see what theory you come up with. You wouldn't even have to travel. Research in-bloody-situ, Edward. Write a five-hundred-page volume, have a glossary, but it will say just one thing—"

"Stop."

"Imbecile!"This is the word people have always used. With each syllable, her palm smacks the table."Im-be-cile!"

Edward reaches across and grabs her shoulders. "Stop it, Elsa. Stop."

Elsa wrenches free, but then slumps lifelessly over the table. She has exhausted everything inside herself.

A tear rolls down the sharp line of Edward's cheek, catching at the top of his beard. He shakes his head as though to disperse it, but this only releases another."Do you want me to be ashamed? I assure you that nothing you say to me can be worse than what I've said to myself." He looks down at the table."I will not protest any accusations you make against me. But don't do this. Not to Alice. You love her, Elsa. I've never for a moment doubted that. But"—he looks up and seeks her eyes—"I don't think you fully understand her."

"I don't understand *you*."

"What would you like me to say? All I can tell you is that this is real. No argument, no explanation, can make it go away. Alice is furious with you, because of what you have and she doesn't."

Alice, in love with him."No,"she says.

"Perhaps you've loved her too much to let yourself imagine what she really feels, to imagine her pain."

Elsa rubs the scratch on her neck, and the salt of her fingers awakens the wound.

"Elsa, I want you to know that I've been firm with her. I've told her that I cannot be like a husband to her. But when I tell her, she says she hates you. Of course she doesn't mean that, but she has a strong sense of what she's missing. She wants the things you want, wants to have the things you have. Elsa, you've known her since she was a child, and you think of her as a child, but she isn't a child. Part of her is a woman. A very despondent woman."

"*Woman?* I think you *have* let desire deceive you."

"You say she understands more than it seems, you *know* she understands, and yet you refuse to consider the fact she may actually understand something of her own deficiencies. Alice knows she's different. No amount of encouragement or kindness or love will prevent her from recognizing what she has been denied."

"Denied?"

"That's not an accusation."

"What is it, then? Since the day she was born, and I do mean that

literally, she has been loved, and cared for, and watched over, and en-
tertained—"

"Don't you see? You think of her needs only in terms of the ones
you can tend to. You believe that her happiness, her health, and her
well-being are completely dependent on you. I know the sacrifices
you've made for her. You could make all the right choices, make endless sacrifices, but, Elsa, no person can provide contentment or safety
to another the way you want to believe you can. Especially to Alice.
She will always have longings and sadnesses you cannot remedy. You
let the boy love her. Biscuit Tin. While you have a husband, a man
you—"

"Allie loves Biscuit Tin," says Elsa, though she knows this is not his
point.

"She wanted to be in the tent with us. She wants a companion."

"Alice. In love with you. With anybody. And jealous of me. After
everything, she hates me."

"She doesn't hate you."

"I did this," Elsa says, gesturing to Edward, to the island, "for her."

"I know," Edward answers without anger. "And . . . I think *she*
knows."

Elsa refuses to believe this. It is too much.

"I do love you, Elsa, no matter what you may feel for me."

She wants to say something kind, something to make him feel
better, but she can't find the energy. She doesn't know what she feels
for him.

"I can't stay in the tent with you," says Elsa.

"Elsa, you have been a good companion."

It is on the tip of her tongue to say she has been a *convenient* companion, but she looks at his swollen eyes, and restrains herself. The
venom of what she's already said rises in her throat.

They sit in silence, the echoes of their conversation hovering
above them. Elsa finally stands and wanders up to the rise above
their camp. She lies down in the rough grass, listening to waves lap at
the shore below. She closes her eyes and tries to picture herself before she came to the island, before she married Edward, before her
father died. What was she like? Was she really kind to Alice? Images
flood her mind: cycling in the afternoon through St. Albans, sitting in
Dr. Chapple's office, walking together through Hyde Park in the rain,
their kiss in the dark. Did she understand Alice? And Alice—was she
happier before Elsa became her guardian? *Guardian.* The word roams

her mind, her memory. A breeze, carrying the chill of descending night, sweeps across her face. Slowly, the sky darkens, blackness seeping like tar to the edges of the horizon.

"Elsa!"

It is the following morning, and Elsa is lying, once again, atop the hill. She knows Kasimiro is awaiting her return, but she is too fatigued to budge. It feels like months since she was at the leper colony, excited simply by the translation of one small tablet. How happy she was, riding back along the coast, the *kohau* in her lap. But it now seems impossible another translation could give her such pleasure, that anything could. She cannot bring herself to go down to the camp again and see Alice, not yet.

"Elsa!" Edward calls from below. She can hear his boots clambering up the hill, can hear him panting.

"I just need to lie here." But she only whispers this to herself, shutting her eyes. The symbols of the *rongorongo* float before her, clouds forming and dissolving.

"Elsa." His voice is directly above her.

"Please. I'll be down soon. I just want to be alone a little longer."

"You must get up."

"Edward—"

"Just tell me I'm not mad. You must see this."

Begrudgingly, she opens her eyes. The symbols vanish, replaced by the gray sky, the grass. She doesn't want to be here. She doesn't care what color tern Edward has sighted, what marking he has found on a *moai*. She doesn't care about his apologies or regrets. She simply needs solitude, but she hasn't the strength to fight him. Edward's face, crooked with bewilderment, hangs above her.

"I must be going completely insane," he says.

"Yes."

"Elsa, please. Sit up."

Elsa sighs. "All right. What?"

"Just tell me. Please. Do *you* see that?" Edward points toward the water.

She props herself up on her elbows and looks down at the sea. What appears to be a fleet of warships is steaming toward the island.

20

The Sociedad de Arqueología de América del Sur had sent word that a small conference would be held on the island in October in which the four researchers would present their work to one another and to any islanders or tourists who wished to attend. To coordinate this, SAAS had sent Isabel Nosticio, a humorless but seductive middle-aged Argentinean woman with thick black hair to her waist, who always wore pink and an abundance of makeup. At the end of any conversation, about overhead projectors or hors d'oeuvres, she would reapply her lipstick. "Remember," she would say, sliding her glossy lips together, "it is in the interest of the island community that we work." Her main task was to make sure the eccentric researchers roaming the SAAS halls came through in the end, making the Sociedad appear efficient, charitable, and, ultimately, pro–Rapa Nui. In the wake of a Rapa Nui petition to Chile demanding land rights outside Hanga Roa, the conference, it quickly became clear, was meant as an appeasement.

Mahina was not impressed. "They ask you to tell us of your work, the work they decide for the island, so that we not complain of their government. *Pasto!*"

Greer was having breakfast in the dining room.

"I'm sorry," she said. She sipped her tea and turned to Mahina, seated at the next table, drinking a tall glass of apricot nectar. Every morning they ate together at sunrise, as Greer was the first to wake of all the guests. Mahina would gather eggs from the yard, pluck fruit from the trees. Then Greer would hear the crackle of eggshells from the kitchen, the rhythmic thump of the knife as a guava was quartered. Greer couldn't help but think that Mahina would have made an excellent scientist. Precision and procedure governed her life.

"It is our island," said Mahina, who, out of some strict sense of professional boundaries, always refused to sit at Greer's table. So they spoke across the space between them like solo travelers. Over the past few months, Greer had learned that Mahina started the *residencial* six years earlier, when the Lan Chile flights began. Before that she had been a schoolteacher, making sure the island's children learned the Rapa Nui language; sometimes, on the street, if they were out walking together, a teenager would approach Mahina with great deference, and Greer could tell the person was a former student. Mahina, she was sure, had been a demanding but inspiring teacher. Her knowledge of the island's folklore was encyclopedic, and she took her responsibility as a storehouse of history seriously; she made Greer write down the legends she recited, then read them back for verification. Over the past few weeks, roused by late-arriving news of the military coup in Chile, they had spoken often of politics, concerned about the new regime's effect on the island. Greer's sympathy for Rapa Nui's predicament increased daily, but she knew little could be done. Chile, no matter who held office, was too large and powerful, Rapa Nui too small to exist on its own. The annual supply ship collected wool from the island's Chilean sheep ranch. If Chile had no wool to collect, why send the boat? Who, then, would bring supplies—cement and furniture and food? Still, their conversations were not about pragmatism but political idealism and the right to live freely. To speak of the logistics, Greer thought, would seem offensive.

"It's an injustice," said Greer.

"You do not have these problems," said Mahina. "In America."

"Oh, we do," said Greer, slicing into her omelet. "Plenty. Long ago, we fought the British for independence. That was cut-and-dry at least. Now we have more complicated problems. The funny thing is, in the U.S., the word *revolutionary* has such a negative connotation. But we were revolutionaries."

"Con-no-ta-tion?"

"A hint. A suggestion."

"A clue?"

"Sort of," said Greer. Mahina wrote the word on the notepad beside her—each morning they exchanged vocabulary: English for Rapa Nui, Rapa Nui for English.

"Con-no-ta-tion," Greer enunciated. "It's a nice word. But I promise, you could travel across the whole U.S. and never have to use it."

"I would like to travel!" said Mahina, suddenly animated. "I would like to have money to go somewhere. People come here now from all over. Germany, Australia, and New Jersey. I am lucky to meet so many different people. I am"—Mahina looked to Greer and pronounced, slowly, one of her new vocabulary words—"*privileged.*" Greer nodded. "God is good to me. But still I would like to go somewhere."

"What about Santiago? Could you go there?"

"It is the money," Mahina said. "I have the old English books. I could sell them, yes?"

"Depends on what they are. There's a market for old books. I could try to find a dealer in the States."

"Yes, but of course I cannot leave. I must wait for Raphael to come back."

"Raphael?"

"My husband."

"Husband!" In the five months Greer had been there, this was the first Mahina had mentioned a husband. "When on earth did you get married?"

"Oh, *treinta y cinco* . . ."

"Thirty-five?"

"Thirty-five years ago. Saturday."

"But where is he?"

"Tahiti."

"Will he be back for your anniversary?"

"I hope so," she said, nodding forcefully. "He said if Tahiti was as lovely as we heard, he would come back and bring me too."

"He's your exploring party."

"*Sí, sí,*" she said, looking out the window. The sun lit her face and she let her eyes drift closed.

"But the *residencial*? Your home? You'd give it up for Tahiti?"

Mahina shrugged, opened her eyes. "No more talk of him." She piled her fork and knife on her empty plate, swiped her napkin across the tablecloth.

"I have to tell you," Greer said, "I think Ramon has a thing for you. A crush."

"Crush?"

"Romantic interest. Love interest. He watches you all the time."

Mahina shook her head. "Ramon is the brother of my husband."

"That doesn't mean he can't think of you that way."

"*Ramon?*"

"Yes, Ramon. Haven't you noticed?"

Mahina gave a quick *hmph.* "And you, *Doctora*? You have a crush as well, I think. *Amor* for the *doctora*, no?"

"Me?"

"*Me?* The *doctora* would like to be so innocent! Vicente, *Doctora*! He is always leaving books, a note, a thing for you."

"He's just a colleague. He's trying to be helpful."

"You are not married. What is wrong? You do not like him? He is too short, you think?" Mahina shrugged. "The Chilean men are tiny, it is true. Not like the Rapa Nui men."

"No, Mahina, he's not too short." He was taller than Mahina, and taller than Greer. But Greer laughed, amused by the suggestion that after months of examining her feelings for Vicente, talking herself out of attraction, it might come down to something so simple, so definable: his height. "I was married, though."

Mahina tilted her head. "Your husband? He left you?"

"He died," said Greer. "He died ten months ago. From a heart attack."

"Oh, my dear *doctora.*" Mahina rose from her chair and moved behind Greer. "So sad." Shifting Greer's hair to one side of her neck, she rubbed Greer's shoulders, then rested her chin on Greer's head. The sweet smell of gardenia washed over Greer, and she felt her eyes drift closed. She hadn't expected to be comforted by this—her admission, the warmth of Mahina's sympathy, by simple touch.

"Thank you," said Greer.

"*Doctora*," said Mahina. "Never feel alone."

❧

What Mahina had said about Vicente was true—he did come by often, with books and journals and articles. He'd supplied Greer with all the reading material she could possibly need. At the weekly dinners, or in passing at the lab, he updated her on his *rongorongo* work and his investigations into the Germans. By now she even knew his daily routines. In the morning he did sit-ups and push-ups on the coast; on the nights the Lan Chile flight arrived, he read the newspaper by the *caleta* with Mario and Petero, exchanging finished pages one at a time, all of them sharing a bottle of pisco. Greer in fact knew everybody's routine. Ramon tended to his garden after tea each morning; he took great pleasure in trimming his avocado and guava trees, in pinching the withered blooms from his flower garden and slowly pacing his rows of manioc bushes. As Greer passed the Espíritu, Sven could be heard singing in the shower. The island had a small-town intimacy. After five months, people knew where Greer went, and when. Twice a week she bought groceries from Mario, the red-haired man she'd met her first day. Once a week she went to the *correo* to post research requests. She found comfort in these rhythms, in the intricate web of greetings that underlay her daily lab work.

At night, after dinner at the *residencial,* Greer would sometimes gather with the other guests to listen to Mahina's island stories, or to offer advice on sight-seeing routes. But usually, she went back to her room, took a long shower, and climbed into bed with a book. She was now rereading Captain Cook's log. He had anchored off the coast in 1774, about fifty years after Roggeveen:

> . . . *As the master drew near the shore with the boat, one of the natives swam off to her, and insisted on coming aboard the ship, where he remained two nights and a day. The first thing he did after coming aboard was to measure the length of the ship, by fathoming her from taffrail to the stern; and as he counted the fathoms, we observed that he called the numbers by the same names that they do at Otaheite; nevertheless, his language was in a manner wholly unintelligible to all of us. . . .*
>
> *Before I sailed from England I was informed that a Spanish ship had visited this isle in 1769. Some signs of it were seen among the people now about us; one man had a pretty good broad-brimmed European hat on, another had a Grego jacket, and another a red silk handkerchief.*

Greer set the book down and watched the curtain billow in a breeze. She looked at the wicker nightstand, the mahogany desk, the plaque of the Virgin Mary hanging above her. It wasn't just the ecosystem; objects as well suffered from the island's isolation. Things didn't disappear, they changed hands. Everything in her room would remain on the island. That red silk handkerchief and the Grego jacket, she thought, were probably in the back of someone's closet.

> *They also seemed to know the use of a musket, and to stand in much awe of it. But this they probably learnt from Roggeveen, who, if we are to believe the authors of that voyage, left them sufficient tokens.*

> *. . . The greatest part of the distance across the ground had but a barren appearance, being a dry hard clay, and everywhere covered with stones . . .*
>
> *On the east side, near the sea . . . three platforms of stone-work, or rather the ruins of them. On each had stood four of those large statues; but they were all fallen down from two of them, and also one from the third; all except one were broken by the fall and in some measure defaced . . .*

Greer had already noted this: Most of the *moai* had been toppled by 1774. Yet Roggeveen had seen them standing. So the statues must have fallen between Roggeveen's and Cook's visits, 1722 to 1774. If a natural disaster brought down the *moai,* it wasn't the same one that wiped out the biota, for even Roggeveen noted barrenness. So what had actually toppled them? A disaster with that kind of force would surely have entered the island's oral history, but there was no such record. Had the islanders themselves done this? After ages of carving and construction and moving? Throughout history monuments were destroyed—churches burned, idols smashed, portraits defaced—but as acts of violence inflicted by an enemy, an invader, a new regime. The Europeans hadn't touched the *moai.* Mahina had spoken of two vying tribes on the island—the long-ears and the short-ears. Could one have vanquished the other? Even so, why destroy the island's greatest achievements? Western investigators speculated endlessly about the building of the *moai,* amazed a primitive people could erect and transport such magnificent idols. But how could a people, any people, allow them to fall? This was the more interesting question. Greer continued:

> *No more than three or four canoes were seen on the whole island; and these very narrow and built with many pieces sewn together with small line. They are about eighteen or twenty feet long, head and stern carved or raised a little, are very narrow and fitted with outriggers. They do not seem capable of carrying above four persons, and are by no means for any distant navigation . . .*
>
> *In all this excursion, as well as the one made the preceding day, only two or three shrubs were seen. The leaf and seed of one (called by the natives Torromedo) were not much unlike those of common vetch; but the pod was more like that of a tamarind in its size and shape. The seeds have a disagreeable bitter taste; and the natives, when they saw our*

people chew them, made signs to spit them out; from whence it was con-
cluded that they think them poisonous. The wood is of a reddish colour,
and pretty hard and heavy; but very crooked, small, and short, not ex-
ceeding six or seven feet in height. At the southwest corner of the island,
they found another small shrub, whose wood was white and brittle in
some matter, as also its leaf, resembling the ash. They also saw in sev-
eral places the Otaheitean cloth plant, but it was poor and weak, and not
above two and a half feet at most. They saw not an animal of any sort,
and but very few birds; nor indeed anything which can induce ships
that are not in the utmost distress to touch at this island. . . .

Again, Greer noted that they had observed *toromiros* and a cloth
plant likely related to the Polynesian mulberry used for making tapa
cloth. Her thoughts were interrupted by voices from the courtyard—
a woman and a man. The woman was speaking Spanish, and Greer
could barely make out the phrases, but she was almost certain it was
Isabel Nosticio. She was staying at Mahina's, and seemed to be out
every evening. Greer pulled two pieces of tissue from her nightstand,
twirled them into small cones, and slid them into her ears.

. . . No nation need contend for the honour of the discovery of this
island, as there cannot be places which afford less convenience for ship-
ping than it does. Here is no safe anchorage, no wood for fuel, nor any
fresh water worth taking on board. Nature has been exceedingly sparing
of her favours to this spot.

Greer marked this last page and closed the book. She was thinking about Admiral von Spee, who had become, as predicted, Vicente's
new fixation, the *rongorongo* for the time being forgotten. Vicente
seemed a man in constant pursuit of obsessions—hot air ballooning,
cryptography, German military history—appetites never quite sated.
For now von Spee's squadron truly excited him, and he spoke of it so
incessantly, wondering what they might have made off with, that
Greer's own imagination had been ignited. A fleet of warships anchoring off the island, scores of German officers wandering among
the *moai*. But the question in her mind as she drifted toward sleep
was: If mariners found the island so inhospitable, why had the Germans stopped, of all places, at Rapa Nui?

At the SAAS dinner the next night outside the Hotel Espíritu, Greer showed Vicente the Cook excerpt. "I'm with you, Vicente. When you think about it, why would anyone come here to provision a whole fleet? How many men were we talking about?"

"Two thousand," he said.

"You couldn't pick a worse spot."

Vicente smiled. "Unless," he said, "you wished to stock up on something other than coal and food."

"Or," said Sven, "if you wanted to lay low and hide. If you haven't noticed, it's a pretty out-of-the-way spot. Not bad for a fleet running from the whole world."

"Soon you will see," Vicente said calmly. "I'm awaiting proof, papers, that will show definitively where the tablets went." This was Vicente's usual retort. It was amazing—he never suffered a moment's doubt.

Still, Greer agreed with his theory. "Just think. Admiral von Spee was a man of the world. A naturalist. He wrote about the flora and fauna of places where he was stationed. Wouldn't he have read Cook's log? His job was to prepare for all possibilities. He wouldn't just drop anchor and play it by ear."

"You shouldn't feed his frenzy this way," said Sven. "You indulge him."

"She happens to be right," Vicente said. "Von Spee came here for one reason: the *rongorongo*."

"So did you," laughed Sven. "But that clearly means nothing."

"All right. New topic," announced Greer. This was how they managed the weekly dinners. Everyone was limited to five minutes of work talk, otherwise they would sit and argue for hours.

"The mysterious cores?" asked Vicente.

"Still mysterious," said Greer. "Same as last week. Same as the week before that. Counting grains. It's a slow and boring process. I'll save you the details."

Greer shook salt and pepper onto her chicken, then reached for Sven's most recent condiment concoction: cilantro and mango sauce. They'd all been eating the same basic meal of chicken for months now, and any new flavor, even a strange one, was a welcome change. She dipped a forkful of chicken in the sauce. It was sugary, with a hint of spice. "Not bad, Sven."

"What we really need is a nice plate of gravlax, maybe some Hasselback potatoes."

"Well, then, the conference," said Vicente. "Señorita Nosticio asked me to make my presentation first, and I'd like to make sure we're all in comfortable agreement on that."

"Do you really think people will show?" asked Sven. "I've an image of standing up there, babbling about my work to just the three of you."

"Just like our dinners," said Greer.

"Touché."

"Kidding." But she hoped people would show. She liked the idea of participating in a conference.

"People will come, Sven. Mario and Petero, and I'm sure Mahina. And others. But first: Are we settled on my commencing the program?"

Just as they arranged the order—Vicente, Sven, Burke-Jones, Greer—Luka Tepano walked by. Greer saw him often, passing Mahina's, or the Espíritu, strolling pensively. Sometimes, if she went to the *caleta* at night to watch the ocean, she would spot him sitting on the rocks. He now held a bunch of daisies.

"That's the saddest bouquet I've ever seen," said Sven. "No woman in the world would be impressed by that. Even women in caves have standards."

"It is the thought that counts," said Vicente. "It is the thought that matters to women."

At this, they all instinctively turned to Greer.

"Speaking on behalf of all women: absolutely."

"Well, for men as well," said Vicente. "For anyone. It's the thought."

"Excellent recovery, Vicente—" Sven grinned. "You should have been a diplomat."

"You'll be pleased to know I've considered it."

"People give flowers because they're pretty. Plain and simple. They signify beauty. Why do artists paint flowers? Because they're pretty. Am I right, Greer?"

"Couldn't say."

"This is no time for the flower expert to go silent."

"Botanist, Sven. Palynologist. You do understand that I'm not a florist?"

"Yes, but science requires too many dull technical terms," he said. "Come on, a little something. One small floral opinion to tide us over."

"All right. In my mind, the only artist who can paint flowers is O'Keeffe."

"What about Van Gogh and his sunflowers?" asked Vicente.

"I think the only true picture of flowers should be of a single flower. Quantity only obscures beauty. Examine one thing closely, and all things will be revealed. One flower. One grain of pollen." She gestured to them. "*Even* one island."

"Be careful," teased Sven, "you speak as though we're doing something meaningful here. People will get the wrong impression."

"We *are*, though." Greer leaned back in her chair and sighed. The strain of her work was catching up with her. "Even though we're all at an impasse, we're asking the right questions. Important questions."

They basked for a moment in this reminder of the meaning of their daily lives, the months of small, tedious tasks. They needed it, especially Greer.

"Let's have Greer go first," said Sven, "get the crowd worked up."

"I'm already thinking of calling in sick as it is," she said. "I've got zilch to report."

Burke-Jones pushed his chair back and stood. "I'm fatigued." Before they could offer good-byes, he began to walk off down the street.

"Isn't he staying here at the Espíritu?" asked Greer.

"Yes, but he likes to roam. It relaxes him."

"An endlessly intriguing man."

"Well, we give him a long rope," said Sven.

"Can I ask why?"

"You haven't told her?" Sven asked. "You bombard her with every detail of Admiral von Spee, dead for sixty years, and say nothing of our living colleague?"

"His wife," Vicente said to her. "She died almost two years ago. And he's been here since, studying the transport of the *moai*. He is, or was, quite a well-known architect in London. He was commissioned to build a new theater. It would have been the largest in London, but when his wife passed on, that was the end of it. He walked away."

"Poor Randolph," said Greer.

They all sipped the last of their drinks, then attempted to rekindle the conversation with complaints about SAAS, predictions about when the Chilean navy boat would arrive with supplies, thoughts on the Pinochet coup. Vicente pulled out his newspaper and showed them the headline: *La Muerte de Pablo Neruda.*

"Five days ago now," he said. "They say it was from sadness at see-ing his homeland fall into the hands of such a dictator. And they say he had just published a poem about Rapa Nui."

This and Burke-Jones's story made them all pensive, and they soon said their good-nights.

Greer went back to the lab to check on a sample soaking in potas-sium hydroxide. In the hallway she saw a line of light beneath Burke-Jones's door. She hadn't spoken with him outside of the SAAS dinners, but now she felt she should check on him. After all, she knew something of grief, of the desire to escape. The door was ajar and she gently knocked, but there was no answer. She eased it open, and saw him hunched over a table at the room's far end; his hands, out of sight, were occupied. Stepping forward, she saw what lay be-fore him: a miniature landscape—the island littered with six-inch *moai*, toothpick ladders, and ringlets of what appeared to be dental floss. There were bottles of opened glue, scissors, cardboard, colored construction paper, and in the corner a bucket of papier-mâché. He hummed forlornly as he moved about, adjusting and altering the miniature landscape.

"Randolph," she called. "It's Greer." But there was no response.

"Randolph," she said again.

Was he simply ignoring her? Or was he so entranced in the island he had built for himself that there was no room for a life-size visitor, who would seem, no doubt, like a giant come to wreck his perfect world?

☼

The conference, as Sven had predicted, was poorly attended. It had rained earlier that day—unusual for October—and the three semicir-cular rows of chairs Isabel Nosticio had arranged were slick with wa-ter, the tablecloths on the sandwich tables were drenched, and the white sheet for the slide projections lay soiled on the ground. Everyone was in good spirits, though, having shared two bottles of pisco sour by the *caleta* beforehand, watching the fishing boats come in. They walked with linked arms along the coast to the conference area, exchanging anecdotes about other symposiums. Sven claimed to have once per-formed the Heimlich on a colleague in the middle of a presentation; Vicente had at one event met three other linguists who'd also made balloon voyages over the Andes. Greer couldn't help but wonder what they would make of her dissertation committee story. As she'd been getting ready in her room at the *residencial* earlier that day, she realized the SAAS conference would be her first public presentation since Wisconsin. Looking at herself in the mirror, she tried to catch some glimpse of that younger woman who had been so fearless and so trusting, a version of herself she could hardly remember.

As they arrived at the site, the wet wreckage of their outdoor conference room brought laughter from all of them, including Isabel, who, when she saw the size of the audience, was beginning to realize the hopelessness of the event.

They took their seats, and Vicente, as planned, went first. He wore a white dress shirt and brown tie, carried a stylish briefcase, and as he stepped to the torchlit podium he looked, Greer thought, almost like an actor, like someone accustomed to attention.

Vicente began with the formalities, in Spanish and English: thanks to the Sociedad, to Isabel, to his sponsors, his colleagues. "Test. Test." Vicente tapped the microphone and smiled. "Can everybody hear in the back?" There were only about fifteen people there, mostly friends, plus a few tourists who'd passed them earlier at the *caleta*. "Way in the back? Row Z, are you with us?" Everyone laughed, even Isabel. "Excellent," he said. "As we all know, ontogeny recapitulates phylogeny. The embryo evolves in the same pattern as life itself. And the same is true in the evolution of the human race." He went on to say that mankind's major turning points—the discovery of fire, the beginning of burials, the cave paintings, and the invention of written language—were all mirrored in personal development. For each individual, he said, there was a moment of discovering fire—a talent, a passion, or a love—and then a moment of learning to bury the past, and then to represent, and to record feelings about the world through writing. He finally stepped back from the podium and said: "The *rongorongo* is a perfect example of how society invents a way to protect its stories."

A clap came from behind the seats and Greer turned to see Mahina in a purple dress. She had let her hair down from its usual bun, and it fanned out in waves over her bare shoulders. Greer beckoned to her, and Mahina waded through the chairs, offering a brief greeting to everyone she passed. She checked that the chair was dry and sat beside Greer.

Sven then strode up to the podium and pitched a torch beside him. He wore blue jeans and a faded yellow T-shirt, carried no notes or cards. He offered a special thank-you to Isabel, then spoke briefly of the geological status of the volcanoes and weather patterns, alluded to his need for satellite data, his abundant supply of ballpoint pens, and thumped both palms against the podium and said, "This is boring the hell out of me." As he sat down, Isabel's high-pitched laugh sprang into the night.

Next, Burke-Jones began what was his most animated display since Greer had met him. He had put on a fresh suit, and the light revealed distinct comb-tracks across his hair. According to island legend, he said, the finished *moai* had walked from the quarry to the coast, a distance, in places, as great as six miles. Since volcanic tuff bruised easily, and since no scrapes appeared on the statues' backs or fronts, the *moai* must have been transported upright. Ropes, Burke-Jones hypothesized, had been lashed around the statues' necks to "shimmy" them to the island's periphery. Then he made his final announcement: He would simulate this in exactly one month. His eyes were full of life as he spoke. He said he hoped the people of Rapa Nui would join him in his investigation of their ancestors' feats.

Greer went last, stepping into her leather sandals that she had let rest in the grass, her pisco buzz now gone. Since her data were still incomplete her talk would be brief. The past few weeks she had been preparing samples, centrifuging, counting the known grains and unknown grains—doing the work it had once taken a team of lab assistants to do. She had ordered pollen books on Polynesia and herbarium samples from Kew, which still hadn't arrived. It would be another month, at least, before she had any comprehensive numbers on the island's former biota.

When she arrived at the podium, she, too, thanked SAAS and Isabel. She thanked her colleagues, and offered a special thank-you to Mahina Huke Tima, whose face registered a sudden burst of pride. The acknowledgment also brought a clapping from the darkness—Ramon stood behind the chairs, watching, not the podium, but Mahina.

Greer opened her folder, and began. "One of the first things that was understood about evolution, about the theory of organisms maturing and changing, was that isolation was key. For significant change to occur, an organism needs to be on its own, separated, so to speak, from its parents. Islands have long been the ideal studies of isolation, and with Rapa Nui, we have an island so isolated geographically, so isolated in its human history, it is, in essence, a perfect test tube for examining patterns of speciation, migration, and evolution. In particular, the island is unique in its utter deficiency of natural resources . . ."

A disapproving silence had fallen over the crowd. Greer looked up to see a frowning Isabel, clipboard held to her chest. What Greer was saying clearly didn't sound very pro–Rapa Nui. She was telling them their island was worse than half-empty. It was completely empty.

"But this deficiency couldn't be more meaningful. More *perfect.*"

She proceeded with the coring details, hoping to bury her negative remarks in a catalogue of numbers. *The ratio of Gramineae to Filices in the base core layer to 26,000 years* B.P. . . . *Forty-three percentage herbs and Pteridophyta at six meters in the primary borehole.* When she at last looked up from her paper, Mahina smiled, but then broke into a yawn. Vicente was rubbing his eyes. Greer thanked them all for their time, their attention, and gathered her things.

"You are an honest woman, Greer" came Vicente's voice behind her. "You said coring was a slow and boring process, and you spoke the truth."

"I think you missed some sleep in the corner of your eye, Vicente."

"It is not my fault. I have a medical condition. When I am bombarded by numbers and statistics, my brain becomes overworked and needs to rest itself."

"Ha-ha."

"I was diagnosed at a cryptography conference when someone gave a five-hour talk on the relationship between prime numbers and cuneiform. Saved by sleep."

"Well, Burke-Jones was very inspiring. I had a tough act to follow."

"Yes, he was excellent, I thought."

They both turned and looked for him, but he'd already left. People were milling about the chairs. Mahina was by the snack table, holding what looked like a potato chip up to the light. Ramon whispered in her ear, and Mahina laughed.

"Your proprietress is having a good time," Vicente said.

"He likes her."

"Ah, Ramon. Since I first came here I could see he was in love with her."

"They seem good together. I was going to encourage her. But I try not to endorse infidelity."

"He's not married."

"No, I mean Mahina. Her husband's away."

Vicente shook his head with dismay. "In . . . Tahiti?"

"Yes."

"Poor, dear Mahina."

"Why?"

"I told you that in the fifties and sixties, when Chile forbade the islanders to leave, men stole boats, built rafts, and tried to sail to Tahiti. Mahina's husband was one of them. Lost at sea."

"But that's over ten years ago. God, she can't really think he's coming back."

"Who knows? But she won't look at another man. Several have tried. And she is quite an attractive woman. It's a shame."

Greer looked over at Mahina. Her hands were clasped behind her back, and Ramon leaned into her. The purple dress brought out a deep flush in her cheeks, and a smile lit her face. Vicente was right— an attractive woman.

"Poor Mahina," said Greer.

A few people began to leave. Two teenagers—Claudio and César—whom Isabel had hired for the evening, began folding the chairs. Isabel and Sven were sitting side by side, their knees touching.

"I guess I should get back," said Greer. "I've got a lot to do tomorrow."

"More counting pollen?"

"What else?"

"Walk with me." Vicente took her hand. "You cannot keep clinging to these foolish American habits of independence."

"It's what my nation was built on. Think of it as my form of patriotism."

"Come, Greer. You must let me at least walk you to the *residencial*. I know my way there very well. Too well, perhaps."

Greer looked at him, his face soft and generous in the moonlight. She wanted him to walk her home, but it would be harder to say good-bye there. "Another night, Vicente. A rain check."

"A rain check? For when the weather is better? I warn you, Greer, summer is upon us."

"Ah, yes. The dry season. I think I can handle that."

"It's funny, I know everything about your research, your acid washes, your pollen counts. I know when you like to work, what you like to eat, to drink. Months we've been here, learning all these little things about each other, but I would like to know the other things."

"Little things are important."

"But I would like to know what your life is like outside of your work. Is that so very awful to ask?"

She had never seen him so sincere. "No, it's not at all awful to ask. But sometimes it's hard to answer."

"It is the way with all the important questions, no?"

"You're right," she said. She gave him a kiss on the cheek. "I'll work on an answer."

And with that she left him.

Greer woke early the next morning to a loud knocking. She pulled herself out of bed and opened the door to Mahina, who announced an urgent visit from Vicente. (Mahina forbade men from approaching the doors of women guests.) The previous night's revelation about Mahina's husband came fuzzily to mind as Greer threw on her robe and followed her through the courtyard into the main room.

There was Vicente, in blue jeans and a white T-shirt. He was waving a piece of paper in the air. He looked buoyant.

"What? No hangover?" Greer asked.

"One of my many talents: pisco tolerance." He handed her the paper. "Not the original, of course. A translation. But direct from the German archives. You see?"

Urgent. Precious cargo onboard. No chance for return. Need safe harbor for drop-off. Cargo cannot remain on ship.

It was a telegram from von Spee's ship, the *Scharnhorst*, dated 22 October 1914. Greer's mind twisted its way through the calculation. "Two days after they left the island?"

Vicente nodded, clearly trying to contain his excitement.

"This is really something. Is there a reply?"

"If there was, it went down with the ship. But there may be another telegram from von Spee. About the 'cargo.' It should arrive soon."

"Oh, Vicente!"

He smiled. "I know," he said. "I know."

And behind him Mahina rested her hands on her hips and tilted her head. "*Doctora*, your *colleague* has brought you another something?"

21

There are eight ships approaching the island. Five appear to be warships, black smoke belching from their cylinders. Three smaller vessels trail behind. From the cliff's edge, Edward and Elsa watch the procession in disbelief. No ship has approached the island since their own arrival. And now eight. Unease creeps through Elsa as the boats steam past Anakena, toward the island's eastern coast.

"They can't actually intend to anchor here," says Edward.

Elsa shrugs.

"Of all things," he says. "Well, we must greet them. They're likely a European fleet. Perhaps British. They may have mail. Or at the very least newspapers."

"German," says Elsa.

"German. British. Japanese. So long as they have newspapers."

German. That's what disturbs her.

Edward heads inland. "I should get off a letter to the Royal Geographical Society. Summarize our work . . . And you should write one about the tablets. Whet their appetites back home. If we send them with the ships, we could catch replies with the Chilean Company boat. Elsa, are you all right?"

Elsa, whose gaze has not left the horizon, turns, finally, and traces Edward's path through the grass.

Edward is by the ponies. "I can't imagine they'll want to stay long." He loosens his pony's rope from the post and mounts the animal. "Well?"

Elsa looks up at him. "Alice?" She has not seen Alice since the day before.

"Asleep."

"But if she wakes . . . I should stay with her." As if on a gust of wind, their argument returns. *Imbecile*—the word leaps into Elsa's mind.

"You don't mind?" he asks.

"Just find out who they are and return soon."

Edward gallops off, and Elsa sits in the grass beside Alice's tent. She closes her eyes, trying to calm her mind. But the warships. She cannot stop thinking of them. What if the fleet is German?

Elsa soon pulls herself up, brushes the sand from her skirt, and wades through the gauzy cloud of netting. Alice is asleep on her cot, her body curled fetal-style. Beside her, Pudding preens in his cage. Alice's hair, having dried from the rain, falls in thick tangles around her face. Elsa lies down beside the cot, listening to the gurgling of Alice as she dreams, and the sound is so gentle, so childlike, Elsa reaches out her hand and strokes Alice's arm. But when Alice stirs, Elsa quickly withdraws. She fears Alice waking up, her anger rekindled. Afraid of Alice—the thought sends a shudder through Elsa. Everything with Alice will now be different. Elsa will have to accept that. And as she thinks this, she feels as though the edges of her being are fraying, as though something has taken hold of her vital thread and is tugging steadily and she can only watch as stitch by stitch she comes undone.

The whinnying of a pony awakens her, and she rises in the gray light of the afternoon. Alice, on the cot beside her, is still sleeping.

"Elsa!" Edward is calling. "Elsa dear, we have visitors."

She kneads her face into alertness. Easing her head outside the tent, she can see on the hill above the beach a dozen figures on horseback. A galaxy of brass buttons on navy blue. She offers a wave.

"You were right, dear! Germans." Edward's voice again. His lecture-hall voice. "They've come to provision, and do a little sight-seeing. I've been telling the admiral what we're doing here and he's most interested in your work on the tablets. I told him you'd be happy to show him one."

"Now?" she shouts. Her tone is rude, but she cannot subdue her panic.

"The admiral was rather hoping to see one today. They've been at sea for quite some time. Starved for stimulus, I imagine." Edward mumbles something to the half-circle of figures and brief, gruff laughter erupts on the hill.

"I insisted."The voice, accent-laced and familiar, addresses her.

She looks up again at the row of figures, but she cannot discern faces beneath the gold-ribboned hats. She will have to make her way up there. Her heart now hammering in her chest, she steps inside her tent, grabs the *kohau* she took to Kasimiro, and stumbles up the hill. In the center of the half-circle, his hat suspending a thick band of gold, is the admiral.

"You've brought a *kohau*,"says Edward."Splendid."

Elsa unwraps the tablet and extends it like a rifle at the admiral. His lips maintain an unflinching line, an effort at gravity, betrayed only by his silvery mustache, whose edges, curling upward, suggest amusement. Elsa asks,"*Was machst du hier?*"

He turns to Edward."The lady speaks German."

"Elsa is fluent," says Edward. Trying to ease the awkwardness, he dismounts and gently pries the *kohau* from Elsa's hands. "You see, Admiral, each *kohau* is carved with a variety of figures. Look. Just here? Some are in the shape of birds, and here—animals. Some are mere squiggles. But Elsa has already catalogued over two thousand characters."

"Your wife is an industrious woman."

"She's made an extensive study of the Rapa Nui language and the *rongorongo*. She's quite close to making a translation."

"And what do these tablets say, Frau Beazley?"

Elsa cannot find words with which to answer.

"We think"—Edward interjects—"they record the island's history. This one, for instance, we have reason to believe explains the moving of the *moai*."

"It could not be, then, a communication of some sort? Like a letter announcing an occasion? A marriage?"

Elsa shakes her head. She won't accept what she is hearing.

"Or a journey?"

"You see, Admiral, our research among the Rapa Nui—and Elsa has interviewed scores—strongly indicates that the tablets record the island's history and mythology. They were composed by special scribes schooled in the script. They were not, therefore, used by the common people for communication. She intends on getting a key, as well."

"Fine. *Gut,*"says the admiral."Now"—he searches his officers—"I would like to ask Frau Beazley if she would accompany us briefly to the town. To assist in some transactions. To translate. Provisions for the men."

Edward turns to her. "It will be dark in a few hours."

"We shall have her escorted directly back, I assure you."

"Dear?"

Elsa looks from Edward to the admiral and back again. The sight of the two men beside each other seems impossible.

"Fine," she says. "Provisions."

"Only if you feel up to it," cautions Edward. "We've had a very long day, you see," he explains to the Germans.

"I'll go," she says. "Check on Alice."

"Of course." He passes Elsa the reins of his pony. "You're sure?" Elsa nods. As she draws up beside him, he whispers, "See if you can't get us a newspaper. He claims they have none, but maybe if *you* ask." She mounts the animal.

"We shall have her back shortly," says the admiral, his boot flickering a kick to his horse's flank.

Elsa keeps her head down as her horse trots ahead of the men, stirring the red dust along the coastal path. Suddenly she wants to race far ahead, to flee.

"Reitet hier weg!" a voice commands behind her, and the sound of all the hooves comes to an abrupt stop. The silence is broken by the sound of one horse, walking slowly toward her. Only when he is beside her does the final eddy of her confusion erupt in one breathless question.

"Max?"

He reaches out and takes her hand. *"Mein Liebling."*

22

By late October, Greer had taken and examined all her cores. She'd sent off her sediment samples for radiocarbon dating to establish the island's ecological timeline. A copy of Selling's *Studies in Hawaiian Pollen Statistics* had finally arrived, along with herbarium samples from Kew that would help her, for the next month, identify the unknown pollen grains.

Vicente and Sven were helping Burke-Jones excavate a *moai* at the quarry—in preparation for his experiment they had to loosen ground beneath the statue—and Greer worked alone in the SAAS building. The hours passed quietly as she pulled her stool between the two microscopes on the lab's long worktables. She had devised an angled platform for her microscope so she didn't strain her neck, and on long days she wore a thin brace. At noon, Mahina brought her lunch, and Greer would sometimes show her the pollen. Mahina had a good eye for the subtle differences—she could spot a small indentation in the exine immediately—and liked to compare what she saw in the microscope to the pictures in the pollen guide.

Occasionally, when they took a break from their work at the quarry, Vicente would stop by to say hello, or Sven would burst in with a joke: "So how are the *Pollen Esians* today?" Sometimes, at night, while waiting for her centrifuge, Greer would stroll down the hall to Burke-Jones's lab, where he retreated at the day's end to fine-tune his miniature worlds.

Greer suspected that her emerging picture of the island's early flora could help him. At the middle levels of her cores, she had found pollen of the *Triumfetta semitriloba,* the tree widespread across the Pacific that was used to make rope. If ropes had moved the statues, she told Burke-Jones, they probably would have been made from the bark of this plant.

"It still grows in Tahiti," she said from the doorway of his lab. He was uneasy with visitors, so Greer never crossed the threshold. "We could have some sent. I'm sure you could get SAAS to pitch in. Talk to Isabel."

He pushed his chair back and surveyed his dioramas. "I do think they used something soft, something fibrous."

"Well, let's get some shipped, then. And we can all help with the weaving. How much do you need?"

Burke-Jones stared straight ahead, as though reading calculations in the air. "One hundred and seventy-eight yards."

"Let's say two hundred."

"Twenty-two yards will go to waste."

"We'll find a use for them. If worse comes to worst, we'll make a *semitriloba* hammock for future SAAS researchers. Shall I write the forest service on Tahiti?"

"I'd like the simulation to be as accurate as possible."

"Then let's have genuine *semitriloba* rope."

He turned to her with a small smile. "That is something to be happy about."

"It certainly is, Randolph."

Other plants as well were emerging from the island's past.

Pollen from the *Sophora toromiro* tree, similar to a Japanese pagoda tree, appeared in cores from all three craters. The *Sophora* genus was known for its bell-shaped calyxes, white and yellow flowers, pinnate leaves. The *Sophora toromiro* was undoubtedly the small tree noted by Captain Cook: *Only two or three shrubs were seen. The leaf and seed of one (called by the natives Torromedo) were not much unlike those of common vetch . . .* The *toromiro*, then, had outlived all its botanical peers.

Other pollen types appeared only in the cores' upper levels: pollen almost identical to *Broussonetia papyrifera*, the mulberry trees whose bark fibers were used to make paper, and like the mulberry used throughout Polynesia for making tapa cloth. Again, Cook had observed: *in several places the Otaheitean cloth plant, but it was poor and weak, and not above two and a half feet at most . . .* The mulberry's pollen, however, was absent from the lowest sediment levels, suggesting it had arrived with the first settlers.

At the lowest levels, the pollen record shifted drastically. Here were spores of at least ten different Pteridophtya, including the expected ferns.

Most interesting, though, was an unknown pollen type clogging the bottom of the cores—oblong grains with a large depression bisecting the center. Whatever this angiosperm was, it had once blanketed the island and had been extinct for several hundred years, the pollen beginning to thin out just as the paper mulberry appeared. Greer would have to send a sample to Kew to see if they had anything similar—but the chances were slim. If this plant had been on the island for thousands of years, it was so far removed from its ancestors that its genealogy would be hard to trace.

And still, the question of wood lingered. Roggeveen and Cook had mentioned canoes with long planks—but neither the *Sophora toromiro* nor paper mulberry trunks could suffice for boat building. Was the pollen at the lowest levels from a large heavy-wood tree?

The Frenchman Jean-François de Galaup, Comte de La Pérouse, visiting the island in 1786, also made note of the canoes:

> They are composed only of very narrow planks, four or five feet long, and at most can carry but four men. I have seen three of them in this part of the island, and I should not be much surprised, if in a short time, for want of wood, there should not be a single one remaining here . . .
>
> The exactness with which they measured the ship showed that they had not been inattentive spectators of our arts; they examined our cables, anchors, compass, and wheel, and they returned the next day with a cord to take the measure over again . . .

Monsieur de Langle, La Pérouse's companion, who made his way inland, observed shrubs of paper mulberry and mimosa, remarking that only one tenth of the island was cultivated, the rest covered with coarse grass. The only birds sighted by Monsieur de Langle were terns at the bottom of the crater. The statues seen through his telescopes had all fallen. None of this, thought Greer, differed from previous travelogues.

What struck her, however, was that Langle and La Pérouse both assumed the island had once hosted different vegetation. Langle estimated the island's human population at two thousand and added: *There is reason to think that the population was more considerable when the island was better wooded.* La Pérouse even accused the Rapa Nui of deforestation. He complained of the lava rocks strewn across the land, explaining:

> . . . these stones, which we found so troublesome in walking, are of great use, by contributing to the freshness and moisture of the ground, and partly supply the want of salutary shade of the trees which the inhabitants were so imprudent as to cut down, in times, no doubt, very remote, by which their country lies fully exposed to the rays of the sun, and is destitute of running springs and streams . . .
> . . . M. de Langle and myself had no doubt that this people owed the misfortune of their situation to the imprudence of their ancestors . . .

Greer was reading this one evening in the main room of the *residencial* when Mahina came in.

"*Iorana, Doctora!*" She cradled several cans of peaches. "Look. *Peti.*" She set the cans, one at a time, on the edge of her desk. "Ramon give us *peti.*"

"*Iorana,* Mahina."

She glanced down at Greer's book. "The *doctora* always work."

"I know. Another European travelogue of Easter Island. Do you know about any tree stories in the island legends? Trees that once grew here? When Hotu Matua came?"

"I've already told you the story of Hau Maka, and of the dream soul who flew toward the sun and found the most beautiful island."

"In that story, were there trees?"

"There was everything." She sat behind her desk. "The fish and the fruit and the flowers. The dream soul sees everything she desires."

"La Pérouse says that the islanders cut trees down. And I've found a strange pollen type in my cores, at the lowest level, and I'm wondering if there's anything in the oral tradition about trees."

"There is one story I heard as a child, but it is only legend, as you say. It is not for your science."

"Try me."

"Well, it is the story of how the big tree came to be. There was a woman, Sina, who loved the man Tuna, but she could not have him. Forbidden. She had many other men, suitors, you say, and the suitors came together to capture Tuna in a big net. The night before they kill him, Sina came to see him, to say *iorana,* and Tuna says the next morning she must plant his head in the ground and it will grow a large tree that will remind her of him."

Greer wrote this down, and Mahina examined it to make sure it followed her account. It was the same motif that appeared in every mythology—the tree-spirit, the Maypole, tales of death and regeneration, sacrifice and growth. Human life was always bound to plant life. In Australia and the Philippines, trees were thought to hold the spirits of dead ancestors. The Russian Kostrubonku and Indian Kangara held funerals for dead vegetation. According to Norse myth, Odin created the first man and woman from two logs he found by the shore.

These stories tried to explain the world, to make sense of the wilderness that surrounded primitive people. Why tell a story of a large tree when none grew?

"It is make-believe," said Mahina.

"Vegetation myth," said Greer. "But useful."

"Myth," repeated Mahina. "Because we have no big trees here." She walked over to Greer and examined the first few pages of the book. "La Pérouse. Yes, it is good."

"A lot of pages wasted complaining of stolen hats."

"Hats?"

"*Hau*," said Greer, pointing to her head. "Every travel account so far describes an almost obsessive theft of hats. The islanders seemed to like them."

Mahina pondered this for a moment.

"Maybe," she said, "they need the shade."

☼

It was the first week of November, summer, but gray clouds hung overhead all morning. The crowd stared expectantly at the sky, hoping that if it rained, it would at least begin soon, before they rolled back their sleeves, wrapped their hands around the fibrous rope, and began dragging the *moai* down the hill.

Burke-Jones, dressed in safari gear, stood over a diorama on the hood of his Jeep. He had assigned each small figure a number correlating to one of the fifty life-size humans awaiting his instructions.

There was a great excitement in the air; Greer could feel it. For the past week everybody had been talking about this day. Burke-Jones's announcement at the conference had, in fact, catalyzed the island. Almost one hundred islanders were now milling about the grassy slopes of Rano Raraku, the *moai* quarry, waiting to see how their ancestors had done it. For Burke-Jones, for Vicente, even for Greer, this was a scientific experiment. But for the Rapa Nui this was not a fact to be filed away, this was their heritage, the epic of their ancestors.

The logistics, however, were daunting. The fifty volunteers first had to stand in a long line that snaked through dozens of fallen *moai* as Burke-Jones handed each one a numbered placard on a necklace of string. He then called people over in groups of five, and showed them on his diorama where to stand. When her group was called, Greer was surprised to see that Burke-Jones had included himself— a small toothpick figure beside a red matchbox Jeep in exactly the position he was standing. She was relieved to know there were researchers more obsessive than she was. He had assigned each group a team leader—toothpicks with red tips. Theirs was Sven.

"Oh, no," said Vicente, sporting a number "34" placard over his tan shirt. He had rolled up the sleeves, and was wearing khaki shorts rather than his usual pants.

"It's about time I got some respect," said Sven.

"There is always room for a coup." Vicente winked. "It's in my blood."

Burke-Jones looked up from the diorama. "Pay very close attention to where you are supposed to stand." He pointed to a row of toothpick figures. "Team two takes up the middle row on the statue's northern side."

Sven turned to Greer and Vicente. "I've been informed that team two will take up position on the statue's—"

"It's hot, Sven," Greer said.

"You see how my subordinates speak to me?" Sven asked Burke-Jones.

"What we won't put ourselves through for science," sighed Vicente.

Burke-Jones stared fixedly at his diorama. "You have your assignments," he said. "Team three!"

"Good luck, Randolph," Greer said.

"Promptly, please!"

The volunteers were clearly put out by this rigid show of authority. Teams three and four walked away from the Jeep disgruntled, and Sven eventually gave up on his own game, threw his arm around Burke-Jones, and said: "No society, no matter how advanced, could have been as organized as you. Let's get started with the shimmying." But Burke-Jones would not be swayed from his agenda.

It took over an hour, but soon everyone had a number, knew

where to stand, and had been assigned a group leader. Vicente, who had brought a camera, took shots of Burke-Jones as he delegated and pointed and examined his diorama, and as he then compared it, with a look of amazement, to the scene before him. It was remarkable, thought Greer: on one hillside, three orders of magnitude. The tooth-pick people, the life-size volunteers, and above them, on the crater, flat on its back, a twenty-foot stone giant to be hauled down the hill to loom above everything.

As things were about to start, Vicente turned his camera over to Mahina, asking her to document the experiment. She stood off to the side with dozens of islanders, the older and meeker who had come to watch. Greer was one of only two women who would be pulling, and she had had to fight Burke-Jones for the chance. He wanted to repli-cate the historic conditions, and it was a near certainty women hadn't helped move the *moai.* Vicente finally persuaded him she couldn't hinder the results. He had pointed to Sven across the dinner table: "Let's face it. They certainly didn't have Swedes to help, or British ar-chitects to coordinate."

Isabel, who had stayed on for the experiment, stood by Mahina in pink culottes and white tennis shoes, her arms crossed. Every few minutes she dipped her head, inched her sunglasses down the bridge of her nose, scanned the volunteers, Sven in particular, and then tapped her glasses back into place.

"Positions!" called Burke-Jones, and the crowd approached the supine statue. A web of ropes, handmade from the *Triumfetta semi-triloba* trees flown in from Tahiti, had been lashed around its neck. For the past several nights, Greer and Sven and Vicente had gathered at the Residencial Ao Popohanga, where Mahina taught them and several of her friends to weave the fibers. They had made over two hundred yards of rope, which now hung in loose lines about the statue like locks of hair.

Burke-Jones blew his whistle three times, and everyone crouched and lifted their ropes, tentacles coming to life. Greer sunk her feet deep into the grass, bent her legs, and prepared herself. Vicente was in front of her, Sven in front of him. The whistle blew—two long, one short—and all the teams heaved. Greer's face flooded with the heat of exertion. Her palms burned around the rough fibers of the rope. She shifted her weight from leg to leg, but no matter her position, every muscle rebelled. All sorts of sounds began springing up. Grunts, moans, a distinct *Mi madre.* Someone on the statue's other side cursed Burke-Jones. Finally the whistle blew, and all of them, dizzied and hot, let the ropes drop and collapsed in the grass.

Several women from the audience waved canteens at the volunteers. Vicente and Greer sipped from their own.

"This will be a long day, I think."

Disappointment had already set in among the volunteers. They drank their water, wiped their foreheads, leaned against the statue. Greer carefully stretched her neck, which was now bothering her for the first time in over a year.

Again came the whistle. They lifted their ropes. Burke-Jones blew again. Greer could feel the furnace of her muscles burning, the skin on her hands chafing against the coarse rope. Again the quit whistle. Nothing.

Burke-Jones had clearly anticipated this. Three of the team leaders were summoned, and a project of collecting stones began. Within an hour a pile of rocks had been wedged beneath the *moai*'s head—this might raise the statue enough to get some leverage on the ropes. While the rocks were set in place, the sun reached its full height. Volunteers tied scarves and bandanas over their heads, doused their necks with canteen water. Only a slight breeze rolled off the ocean. When Greer looked toward the coast, she saw Luka Tepano on his horse at the bottom of the hill. He was studying the motions of the volunteers, the ropes being tested, the stones being rolled. This was a good distance from the woman's cave, and it seemed he'd come simply to watch. He appeared transfixed, but when Greer looked a few minutes later, he was gone.

A team of volunteers flanked the head, seated so their feet could further wedge the stones beneath the *moai* as it was pulled. Again, the whistle blew; this time Burke-Jones had ordered a rocking motion, in the hopes that the simultaneous force of all fifty people would help. *Uno. Dos. Tres. Hee-yaa! Etahi. Erua. Etoru. Hee-yaa!* Then on the opposite side shouts exploded, and the whistle spluttered, the sound of a referee madly calling a time-out. Everyone released their ropes. With Vicente and Sven in tow, Greer ran to the other side: Team number three, five panting men, were heaped on top of a very disgruntled team four. One of the ropes had snapped.

Burke-Jones called a lunch break while he examined the torn rope and made adjustments on his diorama. Mahina had come down the hill to sit with Greer and Vicente, and Isabel stretched out her legs in the grass. They all shielded their eyes from the sun.

"These ropes aren't strong enough," said Vicente. "Perhaps if they were thicker."

"Let's hope it's the ropes," said Sven, "because I don't want to think we're not strong enough."

Vicente sighed. "Poor Burke-Jones. He has been planning this for months."

"Well, Burke-Jones will get the job done," said Sven. "I have faith in the man. He has plans A through Z filed away in his mind. We may be here all day, all week, but he'll get it done."

"Now we can appreciate how hard a task it was to move these things," said Vicente.

Greer was thinking of the tree legend Mahina had told her. She'd been reading further and had found a similar myth from other Polynesian islands—the myth of the coconut palm. Of course, there hadn't been a trace of coconut palm pollen in any of her cores. The unknown pollen was still unidentified—neither Kew nor the Swedish Museum of Natural History was able to name it. They both suggested she send a sample to Strasbourg, France, where a new International Laboratory of Pollen Sciences had just been established, staffed with the best pollen-typing experts from around the world. She'd done just that and crossed her fingers. Whatever it was, the species was endemic to the island, and so far removed from any parent plant, it had lost all traces of its inheritance. But what if it were some sort of palm? A large tree used for construction, strong enough to move the *moai*? Ropes and stones clearly weren't sufficient, a thought that had apparently occurred to Burke-Jones as well, who was now distributing five-foot gnarled planks from specially flown-in Japanese pagoda trees—the closest match to the *toromiro* tree that had once covered the island.

Planks in hand, their numbered placards flipping in the wind, the volunteers looked like a group of marathoners preparing to riot. They dragged their wedges up the grassy hill and reassembled around the statue. Greer doubted this would work—pagoda wood wasn't very sturdy, and the planks were too short to be of much use. What were needed were planks as long as the statue, fifteen to twenty feet, that could slide the statue on its back.

The whistle blew. Half the volunteers were still pulling ropes, team three was still wedging stones, but now two teams were shoving planks beneath the *moai*'s head, trying to use the wood as levers. Then came a crackling as one by one the planks snapped, and then another rope was torn in half. Burke-Jones sounded the whistle, defeated.

Greer sat to catch her breath. Some of the spectators had already left, like fans heading home when their team's score is too low for hope. Mahina, though, remained, taking pictures of volunteers collapsed in the grass. Greer looked at her watch—almost four—and knew that soon Burke-Jones would have to call it a day.

Greer, weary, glanced toward the coastal path where the Jeeps were parked and the horses tethered, and there was Luka Tepano again. This time the woman from the cave was seated behind him on his horse, holding one hand up to shield her eyes from the sun. They slowly approached the site, but stopped at a distance of about forty yards, staring at the scaffolding. Sven, deep in conversation with Isabel, who was dabbing his forehead with a lace handkerchief, didn't notice them. Only Greer seemed aware of their presence, and lifted her hand to wave.

"How many strikes until you're out?" Sven was asking.

"The last time is the luckiest, no?" asked Vicente.

"Forty-eight men, two women, a hell of a lot of rocks, and trees. How many trees did he get, Greer?"

"Ten pagoda," she said, pulled back to the group. "And fifteen *semitriloba* for the rope."

"Twenty-five trees," said Sven. "You can't accuse the man of not trying."

"Poor Burke-Jones," sighed Greer, watching him rearrange his diorama, "soon we're actually going to have to try moving this thing with toothpicks and dental floss. We've nothing else left."

"We have our effort," said Vicente. "And our spirit."

They took their positions once again, now on the *moai*'s other side—Burke-Jones had shuffled everyone around, as though simple rearrangement might offset the ineptitude of their tools. Greer noticed Luka and the old woman were still watching. The whistle blew, the last fragments of pagoda wood were jabbed into the ground, the ropes were held like lifelines, the rocks rolled. Curses flew through the air as the volunteers, on this last attempt, gave their all. But when the quit whistle finally sounded, Greer dropped the rope and stepped back from the *moai* with enormous relief. A silence descended on the scene; the crowd looked to Burke-Jones, whose face, fixed on the statue, was expressionless.

"I think he's going to want the whole bucket of pisco tonight," said Sven.

"He looks ill," said Vicente. They all three wiped the sweat from their faces, and stumbled toward the Jeep.

"Let's call it a day," said Sven, patting Burke-Jones's back.

"Randolph," said Vicente, "you've done a great thing here. We must always test our hypotheses, and follow the answers wherever they lead us."

"I see an ice-cold pisco sour in your hand, my friend."

Burke-Jones's mouth hung open for a moment, then closed. It was as though after six hours of unprecedented activity, he had spent himself. He had, it seemed, nothing left to say.

"Randolph," began Greer, "I think what we saw here today might be related to something else I'm seeing in my cores—"

Burke-Jones nodded slowly, then climbed into the Jeep, started the engine, and drove off. The diorama, which had been resting on the hood, flew into the air and fell to the grass, the matchbox Jeep landing exactly where the actual Jeep had sat, the small toothpick figures scattering in the wind.

When Greer returned to the *residencial* that night, there was a letter from the International Laboratory of Pollen Sciences in Strasbourg waiting beneath her door. She tore open the small envelope. The letter was handwritten:

> *Jesus! I don't have a thing here that resembles that little critter you sent me, but I would bet my ass it's a palm species. Call it an informed hunch. You'll need some proof though, verification (all good scientists do, don't they?). Maybe look for macrofossils. Fossilized leaves, bark, nuts.*
>
> *Easter Island!—I feared you'd dropped off the face of the earth (forwarding address with the p.o. next time? or a phone number? Do they even have phones there?). When I heard about Thomas I tried to get hold of you. Looks like somebody didn't want to be gotten hold of. They should let you run the Witness Protection program! Anyway, I ought to offer my condolences.*
>
> *If you're ever passing through Strasbourg you must come say hi. The pâté is divine, the wine, primo. No scuba diving here, but I*

gave that up anyway 'cause I slipped a disc. I smoke, I don't know, about five packs a day. I'm happy.

I've thought of you often, you know. Please visit.

> *All good wishes,*
> *Josephine (French pals insist—I kind of like it now)*
> *Banks*

P.S. You should think of going by Dr. Sandor. When I saw Dr. Farraday on the analysis request form, I nearly had a heart attack. Also, have you heard about the National Geo expedition to Surtsey in February? Right up your alley. They're looking for palynologists.

Greer sat on the bed and set the letter beside her. She tugged off her boots, peeled off her damp shirt, and looked again at the piece of paper. Jo. Greer thought she'd never hear from her again, that Jo had given up on her. Greer had never blamed her for this, knowing how hard it must have been for Jo to see her accused of plagiarism, humiliated in front of the whole department. Jo, who without a moment's doubt knew what Thomas had done and then had to watch Greer's stubborn denial. Jo must have known her accusation of Thomas would be suspect, that the simple act of defending a friend might seem the jealousy of a spurned lover. In the end, Jo had no choice but to let Greer figure it out on her own. She probably hadn't thought it would take Greer five years.

Greer looked at Jo's signature, the familiar handwriting. This unexpected hello should have made Greer happy, but sitting in the small room where she'd spent the past few months, she felt suddenly edgy. The note brought back too much, too suddenly. Jo, Thomas, the dissertation. Things she'd come here to get away from. That whole part of her life in Madison now seemed incomprehensible. Ever since Thomas's death, the question plagued her: How hadn't she seen it? Why hadn't she realized his betrayal? She was an intelligent woman; she'd graduated summa cum laude from college, had a Ph.D. in botany and palynology. Yet when the evidence was presented, she simply turned away.

Greer looked at the letter once more, folded it, and slid it back in its envelope. She could feel the ache in her limbs, but wouldn't be able to sleep now. She didn't want to lie in the bed whispering taxonomy to herself.

Instead, she changed clothes and went to find Burke-Jones.

The laboratory was dark. Vicente and Sven, worn out, had gone back to their hotels to sleep, and perhaps Burke-Jones, too, was back at the Espíritu. But his silence at the moment she'd last seen him made Greer think otherwise. She turned on the lights and peeked into his room. Everything was in order, but no sign of him. As she now stepped across the threshold, she saw, for the first time, the full scope of his constructed world. The long table against the far wall was just the beginning. Perpendicular to either side of the room, six small tables each displayed their own green papier-mâché islands, small *moai* enmeshed with dental floss and toothpicks. In some places the statues were propped up with piles of jellybeans. She ran her fingertips along one's head, the same grainy texture as the real statues—volcanic tuff. Had Burke-Jones paid a carver to make hundreds of *moai* the size of soda cans? Or had he carved them himself, as he'd so meticulously built everything else?

She walked through the labyrinth of alternate universes—the differences between each were subtle. In some the *moai* were only slightly more upright than in others, and then she realized: chronology. Here was the history of the island laid out on all the tables in the room. On the final table he had included the toppled *moai,* a barren landscape of fallen statues.

Greer flicked off the lights and went back outside. The air was cool now, the sky dark, and she made her way toward the village with her flashlight. She stopped into the Hotel Espíritu, and was told by a groggy Elian, the night watch, that Burke-Jones hadn't yet returned. Elian lifted an invisible glass to his mouth and swigged. "Señor Burke-Jones drink, I believe."

Greer left the hotel and cut toward the main street—no sign of him. Heading out of town she spotted his Jeep beside the road to the old leper colony. She followed the path to where the moon lit the semicircle of abandoned huts. She saw a figure seated beside one of them.

"Randolph?"

There was no response, but as she moved closer she saw that it wasn't Burke-Jones at all, but Luka Tepano.

He sat with his knees bent to his chest, his arms wrapped around his legs, and his hands folded atop his shoes. His chin was tucked, but he now looked up.

"I saw you by the *moai* today," she said. This was the first she'd spoken to him. "*Habla usted inglés?* I'm looking for a friend. The British engineer. The man who arranged the experiment."

He offered a half-smile, but Greer wasn't sure if he understood. He let his chin rest on his knees. He was old, his face deeply seamed but perfectly shaven. His thick hair was neatly parted, and despite the shabbiness of his clothes, he seemed well groomed. There was a quiet dignity to the way he sat. He was apparently lost in thought. If Burke-Jones had come this way, she doubted Luka Tepano had noticed him.

"*Iorana,*" she said, and made her way back toward the coast, continuing farther along the path, toward the cemetery—the same route she'd taken her first week on the island. There, among the scattered crosses, she saw him.

"Randolph, it's Greer. I've just come to see if you're all right."

She moved closer to the crosses, white against the black sky, daisies and nasturtiums scattered before them.

He was leaning against a headstone, his hands in his lap, serene. "Look." He tilted his head back. "One. Two. Three. Four. The Southern Cross."

Greer looked up at the blizzard of stars. "There are some advantages to having few streetlights," she said.

She sat down beside him. The cross before her read: *Te Haha Huke.* 1864–1922. Born in 1864, the year the missionaries arrived, long after the last *moai* had fallen.

"Listen, Randolph, there's something in my work that could be of help to you. Not just the *Triumfetta semitriloba* trees, but palm trees," she said. "There may have been some sort of palm tree on the island. I have fossil pollen from a plant that would have covered this whole island when the settlers arrived, but there's no known match. I suspect palm, a good researcher in Strasbourg suspects palm; but I don't know the exact species. There are an endless number of properties it could have displayed, so without knowing the species, it won't tell us much about island life. But there was more here than the *Sophora toromiro.* That I'm sure of."

"Fine."

"They had more than rope," she said. "Do you see what I'm getting at?"

He shifted toward her now, his face peaceful—she thought he was about to answer, but he pressed his mouth to hers. His lips were warm and dry and moved tenderly against hers. Greer could sense her body's curiosity at this forgotten intimacy.

"I'm sorry," he said, pulling away.

"It's all right, Randolph." She sat back against the headstone. It was her first kiss in almost a year, her first kiss with anyone but Thomas in a decade. She felt strange.

"Have you ever seen Lydia?" he asked. He slowly retrieved from his back pocket a wallet stuffed with small scraps of paper. Without a moment's search he extracted one small photograph, its edges worn; in the dark Greer could vaguely discern the face of a woman. "Lydia," he said.

"She's beautiful," said Greer, holding the picture before her as though the image were clear. "A beautiful woman."

"She once read about Easter Island. A book with pictures. And do you know what she said? She said, 'Randolph, I wonder how they moved those giant things.' " He took the photo back and slid it into the wallet. "Enough of that."

"Randolph," said Greer, standing. "You should go home and sleep." She held out her hands and he clasped them—he sprung from the ground, so much lighter than the statue she'd spent the day trying to budge.

They drove in silence back to Hanga Roa, leaving the Jeep in the street. At the Hotel Espíritu, Elian emerged with a grin, no doubt imagining Greer had found Burke-Jones dead drunk in the road. He rushed forward to catch his arm and guide him inside.

Greer then headed back toward Mahina's, past the other small hotels, the *residenciales;* she looked at the lines of light filtering through wooden shutters, and wondered if behind those windows were other people like Burke-Jones, who had come to this island in search of some impossible answer. At the sign for the Residencial Ao Popohanga, Greer turned left, toward the road that cut to the southern coast. It was almost ten, but she wasn't yet ready to go back to her room, to the letter, to a reminder of what she'd lost.

❀

When Thomas's fraud was exposed, he resigned his chair at Harvard, packed up his lab and his office, and moved everything to Marblehead. Through all of it he was silent, carrying his whole life—twenty years of notebooks stuffed with data, framed awards, press clippings, citations, a letter from Albert Einstein—in cardboard boxes, making lists of where they were going—attic, basement, office—as though to organize the confusion. Greer herself was still trying to grasp what had happened. He had forged his data. There was no Mags. Bruce had exposed him. But where had she been through all this? What was she doing married to a man who cared so little for science? Who cared so little for her that he had, she now realized, years earlier appropriated her equation for himself?

Greer knew she had to leave him. She just didn't know how.

"I don't expect you to stay with me," Thomas said one night.

Greer wanted to laugh—after years of her trying to meet his expectations, he expected nothing.

"I'm not leaving you because of the scandal," she said. "You know why I'm leaving." Her anger was too large to express.

"I know," he said.

He was sitting on the porch, an old Wisconsin notebook in his lap. He seemed strangely calm, as though nothing had happened, as though he owed no apologies.

"How come you never mentioned pollination by deceit?" she asked. "Those intro lectures. Strangler figs. Malay rafflesia. Wormwood. Why not include something about ghost flowers or sun orchids? Flowers that pretend to be something they're not. The mimics. So they can lure the bees."

"Lily, you've a right to be disappointed."

"I've a right to be fucking furious."

"It had nothing to do with you."

"That, Thomas, is the worst part."

Deciding to leave was one thing, arriving somewhere new was another. Greer wrote letters to other universities, inquiring about research positions; she applied for several grants. And then, while Greer was still trying to figure out where she wanted to be, Thomas had a heart attack. He died in the ambulance on the way to the hospital.

She hadn't asked him about the dissertation, but it was clear now he'd taken her equation. What she still couldn't understand, though, was why on earth she'd let him. For months this haunted her. While she packed up his things, arranged the funeral, and waded through the paperwork of insurance, she kept going back to that night in Madison when he returned from his conference and pulled out the champagne, wondering why she hadn't said to him: *You stole from me.*

But finally, after all these months on the island, after the confusion and exhaustion of her grief had settled, Greer now understood why she hadn't. She'd turned away from his betrayal to keep alive the idea of the man with whom she'd fallen in love, clinging to the illusion of him, of their shared past.

Love, Greer thought, or the memory of love, was single-minded in its will to survive, the fittest of all emotions.

Greer wasn't sure how far she'd gone along the path. She was tired, the day's effort lodged in her limbs. She wandered down to where the grass met the rocks, and stretched herself out. A cool breeze swept in from the ocean and she could see the sliver of an opening in the cliff below. So many cracks in this island, she thought, as though the whole place had once been carelessly dropped from a tremendous height.

Her eyes felt dry and heavy, tugging closed. Before her on the dark ground it seemed a miniature crab was moving toward her, its legs jointed and fast. It inched closer, glossy and black in the light of the moon, a flash of red beneath its belly.

"There you are," she mumbled as she felt herself drifting off to sleep.

23

On the rim of the Rano Raraku crater, Max tells Elsa about the war. News of the archduke's assassination and the Austro-Hungarian declaration of war reached him in China and for months his Tsingtao fleet has been trying to make its way back to Germany. Pagan, Ponape, Eniwetok, Majuro, Samoa, Tahiti, Christmas Island—they have already zigzagged through eight thousand miles of ocean. "Eight ships, steaming beneath a constant cloud of black smoke, wholly undetected by the Allied patrols," says Max, looking down into the crater at the scores of half-carved stone faces. At Fanning Island they blasted the cable station. On Bora Bora, they claimed to be French, flying French flags and painting over the ships' names. Max details each anchorage, each brush with danger. After being so long in the company of only his officers, he seems elated to speak freely, to express some small astonishment, and perhaps fear, at finding himself in the middle of a war sweeping all of Europe. He is nothing like the man Elsa remembers from Strasbourg, the man who sat on that bench with such composure while she talked about Alice.

"But you, Elsa, you have been here how long? This island. It must be strange for you."

"Strange, yes . . ." For two years, her life has consisted only of this island—Alice and Edward, Te Haha and Biscuit Tin, the mysterious script, the language. For two years, she has been immersed in novelty, riding a steady current of the unfamiliar. And now looking at Max feels out of place.

"Elsa, are you unwell?"

"I'll be all right. I—I never expected to see you again."

"You are not . . . *unhappy* with it?"

"Simply adjusting."

"But you have thought of me?"

"Of course." But she has not thought of him as she had expected she would. And an awareness comes to her that she has supplanted him, and not with Edward, but with her work. As if her research into the island's past has somehow removed her from her own past. As if the past were simply a quality to which she was bound, a suitcase she was obligated to carry, but which could be filled with anything. Her own disappointments swapped for the demise of a civilization.

"You are even lovelier."

"I think you've been looking at your officers too long."

"Is that . . . yes, I think it is. The hint of a smile?"

"Max." Something in her flutters open, and Elsa reaches out to gently touch his hand. How very odd that she can see herself, three years earlier, in Strasbourg, seated beside him on that garden bench, shielded by hedges and bushes, in that small patch of the world they made their own. Max in a brown day suit, smoking his pipe, explaining to her the various flower species in the garden, their natural habitats, noting how the beaks of the hummingbirds fit perfectly within the long petals of the fuchsias.

A cold breeze chills her face. "It's getting late," she says, standing.

"Elsa."

"I'm sorry."

"Come tomorrow. Come to the harbor where we are anchored. Please. We will talk some more. You will tell me all about your tablets and statues. And, if you like, about your husband."

She climbs onto her pony. As Max hands her the lantern, she is struck by an impossible notion. "You're not here . . . because of *me*?"

"I knew you were here."

"But . . ." She doesn't know what she means.

"We came from China across the entire Pacific, stopping at a half-dozen islands along the way. We needed to gather our forces. And you were on an island. In the South Pacific. You were on this one, *Liebling*. I could not very well decide to coal at Juan Fernández instead."

"I can't believe I'm looking at you. *Here*."

"You need rest, Elsa. It's late. But come tomorrow." He glances over his shoulder, down the darkening slope, and whistles sharply. A heavy cantering tears through the silence and an officer on horseback appears, halting in a salute. Once again, sternness hardens

Max's face. Like magnets, his shiny black boots draw together. His hand cuts a salute.

"Elsa." He turns to her and clasps her arms. "You realize, of course . . . you must say nothing about the war, to anyone." He lowers his voice. *"Anyone."*

She knows, above all, he means she isn't to tell Edward. *"Nicht,"* she says, and rides off back to camp behind the silent officer.

The next morning, she tells Edward the squadron has requested her help.

"They're certainly not shy about making their needs clear." Edward is steeping a cup of tea, raising and plunging the silver globe. They have depleted most of their tea supply, and now brew with only a pinch of leaves, trying to drain every last bit of flavor.

"They want to purchase livestock," says Elsa. "It's best I talk to the islanders. So there's no confusion over payment."

"Yes. Better to assist them. Still no sign of newspapers?"

"I'll try again today."

"For all the help they're asking, you would expect they would offer something in return."

"You would expect."

"It occurred to me," Edward begins, sliding the cup of tea across the table to Elsa. "Their interest in the tablets"—he lifts the pot from the meager fire and pours the steaming water into another cup—"was unusually extreme." He plunges the globe in, stirring contemplatively. "It might not be prudent to show the Germans your work on the translations."

"Edward."

"You cannot say their behavior wasn't odd."

Max's behavior would, of course, seem suspicious to Edward.

"I realize, Elsa, that my maritime experience has been in the sporting class. But even so. There are priorities when one anchors, a certain hierarchy for what one attends to. Wooden tablets? No. I should hate to see your work, our work, revealed by others. And in the event that they're interested in photographing the *moai,* I think it best I hide the excavation work."

To argue that Max's behavior was normal seems pointless.

"The safest place is the schooner," says Edward. "I can have the boat cleaned and brought around here to load. They won't see a thing. I think it best we move your journals there as well."

"Of course."

There is a yelp from Alice's tent, and then the words *"Bad Pudding."*

Edward takes a long sip of his tea. "I want you to know that I have set things down for her. I have explained, in detail, the rules for our relationship. Physicality, of any sort, has been forbidden. Kissing, fondling. She understands it is entirely out of the question. She was quite distressed. She's angry with me. Feels I've . . . rejected her. And I think it's best that for now I stay distant."

"Whatever you think is best," says Elsa, rising from the table. "I'll see she's all right."

"She may not want to see you, either."

"Alice and I had our difficulties long before you came into our life. We've fought before. It will be fine. She will be fine."

But in the tent Alice turns from Elsa.

"Allie. You can't stay cross like this forever."

"Pudding," says Alice. "Don't be cross."

"Allie, look at me. Talk to me."

"Pudding is always talked to."

"Allie, I'm going to Vinapu. Do you want to come?"

Alice releases a huff. "Vinapu. Vinapu. Vinapu."

"You don't have to if you don't want to. I'll come to see you later, when I'm back," says Elsa.

"Pudding never gets to go to Vinapu."

Elsa approaches her from behind, and tentatively kisses Alice's head; Alice sits perfectly still.

"I won't be long," says Elsa. "I'll see you and Pudding in a little while."

Elsa closes the flap of the tent and calls to Edward, "She's fine. She just wants to rest for a while." Then Elsa sets out on the southern coast toward the harbor.

Along the path, the sour smell of burning coal fills the air. She hears the clanging of chains and cables, the rumble of engines, voices rising and falling in waves of German song. Then, mounting the cliff above the harbor at Vinapu, she sees on the water below eight gray vessels. But for the commotion all around them—derricks dripping with cords and lines, wobbly dinghies clogged with sunburned men making slowly for the shore—the ships have the look of vast strips of dead metal. On the side of the largest ship, colliers toss baskets of coal into a row of square bunkers, chanting, *Wem Gott will rechte Gunst erweisen.*

Elsa tethers her pony and edges down the path to the bay, where dinghies, pinnaces, and Rapa Nui canoes clutter the shore. A small supply ship has been almost run aground, lashed to the jetty with ropes and chains. A pyramid of blistering wooden barrels tops its deck. Crates rise in a tower. On the rocks, several yards away, dozens of bulging, sap-stained burlap sacks spill yams, pineapples, and pumpkins. A young officer is tugging one bag at a time across the rocks while trying to smoke with his free hand.

He sees Elsa coming down the path and blows a bored plume of smoke toward the sun. *"Von Spee? Ja?"*

"Ja," says Elsa.

He drops his sack and leads her to a small motorboat. He flicks away his cigarette and tugs the engine to a coughing start. Elsa watches the shore recede behind them, realizing this is the first time in two years she has left the island. They soon pull alongside the largest of the warships, a vast wall of studded metal rising above them. All along the wall, rope ladders dangle like vines, and at a metal ladder, the officer cuts the engine. He stands and extends his hand, gesturing to Elsa and then to the ladder. *"Ja?"* She nods. Wrapping her skirt around one wrist, she climbs, her boots clanging against each rung. At the vast expanse of the main deck, chimneys and derricks rise all around her, between them a web of taut wires, like a colossal game of cat's cradle. She walks along the deck, trying to picture the boat at sea, cutting through frothing waves, abuzz with hundreds of men shouting orders, grabbing lines, taking positions. And guns. They would of course be firing guns and cannons. And would they not, then, also be fired upon?

"Hallo! Hallo!" From belowdecks comes a smiling officer, his white uniform bright in the sun.

"Ich suche Admiral von Spee?" she asks.

At her words, his face, tanned and fleshy, fills with delight. He strides forward and leads her down a ladder, through a labyrinth of narrow corridors lit by naked bulbs. At a black door with gold insignia, the officer delivers four swift knocks. Just before the door opens, he bows to Elsa and whisks his arm into a slow, gallant arc. But as the handle unlatches, he offers a full, sharp salute just as the face of the admiral emerges.

"Max, this is a floating . . . city."

"*Weg,*" commands Max. The officer turns, departs.

Max rests his hand on Elsa's shoulder. "You made it. And you look rested."

"Where is everybody?"

"Shore leave. It has been a long time at sea for them. Come in, sit down."

She follows him into the small cabin. Maps and charts spill from a table beneath the porthole, but the room is otherwise spare. She sits down on a cushioned bench, what might be a sofa or a bed.

"I must confess, I imagined you living in a bit more luxury."

"You should have seen her at Tsingtao. Carpets, paintings, French tapestries. The deck done up with awnings for dances. This cabin had wood paneling. I have had my share of luxury."

"And you redecorated?"

"Everything flammable . . . we left in China."

Flammable. Again the image rises before her of the ship firing its cannons, smoke clouding the decks. She stands and looks out the porthole, toward the shore. "The islanders will be visiting you. Their canoes are out. They enjoy sneaking up on people."

"They've come by already. We gave them some soaps and tinned meats, though we have little to spare. It's costly, this peacetime charade."

"This will go down in Rapa Nui history, you know. They don't get many visitors."

"So long as it does not go out on the wireless."

"There's no wireless—"

"I know."

She turns now to face him, and his eyes meet hers with solemnity. "They are looking for us, Elsa. The British."

"Thank goodness the ocean is so large."

"Germany is thousands of miles away. *Thousands* of miles."

She looks at the charts spread on the table and rolls back the edges of one, then another. "How long can you anchor here?"

"Not more than a few days. We are awaiting one more ship."

What can she possibly say to him? Don't leave? She imagines the plea rising in waves over the whole of Europe at that very moment. She knows its futility, its naïveté.

"Well—" He breaks the silence. "Now you see what I do when I am not leading the children through the forest."

Elsa drops the charts. "And now you know what I've done since I stopped running around after your children."

"He is much older than I envisioned."

"Hah! You're not one to speak."

"Oh, no. Have I aged?"

"Everyone looks older with a battleship."

But as swiftly as their playfulness swells, it subsides. A bird flapping briefly through the room and out the window.

"It is serious, isn't it?" says Elsa.

"Yes, *Liebling.*"

"And you're in real danger."

He takes her hand. "There are almost two thousand men in this fleet. Most of them younger than you. At Samoa, they went ashore, they flirted with the women, they drank, and then they wrote, as they have always done, on the tree trunks and the large rocks. *Fritz was here, 1914, Sailor on the* Scharnhorst. Before we left we sent another party to scratch everything out, all their names, the marks they had wanted to leave." He pauses. "They are hunting us."

She understands now what he is trying to tell her but can't say: He cannot make it home. The odds are impossible. And that is why he has come.

"Tell me, Elsa. What thoughts are in your mind?"

She is thinking of his ship being stripped of all its wood, all its fabrics. She is thinking of the ship aflame. "England," she says. "My father's house. I would like to see it again."

"Yes," he says. "I, too, dream of home. Strasbourg."

"The garden."

"The garden," he sighs. "Your sister is here, is she not? Alice?"

"Alice."

"Is she well?"

"Well? Yes. But different."

Elsa steps to the porthole, Max following, and they look through the glass toward the shore, toward the cliffs, the parched grass, and fallen statues. How small it all seems from here.

"It is an odd thing, this landscape," he says. "It's not what we have seen on other islands. I've never seen an island with so little."

"What have you seen? On the other islands?"

"Breadfruit trees and coconut palms. Turtles and tropical birds. The other islands are like jungles."

"I think this was as well, and then something happened."

"What?"

"It has to do with the *moai*, how they were moved, and why they are like that, fallen on their faces."

"They are like tombs, those statues," says Max.

"They are tombs," she says. "Those platforms they stood on, people were buried beneath them. The statues are symbols of the dead. Ancestors. And I don't think they fell. There are stories on those wooden tablets. Histories of this island. This place was once covered with a forest. It could be just legend, just folklore, but—"

"Tell me."

"You really want to hear it?"

"Why would I not?"

"It's sad," she says.

"Good," replies Max. "Then we know it is true."

❀

For the next six days, Edward dismantles the excavation and moves the *kohau*, their notebooks, her journal with the *rongorongo* translation, and their *moai* sketches—anything the Germans might make off with in the night—onto the schooner, which has been cleaned and brought around and is now anchored off Anakena once again. Elsa helps Max provision the ships. Beef, lamb, and chicken are bartered. She even helps several officers purchase wood carvings.

When finally she and Max say their good-byes, it is in his cabin. In silence, they sit beside each other, listening to the din of the anchor lines, the noise of the waves against the ship's side. It is like the times they sat in the garden, except this past week there has been no need for propriety. As if to simply relieve the need to talk, Elsa kisses him, and soon she can feel his full weight, and in this weight his absence; already she can sense the moment when his body will be gone, feeling all at once his presence and its loss. And it is now, as she lies beneath him, that her mind returns to Edward's house, when she stood looking at her trunk, wondering what lay ahead, as if she has, after a long journey, finally become that future self.

She pulls him toward her.

"Don't cry, *Liebling*."

"I never cry," she says. But she can feel a tear run from the corner of her eye.

When Max finally stands, she can no longer suppress the urge. "Don't go."

In the half-darkness, he smiles. "Finally. I wondered if you might not be trying to get rid of me."

"Stay."

"Impossible."

"Then, when this is all over, we'll see each other. You will come visit me in Hertfordshire. You'll see our gardens in spring. You'll tell me the name of everything in bloom."

"Of course."

"We can take the train to London and see the British Museum."

"Absolutely. The museum." He puts his arm around her and a look of pain washes over his face, a look she has never seen before. As though speaking to himself, his tone expressionless, he says: "Our lives will be filled with great bliss."

❂

"So they're off, then?" asks Edward.

"Yes," she mutters, remembering Max's instructions. "They're headed to Pitcairn to look around for several days, and then on to the Marquesas and Tahiti." That is, in fact, where they have just come from. "It seems they're on a grand tour."

Now the reality of their departure hits her. Max is gone. The fleet is gone. They have returned to the ocean, where they will be tracked down. Elsa tries to remember what lies ahead: Kasimiro, yes, she must return to see Kasimiro. She must get her key. Max agreed that this was of great importance. The tablets, the *rongorongo.* That, at least, is permanent.

"Alice has been upset," he says nervously. "You'll see she's all right?"

"What happened?"

"Nothing. It is the same thing. The rules."

"Has she needed to be reminded of the rules?" Her voice is testy. She does not want to return to this life, this confusion.

"I promise. I've made her understand."

"All right."

"You know, I still find it exceedingly odd that they hadn't a single newspaper or magazine with them."

"Perhaps Germans don't like to read, Edward. Good night." She lights one of the lanterns and carries it with her to Alice's tent.

"Allie," she whispers.

But the tent is empty. "Allie," she calls again into the night. And then she sees the cage, Pudding's cage, in the corner of the tent, its door flung open, a solitary gray feather resting on its floor.

The necklace of beans lies broken on the ground.

Her voice rises now, shrieks into the darkness: *"Allie! Where are you?"*

24

The flush of fever came at dawn, crept across her forehead, mounted her cheeks, then made a slow advance down her neck. It attacked her shoulders, tried to shake her from sleep, but she refused to wake. She pressed herself farther into the cool grass. Her fingers, hot and tense, wrapped themselves around a cold stone, a cube of ice. Her mind slowed, slept, then woke with a start. Images spilled before her: a frog dangling upside down, a seed floating in a jar. An island. A white flower in a field of shadows.

Her tongue swelled, hot and puffy, a loaf of bread rising in the oven of her mouth. Her neck grew firm, her throat thick, every channel hardening until the whine of air struggling through the last open pathway reached her ears. I have become a tree, she thought. She turned then, or thought she turned. Her face met a firm wet surface, her hair, damp with sweat, fell thickly around her. Darkness. Her toes tingled—or was it her fingertips? Where did the crab go? Was it crawling over her now with its thick hot feet—was that the fire she felt moving across her body? Yes, it was so hot here. The sun was rising, spilling its heat like lava. She was in a volcano, tossed by an explosion.

"You need help. Put your arm around my neck. Please, Greer. Try to move. There. Yes, that's it. Perfect. See how easy?"

She was floating now above the grass—was she in a dream? She was searching for the white flower. But she couldn't keep her eyes open, the ground sped beneath her, shook. An earthquake. She could feel the trembling, could hear her teeth click like tossed dice. And then she landed, and water washed over her face. Flooding her eyes and nose and mouth. And then an arrow, a musket, a revolver, a cannonball, shot through her arm, broke through her flesh to invade her shoulder, her neck, her head. . . .

Eyes closed, her breathing thick and strained, she tried to sit up. But gravity, a tidal wave, tossed her back.

Thick blankets weighed against her, and still she shivered. "Cold," she whispered.

"I know. It is the fever. It gives you chills. It will pass."

"When?"

There was silence, and she roused one eyelid from its swollen slumber; a soft yellow light shone on the nearby nightstand—a candle? Or a lightbulb blurred by fever? She barely made out the white wall, the desk, the foot of the bed. Where was he?

Through the blankets she felt a hand squeeze her elbow. "Here," he said, but the voice was miles away. Like a recording of a voice, a recording of a recording. She let her head slip onto her shoulder and looked down. On the floor beside the bed he lay supine, one arm tucked behind his head.

She awoke in darkness to warm water flooding her mouth.

"Greer, you must drink. You must flush the toxins from your system. Please, you must try."

But her lips were heavy, and loose, could barely hold themselves to her face.

A creature now stirred in her stomach, stretched its limbs, somersaulted in the back of her throat, and broke free with fury. Her throat burned, her nose burned.

"Yes, *querida*. That is okay. Your body is trying to cleanse itself."

A rancid smell rose beside her. A towel wiped her face. "*Bueno, Doctora.*"

"Mahina?"

"*Sí, Doctora.*"

Greer forced her eyes open, and saw the speckled light through the curtains. Like shadows, Mahina and Vicente seemed to float through the small room, pouring water in the basin, wringing cloths, folding towels, whispering in Spanish. They moved fluidly together; they looked like dancers, beautiful dancing nurses.

"What day . . . ?" Her throat hurt too much to finish.

"Saturday," said Vicente. "Three days. The doctor says you are improving. But you still must rest. Rest and drink fluids."

"Doctor?"

"Doctor for the *doctora.*" Mahina's voice sang through the room.

"I'm not improving."

"Your color is much better," said Vicente, and Mahina agreed.

"*Sí, sí,*" she said. "But sleep now."

Greer rolled onto her side, her hair snarling. She slowly raised her arm and tried to free it.

"*Momento*" came Vicente's voice. And then she felt his fingers trace three careful seams along her scalp, felt a pleasant coolness as he lifted the hair from her neck and began to weave. With each slow stitch of the braid, her mind blurred.

In her dreams, she saw the emerald-green island. She floated above it, examining each fern, each patch of moss, each white blossom.

When she awoke, she felt a breeze through her window and thought she was there, in the sky above the island, a cloud. But when she opened her eyes, it came back: the room, the *residencial,* Easter Island, her fever.

"Do you still feel the chills?" Vicente was seated on a small stool beside the bed. Stubble matted his cheeks, his pants were crumpled.

"I just feel a little achy," she said.

"Your body exhausted itself fighting the poison." Vicente stroked his chin. "You look much better."

Greer looked down at herself. The sheets were twisted about her ankles. Her pale legs jutted from a wrinkled orange caftan. In her hand was the plaque of the Virgin Mary. Had it been put there by Mahina, or in her delirium had she grabbed it? She set it down.

"The venom," she said. "Is it out?"

"With the spiders there is very little venom. But it is very potent. It had already reached your system. You will be okay though. The color in your cheeks, really, is very good. I cannot tell you. When I first saw you . . . well, it was something." Vicente rose slowly from the stool. "I must find Mahina and tell her you are awake and talking. That the fever has broken."

As he stepped out into the hall, he closed the door quietly behind him.

Greer took a deep breath. Her eyelids were no longer heavy. The fever had lifted from her forehead. The chill on her neck was gone. She raised both arms and bent them effortlessly. She rolled her head in circles, wiggled her toes. How strange and wonderful this body, she thought. Bracing her hands against the wall, she stretched her feet to the bed's edge. Each tendon, each muscle fiber, each nerve, awakened. Never had she been so impressed with her limbs.

Greer looked around her. On the nightstand lay her stack of books and the jar with her magnolia seed. The basin was still on the desk, a pile of folded cloths beside it, and a pitcher of water.

"*Doctora!*" The door swung open and Mahina, followed by Vicente, burst in. She laid her palm on Greer's forehead.

"*Sí, sí,*" she said to Vicente. "*Está mejor.*" Mahina let her pleasure fill the room, then snatched it back. "Why did you go off like that? Outside Hanga Roa! In the dark? You act crazy. For three days you are sick."

"I'm sorry, Mahina. I was out for a walk. I got sleepy."

"You are lucky. Very lucky. This island is not a place to act so crazy. Too many things go wrong here. When you go home to America, then you do crazy things, as many as you like. Here you will stay at Mahina's at night and sleep in bed. Yes?"

"Yes."

Mahina narrowed her eyes.

"Yes," said Greer.

Moving to the foot of the bed, Mahina untwisted the sheet, fluffed it out, and spread it over Greer. "You had many visitors. I did not know you know so many people here on Rapa Nui." She moved to Greer's side of the bed and folded the sheet beneath the mattress. "Everyone says the American *doctora* is dying, and everyone come to Mahina's to see. Mario. Vittorio." She moved to the other side and did the same. "Like a movie, they think. Nothing happens here, nothing to do, so they come to look at my *doctora.*" Mahina gazed at Greer, at her *doctora,* folded back the top of the sheet, and tucked it beneath Greer's arms. Mahina had made the bed with Greer in it. "I told them no, go away." She rested her hands on her hips. "Even Ramon, I told no. I tell them the *doctora* is private person and would not like it."

"But you let Vicente in?"

"Ah, yes." Mahina smiled, clearly pleased that this point had been raised. "But Vicente is your *colleague.*"

"I have many colleagues here, Mahina. But I'm glad you let him in."

"Señor Urstedt and Isabel come by. I say no, and Señor Urstedt come sneak through the window to see you."

"Fortunately," said Vicente, "Sven didn't fit, and Mahina caught him by the legs. I am sorry you missed that, Greer. You would have enjoyed the sight."

Mahina smiled, rubbed her hands together. She liked being part of the joke. "*Sí, sí*. Now I go to fix lunch for Isabel. She is much trouble. She want to be thin and will eat only fruit and vegetable! When you are hungry, Greer, I fix you ten chickens." She left with a small slam of the door and could be heard humming through the courtyard.

"Vicente, listen, I owe you a big thank-you."

"Well, it was Luka Tepano who found you. He brought me to you. And then we all did our part. Mahina especially. You are like family to her. She does not want you to leave," said Vicente, pointing to how Greer had been sealed to the mattress.

"Well, I'm not going anywhere yet. I'm tired."

"Yes, of course." Vicente retreated toward the door. "You need your rest."

"No. I didn't mean . . ."

"I will leave you to sleep. But first, here." He pulled a small object from his pocket and put it in her palm. "You had it in your hand when we put you into bed. You would not let go. I had to pull each finger off." He laughed. "You're quite strong, you know."

"I had it?" It was roughly the size of a walnut. The shell had ossified. "It's a fossil."

"Perhaps that is why you were out so late. You were on the trail of a fossil. There was no time to lose. It was in the caves. And when you found it, when you picked it off the ground, the spider was hiding beneath it."

"I like that story. I like that story very much."

"Now you rest."

He closed the door gently and Greer rolled the nut in her hand, held it up to the light: "Hello, little *angio sperma*."

A few nights later, Vicente came by her room to report that Burke-Jones had decided to leave the island.

"He said he is sorry," said Vicente, standing over her bed. "He asked me to say good-bye."

Greer hadn't seen Randolph since the night in the cemetery. "He couldn't stop by himself? It's not exactly a long walk from the Espíritu."

"You know Burke-Jones. I don't think he is fond of good-byes. But he said he will miss you. Actually, he said"—and now Vicente lowered his head, and muttered—" 'I will miss her.' "

Greer remembered the picture in his wallet. Lydia. "I guess England will be good for him."

"Burke-Jones is going to India."

"India?"

"I know. A surprise to us all."

"What's in India?"

"Other than one billion people?"

"You're definitely in good spirits."

"Oh, but I am!" he exclaimed, sitting on the foot of the bed. "I am awaiting a telegram."

"From?"

"Who else? My favorite German admiral! Another dispatch from his ship."

"I think you've become much more interested in the *missing* tablets than the ones you have."

"This thought has occurred to me as well."

"A sort of scholar's half-empty approach."

"But the glass will fill soon. I'll find those tablets."

"So, India, what will Randolph be doing there?"

"He is interested in something to do with the construction of the Taj Mahal."

"Wait." Greer closed her eyes, raised her hand in the air. "I'm picking up on something. An image of . . . hundreds of miniature Taj Mahals."

"A little universe of marble palaces."

They laughed.

"Well, good for him," said Greer, adjusting the covers. "But I'll miss him. Sven will be sad."

"Señorita Nosticio will help him through his sorrow."

"Isabel? They're really together?"

"I told you. He likes the older women."

There was a gentle knock at the door.

"It's open," said Greer.

In came Mahina, carrying two bowls, eyeing Greer and Vicente with pleasure. She handed a bowl to each of them and pulled two shiny forks from the pocket of her apron.

"Thank you, Mahina," Greer said.

"*Peti*," she sang, closing the door behind her.

"Peaches. Uh-oh. I know what this means. You're in my room, sitting on my bed." Greer pierced the shiny half-peach with her fork and held it up. "I think this is Mahina's idea of a dowry."

"Well, I'm holding out for an *umu* feast."

Greer slid a slice of peach into her mouth and let the syrup coat her tongue. "You know, I've wanted to say something to Mahina. About her husband."

"Not an easy topic."

"She's a friend, though. I should be able to say something."

"What would you say?"

"I don't know. That she should get herself a ticket to Santiago, to Buenos Aires, to Rio, and she should see the world, get on with her life. I see Mahina and Ramon on a romantic getaway, sipping tropical drinks, staying at a hotel where *they* get served breakfast every morning and someone comes to clean *their* room."

"I believe the English word for this kind of wish is *meddling*."

"*Caring*."

"Ah, yes. Another lesson in Greer English. I'll soon be fluent."

"Meddling is a manifestation of caring. There. A compromise."

"Very well," said Vicente. "But where do you see yourself? Where do *you* want to go?"

"Good question."

Vicente now concentrated on his peaches, deftly quartering each one as he spoke. "I mean, how long do you think you will stay?"

"On the island? I don't know." It was odd she hadn't figured this out yet. Her research was nearing an end, but the idea of going home, to Marblehead, seemed unreal; her house, her life there, all felt impossibly distant. "When everything is wrapped up, I guess. I'm just waiting to hear about the fossil. If I can get confirmation on the species, I can write up my results."

"And then you are free to go?"

"Not free," she said. "But yes, then I can go."

The next day Greer felt strong enough to go back to the lab to check on her samples, to make sure everything was in order. She decided to review her notebooks and any untouched reading materials, settling in at one of her lab tables.

The last European account was from the young Pierre Loti, a Frenchman who had visited in 1872, almost a century after Captain Cook. Loti's tone was different from other explorers'. Here was a writer, a poet, who came seeking wonder.

> *I went ashore there years ago in my green youth from a sailing frigate, after days of strong wind and obscuring clouds; there has remained with me the recollection of a half fantastic land, a land of dreams.*

Like all the other visitors, Loti finds his scarves and hats in great demand. He bemoans the theft of a red velvet hat with brass buttons, snatched from his head by a small boy who breaks into song. But Loti is welcomed by the Rapa Nui in a way others haven't been. When touring the island, Loti finds himself sleepy and is taken by an islander to rest in a hut.

> *The roof of reeds which shelters me is sustained by palm branches— but where did they get them since their island is without trees and has hardly any vegetation beyond reeds and grapes. In this small space, hardly a meter and a half high by four meters long a thousand things are carefully suspended; little idols of black wood which are engraved with coarse enameling, lances with points of sharpened obsidian, paddles carved with human figures, feather headdresses, ornaments for the dance or for combat and some utensils of various shapes, of use unknown to me which all seem extremely ancient. . . .*
>
> *But when you think of it, all this dried out wood of their war clubs and their gods, where does it come from? And their cats, their rabbits? . . . The mice that stroll around the houses everywhere. I don't suppose anybody brought them. Where did they come from? The slightest things on this isolated island bring up unanswered questions: one is amazed that there exists a flora and a fauna.*

Loti then drifts off to sleep.

> *Waking like that in the savage's dreary nest I felt a feeling of extreme homesickness. I felt far away, farther away than ever and lost. And I was taken with that extreme anguish which comes with island sickness*

and no place in the world would have given it to me so acutely as right here, the immensity of the austral seas round about me. . . .

Greer set the book down; Loti was right. She remembered that first day in the Rano Aroi crater, standing in the reeds. Even in this "land of dreams" she had felt the momentary anguish of solitude. And how could she not? The island was like a thing of myths, a fear made physical: solitude itself. And that perhaps was one of the reasons she'd come, to explore the geography of her loneliness.

Voices came from the hallway. Isabel and Sven. She could hear the thump of boots approach her door. There was a knock, a muffled laugh, another knock.

"Open."

"Ah, back to work! Definitely a full recovery!" said Sven. He moved in and hugged her. "No surprise, though. You had the best of care."

"I did," she said, feeling herself smile. Even on this isolated island she had found a community: people who checked in on her, acquaintances, friends. She'd nearly completed her first solo fieldwork. She was coming to terms with what Thomas had done. What more did she need?

"When they first carried you back to Mahina's you looked so awful. Really, like a corpse."

"Thanks, Sven."

"And now, color in your cheeks! You had no color. I'm telling you, Greer. Nothing."

"Well, I've been outside, moving around. I pretty much feel back to normal."

"We are very happy for that," said Isabel, clasping Sven's hand. She was easily a foot shorter than he was, and a decade older, but these differences somehow produced a sense of balance.

"We're off for a tour," said Isabel. "Will you join us?"

"Tour of what?"

"The island!"

"Is there really anything you haven't yet seen?"

"Oh," said Isabel, "we've not explored all the coast, the craters. I have always explored on paper. Today, Sven will take me to explore on foot."

At this moment Greer realized how Isabel was dressed—hiking boots, khaki shorts, and Sven's yellow T-shirt, too large, billowing over her belt: *Swede e* π.

"I'm going to stay put and read. But thanks."

"If you need anything," said Sven, "let us know. And if you don't, make something up. Now that Burke-Jones is gone, things feel slow around here."

As they left, she could hear Sven singing in the hallway.

Greer returned to the final section of Loti's account, when an improvised chariot was assembled in the frigate's launch and Loti's shipmates, one hundred of them, began to remove a *moai*. The islanders made no objection, as though the statue were valueless. Roggeveen, one hundred and fifty years earlier, had seen fires lit before the idols and islanders kneeling before them in veneration. Loti sees something different:

> *A great group followed us this morning across the wet grass of the plain, and once arrived they start to dance like dervishes, lightfooted with their hair blowing out in the wind, naked and reddish, delicately tinted blue by their tattooing, their slender bodies moving against the brown stones and the black horizons; they dance, they dance over the enormous figures, placing their toes against the faces of the monsters, kicking them noiselessly in the nose and cheeks. I can't understand what they are singing in the constant racket of the gusts of wind and the surf.*
>
> *The people of Rapa Nui, who venerate so many fetishes and little gods, seem to have no respect for the tombs. They don't remember the dead sleeping below them.*

Or perhaps, thought Greer, they did remember the dead below them. And perhaps they remembered something that made them want to dance across the faces of their ancestors. Might they have felt rage at the dead?

25

"She's upset about what I said to her," Edward says."She's gone to sulk. Perhaps she's gone to the excavation site. She liked it there. But she didn't take her pony. If she's been walking she's probably hurt. I've done this. This is my fault."

"Stop it,"says Elsa."Let's just find her."

They ride their ponies in separate directions, away from the camp-site, shouting Alice's name. Elsa follows the southern coast to Hanga Roa, hoping Alice will have at least kept along the path. She passes the fallen statues at Tongariki as the sun begins to fall, dimming the sea, the grass.

There is nowhere to hide on this island except the caves, and Alice has always hated the caves. She must be somewhere, waiting, ex-posed, hoping to be seen and called back. After all these years, it is as if Alice simply wants to be pinched, as though her life has been one long trance she is asking to be summoned from.

Alice *wants* them to come after her.

The full moon washes the landscape white, but Elsa doesn't need it. How many times she has ridden this path to the village—alone, with Alice, with Biscuit Tin just days before. This land, its distances, have become a part of her.

"Allie!"she calls.

As the horse plods forward through the night, Elsa feels as though this one search is her entire life. This pursuit of Alice—it seems she has lived this instant for twenty-four years. So Alice must be all right, then; Alice will be found. That is always the ending.

Finally, on the cliff above the harbor at Vinapu, Elsa spots a fig-ure—Biscuit Tin, arms slack at his side, staring at the sea.

"*Poki!*" Elsa shouts, leaping down from her pony, running to him. "*Poki,* have you seen Alice? Alice. Where is she?"

Slowly, the boy raises his arm and points toward the water. He does not turn to look at her.

"In the water? Alice is in the water? *Vai? Poki! Vai!* Alice!" She grabs the boy by the collar, shakes him wildly until she sees that he is crying. She releases her grip, lets his body settle.

"*Poki,* where is Alice?"

He points again, down to the water, to where the fleet was anchored, to where the supply boat stacked with crates was lashed to the jetty.

Elsa looks out at the ocean, and stumbles back.

26

When Greer returned from the lab, several children were perched beside the *residencial* sign, peering through the bushes; they scattered immediately at her approach. Then she heard a wave of voices in the courtyard, the sound of doors slamming, of feet racing along the porch.

"*Qué lástima!*" It was Mahina's voice, coming from inside. She sounded distressed. "*Qué lástima.*"

Greer had never seen the main room so crowded. At the far end, the two wicker wing chairs had been pushed together and Isabel lay across them in her khaki shorts and Sven's soiled shirt. Her long hair was matted, her makeup faded. She was sharing a cigarette with Sven, who held her hand. Across from them, a uniformed carabinero was at Mahina's desk, his olive beret resting before him, and he was writing in a notebook. He was young, with a thick curled mustache that looked fake amid his delicate features. Luka Tepano sat on the floor in the corner, his knees held to his chest. He seemed entirely disengaged from the commotion. Mahina was moving between them all, offering reassurances, except to the carabinero, whose appropriation of her desk she clearly found insulting.

"*Doctora!*" Mahina had just seen her.

"What happened?"

"Can you get us a drink of something strong?" Sven called.

"In the kitchen," said Mahina, who was keeping her eye on the carabinero. "You get the pisco."

Greer quickly went to the kitchen, searched the pantry for the bottle, and brought it back to the lobby.

After Isabel and Sven had each taken a long drink, the carabinero stopped writing. *"Su historia, Señor Urstedt, lentamente."* He then turned to Mahina and told her to translate.

Mahina winced at this order, but clearly felt the gravity of the situation outweighed her distaste for Chilean authority. *"Sí,"* she said, disappearing through the beaded curtain. She returned with a chair and seated herself across from the carabinero.

Sven sat on the floor beside Isabel, set the bottle of pisco down, and ran his free hand through his hair. "As I tried to say before, we got the horses from Chico and set out to explore the coast. About halfway to Anakena it begins to cloud over, so we get off the path and look for a cave. We find an opening in the rock face. We have our backpacks with our lunch, so we figure we'll avoid the rain and have our sandwiches there. One thing leads to another, we start . . ." At this Sven's eyes floated up to Isabel, who blushed. "Anyway, then something scurries toward us, like it came from the outside. Isabel leaps up because she's sure it's a rodent. Then, again, something moves in the darkness and I start feeling around on the ground. Well, it turns out to be a rock. This is good because it's not a rodent, bad because who the hell is throwing stones at us. We hear somebody whistling and then comes another stone. So we get dressed, grab our packs, and head for the light. And at the entrance I see poor old Luka Tepano holding one of his plates. And then I realize where we are. 'Luka, I'm sorry,' I tell him, 'we didn't know this was her cave.' But Luka just sticks his fingers in his mouth and whistles. He starts to look very upset, so I ask him what's the matter but he just keeps looking at the cave. Then Isabel starts to feel uneasy about the whole thing, keeps asking me what's wrong with him. I ask Luka if he wants me to go in there with him but he just keeps staring at the cave. So I take him by the arm, but he won't budge. I don't think he'd ever entered. So I told him to wait there, and I got my flashlight and headed in alone."

Mahina translated this last phrase, the carabinero copied it in his notebook, and an awkward silence followed.

"Y después?" asked the carabinero.

Isabel shook her head. Sven looked over at Luka. "That's all. Then I came out and told him she was *muerte*. I sent Isabel to fetch you."

Mahina translated; the carabinero surveyed the room and said, *"Bueno."* When finally he made his way out, Mahina closed the door firmly behind him and resumed her seat behind the desk.

"I can't believe you found the old woman," said Greer. "God, I'm so sorry."

"Well, it was worse having to tell him," said Sven. "I looked him in the eye and said, *'Muerte,* Luka.' Isabel tried to apologize to him. But the poor old guy didn't seem to hear anything we said. He just sat down on a rock beside the cave, I don't know, like he was never going to move."

After the carabinero had left, Greer stayed in the main room while Mahina passed around glasses of guava juice. Ramon had joined them. Luka had fallen asleep in the corner, and Mahina had removed his shoes and draped a blanket over him. It was a relief to see him embrace sleep so completely, but nobody knew what they could do for him when he woke up. Other than the woman in the cave, he didn't seem to have family. Greer still hadn't thanked him for finding her, for getting Vicente, and now she wished she'd done so before all this happened. And she had wanted to ask him about the nut fossil too. She wanted to know if he had seen it in her hand when he found her. She still had no recollection of picking it up. She'd been searching for a fossil, as the only evidence to prove what species of tree had really grown on the island. It was simply too extraordinary to have the final piece of evidence appear that way—a gift from an unseen hand. It was like waking to discover the Rosetta stone on your pillow.

"I feel like such a jerk," whispered Sven. He had been repeating this over and over. "I know I teased him. I didn't mean him any harm. But I would never have knowingly gone into her cave."

"Nobody thinks it's your fault," said Isabel. "Or our fault. It was just an awful mistake."

"She was very old," said Mahina. "For years she was there. Hiding. And she died peacefully. A good death. You should not be upset."

Just then, the door swung open, and Vicente entered. Mahina lifted a finger to her lips and gestured toward Luka.

"Where've you been?" Greer whispered, embarrassed at the urgency in her tone. She had gotten used to him being around, had come to take his presence for granted.

"I've just heard. For a geologist"—he turned to Sven—"you have a very poor instinct for rock formations."

"I'd seen him a million times going and coming. Never there."

"Well, the doctor has said her heart was weak. She was old."

Vicente lowered himself to the floor and leaned against the wall, threw his legs out in front of him. He looked toward Luka.

"I am sorry for him," he said. "It must be so terrible to lose her. I suppose this was not meant to be a good day. For anyone."

Vicente reached into his breast pocket and extracted an envelope. He handed it to Greer.

"Oh, no," said Greer. "Your telegram." She pulled out the thin sheet of paper.

> Forever in your debt. Will unload at F. and send officer with instructions and funds for return to E. I have trust in your vigilance. May God watch over us all.

Vicente said, his voice flat, "This message was sent to an Alfred Heidegzeller, a German expatriate living in the Falkland Islands. He had grown up in Strasbourg with von Spee. A famous yachtsman who had turned down many offers to serve in the navy."

"He got the tablets?"

"This was dispatched November fifteenth, routed through two German merchant vessels so that it could not be detected by the Allies, and arrived at the home of Heidegzeller November twenty-eighth. He never got the cargo."

"The battle," said Sven.

"The Falklands," said Greer.

"Every German ship went down. They were never able to anchor."

"And the tablets? Went down with them?"

"That is the last that is known of his cargo. It was the last personal dispatch von Spee sent."

"I'm sorry, Vicente."

He took the telegram from her, folded it neatly into an airplane, and sent it sailing across the room. It was the first time Greer had seen Vicente defeated.

It was growing dark. Mahina switched on a desk lamp and the light refracted through the hanging globes, casting a row of webbed green moons on the wall. They finished the last of their juice in a silence broken only by Luka Tepano's occasional snores. The telegram, the woman's death, Burke-Jones's departure. It was a somber day.

"It is time for bed," Mahina finally announced. "I will stay with Luka. He must sleep. We leave him in quiet. And everybody else, go now."

"Mahina, you remind me of my first girlfriend," said Sven. "Heidi Larsen. Very regimented. 'Pick me up. Six o'clock.'"

While he spoke, Mahina turned off the lights and opened the front door. "*Iorana*, Señor Urstedt."

Sven took Isabel by the hand and led her out. "Don't worry, Mahina. I loved her madly. Good night, Greer." Vicente and Ramon followed him outside.

"Too many jokes, that Señor Ursedt," said Mahina, shaking her head. Greer decided to linger for a few minutes, helping Mahina carry the dirty glasses to the kitchen. When they tiptoed back into the main room to quietly right the chairs, there was a soft knock at the door. It was Sven with a bundle in his arms.

"Some clean clothes," he said to Mahina. "For the old man when he wakes up."

Mahina kissed him on the cheek. *"Buen muchacho."*

The next morning when Greer awoke she found Isabel in the dining room, in a pink robe, sipping tea.

"The man left," said Isabel. "Luka. He must have wandered off in the middle of the night."

"Where is Mahina?"

"She said to tell you the boat is here."

Greer strolled over to the *caleta* to find the Chilean Company boat anchored in the bay. Hundreds of islanders were milling about the docks, watching, as the first few crates were unloaded. Since it was too crowded to find Mahina, Greer returned to the *residencial,* where all day long, through the windows of the main room, came the sounds of laughter and gasps as people examined each other's merchandise in the street. Supplies on the island that had been diminishing—flour, sugar, tea—were now replenished. Gasoline arrived in drums, enough for a year. There were surprises too. As the boat was unloaded, Mahina popped in with regular updates: two new Jeeps, twenty chairs for the schoolhouse, a new mattress for the governor's bed, which caused no end of discussion about what he had done to wear out the first one. And materials—tiles, panes of glass, two-by-fours, brackets and braces and screws—for anyone who meant to build a house. And then there were the crates of pisco, the cans of peaches, the tires, which Ramon needed for his Jeep.

"Ramon has just put the tires on!" Mahina announced from the threshold of Greer's room. "And now I think I know what will be good for the *doctora*."

"Please tell me it doesn't involve *amor*."

"*Amor, amor*. No. A ride in the Jeep! The *doctora* needs Terevaka. The *doctora* can drive, no?"

Greer rummaged through her duffel for her blue jeans, and pulled them on beneath her caftan. Mahina turned to the door, and Greer smiled to herself—Mahina had tended her fever, wiped vomit from her face, led her to the bathroom during her delirium, but had to turn away while Greer changed clothes. Endless courtesy, thought Greer. She stepped into her sandals, tied a sweater around her waist. "Keys?"

The drive was rugged. As they bounced and bucked, Mahina held her seat, and Greer did her best not to stall, or hit any dips. She felt that Mahina viewed her not only as a woman who could drive but as an expert driver, a *doctora* of driving, and Greer didn't want to disappoint. She tried to look confident. Before they left, she'd made a great show of adjusting the rear- and sideview mirrors, only to find now that with each bump the mirrors shifted. It made no difference, though—there was nothing behind or beside them. They were the only two on the grassy mountain.

It hadn't rained in weeks, and the Jeep's new tires kicked up dust. To keep from coughing, they had tied bandanas around their mouths.

When the Jeep finally reached the top, the sun appeared to hang directly before them. Mahina untied her bandana, flung open the door. "Come, *Doctora*."

Somehow, arriving at the top lacked the grandeur Greer had expected. Terevaka was a grassy hill like all others on the island, only it was the highest.

"Look." Mahina pointed at the sea below them. She spun slowly in a circle. "Horizon. All around."

It was true; for an entire three hundred and sixty degrees, Greer could see the hazy line of ocean meeting sky. This, then, was the grandeur. Other sights were of things: monuments, snowcapped mountains. This view was one of absence: a horizon unblemished.

Greer sat down in the grass and tried to absorb the feeling of vast space. "This was worth the wait," she said.

"And *mira.*" Mahina was beside her, facing the sun, her legs tucked beneath her skirt. She'd taken off her shoes. "The horizon is not a line." Her hand cut a half-circle through the air. "But round."

"The earth's curvature," said Greer, overwhelmed. All that lay around them was the endless ocean. *Te Pito O Te Henua*—"navel of the earth." The name given to the island by the first settlers made sense.

The sun streamed through the clouds in bands of lavender, pink, and opaline. On the water below, the light lay like tinsel.

"How far do you think, *Doctora*? How far you see the water? They say it is fifty miles, at least."

"It all depends on how high we are."

"Five hundred meters above the sea."

The numbers sounded right. Greer had always liked the horizon equation. All a person had to do was imagine standing at one vertex of a triangle. If you knew how high you were above the earth's surface, with a little help from Pythagoras, you could calculate your distance to the horizon. Now she imagined everybody as points on billions of separate triangles, all extending upward from a common vertex, the center of the earth.

"Sounds about right," said Greer. "So if a ship were to appear on the horizon right now, it would be fifty miles away."

"Fifty," said Mahina. "But it looks like hundreds to me. I sit here many times and try to count each mile."

Greer remembered Mahina's husband and wondered if this was where she came to watch for him.

"You spend a lot of time alone, don't you?" asked Greer. "I mean, when you don't have guests who follow you around all the time and make you nurse them in bed for days?"

"There is nothing wrong with being alone," said Mahina.

Greer, sensing Mahina's reticence, leaned back on her elbows and let her hair sweep the grass. "Well, this is nothing like Massachusetts or Wisconsin. This is nothing like anyplace I've ever been."

"You have traveled much, *Doctora*?"

"Yes," said Greer. "But for short trips. Taking my samples and then leaving. Always looking at pieces of earth, segments of land, but never feeling the place. I never realized before I got here that land itself has a character." Greer's hand stroked the ground beside her. "This island, it's a gentle place."

They sat silently as the sun fell further in the sky and the air began to cool. A full moon, paper white, emerged behind them. Mahina's hands were held together, her palms churning, as her mind seemed to run through some memory. Then she stood abruptly, straightened her skirt, and headed for the Jeep. "We go, *Doctora*."

"Mahina, are you all right?"

"Yes, yes. We get back before dark."

"Hey, I have an idea. Why don't you drive us back? Or partway back? Or just for a minute?" Greer shook the key in the air.

"Very well," said Mahina.

"But slowly." Greer settled into the passenger seat and retrieved their bandanas from the glove compartment. They tied them on. "Okay," she said, "go."

Mahina turned the key and the Jeep coughed to life. She stared at the gearshift a moment, then carefully wrapped her hand around it. Her foot pushed hard on the accelerator. The Jeep bucked, but soon steadied. Focused intently on the terrain ahead, Mahina leaned into the windshield. She snaked the Jeep down the hill, crossing their former tracks, until they reached a sharp dip, and Mahina swerved right, then left, shifting the gear but forgetting to depress the clutch. The gears moaned.

"Wait, Mahina," Greer said, but Mahina had already brought the Jeep to an abrupt stop. The Jeep's engine rumbled.

"I think we missed the ditch," said Greer. "Let's put it in neutral for a second and I'll check the front."

But Mahina said nothing, did nothing.

"Mahina?"

Greer saw that her thick eyelashes were collecting tears.

"Mahina." She'd never seen Mahina unhappy. She placed her hand on Mahina's shoulder, a gesture she'd seen Mahina perform many times. "What's wrong?"

Mahina released a jagged breath. Her fist thumped the dashboard.

"What is it?"

"It is the Jeep, of course." Her voice was weary. "It is that I cannot learn to drive."

But Greer knew it had nothing to do with driving, with the Jeep, with her. Mahina was lost in a private sadness. And it was clear she didn't want to be comforted. Mahina's benevolence was infinite, but her intimacy had borders. So Greer had to pretend—she could perform that kindness.

"Terevaka isn't easy driving," said Greer. "I barely got us up here myself."

Mahina looked around them. She untied her bandana and dropped it in her lap. "I am stuck," she said.

"No," Greer answered. "No, Mahina, you're not. Just paused."

27

The campsite is empty. She sees the tent flap is open and moves forward to fasten it. A note is pinned to its edge:

Elsa:
This is all my fault, but it's going to be fine just fine. I found out from the boy that she is with the Germans, and I can make Pitcairn in one week and if I don't meet them there it is only 3 more days to Tahiti. They must drop her off as soon as they find her. I can catch the south wind and it will be fine, Alice will be fine. I'll bring her back to you. Do not worry. She will be fine.

Elsa runs down to the water, strains her eyes. The schooner is nowhere in sight. The dinghy is gone. She hikes up to the cliff above the beach, and looks out: still nothing, only the dark and endless sea. She crumples the note and tosses it down toward the water, but the wind hurls it back toward the shore until it skips along the rim of sand.

She begins to climb down, then stops and lets her body find the cold face of rock. She grabs the rough edges with her hands and leans all her weight forward. She taps her forehead against the hard wall, then again, harder, until it begins to soothe her.

"Alice," she whispers.

Edward, alone in the boat, has gone west.

But the fleet steamed in the opposite direction, toward Chile, then to Argentina, where they plan to invade the Falkland Islands.

The boy has followed her, moves toward her now, shaking with alarm. She closes her eyes, continues to tap her head against rock, and feels, for the first time, his fingers clasp her hand.

28

"I have an idea," said Vicente.

He and Greer were sitting on the stone wall above the *caleta*, drinking pisco sours. It was the usual night for the researchers' dinner, but Sven went out alone with Isabel, and Burke-Jones was gone, his lab room emptied. "It is about Admiral von Spee. I am going to write a book about him. About his journey, trying to get home to Germany. It would begin in China, of course, when the war broke out. With his squadron in Tsingtao. Did you know that the route von Spee and his squadron traveled to Rapa Nui was a similar path to the great Polynesian migration?"

"You never told me that," said Greer. "But what about the *rongorongo*?"

"It is not forsaken; I will simply put it aside for now. I'd always believed we would find more tablets; I'd hoped the answer to deciphering would come that way." He seemed a bit embarrassed. "I envy you your work, Greer. Your commitment to one subject. It's a very hard thing to find in this life. And right now von Spee holds my attention and I must pursue it. Many people know the story of the Battle of the Falklands, but not what led up to it."

"Sounds like the Germany trip is on, then." Vicente had been speaking of a full investigation into von Spee's life.

"I feel I must go. But only for a short time. And you? Where will you be?"

"Well, I went ahead and applied for that National Geo research grant. Keep your fingers crossed. I should hear any day now."

"Ah, Surtsey. It should be fascinating."

"An island smaller and less populated than this one. Next I'll be doing biota studies on deserted chunks of ocean rock."

"And I have no doubt you'd discover something interesting there."

"Probably about myself and my interest in small, out-of-the-way places."

"Travel isn't such a strange impulse. And Iceland, there you'll have the hot springs and geysers. When I was there it was beautiful."

"Vicente, where haven't you been?"

"Your homeland, in fact. The U.S. of A."

She couldn't tell if there was a suggestion in this.

"Well, Surtsey's a very long shot," she said. "You know I don't exactly have the best publication record."

"You are dedicated to your work, and that is what counts. I'll write them. I'll tell them how I've seen you now, for months, in the lab all the time. No personal life whatsoever. No boyfriends, no crazy nightlife. They'll appreciate that detail."

"I'm sure."

"Just short evening naps on the cliffs, which help you to find fossils."

"All in the name of research."

"A true devoted and passionate scientist." He leaned back on his hands. "But doesn't it bother you?"

"What?"

"No personal life. We're all human, even devoted scientists."

"Of course," she said. "But by 'personal life' I think you actually mean 'romantic life.' The two aren't the same. Come on. I have friends here, I have a community. I'm sitting here having a drink with you. What would you call that?"

"I don't know. What would *you* call it?"

"A full life."

"You know what I am asking."

"You're asking why I don't have a boyfriend? Or why I don't want one?"

"A fair question."

"So you want to know why I'm not dating Ramon?"

"See? You merely dance around the subject."

"Oh, Vicente. What do you want me to say? You know I was married, for eight years, and you know Thomas died. And God, you must know that in some way that makes it a little difficult to think about getting into something new."

"I do know these things, Greer. But you never speak of them."

Why not tell him the truth? He was, after all, a good man, a good friend. She wanted to explain about Thomas, about everything that had happened with her dissertation, about their life in Massachusetts, what he'd done with his pollen data, how she'd so misplaced her love.

Vicente was trying to read her expression. "You're perhaps still in love with him?"

"No," said Greer. "Then, at least, I could grieve like a normal person. I don't actually think I even knew my husband."

Vicente raised his eyebrows. Perhaps this was how he'd explained to himself her refusals: She was still in love with her husband. "It is complicated, I imagine," he said. "A marriage, the ways in which two people come to spend their lives together, then watch those lives drift apart. I've never been married. I've never been close to marriage. I have dated many women, but it's always been fun. And when it doesn't work out, it's okay too. I can't pretend to understand what it must feel like to take a relationship so seriously, and to lose it."

"Years ago," she said, "after Thomas and I were just married, when I was a graduate student, he took my dissertation and used it for his own paper. He stole my equation."

Vicente looked confused. "This was his data fraud?"

"No. This was years before. My husband appropriated my work, and then *I* was accused of plagiarism."

"What did you do?"

"Nothing," said Greer. "I did absolutely nothing. I refused to believe it had happened."

Vicente took a deep breath. "Who would imagine such a thing could happen? It's awful. But, Greer, not all men are like that. Very few would ever do such a thing."

"I know. He was an exceptional and rare find."

"It angers you."

"It did. But not so much now."

"Is this why you keep to yourself? Alone with your work?"

"Who knows."

"I suppose nothing is that simple."

The sun was low in the sky, bathing the harbor in an orange light. Five fishing boats had already come in, tied to the docks. In the distance three more were making their way home. Amid them, floating toward the shore, was a green glass globe.

"Ah, look!" said Vicente, springing from the wall. "Come."

He grabbed her hand and led her toward the water; he heeled his shoes off, rolled up his pants. "I'll be right back." He waded out to where the glass orb rose and fell with the waves. "It is perfect!" He lifted it, dripping, above his head. Seawater trickled down his face and he smiled. "A good omen, Greer! A very good omen!"

He waded back, the green globe held before him like a crystal ball.

"A buoy! Once, maybe twice a year, they wash ashore. They are considered good luck."

Greer thought of all the buoys hanging from Mahina's ceiling, of the luck her friend deserved.

When he reached the sand, Vicente handed it to Greer. "For your luck. For Iceland. For the future."

Back on the wall, Vicente rolled down his pants, and Greer examined the globe in her lap, imagining what it would have been like to live there hundreds of years before, to watch the sea for gifts, for visitors, for life. From Terevaka, the island would seem the world's center. Greer took a sip of her pisco sour, letting it roll slowly down her throat.

"You look nice," said Vicente. "Yes, you look very very nice." And Greer was suddenly conscious that she had, for the first time, done her hair up in barrettes. She'd put on a sleeveless dress, the one flattering item in her duffels.

"My field clothes demanded retirement."

"Yes, of course." He tapped the buoy. "Do you like your present?"

"Yes," she said.

"Some men give little tiny stones. I give large pieces of glass."

Greer laughed. "Originality is always better."

"And my idea about von Spee? You think it's good?"

"I do."

"He was a great commander, a man of strong passion." Vicente looked out to the sea. "He was caught in a war where old friends became his enemies, where the lives of thousands of men were in his hands."

"Vicente, you speak just like a man in love."

"It is a new thing for me, this emotion."

But perhaps it was a fleeting passion, perhaps his love for von Spee would pass, perhaps all Vicente's loves would pass. How could one know for sure?

Greer let her hands rest on the glass ball—her gift, her good luck.

✿

A week later, Greer began to stack all her pollen guides and data books in their crates. She sent the seed collection back to Kew Gardens and arranged for her plant samples from the island to be held in the SAAS building for future investigators. She packed her buoy in a crate of its own, carefully padded, hoping it would make its way safely across the ocean with her. The last item left on the long worktable was her paper. Fifty pages of data and analysis, the product of eight months of work. The nut fossil had, in the end, made it all possible. And now she had a real grant; it had come through. She'd be part of an official expedition to Surtsey.

She was wiping down the centrifuge, when she heard a knock at the door. She turned and saw Luka Tepano. Stubble, thin and silvery, matted his face, lending his cheeks the odd shimmer of fish scales. His eyes were fixed on a roll of paper in his hand.

"Luka! I'm glad you're here. I didn't know where to find you. Please come in." Since the night he'd been at Mahina's, Greer had been trying to locate him. She'd gone to the *caleta*, to the leper colony, even to the site of the old woman's cave, but he seemed to have disappeared.

She dragged one of the lab stools out and offered it to him. He sat down slowly.

"Luka, I wanted to thank you. I didn't get a chance the other night. Thank you for finding me and fetching Vicente. I might have died otherwise."

His eyes searched the lab—the empty shelves, the stack of crates, the half-dismantled centrifuge.

"Soy de los Estados Unidos," said Greer. "I've been studying the island's plants."

On the table before them was a photographic book, *Flora and Fauna of the Tropics*. He looked at the cover, and then to Greer. She nodded. He leafed through several pages, examining the plant images.

"Do you understand English? Some English?"

He lifted the rolled paper from his lap and set it on the table in front of her.

"What's this?"

She unrolled the thick paper and flattened it. The face of a young boy stared back at her. His eyes were large, his mouth full and smiling. His neck was narrow, almost too small for the fullness of the face. Greer looked up at Luka. "This is you."

And then, for the first time, she was sure he understood: He nodded.

"When you were little."

She saw in his weathered face that ghost of youth. She could see the boy, the worried eyes, the plump nose, the bright grin. The picture must have been at least sixty years old.

Greer rolled it carefully and handed it to him. "What a precious thing to have," she said.

He took the paper from her, and simply sat there like he was waiting for something.

"Do you sign?" she asked, raising both hands in what seemed to her the natural gesture for a question. "Or write?" She tore a page from her notebook and slid it toward him with a pen, but he made no move to pick it up. Then she went over to her sample box, and removed the fossil and held it out. "This. Do you know what this is? When you found me I had it in my hand."

Luka seemed reticent to take the fossil from her, but when she set it on the table, he lifted it to his eye and examined it with great delight.

"It's turned out to be the most important thing I found here."

He watched her speak with such concentration, Greer thought for a moment he might be reading her lips. He smiled.

"It's a seed from a very big tree. A fossilized seed."

He was still for a moment, then slid off his stool and offered her the nut as though it were a present, then took it back and repeated the motion.

"A gift?" asked Greer. "*You* gave it to me?"

He shook his head, then once more offered the fossil to her.

"A gift from your *someone else*?" she asked. "Did your *amiga* give this to me?"

He held the paper to his chest, nodded, and reached for her hand.

❀

"Ah, *Doctora!* Your work! It is done! I will find a bottle of something good for us."

Mahina had been sitting behind the desk when Greer arrived with

her paper. Mahina now stepped through a curtain of beads and returned with two goblets and an unlabeled bottle. She inspected them
in the light and poured with relish. They clinked glasses.

"To the *doctora*! Who has finished all of her work."

Greer sipped the liquid: brandy.

"Mahina, would you like to read my paper?"

Mahina set her glass down. "It would honor me."

"It's not really standard in scientific papers to have a dedication,
but if I could dedicate it to someone, it would be you."

"*Doctora.*"

Greer then pulled her purse from the floor and set it in her lap.
"And I want to give you something." She took out a thick white envelope. Since she'd left the Lan Chile office earlier that day, Greer had
been wondering how to present this. "Here's a round-trip ticket to
Santiago. Your plane leaves two weeks from tomorrow at one P.M.
Your hotel is all arranged. And Elian at the Hotel Espíritu has promised to come check on everything here while you're away. Isabel will
be staying with Sven, and you have no guests booked for the next
few weeks." Mahina slowly shook her head from side to side; this
was clearly too much for her to absorb. "And if for some reason you
think your husband might come back while you are away, well, we'll
leave him a note." Greer had written, in Rapa Nui, a note that she
now handed to Mahina.

Gone to Santiago. Back in a few weeks.

"Simple. Now, if I were you, I would start thinking about what you
want to pack."

There, she'd done it. Then she grabbed her purse and stood. She
hugged Mahina hastily.

"I have a million things to do before I go," said Greer. "And
actually"—she smiled—"so do you."

29

Palynological Analyses of Easter Island Biota,
South Pacific, Territory of Chile
Submitted to the International Conservation Society
November 1973
Greer Farraday, Ph.D.

One cannot fully examine the extinction patterns and shifts in the biota of Easter Island without taking into account the island's strange history of monument building. The massive stone statues, which for so long have stood silent before archaeologists, offer an important suggestion as to the fate of the indigenous population that constructed them. Though the specific details of how the *moai* were carved and transported remain unresolved, I propose, at least, the possibility that some aspect of their construction and transport detrimentally affected the island's environment.

More than 200 statues once stood along the island's coast, transported from the crater at Rano Raraku, where the statues were quarried from the volcanic tuff. Despite heights as great as thirty-three feet and weights of up to eighty-two tons, these statues were transported as far as six miles from the quarry to their positions on the coast. Over six hundred statues never even left the quarry, lying in all stages of completion. The tallest of these was sixty-five feet, the heaviest two hundred seventy tons.

The *Paschalococos disperta* palm and the *Sophora toromiro* were once the island's most bountiful trees (the only current living sample of *toromiro* is at the RBG Kew) and sediment samples dating from the A.D. 200s indicate an abundance of pollen from both these trees in the island biota at that time. The earliest radiocarbon dates associated with human habitation are A.D. 318, A.D. 380, and A.D. 690. Therefore, at the time of settlement, it seems likely the island was forested with at least two tree species.

The *Paschalococos disperta* pollen and nuts (a fossilized nut was obtained) bear a striking resemblance to the still-surviving *Jubaea chilensis*, the Chilean wine palm, which grows up to eighty feet tall and six feet in diameter. From the tall thick trunks of the endemic Easter Island palm, the early Rapa Nui would have made large canoes, shelters, and even fires with which to keep warm— necessities for the inhabitants. The Chilean palm also yields edible nuts, suggesting the Easter Island palm would also have provided food.

These endemic palms are also good candidates for the solution to the transportation and construction of the *moai*. The *Sophora toromiro* trunks and branches would not have been sufficiently strong to manipulate large weight, but *Jubaea chilensis* wood is notably durable. Several archaeologists have proposed the *moai* were placed on wooden sleds, dragged over lubricated (with the sweet potato) wooden tracks or rollers, and then levered to their final standing positions with logs and ropes—this has not been conclusively tested to date. We do know that the *moai* cannot be moved with ropes alone, and we know that the expedition of 1872, described by Pierre Loti, was able to transport a *moai* to their ship by use of "enormous beams [which] have been put together in a sort of improvised chariot." If the sailors were able within a day to transport *moai* with wooden beams lashed together, we can assume this would have worked as well for the islanders.

It has been proposed, though solid figures are difficult to ascertain, that *moai* construction might have been under way as early as A.D. 500, and that production peaked circa 1400. We know for certain from the record of European visitors that the *moai* stood erect as late as 1722, when Roggeveen visited, but that no construction was under way after 1774, when Captain Cook noted they had mostly been toppled. One fact, however, has been agreed upon: At the time the *moai* were abandoned, when the tools were thrown down beside the statues in the quarry, scores of *moai*, larger than any of those that had been standing, were in the process of being carved. Experts have taken this to mean that there was a flurry of carving activity at the very end. Sometime between 1722 and 1774 most, if not all, of the 200 standing *moai* were toppled.

There is no evidence of natural disaster—in the form of tidal waves or volcanic eruption—to account for the sudden disappearance of the indigenous plants. The palynological data suggest a gradual decrease in pollen content with each subsequent sediment layer. And so we must consider the biota shift as, primarily, the result of human habitat destruction.

It is the *toromiro* and *disperta* palm whose disappearance would have had the greatest immediate impact on the native peoples. As indicated by the use of caves for habitation, the islanders could find shelter in the absence of a strong building material. However, as an island dependent upon the sea for its life, and on boats, specifically the typical Polynesian outrigger canoe, scarcity of wood, therefore scarcity of boats, would impact fishing and water transportation activities. (Roggeveen, Cook, La Pérouse, and Loti all noted the poor quality and small number of native canoes. And many of these visitors were greeted by islanders swimming to them from the shore.)

A major clue to this dearth of functioning watercraft is evident in the travelogues of the European explorers. Roggeveen described the first moment of contact between an islander and his ship: *This hapless creature seemed to be very glad to behold us, and showed the greatest wonder at the build of our ship. He took special notice of the tautness of our spars, the stoutness of our rigging and running gear, the sails, the guns—which he felt all over with minute attention.* On Cook's expedition, the same event occurs: *As the master drew near the shore with the boat, one of the natives swam off her, and insisted on coming aboard the ship, where he remained two nights and a day. The first thing he did after coming aboard was to measure the length of the ship, by fathoming her from taffrail to the stern.* La Pérouse witnesses a whole party of islanders examining his ship: *They examined our cables, anchors, compass, and wheel, and they returned the next day with a cord to take the measure over again, which made me think that they had had some discussion on shore upon the subject.* By looking at the objects that held the greatest fascination for the early Rapa Nui, we can begin to understand what they lacked.

We then must imagine the secondary *human* trauma caused by deforestation—soil erosion would have stunted the crop growth, and a general depletion of timber resources would result in an inability to catch fish. The population, within a matter of years, would have begun to starve.

Other researchers have determined that there was a large population concurrent with the period of *moai* construction; estimates place between seven thousand and twenty thousand on the island (the current island population is approximately three thousand). The natural demand of such a population on the environment—food resources—would have been a stress on the natural biota. Coupled with the rampant deforestation of the palm and *toromiro* for the purpose of transporting the *moai*, this would have created, quite rapidly, an uninhabitable environment. It is likely that the population at first suffered a gradual and natural decline, without any specific understanding of the changes occurring in the environment.

One must then look at the *moai*, the monuments themselves, thrown facedown, for the silent story of the island's population disaster. The earliest known inquiries (Roggeveen, 1722) into the purpose of the monuments indicate the statues were meant as memorials, representations of the islanders' dead ancestors. Though they were not described as religious, or in our sense, protective, statues, it is not unreasonable to suspect that the carvers associated these monoliths with protective qualities— which is to say they believed their task of monument building to be beneficial. At whatever point the flurry of monument building began, we must imagine the arduous labor of building ever larger, ever more difficult-to-transport memorials, coupled with a progressively rapid deterioration of the island. Trees and bushes would have been disappearing, crops would have been failing. The population would have started to decline and, for perhaps the first time, this isolated people would have experienced starvation.

What we can reasonably assert from the evidence is a likely correlation between the increase in monument building and a devastation of the terrestrial landscape. Which is noteworthy as perhaps the only known instance in the history of mankind in which a people destroyed themselves by building monuments to their dead.

But there was something Greer didn't write.

It involved the position of the *moai*. The statues didn't look out to the sea as one would imagine; they faced inward, staring at the island, their backs to the ocean, as if these people, thousands of miles from other humans, had, over generations, lost knowledge of the outside world. As if in building these monuments, megaliths of the past with which to encircle themselves, they had forgotten, or tried to forget, that anything lay beyond their shores.

What, then, would they have thought the day Roggeveen anchored off the coast, the deck of his massive ship topped with goods they had never before seen, the men in a rainbow of brightly colored hats and jackets and epaulets? What would they have thought as they paddled alongside in their corroding canoes, climbing aboard to stroke the sleek sails and trim and ropes? What would they have thought when Roggeveen's men rowed ashore, climbing the rocks with polished pistols and muskets by their sides, which, when raised, seized life in an instant? What would they think, three days later, as they looked at the bodies of their fallen friends while the ship sailed off beyond the edges of the world they had thought their own? Would the islanders have looked around at the barren landscape? The rocks and the reeds and the yellowed grass? Would they remember the trees? Or stories of trees—didn't their mother once tell them of a girl who was told to plant her lover's head in the earth? Would they look at the few canoes rotting in the surf? Boats that could hold no more than four people each, too leaky to make it more than a few miles? Would they know they were sharing the tragic fate of so many creatures, like the intrepid birds that had found their way to such distant shores and awoke one day to find they could no longer fly? Would they then look up at the massive stone giants they and their ancestors spent centuries building? At their own history, now no longer enough to protect them, to keep out their knowledge of another world?

Was this the moment when one furious man gave the command—*Enough! Never again!*—when they knew the dead had betrayed them, when they swarmed the nearest statue, their bodies heaving, angry, frightened by the weight of this massive relic, bleeding themselves for the sake of a new beginning?

30

The plane leaves at one P.M. and both Vicente and Mahina are there to see her off at the airport. Sven and Isabel helped load her bags and said their good-byes at the *residencial*. Now there is a commotion at the cargo bay as her crates and cores are loaded, and they all watch as her work of eight months is sealed inside the plane.

Mahina is strangely silent as the other passengers line up beside the plane, as though Greer's departure is an unexpected betrayal. She has dressed for the occasion, though—a dress of white cotton printed with small yellow flowers; flowers that, Greer thinks, don't exist. Fashion flowers. Around her neck is a shell necklace.

"Thank you for the books," Greer says, tapping her backpack.

That morning, as Greer was packing up her toiletries and sealing her duffels, Mahina came by with a stack of books. "For the *doctora*," she said, and placed them, one by one, onto the mattress. They were leather-bound, a faded burgundy, titles lettered in gold along the spines. The collection from the glass armoire above the desk. Greer lifted one book and opened it. Charles Robert Darwin, *The Voyage of the Beagle*, London, 1839. The front page was embossed:

Ex Libris
E.P.B.

Greer ran her fingers along the pages, the binding.

"But, Mahina. You wanted to sell these. These are Darwin. First editions. They're extremely valuable. I can't take them."

"They are your kind of books. What you like to read. And they are a present. If you refuse my present, well, I refuse yours."

"You are a tough woman," said Greer.

"Yes," said Mahina. "I am a tough woman. And I have enough to try to read with your paper. I cannot be troubled with so much English in my lifetime." And she left Greer to put the books in her pack, calling Ramon to help load the duffels into the Jeep.

But Greer doesn't know how Mahina feels about her own gift. She's said nothing yet of her plans to leave. Greer will have to wait for Vicente to let her know if Mahina used the ticket. Hopefully Mahina will climb onto the plane and wave good-bye to her island, at least for a little while.

Vicente begins pacing. "So, Germany," he says. "I'm sure there is some good wet ground there for coring. Come visit. Call it a research trip."

"Where's your first stop?"

"The beginning. Strasbourg. Where von Spee lived."

"Strasbourg? France?"

"Only after the war. It used to be German."

"I have a friend in Strasbourg I'm thinking of visiting."

"Then you'll have two friends in Strasbourg."

He unwraps a cone of tissue paper and hands her a single daisy. "For my favorite botanist."

"Vicente."

"And the daisy, I am certain, is the flower that means 'I will see you soon.' "

"Precisely," says Greer, saddened by this reminder of all their conversations. How quickly one forms a past, even while trying to escape another. She puts the flower behind her ear. "I'll miss you, Vicente. You've been wonderful."

"We will meet again. I am sure of it. The flower says so."

"I never argue with flowers."

She turns now to Mahina and opens her arms. "And you . . ."

"*Iorana,*" says Mahina. "I mean both now. You come back, *Doctora.*"

"Someday," says Greer. In this good-bye she can hear the echo of every other good-bye she has ever said. "I'll be back."

"You will come back to see the *moai* standing," says Mahina.

Just the day before, they have learned of a new "*moai* restoration project" through SAAS. A team of French archaeologists will spend a year restoring a row of *moai* on the coast to their upright positions. The islanders have mixed feelings—the *moai* have been down for over two hundred years, and everyone is used to them that way.

Greer, too, is undecided—the toppled statues tell the island's true story, of its tragic collapse, but perhaps this project will become part of the island's story as well: rebirth.

"Yes," says Greer. "I must see that."

The Lan Chile stewardess at the base of the portable stairs now waves the passengers forward. Greer embraces Vicente, who kisses both her cheeks, and then her forehead, saying simply "Strasbourg." Then Mahina takes off the shell necklace and places it over Greer's head. "*Doctora,*" she says.

"This is me." Greer picks up her backpack, heavy with her new books.

She approaches the stewardess. It is the woman from her flight here eight months ago. Still smiling.

"*Iorana. Buenos días.* Hello," she says, taking Greer's ticket. At the top of the steps, Greer turns to Mahina, points at herself climbing onto the plane. "See how easy?" she shouts, and with a last wave, she ducks into the plane.

She takes the pillow from her seat and props it behind her neck. She has a long day and night of travel ahead. Santiago. New York. London. Reykjavik. And then the small expedition plane to Surtsey, twenty miles south of Iceland.

She has reviewed the necessary materials for the project. The island is volcanic, like Easter, but new, unblemished—just barely ten years old. It has seen growth, with no corruption yet. Sightings have already been made of sea rockets decorating the island with purple and white flowers, and the small pink blooms of sea sandworts. Even as she sits here, new seeds are pressing toward it. She imagines thousands of fern spores floating on the wind. All the box beans and Mary's beans and morning glories, all the seeds on all the creatures bobbing on driftwood, carried by the current, waiting to take hold, to root themselves, to push through the darkness, into light, where a new life awaits.

The propellers spin and the plane begins to trundle down the runway. Greer looks once more out the window, but now the tarmac is empty, the glass of the airport a blur. Her seat shudders as the engine pushes the plane into the air, onto the current, and soon she is looking down on the island as it fades from view.

Climbing through the clouds, above nothing but ocean, the plane steadies. She glances around the cabin: several American tourists, already sleeping; a young European couple, perhaps German, holding hands; an older woman, Chilean, with two small girls beside her.

Greer pulls her backpack from beneath the seat and removes one of Mahina's books, a copy of *On the Origin of Species*. She sets it in her lap, and falls asleep.

Hours later, on another plane, above another ocean, Greer awakens from a deep sleep and realizes she is almost there. To calm her nerves, she opens the old, weathered copy of Darwin and begins to read. The leather binding is soft, bleached at the corners. The pages are crinkled. There is some faded pencil underlining in the book, which no doubt compromises its value as a first edition, but then again, she has no intention of selling it. She finds the simple statement that has always made her pause:

> *No one ought to feel surprise at much remaining as yet unexplained in regard to the origin of species and varieties, if he makes due allowance for our profound ignorance in regard to the mutual relations of all the beings which live around us.*

And beside the passage, this other reader, this invisible friend, has written in a neat and unmistakably feminine script—letters long and curled—the simple word: *Lovely.*

Greer looks out the window, at the island emerging. There, below her, is the emerald shimmer of newly sprouted plants, a broad-winged bird gracefully circling the shore, a white flower winking amid a thick blanket of green. Everything glistens with the urge to live.

Her hands rest gently on the book.

It is lovely, isn't it?

Author's Note

This is a work of fiction, although several characters were inspired by historical figures:

The eighteenth- and nineteenth-century European voyagers mentioned were all real people. Excerpts of their accounts of Easter Island are from the translations in John Dos Passos's compilation of travelogues, *Easter Island: Island of Enigmas.*

The legend of Hau Maka's dream presented in the book's epigraph is a compilation of legends from various sources, particularly Thomas Barthel's *The Eighth Land: The Polynesian Discovery and Settlement of Easter Island.*

Graf von Spee was the real vice admiral of Germany's World War I East Asiatic Squadron, which did anchor at Easter Island before the battle of the Falklands. Von Spee's actions on the island, however, were entirely invented for the purposes of this story. *Graf Spee's Raiders* by Keith Yates, *Coronel and the Falklands* by Geoffrey Bennett, and *The Long Pursuit* by Richard Hough provided information about the movements of von Spee's fleet. The scene in Tsingtao, in which von Spee learns of the outbreak of war, is a fictional synthesis of several incidents.

The expedition undertaken by Elsa and her family was inspired by the 1914 expedition of Katherine Scoresby Routledge and her husband, wonderfully described in her book *The Mystery of Easter Island.* It is worth noting that the Routledge expedition did not go missing from the island, but returned safely to England.

The ecological history of Easter Island presented is factual. The first thorough examination of the Easter Island pollen record was started in 1977 by Dr. John Flenley. In 1984 John Flenley and Sarah King were the first to publish evidence that Easter Island was once forested by palm trees.

Two books pertaining to island biogeography were of particular importance in my research: *The Song of the Dodo* by David Quammen, a remarkable volume, and *Island Life* by Sherwin Carlquist, published two years before MacArthur and Wilson published their monograph formalizing the field.

Thomas's angiosperm research is based on the work of several people who searched for magnolia pollen in that era. *The Enigma of Angiosperm Origins* by Norman F. Hughes was helpful to me in understanding Thomas's process. As I write this, however, the magnolia is no longer considered the first flower. Through genetic analysis done in the 1990s, Amborellacaea, Nymphaeacaea, and Illiciacaea are now considered the first angiosperms.

In 1955, the first Easter Island *moai* was re-erected by Thor Heyerdahl at Ahu Aturi Huke, near Anakena. Ahu Akivi was restored in 1960, and subsequently Ahu Tahai, in 1967, both by Dr. William Mulloy. Ahu Nau Nau at Anakena was restored in 1978 by Sergio Rapu Haoa. Between 1992 and 1995, the fifteen *moai* at Ahu Tongariki were restored to their upright position by a joint team from the University of Chile and from Japan, with the Japanese TADANO corporation funding the project. Currently, only about seventeen percent of the statues that once stood upright have been re-erected, and most are still in danger of erosion. To protect the statues, an ongoing effort is under way through the Easter Island Foundation and other organizations to raise funds for preservation.

The *rongorongo*, where it originated and what it means, still remains one of the great mysteries of Easter Island.

Acknowledgments

For their invaluable comments on this manuscript I would like to thank Dr. Margaret Davis, Dr. Sara Hotchkiss, and Dr. Patricia Sanford. Dr. John Flenley, whose work on the Easter Island pollen was the inspiration for Greer's work, was of great assistance, as was his paper *The Late Quaternary vegetational and climatic history of Easter Island*. And a special thank-you to Dr. Georgia Lee, Easter Island expert, for lightning-speed answers to my endless questions.

Maururu to Maria Huke Rapahango and family for their great hospitality and kindness, and to Ramon Edmunds Pacomio, Rapa Nui guide *peti etahi* and friend.

For the time to write this book, I am deeply indebted to the James McCreight Fellowship at the Wisconsin Institute for Creative Writing and the Colgate University Creative Writing Fellowship. Particular thanks to Peter Balakian, Frederick Busch, Linck Johnson, Jesse Lee Kercheval, Leila Philip, and Ron Wallace.

I was blessed with several extraordinary teachers along the way: Robert Stone, Caroline Rody, Barry Hannah, Stuart Dybek, and Ethan Canin.

For friendship, feedback, patience, and all else: Emilie Baratta (who read this book more times than a friend should have to), Justin Cronin, Leila Hatch, Aimee Nezhukumatathil, and Richard Powers. For their perpetual good cheer, energy, and time: Margo Lipschultz, Patrick Merla, and Johanna Tani.

A million thanks to my spectacular editor, Susan Kamil. And thanks to Irwyn Applebaum, Nita Taublib, and the wonderful team at Bantam Dell.

And last, but far from least, this book would not exist without Maxine Groffsky, agent extraordinaire and so much more.

About the Author

Jennifer Vanderbes is a graduate of Yale University and the Iowa Writers' Workshop. She was a James McCreight Fellow in Fiction at the University of Wisconsin, and most recently was the Fellow in Creative Writing at Colgate University.